DAUGHTER OF THE HEART

—◦✦◦—

DAUGHTER OF THE HEART

ROBIN STRACHAN

CAMEL
PRESS
Kenmore, WA

CAMEL PRESS

A Camel Press book published by Epicenter Press

Epicenter Press
6524 NE 181st St.
Suite 2
Kenmore, WA 98028

For more information go to:
www.Camelpress.com
www.Coffeetownpress.com
www.Epicenterpress.com
www.robinstrachanauthor.com

Design by Scott Book and Melissa Vail Coffman

Daughter of the Heart
Copyright © 2020 by Robin Strachan

ISBN: 978-1-94189-076-9 (Trade Paper)
ISBN: 978-1-94189-099-8 (eBook)

Library of Congress Control Number: 2019945127

Printed in the United States of America

Acknowledgments

⁓∖∤⁓

IN EVERY AUTHOR'S LIFE, THERE ARE people who leave indelible impressions on our hearts and change us for the better. We become better writers and better people. In my life, one of those special influences is Joseph Matheu, D.O., a family physician in the Chicago area. "Dr. Joe," as I call him, has left his personal and professional mark on a poverty-stricken remote Indian reservation in Browning, Montana. The people there call him "Medicine Eagle."

It was Dr. Joe who first told me about the corps of volunteer physicians he leads each summer to the Blackfeet reservation near Glacier National Park. With my imagination captured by a DVD about his Blackfeet Volunteer Medical Corps, I decided my next book would be about a young female physician, a Doctor of Osteopathic Medicine like Dr. Joe, who moves to the Blackfeet reservation to serve the people. That novel, called *Listening for Drums*, is the story of Dr. Carrie Nelson's adventures her first year on the Blackfeet reservation. As unexpected events conspire to change her life, she is challenged to overcome heartbreak, homesickness, and judgements about what her life used to be or should be moving forward. After that book was completed, I realized that I wasn't finished telling Carrie's story. The result is this sequel, *Daughter of the Heart*.

I also want to thank Blackfeet singer-songwriter Jack Gladstone and his wife Patti for the cultural bridge they provide to the world. I have loved Jack's music for many years. I didn't know he was a Blackfoot—hadn't, in fact, yet been introduced to the Blackfeet reservation. This would come later, when I realized that the familiar music Jack played as part of a Blackfeet Volunteer Medical Corps fundraiser was the same music I had loved for years. Listening to Jack sing and play his guitar now transports me to the Blackfeet reservation and provides instant creative inspiration. I love his song "Tappin' the Earth's Backbone."

As usual, there are many people to thank for getting me from vague idea to finished novel. First, I want to thank Jennifer McCord for her conceptual editing suggestions. She has been a creative force through three books, and her sage wisdom and advice is always spot on. Every other year, Jennifer and I present a workshop for aspiring authors about the magic that can happen when an author and editor work together on a book they love.

But there are other people, too, who have shaped *Listening for Drums* and *Daughter of the Heart*. Dr. Elizabeth Kramer-Brent, a longtime friend, has read advance manuscripts of each of my books and offered suggestions that frequently get me over writer's blocks. (Sometimes I think she knows what's in my head better than I do.) A big thank you goes to Carol Bouma, the soul sister I met through a book group, who is willing to discuss plots and sub-plots—usually over a glass of wine. Charlie Goldsmith, a colleague and longtime friend, offers a helpful male perspective. To Ed Pears: River Man, you are no longer here on earth, but I thank you for introducing me to the music and ideas that inspired these books.

Four female osteopathic physicians have been instrumental in helping with medical background and advice for these books. Dr. Karen Nichols, Dr. Kim Huntington-Alfano, Dr. Nadine Keer, and Dr. Melanie Jessen cheered me on and provided great ideas. I also want to thank David Carney, M.D., one of my best friends from our hometown, for his support of my writing, and for great talks.

To my family, thank you for unconditional love and support. To all my friends, near and far, who share my life and times through visits, phone calls, emails, and social media, thank you for enriching my life with your intellect, wit, kindness, and encouraging words.

Last, but not least, I want to thank all the readers of *Listening for Drums*, who asked for more of Dr. Carrie and Dr. Nate.

Also by the Author

Designing Hearts

Manifesting Dreams

Listening for Drums

Dedicated to all my readers.

You inspire me with your love of stories.

Chapter One

‒◞◟‒

JULY

THE LABOR AND DELIVERY NURSE RAPPED on the door before peeking her head inside the patient room where Carrie Nelson, D.O. lay curled up nearly sideways on the narrow bed, fast asleep. A tendril of blonde hair the color of corn silk fell over one eye, and her hands were wedged under her head for a pillow. One slender bare foot extended beyond the bed.

"Doctor, it's almost time."

Carrie sat up, yawned, and rubbed her eyes, which felt like boiled onions from lack of sleep. This was her third delivery in twenty-four hours in addition to seeing more than the usual number of patients in the family medicine clinic at Blackfeet Community Hospital. The tiny federal hospital on the Blackfeet reservation in Browning, Montana had no full-time obstetrician. For the past two years, in addition to her work in the clinic, Carrie had delivered most of the babies born at the hospital. It was a duty she embraced happily. Yet, on days like today, it seemed that Blackfeet babies planned their arrivals in pairs or even trios.

She hadn't been surprised to hear from one of the older obstetrical nurses the matter-of-fact explanation that "Infant spirits plan their arrivals so they can be together on their earth journeys."

"Thanks, I'll be right there," she said to the young nurse. "And would you please tell that darn stork to stop circling the hospital?"

The nurse let out a quiet, understanding laugh. "The patient is still at seven centimeters. I thought I'd give you a few minutes to get awake."

"She moved quicker than I thought she would. Good for her."

Carrie swung her legs over the side of the bed and stood up. Stretching, she slipped her feet into cushioned clogs, then headed to the sink to splash water on her face. After this baby was born, she could go home.

She peered at her face in the mirror and sighed. The whites of her blue eyes were so red-lined, they resembled a Montana road map. With her long blonde hair pulled into a ponytail and no make-up, she looked every bit the part of a tired, overworked doctor.

She drew in a quick breath at the familiar face behind her, reflected in the mirror. *Dancing Bird.* The elderly Blackfoot patient had died two winters ago. "Whaa-tt?" Carrie blinked twice and whirled around. She would have chalked the vision up to exhaustion, but this wasn't the first time she had caught a glimpse of Dancing Bird, seemingly from out of nowhere. Was there a message in this sudden, repeat appearance of her old friend?

Dancing Bird had died of congestive heart failure after a lengthy illness. As Carrie worked to offer her the best of quality of life possible in her final months, she had come to love the gap-toothed old woman with her twinkling eyes and kind sense of humor. Carrie had mourned her passing. Here, on this close-knit reservation, her patients were neighbors and friends.

Though she came from a background steeped in academic medicine and science, life on the reservation had opened Carrie's mind to the viewpoints of Native Americans. She no longer found it impossible to believe that Dancing Bird might still be looking in on her. After all, the old woman had possessed special gifts allowing her to see, hear, and sense information that she freely shared with others. She was well-known as a seer on the reservation and had predicted that Carrie would marry soon, though this seemed unlikely at the time. Yet, within the year, through what could only be described as a seemingly miraculous turn of events, Carrie became engaged to the man of her dreams, Dr. Nate Holden. They had progressed from being colleagues at the hospital and the closest of friends to marriage the following year. There was no doubt that Nate was the love of her life. Butterflies still fluttered in her stomach at the thought of him.

As she splashed cold water on her face and dried it with a paper towel, Carrie recalled a dream she'd had as she napped on the hospital bed. It had been so vivid, as real as life. The old she-wolf was there—had spoken to her as she had in dreams past. In this dream, in a Native American lifetime, Carrie was a member of the Blackfeet tribe. But was the she-wolf in the dream the same wolf that had visited Carrie in real life nearly every week since she moved to the reservation two years ago?

In this dream, the wolf walked with Carrie to a tipi before turning around to retreat into a grove of fir trees. Carrie pushed aside the flap of the tipi and stepped inside. A fire burned, warming the cold night air. Medicine Owl, the tribal medicine woman, greeted Carrie and handed her a tightly wrapped bundle.

Curious, Carrie opened the blankets with great care, sensing new life. A baby blinked up at her. Whose baby was it?

Carrie and Nate wanted children and intended to start a family right away. They had been married just shy of two weeks, although truth be told, they had been lax on birth control for a couple of months. Yet, success had eluded them so far. No doubt, their challenging work hours and stress were a factor. Carrie's desire for a child had only intensified over the past two years, especially after she delivered her best friend Gali's first baby, a boy named Charlie.

Gali and her husband John Leathers were Carrie and Nate's best friends. Seeing the joy that Gali experienced as she gave birth and embraced motherhood—witnessing the happiness that Gali and John shared with their first child was something that Carrie and Nate longed to experience. At her age, Carrie knew that if she wanted more than one child, she needed to start soon.

She blew out a frustrated breath and walked down the hall to labor and delivery, making a mental note to ask Medicine Owl and her grandmother, who was also a doctor, for fertility advice. Like Carrie, Gran was a licensed osteopathic physician and a fifth-generation healer who used plant-based remedies in her work. Gran had an innate appreciation for the work of the medicine woman. Carrie had grown up watching Gran blend her knowledge of healing plants with her academic medical training to treat grateful patients. This fascination with historical plant-based therapies was the primary reason Carrie had applied and been accepted to the Mayo Clinic in Rochester, Minnesota for residency. Mayo had a strong program in complementary and integrative medicine.

As an O.B. nurse helped Carrie into a sterile gown, mask, and gloves for the delivery, it was time to focus on the new life about to enter the world. The delivery was uneventful—except for a moment when the baby's shoulder caught in the birth canal. When Carrie placed the nine-pound newborn on his mother's chest and gazed at the awe-struck expression on the girl's face, she wondered how long it would be before she would feel this joy.

An hour later, with the newest male member of the Blackfeet Nation howling in the hospital nursery and his teenage mother resting comfortably, Carrie headed to the emergency department, hoping to give Nate a ride home. But he was nowhere in sight.

"Hi, Dr. Carrie. Dr. Nate's in the O.R. with a hot appendix," the male Blackfoot physician assistant informed her.

"I wondered why he didn't answer my text." Carrie shook her head. This was the reality of their relationship. Nate was the only surgeon in the entire region. It was lucky they had any energy left over to be newlyweds.

Stepping outside the hospital, she took in deep breaths of the crisp evening air that smelled of fragrant wood smoke from a distant bonfire. Despite the hour, nearly nine-thirty, it was still light outside. Daylight lasted eighteen hours here in northwest Montana, which was just fine with Carrie. She needed all the daylight hours she could get. But she also imagined the sun couldn't bear to set on so lovely a scene.

It had been another gorgeous day for visitors at the Glacier National Park. Gazing out over the lush green and gold prairie, she admired the Northern Rockies rising in front of her. The sky had deepened its hue, beginning to show stripes of a deeper lapis-blue with streaks of gold, coral, and scarlet. The wind rustled and lifted her baby-fine blonde hair as she rubbed the gooseflesh on her arms. Even in mid-July, the nights got cold this far north. By the end of September, winter would return.

Her thoughts turned to her parents, Dr. Mark and Lynne Nelson, who had just returned to Philadelphia after ten days on the reservation. She already missed them. They came for the wedding and to enjoy North American Indian Days festivities in Browning, then stayed to volunteer at the hospital. Her dad, a cardiologist, and Gran, his mother, who was an internal medicine specialist with additional training in diseases of the kidneys, were an important part of the volunteer medical corps serving the Blackfeet people.

To Carrie's delight, Gran had decided to remain a few days longer than her son and his wife, saying she wanted to spend more time with the medicine woman. The two had become fast friends. They spent hours picking and studying plants, discussing their array of uses.

With Nate still in surgery, Carrie drove home from the hospital, watching intently through her windshield as the sky changed ever so gradually from blue-gray streaks to a clear cobalt blue. She parked her aging Subaru in the circular gravel driveway, looked up to see a few twinkling stars emerge, and entered the house on tiptoe. She half-hoped Gran might still be awake in the downstairs guest room, but no light was visible under the door.

Annie, Carrie's old hound dog, rose from her bed by the fireplace, to greet her. "Hey, girl," Carrie said, kissing her long nose and caressing the velvet ears. "I thought you'd be asleep with Gran tonight. Sorry I woke you up."

With Annie trailing at her heels, hoping for a late-night snack, Carrie entered the spacious kitchen and opened the freezer, pulling out an assortment of frozen wedding cookies. A smile crossed her lips. Her mother had baked enough for an army: nut rolls, crescent-shaped almond cookies, peanut blossoms, brown sugar cookies, jelly thumb prints, and chocolate chippers.

Although Carrie and her mother shared many physical and personality traits, a love of cooking and baking was not among them. Nate was the cook in their relationship. Surveying the plump bags tucked into the freezer, she could see that there were enough cookies to last most of the winter.

She fixed a cup of chamomile tea sweetened with honey from local bees to go with her small plate of cookies and sat down at the kitchen table. She handed

Annie a piece of a peanut butter cookie and was rewarded with a kiss on her hand. While she waited for Nate to come home, Carrie read a journal article on growing opioid abuse, as big a problem on the reservation as it was everywhere else in the country. She worried that the problem would get worse, with so many Blackfeet out of work and living in poverty. There were fewer resources here to deal with the problem.

She heard a toilet flush in the upstairs guest room followed by the whoosh of water in the sink and then a low male cough. *Dr. Jim.* Carrie's mentor Dr. Jim Miller and his wife Lois were staying with Carrie and Nate for the summer. The house had formerly belonged to them.

Dr. Jim, as he was fondly known, was the founder of the Blackfeet volunteer medical corps and so beloved by the people, he had been given the tribal name of Medicine Wolf for his good works. Lois possessed the same drive and spirit of service as her husband. Lois's forte was in managing details, making her the ideal partner for Dr. Jim.

"The devil is in the details," Lois always said. She left nothing to chance and had energy to spare. She cleaned the house as if she still owned it.

A few months ago, Carrie and Nate had begun making plans to build a new home close to the one owned by Dr. Jim and Lois. They were overjoyed when the Millers decided to sell them their rustic three-bedroom split-level log home. Carrie loved the house—had, in fact, lived there the past two years rent-free. It felt like home, and there was plenty of room to expand the place as their family grew. Now they had a beautiful house in which to start married life. Dr. Jim and Lois would have permanent visiting rights, of course.

Nate had proposed last July while her parents and Gran visited the reservation for the first time. The year had flown by, thanks to their heavy, unpredictable work schedules. Still, the couple had made joyful plans for their lives together.

Nate. Just the thought of him brought about an automatic heart flutter. A skilled surgeon, Nate Holden, D.O. was as handsome as a film star, even if he didn't quite see himself that way. His laidback personality and humble manner combined with kindness and a witty sense of humor made him popular with everyone. Carrie not only loved him, she admired and respected him.

It was eleven-thirty before Nate arrived from the hospital, looking every bit as tired as she felt. He leaned over and kissed her. "I can't believe you're still awake," he said.

She noted the bluish circles under his eyes. "I haven't seen hide nor hair of you today, bud."

"I thought about calling earlier, just to catch up, but things got crazy." He bit into the snickerdoodle she handed him, closed his eyes in ecstasy, and took a deep breath. "Hey, guess what."

"What? You love me?"

"You know I do." She stood up, and he took her in his arms, running his hands down the length of her silky hair and settling his hands on her hips. "Tomorrow, we will officially have been married two weeks." He kissed her in that way that never failed to elicit a response from her. All the exhaustion vanished. She knew they'd make love before they went to sleep tonight.

"I know, right?" Carrie finally said, letting out the breath she had been holding. "You're stuck with me till death do us part."

"Which hopefully won't happen until we're too old to risk bodily contact for fear of breaking a hip." Nate grinned.

She slapped him on the arm. "Hey, aren't you a surgeon? There are always hip replacements. I'm not letting you off the hook that easily."

THE NEXT MORNING, THE MELODIOUS SOUND of drums in the distance woke Carrie from a sound sleep. Even with cell phones, drums were still a primary way that Blackfeet communicated on the reservation. She peered between the blinds in the master bedroom, marveling at the powder-blue sky with a hint of snowy cotton ball clouds.

From downstairs came the tantalizing aromas of fresh coffee and sizzling bacon. Lois was a big believer in substantial weekend breakfasts. Carrie leaned in to kiss Nate's rough bearded cheek and decided to let him sleep. Pulling on a pair of sweatpants and a tee shirt, she headed downstairs.

"Good morning," she said, wrapping her arms around Lois, who hugged her back. "Where's Dr. Jim?"

"He went over to the hospital. The E.R. called, so Jim decided to make himself useful." Lois wore a fitted blue-checked flannel shirt over a tee-shirt and jeans. Hand-beaten silver Native American jewelry adorned with green and sky-blue turquoise flashed at her wrist and ears. Her auburn hair was styled in a chin-length bob.

"Nate is exhausted. It's nice of Dr. Jim to help out today."

Lois stepped back, poured Carrie a mug of coffee and handed it to her. "Don't let him fool you. It's purely selfish on his part." She grinned. "Since he began transitioning into retirement, he complains that he doesn't have enough to do. Fairly drives me crazy, I tell you." She picked up a dish cloth and wiped down the countertop. "Gran is already outside taking a walk with Annie. Why don't you go find her? When you get back, we can all have breakfast together. I'll make us a big frittata with some of those fresh herbs from the garden."

Carrie caught sight of Gran walking with Annie farther out on their property. Gran's snowy white hair was fashioned into a twist, secured with a jeweled comb. She was slender and fit, dressed in khakis and a long-sleeved periwinkle-colored shirt. Still beautiful, Gran appeared at least two decades younger than her eighty-seven years.

Annie stopped to sniff the ground every few feet as if recommending plants for Gran's attention. As Carrie made her way across the yard to join them, she gazed out over the prairie fields, looking for her wolf, certain the animal was somewhere nearby, hidden in the tall grasses. She had been told by the medicine woman at their first meeting that the she-wolf was her spirit animal.

"Hey, you two," Carrie called out. "Find anything unusual?"

"Just some wild carrot. Annie loves the scent," Gran said.

"I do, too," Carrie said. Wild Carrot, a white flowering plant also known as Queen Anne's Lace, had medicinal uses.

It was the perfect day to enjoy the sights and smells of dew-drenched grass, blossoms, and bracing mountain air. Carrie allowed Annie to stretch her retractable leash as far as possible while the old dog sniffed all the irresistible smells on the ground. As they walked through the field, Carrie and Gran investigated high-summer plants growing in abundance. Many had uses in common plant and herbal remedies. Gran plucked a purple coneflower, also called Echinacea, sniffing it and examining its petals and stamen. These flowers grew in her greenhouse, always available for distillation into a tincture to treat early colds.

A cool breeze rustled the fir trees nearby with a gentle whoosh, causing the tall grasses near them to sway. Smoothing a wisp of hair that had escaped her French braid, Carrie lifted her face to the warm sun. In the distance, the mountains shone lapis-blue and lavender with sunny sloping areas of jade-green and peach.

She continued scanning the landscape around them in every direction, looking for her wolf. She always felt better somehow when the animal showed herself. *There she is.* The creature paced slowly from a grove of trees, walking deliberately toward them, yet keeping a protective distance. Carrie held tightly to Annie's leash, but Annie had grown accustomed to the nearness of the wolf, sensing there was nothing to fear. The biggest danger was that Annie was a runner and might want to join the wolf for an adventure.

"Look," Carrie said, indicating to Gran with a nod of her head to remain still. "There she is."

Gran took in a quick breath. "Oh my," she said. "The sight of her still gives me chills." She rubbed her arms. "It's amazing to know that she is a creature in the wild. Yet, she comes to you in friendship."

"She's been visiting me regularly for so long, I'd be lost without her," Carrie said. "I can still hardly believe how she has befriended me. But I worry about her, Gran, you know? She is one of the oldest females. Medicine Owl said so. I fear someday she won't come. I guess, in a way, I rely on her. When she's here, all is well." Carrie met the eyes of the she-wolf, who took a few more steps and then lay down in the grass. She sent the animal silent good wishes and turned back toward the house.

Nate was seated at the kitchen table drinking coffee and munching a slice of bacon when Carrie and Gran returned. "Good morning, sleepyhead," Carrie said, kissing him on the top of his unruly golden-brown curls. "Did you sleep well?"

"I did. I don't remember anything after . . . well, you know." He grinned conspiratorially at her behind Lois's back. Then he rose from the chair and took her in his arms while Lois finished placing serving platters on the table.

Carrie leaned in, wrapping her arms around Nate and resting her head on his chest. She felt the vibrating buzz of his pager before fully registering the sound. He stepped back and glanced at it. "Oh, geez," he said. "I wonder what this is."

Nate punched in a number on his phone and identified himself. Then he listened, his eyes registering increasing concern by degrees. He looked up from his phone. "There's a trauma case, a male with multiple gunshot wounds. We'll probably end up having to airlift this guy to a trauma one center. But I'll need to stabilize him first. I hope Dr. Jim can stay put in the E.R. until I'm finished. I'll take care of this as quick as I can."

While he changed into clean scrubs, Carrie quickly fashioned a sandwich for him out of a toasted English muffin filled with part of the frittata and wrapped it in foil. "I'll head over to the hospital in a little bit to help out, too. Here," she said, handing him the breakfast sandwich. "Eat something. It might be hours before you get a break."

"Thanks. I'll call when I can," he said and gave her a quick kiss.

Dismayed, she watched him race to his SUV, gun the engine, and speed down the road, trailing clouds of dust. They had wanted to spend the day together, maybe take a hike into the foothills. This kind of medical emergency wasn't an unusual turn of events, especially on a summer weekend in a national park. More outdoor activities translated into more injuries.

Last weekend, there had been a grizzly attack on a lone hiker. She flinched, remembering the woman's horrific injuries to the head and neck. She shouldn't have been walking alone so far from civilization. Even bear spray wouldn't have been much of a deterrent in that case.

Gran sat at the table and helped herself to a small amount of the frittata in the large cast iron skillet Lois set on the table. "I don't know how Nate does it," she said. "That's a lot of surgeries for one person. But I guess if we wanted normal lives, we shouldn't have become doctors, eh?"

"I have no doubt he'll do what he can here to ensure the patient survives the flight," Carrie said. "As good as Nate is, we have our limits here." This was the grim reality of Nate's status as head of emergency medicine and lone surgeon on the reservation.

Gran finished her breakfast and stood up. She went to the hall closet and withdrew her black medical bag. "Lois, that was a wonderful breakfast. Thank you. I hate to eat and run, but I must. Medicine Owl and I are seeing patients together today. I was thrilled that she invited me. It's sort of a dream come true, actually."

"Tell her I said hello," Carrie said. "I'll get over to see her as soon as I can."

At half past ten, Carrie donned a set of clean scrubs and drove to the hospital, feeling the need to do her part to help in the emergency department. Dr. Jim had texted that the waiting area was overflowing. Of course, most Blackfeet patients arrived with a troupe of family members, so who knew how many actual patients there might be? But when she arrived, it was clear that Dr. Jim had his hands full.

"Glad you're here," he said with a cheerful grin. "Would you mind handling the kid who needs his stomach pumped?"

Carrie rolled her eyes. "Sure, save the disgusting stuff for me," she quipped.

"Hey, I lanced a nasty boil, set a broken wrist, put a shoulder back in place, and stitched an ugly head wound," Dr. Jim said. He pumped his fists in the air. "I haven't seen this kind of action since I was an intern."

Carrie laughed. "Got to love your enthusiasm. I would have appreciated a day of more routine stuff. Laundry. Helping Lois clean my house. She's a whirling dervish."

"You can't stop her. You can only hope to contain her," he joked.

Carrie and Dr. Jim had enjoyed working together since she was a fourth-year medical student volunteering on the reservation. Now they had a natural rhythm and managed to triage and treat a steady stream of patients presenting with every conceivable malady. As usual, the day flew by. But by four o'clock, Nate had not yet appeared. Carrie grew more anxious. What was taking so long?

At five o'clock, she glanced up from entering information on the medical records system to see Nate as he walked into the emergency department, looking exhausted and elated at the same time. Spatters of blood could be seen around the collar of his scrub top and on one sleeve.

"How'd it go?" she asked, standing to greet him. "That sure took a long time."

"There were a lot of problems to fix," Nate said, kissing her quickly on the lips. He began explaining the surgical case that had taken him the better part of six hours to complete. "I *had* to operate, Carrie. He wouldn't have lived through a helicopter ride. There were gunshot wounds to the shoulder and chest, upper arm, and one leg."

"Jeez, what happened?" Carrie asked.

"The victim's brother-in-law was the shooter—some sort of domestic dispute." He raised his eyebrows. "I was able to repair everything. The guy was lucky we had enough of his blood type."

Carrie considered the patient's prognosis. Blackfeet Community Hospital had no intensive care unit. "And he's stable enough to keep here?"

"I'd say yes, although if things go south suddenly, we'll have to send him by helicopter over to Great Falls. He wouldn't have made it there without immediate surgery; that's for sure. I could have used another trauma surgeon to help with that mess. Thank heaven for our nurses."

"THERE'S MAIL FOR YOU ON THE dining room table," Lois said when they walked in the front door later that afternoon.

Nate rifled through the stack of envelopes and newspapers on the table and handed a large white envelope to Carrie. "Looks important."

She tore the envelope open and read through the cover letter before raising astonished eyes to his. "I can't believe it."

"What?"

"You know that publisher in Seattle where I sent my book manuscript? They want to publish my book! My research study about Native American medicine is about to become a real book!"

"That's great!" Nate wrapped his arms around her. "Hey, my wife is an author!"

"Carrie, that's wonderful," Lois said, hugging her. "What's the title?"

"The working title is *A Natural Approach to Healthcare: The Confluence of Native American and Modern Medicine*. Medicine Owl is co-author."

"Well, isn't that something?" Lois smiled broadly. "And to think that you and Medicine Owl did that research project together."

"I haven't told her yet that I added her name as co-author. I didn't want to disappoint her if it didn't get published."

Later that week, with Gran on a plane back to her medical practice in Philadelphia, Carrie borrowed a horse from a neighbor's ranch and rode into the foothills to see Medicine Owl. The old woman often retreated to the ramshackle hut a few miles away. It never ceased to amaze Carrie that the hut, little more than plywood sheets with a tin roof, withstood such long, harsh winters. Yet, Blackfeet friends assured her the hut had been standing for as long as they could remember.

Carrie tethered her horse to a tree and rapped on the door. When Medicine Owl answered, a sweet smile broke on her wizened face. Standing less than five feet tall, she walked with the aid of a tall hand-carved stick. She greeted Carrie with a warm cheek-to-cheek embrace and took her hand. "Come in, come in," she said. "I was hoping to see you. I enjoyed time with your grandmother. She is a good medicine woman."

Carrie smiled. "What you just said would mean the world to her. She admires your work, too."

"And how is your new husband?"

They sat on pine benches facing each other. "He's fine," Carrie said. "He sends his regards."

Medicine Owl tilted her head and smiled. "I like his face. And you are happy?"

"Oh, yes. I couldn't be happier," Carrie assured her. "He'll be a wonderful father, too."

"Yes, yes. It is your time to be parents, too."

"I hope so," Carrie said. "I don't want to wait much longer."

She watched as Medicine Owl rose from her bench and went to a table where she kept a large box filled with dried herbs and flowers. She turned and handed Carrie a cloth bag tied with string. "This is a tea for you. It will help with your cycles."

Of course, Medicine Owl knew. Never mind how she knew; she just did. Carrie had never told Medicine Owl that her monthly cycles had been erratic for a few years, likely as much from work-related stress as any other cause. She had long ago given up wondering how the medicine woman always seemed to know what was happening in her life before she even had a chance to tell her.

"Yes, that is an issue for me," she acknowledged. "Thank you."

"It is important that you rest more and take time to be still each day, even if it is only for a little while," Medicine Owl said. "You have much to do, yes, but to prepare for a child, you must be in the best possible condition." Carrie nodded at these words, comprehending the deeper meaning that stress was a factor. "Drink this tea before bed," Medicine Owl said. "If you are still not with child in a few months, I will prepare more for you. You are soon to be a mother."

"My own mother had difficulty conceiving me," Carrie said. "My dad told me that Gran gave her a tea. Worked like a charm, he said."

"Your grandmother and I agree on many medicines," Medicine Owl said. "Hers may be a little different from mine, but I am sure she would agree with what I am giving you: chasteberry, red clover, nettle leaf, peppermint, red raspberry leaf, and ladies mantle. It is pleasant to drink." She smiled, her eyes twinkling. "Just one cup. More will not help you get pregnant quicker."

Carrie sniffed the herbs before tucking the bag in her pocket. "Oh, I almost forgot." She unfolded the letter from the publisher that she had carried with her. "The book I wrote with your help will be published. I want your name to be listed with mine on the cover. You're an author, too."

Medicine Owl fingered the letter as the tiniest smile crinkled the corners of her mouth. She looked up, clearly pleased. "I have never imagined such a thing was possible," she said with such humility that Carrie was doubly glad they could share this honor. "I have never had the kind of schooling that you have had. This is a great honor."

"Maybe you never went to medical school, but you have information that is important for others to know, Medicine Owl. Now we can share that knowledge with the world. This book would never have been possible if you hadn't taught me what you know from your work," Carrie said. "You and I are a team."

"We are a team, yes," the medicine woman said, nodding. "But you are more than that to me. You are my daughter of the heart."

Carrie's throat constricted with emotion. "Daughter of the heart," she repeated. "I love that."

Medicine Owl patted Carrie's cheek. "You will soon have your own daughter to love."

Chapter Two

—⁂—

SEPTEMBER

A S SHE LEFT THE HOSPITAL THAT afternoon on her way home from work, Carrie looked out onto the mountains, the summit barely visible through the thick cloud cover. Snowflakes drifted aimlessly through the air, although none had yet stuck to the ground. Even so, Medicine Owl must have known the weather was about to change. She stopped going to her hut in the foothills and moved back in with her grandson in town. This was a message to tribal members that winter was here.

Carrie wished she had time to see her today, but it wasn't possible, not with so many patients. Spending time with the medicine woman always filled her with peace and a sense of wellbeing. Today of all days, she could use some comforting.

She had delivered a baby girl to a mother who was older than many first-time mothers on the reservation. She was Carrie's age. The baby was beautiful with long dark lashes and a perfect rosebud mouth. As she watched the newborn latch on at her mother's breast, and saw the joy on her patient's face, Carrie quickly excused herself. In the privacy of her office, she wiped her eyes and blew her nose, fighting to regain a professional detachment. No one could see her like this.

She thought of Gran's and Medicine Owl's advice to be patient and allow nature to take its course. After all, it hadn't been very long since she and Nate had started trying to be parents. They were newlyweds, and it was important to enjoy time together as a couple before children came. Everything would work out fine. It always did.

THAT EVENING, CARRIE SAT CURLED UP on the sofa, one leg tucked underneath her, a laptop perched on her knees, as she researched fertility doctors in the region. There was a good one in Missoula a few hours away. She bit her lip as she read the doctor's information online. Was this the time to take such drastic measures? Nate thought they should give it another few months. Admittedly, patience had never been Carrie's strong suit.

It was seven-thirty when she heard Nate enter the house and drop his keys on the table in the foyer. She quickly shut the laptop. Although she longed to have a discussion with him, she was afraid that if he saw what was on the screen, he'd say something wise and comforting, as he always did, and she'd break down. Her emotions were too close to the surface these days.

"Hey," he said when he saw her. "You won't believe what I heard today." He leaned over to give her a quick kiss and then headed straight to the kitchen. She heard the refrigerator door creak open and close with a thud.

"Don't keep me in suspense," she said mildly. "By the way, we're on our own for dinner tonight. Lois left a pan of enchiladas, though. She and Dr. Jim went over to see friends in St. Mary. This might be the last chance they get before they have to go back to Kansas City."

"Good idea. There will be serious snow any day now." He returned from the kitchen with a bottle of water, taking a long pull from it. "Okay, so get ready for this: I heard today that someone is moving into my old rental house next week. The unbelievable part is it's a surgeon." He sat beside her on the sofa and wrapped one arm around her shoulders.

"You're kidding." Her eyes widened with curiosity. This was big news. There were never enough doctors in such a remote area, which was why the hospital relied on nurse-practitioners and physician assistants. What were the chances another surgeon would show up unannounced? "When will he or she arrive?"

"*She's* here now. Margaret Blue Sky said she requested another surgeon, and then, she heard we were getting one." Margaret Blue Sky, a nurse with graduate degrees in business and public health, was the hospital's chief executive officer.

"That's fantastic. I'm happy for you."

He chuckled. "Said with just the right amount of insincerity."

"No, I mean it; I *am* happy for you," Carrie said, slapping him lightly on the knee. "It's just that while she's working staffing miracles, do you think there's any chance Margaret can wrangle up at least a part-time O.B., too? Do you have any idea how many deliveries I've had in the past three days? Seven, and that's on top of my regular patient load."

"I know," he agreed. "You're long overdue for help." He stretched his long legs out in front of him, resting his feet on the coffee table. "Okay, so here is the weirdest part. I already know this surgeon. Her name is Beth Bradley. We worked together in Kansas City. She taught me when I was a resident."

"And she wanted to come here because . . .?" Carrie's brows knitted together. "She loves Glacier National Park? She's always had a passion for serving indigenous people?"

"Maybe she does." Nate said. "But I wouldn't have pegged Beth as someone likely to come to work here." He raised his eyebrows. Practicing medicine in Browning, Montana went a step beyond rural medicine and was often referred to as frontier medicine. Most physicians who came and stayed were intent on a career in wilderness medicine.

"That *is* weird," Carrie said. "Did she know you were here?"

"I would assume so."

"It's strange that she wouldn't call you and sort of feel you out about this place. It isn't for everyone. Is she a big outdoors lover?"

"I doubt it." Nate raked his fingers through two days of beard growth. "She has my cell phone number, which hasn't changed since I lived in Kansas City. But today was the first I heard about this. You could have knocked me over with one finger."

It did seem odd that yet another surgeon from the same medical center in Kansas City would end up in such a remote location. Surely, it wasn't for the same reason that Nate had come here. Carrie's stomach did a back flip. Her gut told her something was up.

"Maybe Beth wanted to surprise you," she suggested. "Although, why she would want to do that is beyond me. You'd think she'd want to know details about what she's walking into. For one thing, that rental house leaves a lot to be desired."

Nate looked bewildered. "True that. But with Beth, who knows?"

"Nate, what is it?" Carrie asked. "I know that look. You want to tell me something but aren't sure how to say it."

"I guess I'm a little uncomfortable with the whole thing. I don't know why she's here. It doesn't make sense, from what I already know about her. I'm glad she's here, but I'm also wary."

Carrie studied him for a moment. "Well, let's not look a gift horse in the mouth, as they say. We need another surgeon. We've been wishing for this forever." Her eyes met his. "Maybe she had a crush on you."

"On me?"

"Nate, most of the women who work here have a crush on you, and probably a few of the men, too. I had a crush on you. This is not news."

"I married you. Why would you say that?"

"I'm teasing you." She had always known he was a man she could rely on and trust.

Nate took her hand. "You're right. I ought to feel relieved that Beth is here instead of overanalyzing the reason why. She's an experienced surgeon who has worked in an E.R. Plus, I want more time to spend with you."

Carrie smiled. "That's more like it."

She felt certain there was more going on behind those arresting sapphire-blue eyes than what he was telling her. If Nate was concerned about Beth Bradley joining the hospital staff, there might be another reason. Beth was a reminder of what had happened three years ago in the emergency room in Kansas City, when Nate had nearly lost his life. She hoped that wasn't what was on his mind now. She wanted their marriage to start off on the best possible footing with no memories of the past to mar their new life together. Yet, as she watched the expression on Nate's face, she couldn't help feeling anxious.

Before slipping under the covers that night, she turned on her laptop again and googled Beth Bradley's name. She was there on Linked-In, but without a photo. A faceless Dr. Beth Bradley had a physician profile on Health Star, and there were numerous patient reviews with an overall score of three-and-a-half stars. *Dr. Bradley is a gifted surgeon, although her bedside manner leaves a lot to be desired,* said one patient reviewer. Another patient reviewer commented; *Dr. Bradley saved my life after a head-on collision.* There was nothing to indicate that Beth was anything other than an exceptional surgeon. But wait, here was another review. *Beth Bradley killed my friend. This woman should lose her license.*

Carrie's eyes flew open. She searched for more information but found nothing. It wasn't unusual these days for a grieving family member or friend to write a scathing online review about a physician. It was a sign of the times. She searched for Beth's name under the hospital's physician directory and found her still listed as a member of the surgical staff. Was she on sabbatical? Or did the directory just need to be updated? She clicked on the link for Beth's email, but it went directly to the hospital's human resources department.

With her fingers poised over the keyboard, Carrie let out a long breath. It was late, and she needed to get some sleep. Whatever it was that had brought Beth Bradley to their tiny hospital was a mystery. Surely, Nate could find out more details later. She shut off the light beside their bed and snuggled under the covers, moving closer to Nate who was already asleep.

Annie jumped onto the foot of the bed, anchoring Carrie's legs in place. Carrie lay quietly, listening for the wolf and breathing in the sleepy scent of Nate. She gently pressed her lips to his shoulder, loving him. There was a howl in the distance, answered by another, then another. Those unearthly-sounding cries had once given her the creeps. Not anymore. Now, the howls were as familiar as drumbeats. Within minutes, she was asleep.

ON FRIDAY, THE TWENTIETH OF SEPTEMBER, Carrie opened the blinds in their master bedroom, and her eyes widened at the sight of two inches of powdery snow on the ground. Winter was officially here. It had been an even shorter summer than usual.

Dr. Jim and Lois would need to leave in the next day or so to return to Kansas City. The mountains in Glacier National Park were no place to get stranded in a snowstorm. She dreaded the time when they would leave, when winter would stretch out unendingly. She and Nate had grown accustomed to having them in the house.

"We're just like the Waltons all living together," Lois quipped.

The four of them had plans for a special dinner tonight to celebrate Nate's thirty-fourth birthday. Carrie had already purchased and wrapped an oil painting by Earl Leathers, a regionally renowned artist whose oil paintings of nature and his beloved Blackfeet people could be found in many museums, art galleries, and gift shops. Earl's paintings often depicted actual Blackfeet people engaged in everyday activities on the reservation. Carrie was the proud owner of one of his earliest paintings of a Blackfoot mother and her young toddler daughter. She loved Earl's work and intended to buy another of his paintings for Nate's birthday.

With another long winter approaching, Carrie had thought Nate would appreciate this painting to remind him of summer. Earl's painting featured a pristine cobalt-blue lake dotted in white caps and surrounded by a meadow of colorful flowers waving in the breeze. The 'Shining Mountains' in the distance were navy-blue, lavender, and rose. Nate would love it.

She had hoped to have another birthday surprise for him, but was disappointed that again this month, she wasn't pregnant. For someone accustomed to achieving every goal she set for herself, pregnancy was a new challenge for Carrie to master. It was a matter of biology, and Nate was doing his part. With so many unplanned pregnancies on the reservation, Carrie began to feel resentful of the ease with which teenagers conceived babies they couldn't afford and were too immature to parent properly.

It was even more frustrating that she had spent years trying not to get pregnant while she was in medical school and residency. Then, when she was finally ready to have a baby, her body seemed reluctant to cooperate. She brewed a cup of tea each night from the mixture of leaves and flowers Medicine Owl had prepared for her. She meditated, although her busy brain fought this quiet time. She took time to eat regular meals and healthy snacks. Unless she got called to deliver a baby, she tried to get at least seven hours of sleep. She monitored her temperature each day to determine the ideal time to conceive.

"You might be thwarting Mother Nature by trying too hard," Gran had advised in her matter-of-fact way, when Carrie mentioned her worries during a phone call. "Stress can have an impact on fertility. Relax and trust that your body knows what to do."

Carrie continued her efforts to eat well, get enough sleep, and envision how she would decorate the nursery for their first baby. Part of her frustration and sadness, she acknowledged, was that it was difficult seeing so many expectant mothers on a weekly basis and delivering their babies. Every time she heard a heartbeat on the fetal monitor, saw a little face with a thumb in its mouth during an ultrasound, or lifted a newborn into the world, a part of her soul yearned to experience that same joy.

Nate, on the other hand, took the matter in stride. He assumed they'd be parents within the year. Carrie hoped that by some fluke of nature, they wouldn't be denied their chance. If she got pregnant soon, they'd still have time for at least a couple of kids.

THE WEEKEND BROUGHT FOUR MORE INCHES of snow, along with winds that gusted to as high as fifty-five miles per hour. Dr. Jim and Lois reluctantly left the reservation, headed home to Kansas City. For the first time since the wedding, Carrie and Nate were on their own. That afternoon, they made their first trek on cross-country skis across their property. Afterward, Nate made a pot of chili, and they watched movies until bedtime. They felt like an old married couple.

Monday was a long, difficult day at the hospital, with an unexpected patient death from a condition that had been entirely treatable. The patient had refused to take his high blood pressure medication and suffered a catastrophic stroke. Carrie knew that he had seen Medicine Owl who had encouraged him to allow the golden-haired lady doctor to help.

Just before five o'clock, one of Carrie's long-time patients had to be admitted for diverticulitis, an acute infection in his digestive tract. He was in severe pain, so Carrie remained with him to get an I.V. started, making certain he was tolerating the pain medication and resting comfortably.

Afterward, she walked over to the emergency department, looking for Nate. As luck would have it, he was finishing up for the evening. He removed the paper mask hanging around his neck and tossed it in a trash can.

"Hey, beautiful," he said, his eyes lighting up. "Will you go home with me tonight?"

"It depends," she said. "Will you cook me dinner?"

"You bet," he said, giving her a quick peck on the lips. "I'll even unscrew the cap on a new bottle of wine."

"You sure know how to show a girl a good time," she said cheerfully, linking her arm in his.

As they made their way toward the front door of the hospital, they heard a female voice exclaim, "Dr. Nate! Dr. Carrie! Don't go!"

Turning, they saw one of the nurses from the inpatient unit. She was in distress as she hurried toward them, carrying a cardboard box. "I heard a sound by the side door. It sounded like an animal crying," she said in a breathless voice. "Look what I found."

Carrie gasped as she saw a newborn baby partially wrapped in a filthy, bloody, frayed bath towel. The infant's cry was raspy and frantic, a cry of distress. Carrie knew the baby had been crying for longer than a few minutes.

"Poor little thing." Carrie's heart contracted at the sight of the helpless, shivering newborn. She wondered how anyone could abandon an infant, especially on a cold night. She quickly realized that whoever had left the baby had at least chosen a safe, warm place. In an instant, her mind did a quick search through the names of obstetrical patients for those due to deliver soon. There were at least four possibilities. Why hadn't the mother come to the hospital to give birth? Where *was* the mother?

Nate gently lifted the baby from the box and held the infant to his warm chest as they hurried back to the E.R. "We've got you now, little one," he said in a soothing voice.

The nurse who had found the baby alerted hospital security. Meanwhile, Carrie began efforts to assess the baby's physical condition. As she unwrapped the yowling newborn from the towel, she saw that part of the umbilical cord was still attached, and yes, this was a little girl. The baby was still covered in amniotic fluid and blood. She guessed the infant to be less than two hours old. Luckily, the baby was in good condition and looked to be full-term.

"You've had a tough birthday," she said softly, swaddling the baby in a receiving blanket and holding her to her chest. She fondled the downy head covered in dark hair and swayed gently back and forth. A nurse held out a tiny bottle of formula, motioning with both hands that she would take the child. But Carrie shook her head.

"I've got this," she said, touching the nipple to the baby's mouth until she began feeding.

Lowering herself into a nearby chair, Carrie's fingers closed around the tiny body as she nestled her face against the soft forehead, sniffing the divine smell of newborn. Her heart contracted in sympathy for the helpless baby girl. The nurses would do what they could for the child while she was in the hospital, but there was no mother to bond with her. Carrie decided to seek out a nursing mother willing to provide breast milk for the baby.

She would do her best to ensure the baby remained in the hospital nursery until her family could be identified or a suitable foster family could be found. But oh, in the meantime, Carrie longed to take her home. She would help the baby understand that she was wanted—that someone cared about her.

"Looks like she found a soft place to land," Nate said as he stood over the chair where Carrie sat holding the baby.

"We need to keep her here until we find her birth family or a good foster family," Carrie said, meeting his eyes. "I wish we could take her home."

"She needs to stay here until a Native American placement can be found," Nate reminded her in a gentle voice, resting his hand on Carrie's shoulder. "It has to be that way."

"It may be the law, but it doesn't seem right—not right now, anyway." This was a federal regulation for the child's own good. Carrie understood the law, even if she now struggled to reconcile it with her emotions. The Indian Child Welfare Act of 1978 had been enacted to protect Indian children from being placed in non-Indian homes. This was intended to protect the rights of an Indian child to live with a native family and grow up with an understanding of Indian life. It was also intended to ensure tribal continuity.

"She's a baby. She needs to be held, not shuttled from a hospital to some agency office to someone's temporary home. Oh, and what about her mother? Nate, whoever gave birth to this baby needs medical care."

Nate's brows knitted together. "The police were notified. We'll make sure anyone who comes in with complications from childbirth is questioned. I'll also call around to E.R.s in other towns and let them know, too. If the birth mother is anywhere on the reservation, we'll find her."

An hour later, with the baby girl fed and tucked into the hospital nursery, Carrie and Nate headed home. Carrie was barely conscious of Nate helping her out of her coat or tucking a blanket around her legs as she sat in a chair by the fireplace. Nor was she fully aware of the glass of wine he handed her, or of the kiss he pressed into her hair. After heating up leftover chili and whipping up a pan of cornbread, he arranged a plate on a TV tray as she sat staring into space, lost in thought.

"Can I get you anything else?" he asked.

She shook her head no before giving him a wan, sad smile. "Thank you."

But she didn't touch her food. He sat down on the footrest, facing her. "What are you thinking?"

"I was wondering about the baby's mother, what reason she could possibly have had for leaving her baby, especially so soon after giving birth. Was she alone when she delivered? Was she being threatened, in some way? Is she okay now?"

"I wonder if she'll come back for her baby," Nate said, helping himself to a bite of her untouched cornbread and wiping a dribble of butter off his chin. "She might have gotten scared and made a decision she'll regret."

Carrie pursed her lips. "It would be best if the baby could be reunited with her mother, assuming there's a chance of that, and the home environment is safe. But if there isn't a chance, for whatever reason, I don't want her to go to foster care with someone who doesn't live here in Browning. Someday, that little girl might want to know her mother and her birth family."

"There's a chance the mother was just passing through, stayed to give birth, and moved on," Nate pointed out.

"I don't think so," Carrie said. "I have a feeling something bad happened."

After they went to bed, he held her close. As troubling thoughts paraded like stormtroopers through Carrie's head, she knew her concerns about the baby were fueled by fears that she might not be able to have a child of her own. She should have been pregnant by now. What was preventing her from conceiving?

It didn't matter how much she knew about biology. She was a doctor who understood the vagaries of fertility, but she was also a woman who desired a child. Emotions won out over textbook knowledge every time.

Chapter Three

⚊⚬⚊

THE NEXT MORNING, CARRIE HURRIED TO the nursery to visit the baby. She hadn't been able to get her out of her mind most of the night. To her delight, she saw Medicine Owl conferring with two nurses. In all the time Carrie had lived and worked on the reservation, she had never seen Medicine Owl at the hospital.

"Medicine Owl!" she said. "I didn't expect to see you here." She touched her cheeks to either side of the woman's weathered, wrinkled face. "I'm glad you came."

"I would like to talk with the doctor alone," Medicine Owl told the nurses.

They looked surprised, but complied with the request, leaving Carrie and the medicine woman standing in front of the baby's bassinet. Carrie watched the infant's mouth make sucking motions in her sleep. The baby had long eyelashes and a cap of fine dark hair.

"This is a lucky baby. She might have died," Medicine Owl said. "I am glad someone brought her to the hospital."

"We haven't been able to find the mother yet," Carrie told Medicine Owl. "In the meantime, this baby needs a place to live. We can't keep her here much longer."

Medicine Owl took Carrie's arm. "This baby belongs with you," she said in a firm voice. "She needs what you have to give her."

Carrie felt her knees weaken. Of all the statements the medicine woman could have said, this was the most unexpected of all. "Oh, but I can't," she said, her eyes wide with disbelief. "Medicine Owl, it's the law. I can't take this baby home. I am not one of your people. I'd have to at least be Native American, wouldn't I?"

"She is better off living with you," Medicine Owl said in a firm voice. "Her family is nearby. I know that."

"Do you know who the parents are?" Carrie took in a deep breath. Medicine Owl knew everyone.

Medicine Owl opened her mouth to speak, then closed it. She seemed to be weighing her response. "I know this baby needs the kind of care you can give her." Medicine Owl's expression was resolute. "You want a baby, and I know that you and your husband can take care of her. I will talk with the tribal elders. They will listen to me."

"But what about the authorities? Even if the tribal elders agree with you, the social service people won't think it's a good idea. And the government . . ."

"Yes, yes, I know. The government." Medicine Owl's lips pursed, and her jaw worked back and forth. "The government does things to people, especially our people. The government does not care about this baby." Medicine Owl tightened her hold on Carrie's arm. "The baby will live with you. You are the best one for her. We will find a way."

THE NEXT MORNING, CARRIE SLUNG HER stethoscope around her neck and knocked lightly on the door of the examination room. She had just vaccinated screaming infant twins and couldn't have been more relieved that her next patient was an adult. Earl Leathers, the artist whose painting Carrie had given Nate for his birthday, was waiting for her.

A new thought flashed through Carrie's mind. Earl was a newly elected member of Tribal Council. His opinion would be critical if she and Nate were to apply to foster—and perhaps even to attempt to adopt—the Blackfoot baby girl. But would he agree with Medicine Owl that the baby belonged with Carrie and Nate? Nate had cautioned her against thinking this was a sure thing. They might be friends of the Leathers family, but they were not Native Americans.

"Blood is thicker," he had said the night before as they lay face to face, a full moon illuminating their features. "I don't want you hurt by this process and how it is probably going to turn out."

"But Medicine Owl thinks this is best. She knows something about the family, Nate."

He caressed her cheek with his fingers. "I'm sure she knows who gave birth to this baby. She knows everyone here," he acknowledged. "She's not saying who it is, and I'm sure she has a good reason." Nate was silent for a moment before continuing. "I know what's in your heart, Carrie. You want this baby to be loved. *You* want to love this baby, and that's a good thing, but we know about the law."

"Are you afraid to love her?" Carrie asked in a low, soft voice. "Because I'm not."

"Maybe I am," he admitted. "I'm not saying I don't want to take her. I'm just saying we need to think about it more."

Carrie understood what he was saying. Yet she also knew that situations happened in ways that seemed random, without purpose, resolving themselves in ideal, often unimaginable ways. Even the bad stuff turned out for the best.

How, then, could she doubt that this baby's appearance in their lives was significant, though she might not yet understand the why's or the how's of what might happen?

Carrie opened the door to the exam room. Earl Leathers sat on the table answering questions posed by Carrie's nurse, Peg Bright Fish, R.N. A handsome man in his fifties, Earl was a stockier version of his handsome sons. And, like many Indian men, he wore his salt-and-pepper hair long, tied back with a leather band.

"Good morning, Earl," Carrie said with a smile when she entered the exam room. They shook hands. "I'm glad to see you. Nate and I want to thank you again for coming to our wedding."

"My wife and I were happy to be part of your big day," Earl said. "My son John and his wife Gali were honored to be part of the ceremony."

"We wouldn't have been able to do it without them. They're our best friends," Carrie said. She chuckled. "Your grandson is certainly getting to be a handful." They laughed easily together, remembering the temper tantrum that had finally sent John and Gali home for the evening with their screaming baby boy Charlie.

"He reminds me of his father," Earl said. "John might seem well-behaved now, but it was not always the case."

Carrie laughed and shook her head. Earl gave her a lopsided smile. She hoped he'd still have a smile for her at the end of today's visit. She had unfortunate news for him. It would be as difficult for her to share this news as it would be for Earl to hear it.

Leaning against the counter, she reviewed her patient's chart, noting differences in blood chemistry levels from Earl's past clinic visits. Peg sat on a desk chair next to the examination table, entering his vital signs on the electronic medical records system. She carried on a mostly one-way conversation with him. Carrie suspected that Peg already knew the answers to the questions she posed to Earl regarding his dietary habits. Nevertheless, her nurse kept up the pretense of professional detachment.

Carrie understood that Peg knew more about their patients than anything Carrie could read on a chart or learn from laboratory tests. When Carrie diagnosed a patient's condition and drew up a treatment plan, Peg knew the psychological and spiritual aspects of the patient's life. She often shared that a patient needed the sweat lodge or that Carrie ought to confer with Medicine Owl. Carrie learned to take her at her word.

Peg and Earl's wife Nadie had known each other since childhood and were good friends. Occasionally, as Peg asked questions of Earl, he nodded or gave a one-word answer. Peg would hesitate a moment before typing in a more detailed answer. Watching and listening, Carrie smiled and bit her lip. Peg likely possessed information gained from Nadie from more casual conversations.

Carrie went to the sink and washed her hands. As she lathered up, she thought about Earl's time on Tribal Council this year. He had demonstrated an ability to be progressive even as he worked to protect the rights of his people against attempts to undermine their culture. Everyone in town agreed that Earl was the best choice to serve on the council. He was a natural-born leader, and people respected him. Quiet and introverted, he had been a strong advocate for his paintings, able to navigate the art world outside of the reservation with relative ease. When Earl spoke, others listened. Although Carrie hadn't known him long, she found him much like his son John: genuine, a man of his word.

Over the past two years, the entire Leathers family had become the dearest of friends to Carrie and Nate. In addition to John, the middle son who was superintendent of the Browning public schools, Earl and Nadie also had a daughter Cheryl who worked with her mother making moccasins. The Leathers' oldest son Mike was a recovering alcoholic who had turned his life around and become a well-respected artist like his father.

"My husband loved your painting," Carrie said, returning to Earl's side. "Now we have two of your paintings in our home."

"I am glad you enjoy it," Earl said. "Since my election to the council, I have had much work to do to help my people. It has cut into my painting time."

Carrie curbed the impulse to ask if Medicine Owl had spoken to him of any matter involving an abandoned baby. Now was not the time. She did a visual assessment of her patient noting that he was carrying extra weight around his middle. She took his hands and examined his fingers and fingernails. His skin was dry and cracked. Pulling her stethoscope from the pocket of her white coat, she listened to his heart and lungs and performed a physical examination

When she finished, she tucked the stethoscope into her pocket and leaned against the counter. "Earl, I see that your blood pressure is under control now. That's good. I wish I had better news for you, though. Your A1C is ten. You were pre-diabetic last year. Now you are considered diabetic." He grimaced. "The A1C test of your blood measures blood sugar over a three-month period and is very accurate. This means your body is not able to use up the sugar in your bloodstream. We will need to begin medications to get your blood sugar under control."

Earl considered her words for a moment. Carrie watched the expression on his face. He clearly tried to project an air of calm, but the anxious look in his eyes was unmistakable. She started to speak, but he held up his hand. "Will I need the shots?" he asked.

"I will start you on a very effective oral medication and see how you do. But you'll need to check your blood sugar regularly with the little glucose monitor we'll give you today. There is a quick sting to your finger, but I'm told by many patients that they quickly get used to it. Peg will show you how to test your blood with the paper strips, and you can practice while she watches. I know this isn't news you want to hear, and I wish I didn't have to say it. The sooner we get your blood sugar under control, the healthier you'll be."

Earl was silent, processing this information. She studied him for a moment, wishing she could read his thoughts. "I think it would be good for Nadie to come with you here tomorrow," she added. "We can talk with both of you about the diet we want you to follow. I know she will want to help you eat healthier and lose a little weight."

Earl nodded. Carrie patted him on the arm. She knew that the typical Blackfeet diet of processed, refined foods was a primary cause of much of the diabetes and hypertension she saw in her patient population. Add to that the fact that Nadie Leathers was a wonderful cook and baker, and she could see why Earl had become overweight and diabetic. Yet Carrie had little doubt that Nadie would adjust her cooking habits to suit her husband's need for a diet with less refined foods, more lean protein, vegetables, and fruits.

"You can still enjoy your favorite foods—in moderation," Carrie hastened to add. "What does Medicine Owl say? 'A little is just right. Too much is not good.' You'll just need to be careful how much you eat of Nadie's good cooking, and plan for when you eat those things. For now, Peg will help you learn how to use the glucose monitor. If you have questions, you can call me anytime. I'd like to see you more often until we know how you're tolerating the medication and whether you need more help from us."

She left the exam room with a heavy heart. She had nothing but sympathy for what Earl was experiencing. In her role as a primary care doctor, she had the opportunity to know family members across generations. In the case of the Leathers family, she had been their family's physician for the past two years, seeing grandparents, parents, children, uncles, aunts, and cousins. She had delivered one grandchild and would deliver his sibling next March. Earl's diagnosis would be a concern to all of them. With any luck, his condition would provide her with opportunities to share information about diet and exercise to help others in the family avoid the same plight.

"Nadie has her work cut out for her," Peg said afterward, letting out a huge sigh. "Earl, well . . . he doesn't like needles, and she'll have to make sure he keeps up with his testing. That won't be easy. Men can be mules. My Ken is like a grizzly with a sore behind when he has to test his blood."

Carrie laughed, nearly snorting a mouthful of coffee. Peg ruled the roost in the clinic and at home. Ken would have little choice but to cooperate. "I haven't known Nadie Leathers as long as you have," Carrie said. "But from what I know about her, she runs a tight ship at home. Earl will have hell to pay if he doesn't cooperate."

"Let the games begin," Peg said.

"NUTTAH," CARRIE SAID TO THE BABY. "I think that should be your name." Nuttah was a Native American name that meant *my heart*. "How do you feel about that?" The baby had a serious look on her face as if considering her options.

Carrie unwrapped her from the receiving blanket and examined her, noting that her skin had a slight yellowish pallor. "And you, my dear, will need to be under the bilirubin lights for a bit. Think of it like a vacation to some place warmer than here."

As she wrote instructions for the nurses, Carrie thought of the three young Blackfeet mothers who had come forward to provide breastmilk for the abandoned baby. They had arrived separately at the hospital throughout the day, telling the receptionist at the front desk that they were there "to feed the new baby." When Carrie asked the first volunteer how she knew about the baby who needed milk, the young woman said, "Medicine Owl told me to come."

"Ah, yes. I should have known," Carrie said, smiling. "Well, right this way. The baby thanks you, and I thank you."

She called for a nurse experienced with lactation to help supervise collection of the milk for Nuttah. What a stroke of luck it was to have these young mothers willing to help. This was one less thing to worry about. Nuttah would get all the benefits of mother's milk, at least for a while.

Two days passed, and no family member stepped forward to claim the baby. There also was no foster family with room to accept a newborn. Even more worrisome, Margaret Blue Sky, the hospital's CEO, said they could not keep Nuttah indefinitely in the nursery. Time was running out.

"Nate let's do this," Carrie said. "Let's give it a shot."

"I don't know, Carrie," Nate said, looking worried. "What if . . .?"

"I understand what you're thinking," Carrie said. "What if we take her and then lose her right away? You're wondering if we'll be okay with that outcome. The answer is that I'll be terribly sad, but I'll also know that, at least, we tried."

In the end, Nate agreed, and they went ahead with their formal application to be foster parents. Carrie understood that if a Native American family came forward, they would not be approved. Still, she had faith that Medicine Owl's assurances that she and Nate should have the baby would be taken seriously by social services and by the Tribal Council.

That afternoon, after stopping by the nursery in time to give the baby a bottle, Carrie left the hospital and drove through the center of Browning's tiny downtown, intending to stop at one of the grocery stores. She wanted to learn how to make a proper meatloaf, one of Nate's favorite meals. His mother had given her the recipe Nate had grown up eating, and Carrie was determined to master it.

As she drove along Central Avenue, she saw an old Chevy truck belonging to John's older brother Mike. It was parked in front of the heritage museum and bore a bumper sticker, "Friends of the Wolves." Mike loved wolves and had taken on the role of leader in preservation activities.

But there was an even more interesting piece of news. Carrie had just heard a rumor at the hospital that Mike was engaged. She hoped it was true. He had worked hard to turn his life around after losing so many years to alcoholism. She decided to stop in to say hello and congratulate him.

She found him in the art gallery, hanging a large watercolor of sacred Chief Mountain, a high mountain with a flat top that played a ceremonial role in the life of young men in the Blackfeet Nation. It was on Chief Mountain that Blackfeet braves tested their manhood. Stripping themselves naked, deprived of food and water, they climbed the mountain in a test of bravery and survival. The fact that it was darned cold on the mountain at night further tested their mettle. Carrie had heard these stories from John and others, who had earned their feather after climbing Chief Mountain. She had never heard Mike tell his story.

"You probably know that mountain better than most artists who have painted it," she said, coming up behind him.

He turned and greeted her with a shy smile. "Hello, Dr. Carrie." He chuckled. "Yes, I spent a long night on that mountain and lived to tell about it."

"This is beautiful, Mike," she said, gazing at the painting. "By the way, I still have the painting you did of my wolf. I admire it every day."

Mike had presented her with the watercolor of the she-wolf several months after going into treatment for alcoholism. A high school drop-out with no job, Mike had nearly died from alcohol poisoning one night. With courage and determination, and with the help of his close-knit family, he had grown stronger and had maintained his sobriety. Painting had replaced alcohol in his life.

"Is the wolf still alive?" he asked.

"Yes, but she is very old." She was quiet for a moment. "I know she can't live forever."

Mike nodded. "A wolf is devoted to her mate and her young," he said. "When a she-wolf loses her mate, or she can't contribute to the pack, her life loses meaning."

"Just the way it happens with people sometimes," Carrie mused. She had often thought that the emotional lives of animals and humans were much the same. "Sounds silly to say, but I hoped that looking after me meant something to her. One thing I know is my life wouldn't be the same without her."

"I am working to save the wolves, as many as I can," Mike said, a look of determination on his face. "Ranchers want to kill them because they act as wolves do." He shrugged. "I cannot let that happen. I am organizing an even bigger protest group."

Carrie's eyes opened wide with surprise and delight. "Mike, that's wonderful! The wolves need someone like you to care about them." She took a deep breath. "I have also heard other news from my nurses that you are engaged to be married. Congratulations!"

"Thank you. Yes, I am marrying Naomi Prairie Hen in a few weeks." His mouth turned up at the corners, and he shrugged again, but Carrie could see the unmistakable joy in his eyes. "She knows me and yet, she still wants to marry me."

"Well, of course she does!" Carrie had to chuckle at Mike's self-deprecating comment. "You're a wonderful man—a successful man. She's a lucky woman."

Naomi Prairie Hen was the daughter of another dear friend of Mike's mother. The two women had planned from the time their children were born for Naomi and John to marry. But after going away to college in Boston, traveling in Europe, and completing post-graduate degrees, John had not been interested in marrying Naomi. Instead, he had fallen in love with Gali, a Cherokee math teacher he met at an education conference. Carrie knew how hard it had been for John to disappoint his mother. But having met Naomi, Carrie believed she was a much better match for Mike. He had worked hard to turn his life around, and Naomi was a wonderful woman. This seemed like the best possible outcome.

"Mike, something tells me that you and Naomi are soul mates like Nate and me," she said, giving him a hug.

Chapter Four

_⊸⊱⊰⊸_

The hospital grapevine buzzed like a hive full of honeybees. Dr. Beth Bradley might be beautiful to look at, but she was not as pretty on the inside. The nurses found the new surgeon difficult and overly demanding—not like Dr. Nate who was always so pleasant and respectful of others. Rumor had it, Dr. Bradley had taken an instant dislike to Dr. Carrie who was "as sweet as summer fruit."

It had not escaped Carrie's notice that Beth seemed to avoid her, whenever possible. In fact, Beth seemed to dislike her, which confused Carrie because she was glad to have Beth on staff. On the day they met, Carrie saw Beth in the hall and held out her hand in greeting. "Hello! You must be Dr. Bradley," she said. "I'm Carrie Nelson from Family Medicine."

"Oh, uh, nice to meet you." Beth had offered her a cool, thin-lipped smile. "You're Nate's wife."

"For almost three months." Carrie smiled. As they stood together, she understood why the nurses were so complimentary of Beth's beauty, although it seemed odd that Nate had never commented on her appearance. Beth was gorgeous, with long waves of dark-brown hair, eyes the color of blue ice, and a face that was beautiful even without make-up. The voluptuous curves of Beth's figure were clearly visible, even under baggy hospital scrubs.

"Congratulations on your marriage. You got yourself a good one," Beth said. "I guess Nate probably told you that we worked together for several years."

"Of course." Carrie smiled. "He also told me you were the one who saved his life after the shooting. For that, I will always be grateful to you."

"Thanks. He would have done the same for me." She studied Carrie with an expression that made Carrie so uncomfortable, she ran her tongue over her front teeth and crossed her arms over her chest. "Well, excuse me," Beth said. "I have a patient to check on." She turned on one heel and walked away.

As she watched Beth make her way down the corridor, Carrie sensed that she was under scrutiny and had been found lacking. She felt snubbed by Beth's abrupt departure. Yet, she reasoned, sometimes surgeons could be standoffish. She decided not to take it personally.

But the next day, when the medical staff met in the conference room to discuss several patient cases, Beth ignored Carrie's invitation to sit beside her and chose instead to sit across from Nate. Throughout the hour-long meeting, Beth made frequent eye contact with Nate, raising her eyebrows at something Margaret Blue Sky said, winking at Nate when he made a joke, and smiling conspiratorially at him when Carrie talked about one of her patients who needed surgery on his arthritic shoulder.

It was beyond rude for Beth to talk directly to Nate, refusing to engage in discussion with Carrie about her patient. It was downright unprofessional. As the meeting wore on, Carrie began to seethe.

Not wanting to make a divisive comment, she held her tongue and didn't say the first thing that came to mind. But when Beth ignored her comments the third time, Carrie made direct eye contact with her and said, "I'm sure you'll find the longer you are here, that we as physicians work together for the good of the patients, and that we respect each other enough to find common ground."

"As long as that common ground makes good medical sense," Beth said, narrowing her eyes at Carrie. "We have other patients to discuss."

"We're not finished discussing this patient," Carrie said in a level voice.

She was beyond furious. This discussion was too important to postpone. Her patient had unrelenting pain affecting his livelihood, and Carrie was worried about having him on prescription painkillers for too long. If she gave in to Beth now, it would be a slippery slope, perhaps making it more difficult to make her point at future meetings regarding other patients' needs.

Nate glanced from Carrie to Beth and back to Carrie. Then he placed his palms face-down on the conference table and cleared his throat before speaking. "For the record, I've examined this patient. There is so much arthritis, the patient has almost no mobility in that shoulder. The tendons are shredding because of bone spurs. Surgery now will make a difference and, I believe, will be more difficult to perform if we wait."

"Thank you," Carrie said, still not breaking eye contact with Beth

She recognized that, in Beth's view, it could appear that Nate was siding with her because they were married. Nothing could have been further from the truth. But this type of confrontation clearly put Nate in a difficult position. He couldn't be mediator in every challenge Carrie faced with Beth.

"I don't trust that woman," Peg commented that afternoon. "You shouldn't, either, Dr. Carrie."

"What do you mean, Peg? That I shouldn't trust her with my patients? Nate says she's very good. She's just prickly, that's all."

"You know what I mean." Peg lowered her glasses on her nose and looked over them at Carrie. "Dr. Nate would never be interested in the likes of her, but then again, men are mere mortals."

"I completely trust Nate," Carrie said, unable to suppress a chuckle. "Besides, Beth has known him for years. If something was going to happen, it probably would have happened already."

"She reminds me of an ice queen," Peg said. "One of those characters who freezes people with her eyes." Carrie sputtered at the mental image. "Well, she *does*. Those eyes are the color of ice on the glacier."

"Whatever happened to 'We have the two most gorgeous surgeons in the country?'" Carrie asked. "That came straight from your lips, Peg Bright Fish."

"That was before I saw her in action. Now I think she's trouble."

Carrie had to acknowledge that Peg might have a point. In a hospital this small, even one disruptive personality could cause problems for everyone. Nate rarely spoke of Beth, although she had called him a few times at home. He had taken the calls openly, and they certainly sounded work-related. Yet Carrie had to admit that while Nate was normally talkative about his days at the hospital, where Beth Bradley was concerned, he was oddly quiet.

As they waited to receive word about their application to foster the baby, Carrie had more serious concerns about Nate. He had begun having nightmares that left him soaked with sweat, his heart pounding so hard, she automatically reached over to check his pulse. The first time it happened, she had been able to rouse him by gently touching his shoulder. But the nightmares had become a nightly occurrence. She tried to make sense of the words he spoke as he thrashed around.

"Nate, honey . . . Nate!" she said on the third night. "Wake up. It's just a nightmare."

Nate threw an arm across his face, breathing hard. "I'm still here."

"You *are*. You're here with me. Do you remember what this one was about?" Carrie raised herself on one arm, placing her hand on his chest to calm him.

"It happens too fast to be sure. There are bits I recognize. I'm in the O.R., looking down at the patient."

"Are you the surgeon or the patient?" she asked in a flash of insight.

He was silent for a moment. "I'm not sure. I'm looking down at the patient, but it's as if I'm looking down from a higher place. It could be me, but I can't see the patient's face clearly. All I know is the outcome isn't good. There is a surgeon there, and I get the impression he—or maybe it's a she—shouldn't be performing the surgery."

"You mean . . .?"

"I don't know what I mean, Carrie," he said, rolling over and pulling the covers up to his chin. "I know it's not good. I can't help wondering if it's a premonition or something."

"Well, for someone's sake, I hope not," she said, wondering if Nate was reliving the night of his own trauma surgery. Or maybe the nightmares were a manifestation of too many surgeries catching up with him, and he was worried about making a fatal mistake. Whatever it was, she was glad Beth was taking some of the surgical load from his too-full plate.

The next morning, as they got ready for work, she said, "I think you should talk to someone about the nightmares."

"A psychiatrist, you mean? We don't have one here." Standing at the bathroom sink, wearing just his scrub bottoms, he ran an electric shaver over his cheeks and chin.

"That's why we have telemedicine," she said, caressing the small of his back with her hand. "You can have a session via Skype. All that's missing is the leather couch."

Nate chewed his top lip. "There is someone in Kansas City I could call. He was the one who counseled me after the shooting. He was pretty good."

"You can't keep losing sleep like this."

"I know. Neither can you. I can crash in the guest room until the nightmares stop. No point having you sleep-deprived, too."

"I would hate that, and so would you." She leaned in and raised her face to his, kissing him. "Whatever this is, we'll figure it out."

"You're right." He returned the kiss, drawing her face closer. "I'm sorry."

"You don't need to apologize."

"Sure, I do. I've kept you awake for three nights. Let me make it up to you. Let's go out for dinner tonight. We could go to Two Medicine Grill, make an evening of it."

"I can't say no to that. But, hey, promise me you'll talk to someone about the nightmares," she said. "If, as you say, there's no problem, then you can probably get to the bottom of this fairly quickly."

He cupped his hand on her face, caressing her cheek and chin with his thumb. "I don't want you to worry about this. I'm handling it."

"I know you are." Yet, as she thought of Beth Bradley's sudden appearance on the reservation—in Nate's life—she couldn't help feeling uneasy. This gut sensation was something she had learned to heed over the years. Shaking off the troublesome thoughts, she took in a deep breath. They were newlyweds, as happy together as it was possible to be, and she intended to look forward with hope for their future. Even if they didn't get permission to foster Nuttah, she might be a new mother by this time next year.

Chapter Five

—✦—

"A RE YOU SURE EVERYTHING IS OKAY with the baby?" Gali asked at her next prenatal visit. "I was never this sick when I was pregnant with Charlie. I'm worried that because I can't keep anything down, I'm hurting the baby."

Carrie washed her hands at the sink and dried them. "This is actually pretty common. I wouldn't stress too much if I were you. Everything looks good. Your blood pressure and lab results are fine. I'm concerned, of course, that you stay hydrated and get whatever nourishment you can tolerate until this is over. Ice chips help," she said. "Crackers before you get out of bed in the morning."

"Ice chips." Gali nodded.

"Ice chips are good because you take them in more slowly. Even if you throw up a while later, you're still getting at least some liquid. You said the nausea and vomiting don't last all the time, so if I were you, I'd try to drink more fluids when you're feeling okay. Let's give it another few days before we consider anything else."

"Won't I get malnourished if I don't eat? All I can stand is peanut butter toast and baked potatoes with butter and salt."

"Eat whatever tastes good to you whenever you feel well enough to eat. A lot of my patients say fruit smoothies stay down when they don't feel like eating solid food. Make it with almond milk, yogurt, fresh or frozen fruit, and some ice."

"I hadn't thought of that." Gali pursed her lips. "Charlie likes banana smoothies. John can fend for himself for a while. Right?"

"He's a big boy. He can manage. This nausea won't last forever. At least seventy-five percent of pregnant women have some nausea and vomiting in pregnancy. The future Queen of England had the same problem. I'd say you're in good company."

Gali let out a big sigh. "Between taking care of Charlie and working, it's much harder this time."

"For the record, I'm all for pregnant women doing whatever they need to do to take care of themselves. If you really don't feel well enough to teach, speak up. You're married to the superintendent. Surely that counts for something. John can find a substitute on those days when you can't make it to school," Carrie said. She leaned against the counter and studied her friend. "I know, I know. You'll be stressed over what you're missing at work or which kid needs you."

"We don't have substitute teachers for my math classes." Gali eased off the examination table. "But if you think this sickness will stop soon, and the baby is fine, I can deal with it. I don't have much choice. My students need me."

"If the nausea and vomiting get any worse, call me right away." Carrie thought for a moment. "Medicine Owl has a natural remedy she gives to pregnant women." She pulled a small notepad from her white coat and wrote down the ingredients. "Brew a cup of tea—black or raspberry, whichever you prefer. Add a quarter teaspoon of sea salt, a quarter cup of fruit juice, and a tablespoon of honey. Then sip it slowly."

Gali smiled, looking relieved. "I'll try it. I felt so lousy the other night, I wanted to call you. But I didn't think it was fair to call you at home."

"What do you mean? We're friends. You can always call me."

"You're also my doctor. You work hard, and you deserve a life."

"I have a life. Anyway, I'd much rather you call me if you need something." She squirted a dab of moisturizer on her hands and rubbed it in. "You're my best friend. I can't get along without you."

NATE WAS LATE GETTING HOME FROM the hospital that evening. A head-on car accident on a road outside of town had resulted in two critically injured patients including a teenage girl. Then the owner of a bar in a neighboring town was shot in a bungled robbery attempt by two young men from the reservation. Nate and Beth handled the surgeries together. All three patients were doing well.

"What's it like working with Beth again?" Carrie asked as she ladled chicken noodle soup into a bowl for him. She was more curious than ever about Beth and wondered how Nate felt being in the operating room with her again. Had it brought back old memories? She considered mentioning the troubling review she had seen online about Beth but decided to take the high road and give her the benefit of the doubt. The internet could be a mean place.

"Like the old days. She and I always worked well together." He considered the question for a moment. "I can't put my finger on it, but there *is* something different about her."

He took a large bite of the thick grilled cheese sandwich Carrie set in front of him. "We should have her over for dinner some night soon. I think it might help your relationship with her."

Carrie doubted this but thought better of saying so. "If you cook," she said with a grin. Nate did most of the cooking. "Grilled cheese is my forte. Let's not make things worse."

Carrie sat across from him at the kitchen table, watching as he ate the simple supper she had prepared. She smiled, loving the sight of him. *My husband.* Not even exhaustion could dim those eyes, as blue and clear as an alpine lake.

"The guy who got shot in the bar today had an injury that was similar to mine," Nate said conversationally as he took another spoonful of soup. "Beth told me it looked the same."

Carrie flinched. She didn't like thinking about what had happened to Nate three years earlier. While assessing gunshot wounds on a young male injured in a gang shooting, a rival gang member entered the emergency department, forced his way into the area where the patient lay dying, and held a gun to Nate's head. He told Nate to step away. But Nate instinctively threw himself over his patient, and the gunman shot him in the back of the leg, nicking a branch of the femoral artery. Then the shooter finished what he came to do by killing the patient with a point-blank blast to the head.

"That must have brought back memories. What went through your head when you actually saw the injury in someone else?" She watched his expression, but it didn't change.

"I was too busy getting the bleeding under control to think much about it," he said, concentrating on his soup.

"But you just compared the patient's injury to yours, so it must have affected you on some level, actually seeing it."

He let out a long breath. "I'm sorry I brought it up."

"Talking helps, Nate. If you deal with issues upfront, instead of pushing them to the back of your mind, you might not have to dream about them."

"Not everything has a deeper meaning. When I was little, I used to dream about a scary clown that broke into our house. It didn't mean anything. I grew out of those dreams."

"I would have to say that on some level, you were working through a fear of clowns." Carrie replied, twisting her mouth. "Medicine Owl thinks you know something about a surgery where there was a question related to its outcome. There are concerns about some aspect of what happened. She says you try in the night to make sense of what you know."

He let out a long breath. "I don't know anything, Carrie. Couldn't it be that it's just a random nightmare?"

"That keeps reoccurring every night?"

"Maybe Medicine Owl has an herb tea that alleviates nightmares," Nate said, throwing his hand up in the air.

"Maybe she does. Nate, she just *knows* things. I didn't even tell her you were having nightmares. She was the one who brought it up."

"Carrie, there's no point in trying to make sense of it. Stuff just happens. We deal with it the best way we can."

"That's exactly my point."

"Okay, I'll call the therapist in Kansas City and see what he thinks. Happy?" He nudged her under the table with his bare foot.

"I won't be happy until you can sleep," Carrie said and nudged him back. "I'm worried about you."

This was an understatement. The nightmares continued, with Nate mumbling incoherently and sweating profusely. Each time, Carrie held him close, murmuring reassurance until his heart and respiration rate returned to normal. He had gone to sleep on the sofa two nights in a row, but she had insisted he come back to bed.

"I don't want you to wake up alone," she told him, stifling a yawn.

Nate's nightmares were beginning to take a toll on her, too. She still believed it was Beth's appearance on the reservation that might have brought on latent memories of the shooting in the E.R. It made sense. Nate was a surgeon, but he was also the victim of a gruesome crime that had left another man dead. How did anyone, even a strong surgeon used to blood and guts, recover emotionally from something like that without help? There was bound to be post-traumatic shock, and Beth might be a reminder.

Unfortunately, this theory of Beth as the catalyst for Nate's nightmares became the trigger for a near-argument with him that left Carrie feeling anxious for days. Why was he so sensitive when it came to Beth Bradley? She replayed their discussion over and over, wishing she hadn't brought up the idea that Beth might, in any way, be to blame for his nightmares. She would never do it again. Nate was profoundly grateful that Beth was on staff, and he was protective of her in a way that surprised and unsettled Carrie.

She had posed the matter conversationally as they sipped coffee in the kitchen. "I think you have to at least consider the possibility that seeing Beth again might have led . . ."

His eyes met hers. "Let it go, Carrie," he said. His tone was even, his expression serious. "Don't create a problem where one doesn't exist. She isn't to blame. This is my problem, and I'm dealing with it."

"Nate, this is *our* problem. We're married now, and if something is bothering you, we need to handle it together. I only suggested it because she was there when you were shot. She was the trauma surgeon who fixed your injury. She's here now. You've started having nightmares. It stands to reason."

"Okay, I get that." He ran a hand across his eyes. "Look, I'm sorry," he said and kissed her on the forehead. "I'm a little tired."

"What can I do to help?"

"Nothing. Just give me time to work through this. I said I'd talk to a counselor, and I will."

Talk to me. What concerned her most was that it was uncharacteristic for him to clam up like this. He was reluctant to share what he was thinking or experiencing. This was not the Nate she knew, the man who had always been an open book. As he stood with her in the kitchen, the tension between them so thick it felt like a wall, Carrie wrapped her arms around him, not wanting their time together before work to end with an argument.

"I love you," she said. "What affects you, affects me, too."

To her surprise, he countered with, "I know you two don't like each other."

She felt her stomach flip-flop. "I don't know Beth well enough to truly dislike her," she said in a measured voice. "And, anyway, I don't have to like her. It's not about her—or me. It's about our patients. But surely you can tell she dislikes me. I say hello, and she ignores me. I try to strike up a conversation, and she walks away. She questions everything I say. So, yes, she's not on my list of potential girlfriends."

"I've seen her do that to you," he acknowledged. "This isn't the Beth I used to know." He shook his head. "I think she's had trouble adjusting to our culture at the hospital. Our nurses don't like her. A big part of that is her manner with them. I've talked with her about it. She needs to make stronger connections with people here." He paused before continuing. "Beth thinks the nurses don't like her . . . because of you."

"Me? She said that? You've *talked* about this?" Carrie stepped back, not comprehending the meaning of this remark, only that they had discussed her.

"She thinks the nurses won't give her a chance because they all think you walk on water." Nate looked directly at Carrie, who bristled. "She thinks you're turning them against her."

Beth Bradley has some nerve. Carrie let out a sarcastic little laugh and crossed her hands over her chest. "I would never do that! And this is not some high school popularity contest. I had to earn my stripes around here, just like you did. Beth needs to do the same." Seeing the look that crossed Nate's face, she softened her tone. "The truth is, I'm happy she's here because her presence makes your life easier. You and I have more time together."

"She's a nice person once you get to know her," Nate said. "We need her. I need her because I don't want to carry the entire surgical load plus the E.R. anymore. I can't."

Carrie heard defensiveness in his tone. She let pass the next remark that came to her lips and chose another more conciliatory one. "If you say she's nice, I believe you." She hesitated, thinking over her remarks and how she viewed Beth. "Okay, we've been talking about having her over for dinner. Now might be the time for you to invite her. Maybe if she and I get to know each other outside the hospital, we can start over and have a better relationship."

"Why don't you invite her?" he suggested. "It would mean more coming from you. Think about the changes she's made in her life. It's tough to live and work here. The cultural differences alone are like day and night from what she's used to. She wasn't prepared for this," he said. "We should be willing to do more to help her."

Carrie bit her lip. She suspected an invitation to dinner from Nate would mean far more to Beth, but she held her tongue. Nate had a point about the difficulties Beth might be feeling, working here. "If she's experiencing doubts about what she's doing here, I think that's normal," she said. "Has she ever talked to you about *why* she came here?"

There had been moments during Carrie's first year on the reservation when she had questioned everything about her life, missing Gran and her parents so much, she cried herself to sleep. Nate was Beth's only link with the life she knew in Kansas City. It was only natural she would gravitate more to him than to Carrie or anyone else.

"She doesn't say much about it, other than she has some things to figure out. She thought this would be a way to give back, to remember why she became a surgeon. Her reasons are as valid as yours or mine."

"Of course, they are. I'm glad to hear that about her. Are you concerned that she's miserable here and will leave after her contract is up?"

"It's more than that. I think she's going through something really hard right now." He took a deep breath and let it out. "Could you please try to overlook how she's behaved so far? I know it's not your problem, and I'm sorry if you thought I was mad at you." He glanced at his cell phone and his forehead creased. "I have to get going."

"I'll try harder to make Beth feel welcome," Carrie promised, handing him a travel mug of coffee.

"Great. I should be home by six," he said. "Thanks." He was out the door in a shot without kissing her good-bye.

As she watched him get into his SUV, it occurred to Carrie that the only question on her mind now was the one she should have asked earlier. "Is everything okay between us?"

Chapter Six

—⁓—

ANOTHER WEEK PASSED WITH NUTTAH SAFELY tucked into her bassinette in the hospital nursery, courtesy of Margaret Blue Sky. Carrie knew Margaret was as worried about the baby's placement in foster care as she was. Margaret might be all business with an eye on the hospital's bottom line, but she was also a former pediatric nurse and had a soft heart for Nuttah's plight.

"I have made inquiries," Margaret told Carrie. "We should know something soon about your application to be foster parents."

"Margaret, you've gone above and beyond to help," Carrie said. "Nate and I can't thank you enough."

She went to the nursery to examine the baby, rocked her, and fed her a bottle. Then, with Nuttah fed, dry, and asleep in her little bed, Carrie returned to the clinic. She had patients waiting for her. As she walked through the clinic door, Peg emerged from an exam room, looking grim. "You won't like what you see in there," she said.

"Judging from the look on your face, it must be bad." Carrie followed Peg back into the room, where her next patient waited.

The elderly man appeared gaunt, displaying severe complications of diabetes. The toes on both feet were badly infected, the result of diabetes and neglect of his feet. The toes were in such bad condition, they would have to be amputated.

This was a patient Carrie had seen once before, over a year ago. At the time, she had been concerned about the man's non-compliance with his medication and the condition of his skin. Because he had been reluctant to communicate with her, she had thought it best to refer him to a Blackfoot nurse-practitioner for further care. Now she knew she had been right to be worried.

A quick check on the hospital's medical records system showed that the patient had seen the nurse-practitioner two more times and then stopped coming to the clinic. While examining the man, she learned that he had not followed dietary advice, and did not take medication as directed. Patients with diabetes needed to be especially careful with foot care. One little break in the skin could result in a serious infection.

Minus the toes on both feet, the man would have difficulty walking and could require a walker or even a wheelchair. If he didn't start taking better care of himself, he would have more serious problems, if he survived. She admitted him to the hospital and called Nate for a surgical consultation.

It was Beth Bradley who ended up being assigned as the patient's surgeon. Carrie called her to discuss the case, but Beth didn't return the call. So, Carrie went looking for her and found her in the E.R.

"Beth, I'd like to know what you think about my patient with the infected toes. How much of each foot can you save?"

"He won't be able to walk, anyway, so I'm taking off both feet. I'll cut above the ankles," Beth said. "Cleaner that way."

"It doesn't appear that the infection has gone that far. Can't you leave him with at least partial feet so he can remain mobile with a walker? If you take both feet, he's definitely going to be wheelchair-bound."

"No, I can't," Beth said, giving Carrie a condescending look. "I mean I could, but I don't see the point."

"Of course, you don't," Carrie said and walked away. Then she stopped and turned around. "I'm not sure Nate would agree with you. Margaret Blue Sky won't either."

"Do what you have to do. I'm the surgeon. I'll do what I think is best."

MARGARET BLUE SKY STOPPED BY CARRIE's office that afternoon. "I have called for a meeting to discuss the surgical case you're concerned about. Nate will give his opinion. Dr. Bradley will need to justify her reason for such extensive surgery. I've seen the condition of the patient's feet. I agree that what Dr. Bradley intends to do seems extreme."

"Thanks, Margaret. I believe Nate would take a more moderate approach, and I'm hoping he can convince Dr. Bradley to consider doing the same."

"I agree. This won't help your working relationship with Dr. Bradley, but I understand your position." She smiled. "I also came by with good news. The baby is going home with you, if you still think that's what you want to do. We have received permission from the state to release her in your care. I am told that you should also be hearing within the next week that you and Nate have been approved to be foster parents of this baby."

"That's fantastic!" Carrie jumped up from her seat, her face beaming. "I would take her home tonight, but I'll need a little time to prepare. Is tomorrow okay?"

"Tomorrow is fine. It is unlikely permission would have been granted if you and Nate were not doctors living and working on the reservation," Margaret said in a firm voice. "You have wonderful reputations and are well-respected. And since you own a home on the reservation, you aren't likely to remove the baby from the reservation. I'm satisfied with this arrangement, and I've spoken with the authorities."

"Thank you, Margaret," Carrie said. "I know this is highly unusual and that you went out of your way to go to bat for us. We're thrilled to be able to take her home, even if it's short-term."

Margaret's expression was somber yet full of compassion. "Carrie, you can apply to adopt the baby, but I don't hold a lot of hope that your petition would be accepted. The best we can hope for, in this situation, is that she will be allowed to remain with you until a Blackfeet family is found. Don't get your heart set that anything more is possible. This is a highly unusual situation, and you have friends who have spoken up for you. I say this for your sake—because I care about you and Nate."

Carrie nodded. "I understand." And she did. She was aware that the natural mother could reclaim her child. Another family member could step forward and volunteer to take the child. A Blackfeet foster family might have an opening for an infant. Living with Carrie and Nate would be a temporary solution for Nuttah, but Carrie was certain she could do what was right—what was best for the baby.

Margaret smiled. "Most people have nine months to prepare for a baby. You are only getting one day. Let me at least give you an infant car seat to transport her home."

"I appreciate that," Carrie said, a moment before a look of pure panic crossed her face. The gravity of what Margaret had just said began to sink in. "There are so many things we need. We don't have a crib, changing table, blankets, clothes, diapers, bottles . . . um . . . anything."

"Something tells me you'll enjoy that part," Margaret said as she turned to leave. "I think you're also going to require some time off. We'll make it work with one of the nurse-practitioners and the physician assistant until you get back." She accepted the hug Carrie gave her. "Now scoot," she said. "You've got a lot to do."

Carrie rushed home from the hospital, intent on driving to the nearby town of Cut Bank to shop for everything Nuttah needed. She changed out of her scrubs and into jeans and a sweater and headed to her car as John and Gali Leathers pulled into the driveway. Gali waved at Carrie while John backed the Jeep up to the garage and raised the tailgate. The back of the vehicle was full of baby paraphernalia.

Gali removed Charlie from his car seat. "We know this is happening fast, and you need everything," she said. "The only item that isn't new is the porta crib.

We don't need it until March, when the new baby comes, so you're welcome to borrow it."

"It's probably not everything you'll need, but it'll get you started, at least," John said as he removed an infant seat that doubled as a carrier and reclining seat.

Carrie's eyes filled with tears. "I was wondering how I could possibly get everything we need *and* prepare the baby's nursery before I bring her home tomorrow. But how did you know?"

"We heard," John said. "News traveled fast. The drums. Remember?"

"Of course." Carrie grinned. "I guess I missed the community update."

They unloaded the Jeep and took everything inside. In addition to the porta crib and infant seat, there were fitted sheets and blankets, a blue infant bathtub in the shape of a whale, newborn onesies, tiny booties, an enormous package of newborn diapers, bottles, lotions and baby wash, and even toys. "This is amazing," Carrie said. "You just saved me so much time. Let me write you a check for all this stuff."

"Absolutely not. This is our gift to your family—to thank you for all that you and Nate do for us—for everyone here. It's also our way of welcoming Nuttah into the Blackfeet tribe and making sure she has a good start," John said.

"Thank you," Carrie said, hugging them. "I'm excited to bring her home!"

"Will you be able to stay with her the rest of this week?" Gali asked.

"I can be with her for the next three weeks. After that, I'm going to need to find someone to care for her while I work, assuming that is, that we still have her." It would be important to choose a member of the Blackfeet tribe so that they were following recommended guidelines for the baby's wellbeing.

"If I think of anyone, I'll call you," Gali said. "Maybe Medicine Owl can help you find someone to babysit. She knows everyone on the reservation."

That evening, as she cleaned the bedroom that had quickly been converted to a nursery, Carrie remembered Medicine Owl's statement, "This baby belongs with you."

As it turned out, the medicine woman's message was literal. Late morning the next day, a few hours after Carrie brought Nuttah home, Medicine Owl came to visit. As Carrie gave Nuttah a sponge bath, treated the umbilical cord stub, and fastened on a clean diaper, the medicine woman held the infant and prayed over her.

Laying a hand on Carrie's arm, she said, "You understand our ways. We will help you raise her so that this baby understands what it means to be a Blackfoot."

"Are you actually telling me that you think we should adopt her?" Carrie asked as she dressed Nuttah in a fleecy onesie and zipped it up. "From everything I've read and been told, that would be an uphill battle and there would be almost no chance of success."

"We must do what is best for the child. The Great Spirit has seen fit to bring her to you. I will help you, too," Medicine Owl said. "We will show everyone that the baby is living as a member of the Blackfeet tribe. She is surrounded by Blackfeet people who care for her."

Carrie felt humbled by the medicine woman's words, in her faith that a white woman could mother a Blackfeet child. "Thank you. Of course, I'll need to talk this over some more with Nate. I know he'll want what is best for Nuttah. He was fine with being a foster parent, but I don't know if he will agree that we should adopt her. It's a lot to think about. We haven't even been formally approved as foster parents yet."

Carrie wrapped the baby in a blanket and put her in Medicine Owl's outstretched arms. She wondered what Nate would say when she told him. "If he does think we should keep her, I want to start the adoption process right away. It would be awful to have her for months or even a year or more and then give her up. It would be traumatic for Nuttah, too."

"It is better for her to be with you," Medicine Owl repeated. "That is all I have to say about that."

Carrie was ecstatic later that week when the social services caseworker managing Nuttah's placement phoned to say that she and Nate had been approved as foster parents. They had gotten the nod much sooner than Carrie believed possible. In addition to Margaret Blue Sky, Carrie guessed that John Leathers had put in a good word for them. As superintendent of schools, his word had a lot of sway.

Carrie called Nate immediately. "We passed!" she exclaimed when he picked up. "We're officially foster parents!"

"We passed? Are you sure?"

"I just got the call," Carrie said. "I'm so relieved."

"That's great," Nate said, his voice trailing off. "Wow."

"What's wrong?" Carrie asked, tucking the phone under her chin as she fed Nuttah a bottle.

"Nothing is wrong. I'm just stunned." He was quiet for a moment before letting out a slight laugh. "Whaddya know? We're parents."

When Nate got home from the hospital that evening, he made a beeline for Nuttah, scooping her up from the infant seat and holding her against him. "Did you have a good day?" he asked the baby, whose large brown eyes were open, seemingly fascinated with his face, though Carrie knew she was too young to focus clearly on his features. He turned to his wife. "Did *you* have a good day?"

"I have no idea where the time went," Carrie said, dabbing spit-up from her shoulder with a cloth diaper. "Between feedings and changings, I haven't had time to think. It's been fun, though." She grinned. "Oh, and you're getting pizza for supper."

"Pizza works for me," Nate said, nuzzling the baby.

"And how was *your* day?" Carrie asked. "Didn't you have to do a hysterectomy this morning? How did that go?"

"I gave that case to Beth," Nate said. "I needed to re-break a guy's leg and set it properly. His brother thought he could fix the leg himself. Let's just say the results weren't good."

"Yikes. That's one of those 'don't try this at home' situations," Carrie said. "How did Beth take the news that she couldn't just amputate my patient's feet at the ankles?"

A line formed across Nate's forehead. "It didn't endear you to her, but I'm guessing you knew that. I agreed with you, so she backed down."

"I noticed when I saw her the other day that she wasn't dressed warmly enough," Carrie said. "I want to lend her a jacket. But I'm sure she would prefer something more stylish than what I have. I hope she's prepared for how long our winters last here."

"She has to return to Kansas City in a few weeks for some sort of meeting at the medical center. I'm guessing she'll come back with what she needs then."

"She must be on leave, if she's going back there. I thought she resigned." Carrie placed a frozen pizza laden with toppings on a cookie sheet and slid it into the oven.

"I'm not clear on her actual status there. She did say that she is going through the motions of defending herself in a 'frivolous lawsuit'—her words. She asked if I'd go with her for this meeting."

"Huh? Okay, first, you shouldn't both be gone at the same time. Second, why would she think it was appropriate to ask you to go with her? That's weird."

"She said it would help her case if I'd be a character witness for her."

"Nate, it might be a frivolous lawsuit, or it might not. What if she really did something wrong—like cut off someone's feet when that person still needed them? Would you want to defend her?"

"I don't know enough about the situation, but it doesn't matter. I told her I couldn't go, that we're taking care of the baby who was abandoned at the hospital—which she thinks is a bad idea, by the way."

"As if I care what she thinks," Carrie said, sniffing. "It's our decision, and I think we're doing the right thing. Oh, and by the way, Medicine Owl came over again today. She said she has talked with the tribal elders about us adopting Nuttah."

Nate put the baby back in the infant seat. "And what did they say?"

"I don't know. Medicine Owl told them it was important for us to keep her."

"She's adamant about that. Has she said why?"

"She won't go into detail. She just said she'll help us."

"Okay." He sat down with Nuttah and stretched her across his lap. "Let's talk about this. I know that you're anxious for us to start a family, but I'm still not sure that this is the best course of action. It's going to be a long, complicated process, and our chances aren't good. You heard the caseworker." He studied her. "Honey, we've only been trying to have a baby for a few months. What if you get pregnant soon?"

"If Nuttah hadn't been left at the hospital, I wouldn't be thinking about adoption, either—at least, yet. But she's here now, and I want what's best for her. If I get pregnant, it'll just be double the fun."

"But what's best for Nuttah might not be adopting her. Maybe she belongs with her own family."

"The family that abandoned her?" Carrie raised her eyebrows at him.

"I wasn't going to tell you this today because I don't know for certain. A teenage girl was brought to the E.R. over in Whitefish. She was in bad shape—seizures. The E.R. staff realized she had given birth recently. She also had a rough delivery, from what I heard, and she lost a lot of blood. She died of eclampsia. I'm thinking that girl may have been Nuttah's birth mom."

"Oh, no," Carrie said, wincing. She sat down on one of the kitchen chairs. "How horrible for that poor girl." She had never considered the possibility that the baby's mother might be dead. "But why drop off the baby and not get medical attention for the mother in the same place at the same time? Whitefish is at least two hours away from Browning. That doesn't make sense."

"Like I said, I don't know any more details. But I'm sure we'll hear something soon. You know how word gets around here. The girl lived with her parents and siblings here in Browning."

"So, that would mean there is no birth mother to claim her."

"If the girl was Nuttah's birth mother, her parents may want the baby," Nate said in a calm voice. "Their daughter is dead now. This baby is all they have left of their daughter." He studied Carrie's face, putting his hand over hers. "We have to allow this to go through the proper channels. If the authorities think Nuttah should be returned to her birth family, we won't have much to say about it."

"You're right. But I still want to try to adopt her, Nate. If Medicine Owl is okay with this, then I think we stand a chance. She's adamant that the baby needs to stay with us. I think she has her reasons."

"Carrie." Nate shook his head. "You've fallen in love with this little girl. But this could end in heartbreak . . . for you . . . for us."

"I know that. But just hear me out for a sec. We can talk with an attorney specializing in Native American cases. We can at least hear from an expert about what might be possible. And if we're told there is no chance, it will be easier to accept coming from an expert."

"Fair enough," Nate said. He put the baby back into her reclining carrier. "I want us to have babies, too. I guess I'm having trouble seeing this situation having a good outcome—for us. But you're right: we need to explore all the options. This is important to you, so it's important to me, too."

"I love you," Carrie said, wrapping her arms around him. She rested her head against his broad chest, listening to the strong, steady beat of his heart. "I promise I'll listen and do as I'm told."

Nate chuckled. "That would be a first."

Chapter Seven

—⦁—

"VIOLET, I WAS WONDERING IF YOU'D be willing to take care of Nuttah when Nate and I are at work," Carrie said. "You're such a good mom, and Peg told me you take care of little ones in your home. Plus, your boys are older, so Nuttah would be the only baby."

Violet High Tower, a cousin of John and Mike Leathers, was a patient of Carrie's. Over the past year, as Carrie helped Violet improve her diet and lower her blood pressure, her patient's health had improved. She had lost weight, and she had less pain. Violet had polycystic kidney disease, commonly called PKD, a genetic condition characterized by a proliferation of cysts on her kidneys. Although the disease might someday mean Violet would suffer the full effects of kidney failure, she was still in good health and wanted to pursue her dream of a career in childcare.

Peg had been the one to suggest Violet as the baby's caregiver, and Medicine Owl had been quick to say she was in favor of the idea. "She would be good," Medicine Owl said. "Her boys mind their momma, and it would be nice for the baby to be around other children."

Originally, Carrie wondered if Violet might be a possible candidate to be a foster or adoptive parent for Nuttah. But now that she and Nate were intent on adopting Nuttah, it was still important to choose a Blackfoot caregiver for the baby. She also had to consider that if their petition to adopt Nuttah failed, Violet could assist in the transition for Nuttah to another home. Even better, she might bond with the baby enough by then that she might agree to adopt her. The social services caseworker managing Nuttah's placement with Carrie and Nate gave her blessing to the infant care arrangement.

"I would enjoy having a baby around, especially a little girl," Violet said. "My husband does not want more children. He says our two boys have put him through enough. But he says it is fine to take this baby."

"Here's the thing, Violet. I might need to drop off Nuttah at night if I get called to deliver a baby and Nate isn't available. His hours are unpredictable, and so are mine. Is that okay?"

"That is not a problem. I still have the crib my boys used."

"We need to make sure it's up to today's safety standards. If not, I can buy another one for you to have here," Carrie said. She felt comfortable with the amount of space available in the small home, and with Violet's housekeeping. With these important arrangements made, Carrie knew she could go back to work, confident that Nuttah was in good hands.

"This is a huge relief," Carrie said later to her mother on the telephone. "Violet is a wonderful person, always smiling with a good sense of humor. She's excited about caring for Nuttah."

"I'm happy things are working out. It concerns your dad and me that you might not have smooth sailing in the adoption process," her mother said. "But where there's a will, there's a way. We'll hope for the best outcome in the shortest amount of time possible." She paused. "I trust I'll have a chance to meet this little girl soon."

"We're planning to come back to Philadelphia after Christmas," Carrie said. "Nate has a surgical conference in Baltimore, so Nuttah and I will stay with you and dad—that is, if we still have her. Nate can drive over when the conference is finished."

"Perfect," her mother said. "Let's hope for the best. I'll have such fun shopping for clothes and toys. It's been years since I had a little girl to spoil."

For a moment, Carrie felt guilty. If Nuttah was removed from their home, other family members would be disappointed, too. Her mother clearly wanted grandchildren. "Thanks, Mom. Thanks for not saying the things you could say."

"Like what?"

"That Nate and I could have our own child, that raising a Native American child comes with different challenges, and that we stand a good chance of losing her." Carrie let out a long puff of air. "Believe me, I've thought of all those things, and it's still worth it to us to try and adopt this baby. It feels right. Nate agrees."

"I'd say that if anyone else has an opinion about this, they ought to keep it to themselves, unless you ask them," her mother said. "You two live and work on the reservation. You understand better than most what the challenges are. As for having your own child, while you are caring for her and loving her, she is your child. I believe Medicine Owl was right. She belongs with you."

PEG STOPPED BY THAT EVENING, BRINGING a gift for Nuttah. "This is from all the Bright Fishes," she said. "Ken picked it out. I think he did good for a man who doesn't like to shop."

Carrie opened the package and found a tiny white dress with tiers of white lace. As she unwrapped the tissue paper and lifted the frilly dress from the box, she felt a warm sensation around her heart. "Why, it's a . . . a baptism dress!"

"No matter how she came to be here, she's a gift from the Great Spirit," Peg said. "I was hoping you and Dr. Nate would see fit to allow her to be baptized at Little Flower."

"The Catholic Church." Carrie paused. Carrie was a Quaker, Nate a Lutheran. Yet, she knew most Blackfeet in Browning attended Little Flower Catholic Church. It was only natural that Peg would think Nuttah should be baptized Catholic.

"This has all happened so fast." Carrie fingered the soft fabric, a smile on her face. "I hadn't even thought about baptism. Of course, we should do that." She tucked a strand of golden hair behind her ear. "There's so much I haven't thought about yet."

"One day at a time," Peg said, taking a quick peek at the sleeping infant in her seat. "She's so perfect, so pretty. It is sad that she was abandoned, but I believe that good has come from it."

Carrie smiled. "I feel lucky to be able to care for her."

Peg smiled. "You've taken on a special job, Dr. Carrie. Not every woman would care for a baby from a different kind of people. But I guess, now that I think of it, you're one of us. At least, we think of you that way."

Tears filled Carrie's eyes as she embraced her nurse. "You couldn't have said anything more special to me, Peg. Thank you. I'll do the best I can to raise her to be a proud member of the Blackfeet Nation—that is, if I get that chance."

"I don't believe anything happens by accident," Peg says. "It was a miracle when you and Dr. Nate came here to help our people. Maybe the whole point was for you to be a family."

Carrie considered this. "I remember before I moved to the reservation, I had a dream about my wolf. She spoke to me. I was a Blackfoot in the dream; I'm sure of it. Before Dancing Bird died last winter, she told me I had been a Blackfoot in a previous lifetime and that I came back to finish my journey here. She said Nate and I were connected by spirit and were meant to be together."

"And now, you and Nate are married, and here is this baby who needs you." Peg's eyes grew moist. "I came here to see the baby. But I also have some news to tell you. It is not good news."

"What is it, Peg?" Carrie's brows drew together. She locked her knees in place, feeling a lump form in her throat.

"We know for sure who Nuttah's birth momma was. She was called Kimi."

"Kimi." Hearing the name made the birth mother more real for Carrie. "Nate told me there was a chance that the fifteen-year-old girl who died of eclampsia over in Whitefish was Nuttah's birth mom." Carrie took in a deep breath, feeling queasy.

"Her boyfriend took her to the hospital over there because Kimi said she didn't want her mother to know she was pregnant. Kimi was very sick, and the boyfriend couldn't take care of her and the baby, so he dropped off the baby at our hospital, then took Kimi to Whitefish. She started seizing on the way and lost a lot of blood. It's not a federal hospital, so poor Native Americans don't usually end up there. The staff didn't hear about the Blackfoot baby at our hospital until later."

"Oh." Carrie sank into a nearby chair. "That's awful. How that poor girl must have suffered."

"She had a rough time with the birth. She was with her boyfriend when she went into labor, and it took a long time. She had the baby in the bathtub, so they could clean up the mess easier."

"Oh, God. The towel they wrapped Nuttah in was covered in blood, and it was filthy, too. Fifteen years old." Carrie shook her head. "She had to be frightened and nearly out of her mind, giving birth without a doctor or midwife there to help. It must have been terrible for the father, too. Did she live with her parents?"

"She lived with her parents and about seven or eight brothers and sisters. It's not the best home situation, if you ask me. But no one is asking me."

"I'm asking you. What do you mean, 'It's not the best home situation?'"

"I know the grandma. She can be a nice person, but her man drinks and uses drugs. Their kids have been in trouble. This one, the baby's mother, was not a bad kid. She had a hard life. Like a lot of people here, the family is very poor. They do what they need to do to survive."

Carrie chewed on her upper lip. "For a lot of reasons, it's good that we know the identity of Nuttah's birth mother. It's good to have a known medical history, for one thing. And it's important for a child to have the chance to know her birth family." Carrie's breathing became shallow at the next thought. "This could mean her family might want the baby back since their daughter is dead. Did the mother have any idea at all that her daughter was pregnant?"

Peg looked down and shook her head. "She would not say." When she spoke again, her voice sounded solemn and pained. "Grandma wants to see the baby."

THE WOLF CAME TO VISIT CARRIE just before nightfall. Carrie was so glad to see the animal, she instinctively moved forward, wanting to get closer. In an instant, the animal's stance changed from relaxed to watchful, as if she might bolt. Carrie stopped. The wolf might not be alone. She was part of a pack. Still, Carrie was relieved to see her. The animal's presence was a comfort to her. The wolf always showed up during times of stress. Especially today, with the announcement that Nuttah would be meeting her grandmother for the first time, Carrie wanted to believe that the wolf's presence was intended to let her know that she was here for her.

"Thank you," Carrie said out loud. "I wish I could do more to help you." She had considered leaving meat for the she-wolf to ensure she wouldn't starve, but Mike Leathers had said this was a bad idea. The wolf was wild and needed to live as wolves were meant to live, hunting for her food.

"You don't want a wolf taking food that is left out for her," Mike Leathers had said. "You might get more wolves and other wild animals coming closer to your home. It also can be deadly for animals to take food from humans. She is your friend. But it is best if you let her be a wolf."

"Of course," Carrie said, horrified at her own naivete. "I wasn't thinking. But I still worry about her."

Mike's wolf protection movement was gaining public support. He had even begun speaking at rallies. She had seen a story in a Kalispell, Montana newspaper quoting him, and was impressed with the passion in his message. John, however, had confided in Carrie that what Mike was doing was dangerous.

"I am proud of my brother, but what he is doing could get him hurt or killed. Ranchers don't want the wolves around. They want them dead, and they will stop at nothing."

"I should pay closer attention to this issue," Carrie said. "This is personal to me."

"At one time, wolves were nearly extinct in national parks, and the entire balance of nature changed. We are glad to see the wolf population return," John said. "When animals are driven out or killed, all of nature suffers."

CARRIE WAS RELIEVED THAT SHE WOULDN'T be forced to meet Nuttah's grandmother, at least not yet. The caseworker picked up Nuttah at Violet's house and took her to a neutral location where the visit could be monitored. All that long morning, Carrie waited and wondered. Would the grandmother fall in love with her new granddaughter and want to take her home? If so, how long would it take to determine whether the home environment was suitable? Or would it even matter? Did the fact that the birth family was Native American trump all other considerations?

She felt sorry for this woman who had lost her daughter in such a tragic way. Try as she might to put aside her feelings and think about the good that might come from Nuttah being raised by family members, she wasn't yet ready to do that. The feelings were too raw, too painful. Medicine Owl thought *she* was the best person to care for the baby. There had to be some reason for the medicine woman, of all people, to believe that Carrie, rather than a member of the Blackfeet tribe, should have custody of Nuttah. Perhaps Medicine Owl knew something about the family that she couldn't yet share. She decided to broach the subject carefully the next time she saw her.

To ease her frazzled nerves while Nuttah was with her grandmother, Carrie went to the clinic and threw herself into her work, reviewing patient notes from the nurse-practitioner and physician assistant who were filling in for her while she was at home with the baby. The staff, already overworked, was spread way too thin with Carrie taking time off. They were seeing more patients than Carrie thought was wise. She needed to get back to work as soon as possible.

"We're glad you have this time with the baby," Peg said. "But we'll be glad when you come back. It's been a three-ring circus without you."

"I'll be back Monday after next," Carrie promised. "I'm glad you thought of Violet High Tower. She's been keeping Nuttah a few hours at a time while I run errands. I wish there was childcare here at the hospital, so I could see Nuttah throughout the day. That would be ideal."

At eleven a.m., Violet called. "The lady from social services just dropped off the baby. I asked how it went, but she wouldn't tell me."

"She probably isn't allowed to say anything. How is Nuttah?"

"Sleeping like an angel. Dr. Carrie, I went to school with the baby's great-aunt, who is the sister of Grandma. I don't know Grandma very well, but maybe I can find out something more for you."

Carrie hesitated. She wanted more than anything to know as much as possible about the birth family. But she also knew that the perception of interference with Tribal Council or other powers-that-be on the reservation would be foolhardy. When she picked up Nuttah and settled her in the car seat, she said, "Violet, I appreciate your willingness to help get information about Nuttah's family, but we don't want to do anything to upset anyone. If you happen to hear something, I'd love to know, of course. But please be careful. We need to trust the process and hope that things turn out the way we hope."

"We will ask the Great Spirit to help us," Violet said.

"Absolutely. Violet, you know, don't you, that I couldn't do this without you," Carrie said, reaching out to offer Violet a quick hug.

"Medicine Owl says everything will turn out fine," Violet assured her. "If she says the baby should stay with you, the others will agree. Everyone listens to her."

"It's probably going to take a long time for a decision to be made. I doubt we'll hear drumbeats anytime soon, telling us what's going to happen," Carrie said, an attempt to lighten the mood.

Violet looked serious. "You have not yet learned the language of our drums. I will tell you what I hear."

Chapter Eight

—ᴗᐟᐣᐤ—

During the remaining two weeks of Carrie's maternity leave, an idea took root. She began working on a proposal to Margaret Blue Sky, asking that the hospital consider allocating space for a twenty-four-hour childcare center. She also identified Violet High Tower as a potential employee in the new center. Surely, other employees needed this type of benefit, too. Regardless of what happened with Nuttah, Carrie thought it was important to do something constructive for other working parents. Besides, she and Nate wanted more than one child.

Margaret Blue Sky's reaction was uncharacteristically animated. In place of her usual no-nonsense expression, her eyes lit up and she looked as happy as a six-year-old at recess. She took off down the hallway like a shot. "Come with me," she said, a look of pure mischief on her face. She motioned for Carrie to follow her. "Look," Margaret said. "This room used to be a lounge and private lunchroom for the doctors. No one ever used it."

"A lounge just for the doctors? We don't have that many doctors," Carrie pointed out. "Anyway, Nate and I would want the P.A.s and nurses to join us."

"Exactly. No one has time to lounge around here," Margaret said, rolling her eyes. "This space is large enough for an infant nursery. I think we could have at least four cribs in here and a couple of rocking chairs." She crossed the hall and unlocked a door. "And in here is a storage room that we can turn into an activity space for older children."

"Margaret, this is amazing!" Carrie said, a smile lighting up her face. "If we get started right away, how soon can it open?"

"I'll need to talk with the board first," Margaret said. "Then we will need permission on every level, state and federal. But I think I can find some money for the furniture. Optimistically, I would say by spring."

NOVEMBER

AS FAT SNOWFLAKES DRIFTED LAZILY TO the ground outside her office window, and the navy-blue mountains grew hazy in the distance, Carrie sat at her desk reading an email, one leg tucked underneath her as she sipped a cup of tea. The email, along with several attachments, had been sent from her publisher. She studied one of the attachments and frowned. Who knew so many details were involved in publishing a book?

The manuscript had taken considerable time and effort to complete, requiring countless revisions. Yet, it seemed the most daunting part of publishing happened *after* the manuscript was accepted and the contract signed. From cover design to line editing, proofreading, setting up a website, blogging, spreading the news through social media, planning a promotional campaign, and seeking colleagues willing to provide reviews, the to-do list seemed endless. Still, it was a process she embraced enthusiastically.

"It takes a village," her publisher joked.

The next step toward hitting an early winter release date the following year would be a meeting in Missoula with the publisher. There was much excitement about involving the medicine woman in the promotion of the book. Would Medicine Owl agree to a book signing? To Carrie's delight, Nate asked if he could go with her to Missoula. They planned to stay overnight at a hotel and enjoy a romantic dinner for two—well, three with Nuttah.

The trip was especially timely because there was an attorney in Missoula who had successfully helped three other Caucasian couples and individuals adopt Native American children. Carrie had found Joseph Red Feather online. She hoped he would agree to represent them in their adoption proceedings.

Carrie requested and received permission from the caseworker to take Nuttah off the reservation, a formality made slightly easier because they were approved as foster parents by the state. It helped that she and Nate owned a home on the reservation and worked as physicians at the federal hospital.

"In other words, we aren't a flight risk," she said to Nate.

Being credentialed to work at a federal hospital required a lengthy background check for new physicians. The fact that she and Nate had passed this process before coming to work at the hospital meant that the state would have no reason to be concerned about character or any past criminal history. The other important consideration in requesting to take Nuttah off the reservation was that there were no doctor's appointments or visitations with the grandmother to complicate their plans.

"This trip to Missoula is just what the doctor ordered," she said to Nate. "We can use a change of scenery. I've never been to Missoula. Have you?"

"I went there for a conference a couple of years ago," Nate said. "With another surgeon on staff now, it's easier for me to get a few days away."

Nate seemed more relaxed lately, almost back to his normal laidback self. He had begun talking with the same psychologist in Kansas City who had helped him deal with the after-effects of the shooting in the E.R. there. The nightmares were beginning to wane in frequency and severity, much to Carrie's relief.

"They're not anywhere near as graphic now as they were before," he told her. "At this point, I think it's more about figuring out who is the villain in the dream, or whether there even *is* a villain. I'm not even sure the dreams are about me."

Perhaps with a little more time, these episodes would disappear altogether. Sensing that he needed space to explore repressed emotions, Carrie didn't press him to talk about his sessions with the counselor. She knew eventually, he would share the details with her.

She was learning that even in a close, loving marriage, partners needed emotional space. She hoped that giving Nate this freedom would only strengthen their relationship. Although she tried not to feel threatened, she couldn't help but resent that Beth had such a stronghold on a time in Nate's life when Carrie had not known him.

Nate and John occasionally played basketball in the evenings at Browning High School's gymnasium. It was strictly a pick-up game with anyone who showed up to play—a hodgepodge of hospital personnel and young men from the reservation. Nate loved to shoot hoops, and it was important to burn off stress from surgeries. Carrie encouraged him to have fun with his friends. It gave her time to visit with her parents and Gran on the phone.

Afterward, John usually stopped by the house to have a beer and visit. Although Carrie felt this was "man time," John always included her in whatever discussion they were having. A few nights earlier, after Nate and John returned from playing ball, John said he needed to talk with her about the health class she taught each spring at the high school. Nate excused himself to shower, and John and Carrie sat at the kitchen table, ironing out details for the series of three classes she wanted to teach. They talked about sessions on reproduction, sexually transmitted diseases, and birth control.

She hoped the girls would abstain from sexual activity, but she had to be practical. Knowledge was power, and she wanted the girls to understand their bodies and how easy it was to conceive a child. *Easy for them, not me.*

If Gali had mentioned Carrie's frustrations over not being pregnant yet, John gave nothing away. Gali, too, had urged her to be patient. "It will happen," she said. "Probably when you least expect it."

It was a treat to have this one-on-one time with John, and Carrie needed his advice. She had come to rely on his valuable insights over the summers she volunteered at Blackfeet Community Hospital before moving to Browning. During her first year on the reservation, when she had so many questions and while she was so homesick, he had been a source of encouragement and stability.

The truth was that she was still here because John believed in her and had provided the encouragement and connections she needed.

As school district superintendent and a leader among his people, John was the obvious choice to ask about adoption of a Blackfeet child. More important, John's opinions mattered a great deal to Carrie because she trusted him. She needed to know that he was behind her and Nate in these adoption proceedings. Caring for Nuttah until a Blackfeet family could be found was one thing. Raising her as their own daughter was entirely another. If John raised any concerns, she and Nate would have to consider them.

She laid down the pen she had been using to take notes and took a breath. "John, I'm guessing Gali has told you that Nate and I are planning to adopt the baby."

"Gali has mentioned it, yes. I first heard about it from my grandfather. He is a good friend of Medicine Owl's. You have a strong ally there. If it were not for Medicine Owl's belief that this is in the best interests of the child, it is doubtful the tribal elders would have agreed to allow you to take her home. That influenced the state's decision to let you foster her, too. Even my dad would have balked, and you know how much he likes you."

"I'm grateful Earl is supportive." Carrie looked down at her hands clenched into balls in her lap. "Do you think we can really do this? John, are you in favor of Nate and me keeping Nuttah? It's important for me to know how you honestly feel."

John stared off at a distant point through the dining room window. Outside the moon cast a silvery glow over the blue and gray shadows on the snow. "If it were anyone but you, I would not be in favor," he said. "I would want the child to be raised by our people. But," he said, with a toothy grin, "You're sort of one of us now."

Carrie smiled and laid a hand on his arm. "Thank you, my friend. It took time, but now we can't imagine living and working anywhere else or raising our children anywhere else. We promise you, John, that if we can keep her, we will raise Nuttah on the reservation, and we will take full advantage of all the help and support your people can offer. We will enroll her in the Blackfeet school. Maybe she'll even get to know other children who are related to her. It's been stressful, thinking about all of this, but we want to do the right thing."

John raked his long fingers through his hair. "I know you do. It is inconceivable to me that you would not have considered all the ramifications. Remember, I was the first one in my family to break with the culture and marry an outsider. My children are only half Blackfeet. If my mother and father can learn to accept my Cherokee wife as a daughter-in-law, then I should be willing to think about what is best for Nuttah being raised by people who are not Blackfeet. In this case, I'm thinking that Nuttah couldn't ask for better, more loving parents than you and Nate. Count on me for whatever support you need."

As they heard the whoosh of the shower upstairs, John's eyebrows went up and he let out a deep breath. "That guy really worked up a sweat tonight. If we were playing in a league, he would have been benched tonight. Taking out his frustrations, I guess."

Carrie's radar went on red alert. "What frustrations?" she asked.

"What? Oh, nothing. It's just an expression," John said. "I'm just saying he seems to have a lot on his mind."

"He does." Carrie looked so serious for a moment that John leaned forward in his chair.

"Is everything okay?" he asked. "You look worried."

"Everything is fine," she answered quickly. Even if John was a friend, she didn't think it was her place to share that Nate was having nightmares. "We have a new surgeon at the hospital who is a bit of a pill," she said, and left it at that.

"I have heard that from my mother who heard it from Peg." John's brow furrowed. "There is one more thing I wanted to talk with you about. I shouldn't, I suppose. My dad wouldn't be happy with me."

"What is it? John, does it have to do with your father being on Tribal Council?"

"No. My dad isn't doing well with the blood-testing. My mother does it for him. It's a daily battle between them, and she is losing."

"I'm not surprised. Maybe he needs to come back for more practice sessions," Carrie said. "It can be tough to wrap your head around diabetes when it's first diagnosed. There are changes to the way you eat, and it's important to have a routine schedule—which, I might add, and I'm sure you will admit—is the hardest part for people on the reservation. People here tend to take schedules with a very laissez faire attitude."

"He resists testing his blood."

"Finger sticks are no fun. But some patients take insulin shots, too. Your dad is lucky that he's on oral medication. I'll call him tomorrow and see what we can do to help."

"He does not take the shots. Does that mean my father's kind of diabetes is different?" John asked. "I don't know as much as I should about the disease, I guess."

"It means that he's on oral medications now in hopes that he can make some diet and lifestyle changes, lose some weight, and avoid needing insulin shots in the future," Carrie said. "From what I've experienced with other patients, this is an ideal time for the entire family to adjust their eating habits, so everyone can have better health. Look at it as a wake-up call."

John patted his own stomach, which had been as flat as a washboard for as long as Carrie had known him, and that now showed evidence of a happy marriage with a good cook. "Guess that goes for me, too," he said. "I've got the same belly as Gali."

THAT WEEK, WHEN SHE TOOK NUTTAH to visit Medicine Owl, Carrie had an agenda. She wanted to better understand why the medicine woman was so adamant that Nuttah stay with them rather than being returned to her birth family. It was the very opposite of what most people would expect from the tribe's medicine woman. Yet everyone knew that Medicine Owl's decisions were always made with the best intentions for her people.

"Medicine Owl, you know Nuttah's birth family," Carrie said as she laid the baby in the elderly woman's waiting arms. "I want to be compassionate toward them. I can only imagine how hard it must be to have lost a daughter and to know that her baby girl is in the care of a white couple."

Medicine Owl stroked Nuttah's cheek with one index finger. "She is doing well in your care," she said. "She is happy and well-fed. You are able to do more for her."

"We will make sure she has everything she needs," Carrie said. "I give you my word."

"I have my reasons for thinking she should remain with you," Medicine Owl said. "Just as you have rules about talking about your patients, so do I. There are things about the family that cause me concern."

"Is there something I should know about?" Carrie asked, pulling her chair closer to the sofa where Medicine Owl had undressed the baby down to her diaper. She was performing her own well baby check-up, and Carrie was grateful to have such an experienced second opinion.

"There are sad things that can happen with families. Sometimes more than once." She didn't elaborate.

Carrie knew this was all Medicine Owl would say. If more information was forthcoming, it would be revealed in due course. For the time being, it was important to continue to allow Medicine Owl to see Nuttah regularly. Her input on the baby's welfare was critical.

Like any new mother, Carrie occasionally felt overwhelmed. Even a doctor had moments of concern about her child, questioning whether she was doing everything right as a parent. "I couldn't do this without you, Medicine Owl," she said. "What do I know about raising a Blackfoot child?"

"You know more than you think. You have had many experiences here that have taught you well. You understand our ways better than many others who have come here to help us." She smiled. "You have our best interests in your heart. I know that you are the best mother for our Nuttah."

NATE STOPPED THE SUBARU ON THE side of the road so that Carrie could take Nuttah out of her car seat and feed her a bottle of formula. They were on their way to Missoula. The baby's cheeks were warm and rosy from being bundled up against the Montana cold. The cotton-candy pink sleep sack she wore for extra warmth only enhanced her mocha-cream-colored skin. Her dark eyelashes brushed her chubby cheeks, giving her the appearance of a cherub. Carrie nuzzled and kissed the baby's head as she took the bottle, loving the scent and feel of her skin.

She was scheduled to meet later that afternoon with her publisher who was at the University of Montana for a writing conference. Afterward, she and Nate planned to have dinner at a restaurant John had enjoyed while completing his doctorate there. Tomorrow morning, she and Nate would meet with Joseph Red Feather, the attorney they were counting on to help them win their adoption case.

Nate glanced over at Carrie and smiled. His gaze fell on the baby, her soft fingers wrapped around Carrie's pinkie finger. "You've been so quiet," he said. "What are you thinking?"

"I wasn't," Carrie answered. She let out a quiet laugh. "I know you don't believe that."

"You're right. I don't," he said. He laid a hand on her knee. "We haven't talked at all about what we might hear tomorrow. Are you worried?"

"It just occurred to me that for the first time in weeks, I'm not worried. I have this sense that all of this has a purpose. The baby showed up in our lives. Medicine Owl gave her support. We were given permission to foster her. Now we're taking the steps necessary to keep her. What more can we do?"

"I'm glad to hear you say that. You sound more objective, less scared," Nate said.

"Maybe it's because we're away from the reservation. It's just the three of us. It feels so normal. At least for now, we're a mom and dad traveling with our baby. It's nice."

"I've got to admit, not much has felt normal lately," Nate said. "We do have to consider how we'll deal with hearing news that might not be what we want to hear."

Carrie knew this wasn't easy for him to say. The night before, she had seen evidence of Nate's surreptitious online searches about adoption cases involving white couples and Native American children. She had read a few of the stories. Now that they were beginning a similar process, it was impossible to feel detached from these cases. These were people just like her and Nate, who loved a child and wanted to be that child's parents. Not all were successful in their court cases. But surely, these couples hadn't had the medicine woman on their side. Carrie wanted—no needed—to believe that everything would turn out fine.

"Gran always tells me to 'think up.' That means stop looking for what could go wrong and be glad for what's going right. Envision what I want, not what I don't want. But it's harder than it sounds. I always think if I don't think about all the stuff that could go wrong, I can't prepare for them. You know?"

"That probably comes with being a doctor. My point is, we've got to consider all the possibilities. Nuttah has a family in Browning. It surprises me sometimes that we still have her."

"I've said I want what's best for Nuttah, and it's true." Carrie took in a ragged breath. "But now, even with the little I know, I can't stand the thought that she might go back with her grandparents and live in a house with a grandfather who has substance abuse issues. She'll be living in poverty. Her aunts and uncles have had serious brushes with the law. I want her to have the best life possible, and we can give her that."

"If she *is* given back to her birth family, you'll still see her. It won't be easy, but you'll still be an important part of her life, caring for her, making sure she's healthy."

Carrie's eyes filled with tears. She blinked them back. "Oh, God, Nate, that would be so hard. I'd see her at well baby check-ups, and I wouldn't want to let her go."

"But you would let her go, babe. Because you do love her so much, you'd do the right thing and support her family and make sure she received the best care possible." Nevertheless, his eyes were sad. "And as Nuttah grows, she would know that you are someone special in her life. I'm sure of that. We have to hope for the best but prepare ourselves for the worst."

After the baby drained the last of the formula, Carrie put the drowsy infant over her shoulder and patted her back. "I guess we'll know more soon. For now, let's just enjoy her."

"You're right. For however long she's with us, we'll give her the best love and care possible." Nate grew quiet, thinking.

When they arrived in Missoula an hour later, Nate dropped Carrie off at one of the academic buildings at the University of Montana while he took Nuttah to their hotel room. Carrie was impressed with the campus and even more delighted when she met the people responsible for turning the manuscript into a book. Discussion focused on promotion of the book through medical organizations and at scientific conferences. Carrie was advised to set up a website so that readers could contact her with comments or questions. Reviews of the book would be available on the website with links to the online book sellers. She was urged to consider starting a blog with information about Native American traditional remedies.

"Medicine Owl could help me with blogs about Native American remedies," Carrie said. "She might actually do it. And maybe she'd agree to a book signing."

It would be such fun to take Medicine Owl off the reservation to a bigger city like Missoula just to see her reaction to the world beyond Browning. But would Medicine Owl agree to leave the only life she knew? It sure would be fun to find out.

Carrie's head spun with information by the time she returned to the hotel. Nate had changed out of his jeans and into a pair of gray slacks and a dress shirt. She laughed as she watched him wrestle a wriggling Nuttah into a hand-embroidered dress Carrie's mother had sent. The dress probably cost a small fortune, and Nuttah would outgrow it after one wearing. But it was sweet that her parents took such an interest in a baby they'd never even met. Nate's parents in Kansas City had yet to acknowledge that a baby lived with their son and his wife.

Nate had made reservations at a nearby steak house, the one John raved about. Although she had dressed for her business meeting in a skirt, silk blouse, and blazer, Carrie changed into a black sweater dress and high-heeled black boots. She intended that this would be a romantic dinner with her handsome husband.

"We don't get that many chances to eat dinner at a restaurant this time of year," Nate said when they were seated in the spacious dining room. Most restaurants in the Glacier Park region closed in September for the winter. "I didn't anticipate sharing the occasion with a Blackfoot baby."

"Please note that she's on her best behavior." Carrie accepted the glass of chardonnay their server poured for her. "Taking a baby out for dinner isn't as hard as I thought it would be."

"We haven't ordered yet," Nate pointed out. "Cheers," he said, holding up his glass of wine. "To my beautiful, brilliant wife, the author. To future success in publishing!" He clinked his glass against hers.

"To husbands who are great partners," Carrie offered in response, touching her glass again to his.

"To wives who never disappoint," Nate said with a gleam in his eye. "Starting with tonight."

Carrie laughed. "No worries on that score. Besides, it's an ideal time, if you get my drift."

"Conditions are ripe, then?" he responded, raising his eyebrows and offering up a dimpled grin. He took a sip of wine and set down his glass. "Now that we have this little one hanging out with us, are you sure you want to care for a baby this young and be pregnant at the same time? We sort of have our hands full now. Or rather you do. I'm mostly around for the fun parts."

Carrie glanced down at the sleeping Nuttah. "Are you wondering if I'm hedging my bets?"

Nate shrugged. "Maybe. If you are, it's okay."

"I do think we have a reasonable chance of being able to adopt her, especially with the blessings of Medicine Owl and the tribal elders. We have a good support system around us, and we can prove that. If I get pregnant and we find out she can stay with us, it'll be like having Irish twins."

Nate laughed. "I like the way you think."

THE WAITING AREA OF ATTORNEY JOSEPH Red Feather's office was light and airy with Danish furniture and splashes of bright color on cushions and art prints. When he exited his office to greet them, Carrie was surprised that Joseph Red Feather had a light complexion.

"My father is from the Salish tribe. My mother is Swedish," he explained later. "My father was career military, so we moved around a lot. Even so, I spent time with my father's family on the reservation as often as I could, so I grew up with a sense of my Native American roots. It was important to me as a child. It *is* important," he corrected.

Carrie and Nate exchanged glances. "We live and work on the Blackfeet reservation, Mr. Red Feather," Carrie said. "In every way, we are part of the life of the people there, except we're not Blackfeet."

"I don't want to gloss over the difficulty factor here," Joseph said. "You've researched the legislation, I presume. If a Blackfeet or other Native American family is available—or even a Native American individual who wants to adopt this child—there may not be much you can do."

"Her grandparents live on the reservation," Carrie said, exchanging a glance with Nate.

Joseph Red Feather's face grew serious. "Have they said they want the baby?" he asked.

"There was a visitation with the grandmother," Carrie said. "The family has had its share of problems, and I have heard the grandfather is a drug abuser and that other members of the family have been involved in criminal cases. It's not the ideal home life."

"That is not a unique story on a reservation," Joseph Red Feather said. "They are still her family."

"Yes, but their daughter died after giving birth in a bathtub with only her boyfriend present. Her parents didn't even know she was pregnant," Carrie said. She swallowed hard. "They didn't know she was dead for about two weeks after the baby was born. What kind of parents don't look for their daughter when she is missing that long?"

Joseph Red Feather shrugged. "I am guessing the daughter didn't have identification. The boyfriend was probably scared. At least, he left the baby at a hospital. I'm playing devil's advocate here."

"We received permission to be her foster parents because there was no other foster family available when she had to be released from the hospital," Nate hastened to explain. "The baby would have had nowhere to go if we hadn't stepped in to take her. The tribal elders, led by the medicine woman, thought we were the best ones to take care of Nuttah. The medicine woman is a dear friend to my wife. She said the baby belongs with her. That's why we have her."

"It is good that the medicine woman supports you on this. The fact that you own a home on the reservation and that you are doctors will be viewed positively. Still . . ."

"Our best friends are a married couple—a Blackfoot man and a Cherokee woman," Nate said. "Beyond them, we have a supportive circle of friends who have said they will help us."

"You realize that I can't predict the future." Joseph made direct eye contact with Carrie who was sitting forward in her chair. His eyes were kind, his expression sincere. "I'm in your corner on this, but it could go a different way than you hope. Still, I like what I'm hearing, and I think you have a shot at this. It won't be easy, though."

"We want to retain your services," Carrie said, and Nate nodded. "How long do you think it will take to finalize an adoption?"

"In Indian time?" Joseph smiled. "I'd say you'll need to be patient."

Chapter Nine

‒·✳·‒

DECEMBER

A WEEK BEFORE CHRISTMAS, SEVERAL MORE FEET of snow fell on the reservation, making anything except local travel impossible, unless you were lucky enough to own a vehicle with a snowplow. Fortunately, a thoughtful neighbor kept Carrie and Nate's driveway cleared so they wouldn't be delayed getting to the hospital in case of emergency. The heavy blanket of white across fields and foothills was broken only by the tallest brown grasses that peeked through the snow, or the occasional fence post that appeared between properties. Majestic fir trees dusted in white powder swayed alarmingly in the frigid winds. Despite the hardships associated with a Northwest Montana winter, it was breathtakingly beautiful. Most days, the Northern Rockies appeared luminous, blanketed in snow that changed gradually from white to blue or lavender, depending on the light and shadows.

Carrie longed to go out into the fields on her cross-country skis or snowshoes. But between hectic days at the hospital and care of the baby, she had little time for much else. Scanning the fields behind their house, she watched for her wolf. The animal usually appeared at least once a week, walking through the trees on the edge of their property. She listened at night for wolves, wondering if it was her wolf that howled such a mournful tune.

The following week, when she took Nuttah to visit Medicine Owl, she was surprised when Medicine Owl asked, "Have you seen your wolf lately?"

Carrie startled. "Not since last..." She searched her memory. "Last Tuesday. I've missed her this week. Why do you ask?"

"She is your spirit animal. She is always with you, even if she doesn't walk the land."

"Are you saying something happened to her?" Carrie set down the cup of tea Medicine Owl had brewed for her. "She's very old."

"Yes. She risks her safety coming so close to humans." Medicine Owl grew silent for a moment, thinking. She seemed to be viewing a scene.

"What is it, Medicine Owl? You look troubled. Is it about my wolf?"

"You will have a sad moment finding out something. I cannot tell you more at this time."

A sudden thought occurred to Carrie. "I had a dream about her the other night." She searched her mind for details of the dream, which had been so vivid, she had awakened afterward. "I was walking with her through the snow. I was wrapped in something that looked like the buffalo hide you keep at your hut. It's the same kind of dream I've had about the wolf before. She talks with me and tells me important things."

"And what did she tell you this time, daughter?" Medicine Owl sat on the edge of the sofa, Nuttah stretched across her lap. She patted the baby's back, helping to relieve a gas bubble.

"She said something about my work lasting many years. She wanted me to remember that no matter what outcome someone may have, my care of them is still important. I can't always save someone's life. I took that to mean that I might lose a patient."

"Yes, you will lose people you care for. I lose people, too." Medicine Owl began a lullaby as Nuttah's eyes began to close.

"That is the hardest part of being a doctor," Carrie said with a sigh. "I'm trained to help them get well. But sometimes, I can't. Knowing that doesn't make it any easier to lose someone."

"You are not losing them. They are merely going beyond this place. You will see them again."

"Tell me, Medicine Owl. What do you know of the afterlife?"

"I know that this life is just another one of many we have. We come back to earth to take care of each other on our journeys."

Carrie joined the old woman on the sofa and put one arm around her. Physical affection between them had increased over the past year. To Carrie, the closeness they felt was almost as special as what she felt for Gran. She felt her throat constrict with emotion as she said, "Since we met, I have always felt that we knew each other before. I was glad to see you again."

"It is why I call you my daughter. And when I leave this reservation, I will always be with you."

As THE COUNTDOWN TO CHRISTMAS CONTINUED, garish colored holiday decorations and shiny tinsel adorned shabby store fronts along the main street in Browning—remnants like ghosts of Christmases past. Even so, the gaudy display was not without its charm. Beloved holiday carols played nonstop on the radio, defying anyone who listened not to sing along. As Carrie drove Nuttah to Violet's house one morning, she sang "Jingle Bells" and watched in the rearview mirror as Nuttah wriggled in her car seat, reacting with delight to Carrie's lilting soprano.

Christmas was Carrie's favorite time of year. Back in Philadelphia, this meant ice-skating with family and friends, pick-up ice hockey games or ice-skating parties at an outdoor rink, roaring fireplaces, hot cocoa topped with gooey miniature marshmallows, and her mother's endless supply of cookies. On Christmas Eve, the family gathered for shrimp scampi and even more cookies, and they shared gifts while listening to holiday carols from her father's impressive collection of vinyl records.

It was always touching and inspirational to Carrie to watch as Gran reveled in the hand-made tatted lace, clove-studded orange pomanders, and other items her patients made for her—a testament to how much they appreciated the excellent care she provided throughout the year. It had been this example of patient devotion that had inspired Carrie to be the same kind of doctor, someone her patients considered part of their families.

This would be her third Christmas on the reservation. The first year, she had been homesick and sad at a deep fissure in her relationship with her father that kept her away from home at the holidays. He had not approved of her decision to work on the reservation rather than joining him in his group practice in Philadelphia.

The second year, she and Nate were engaged and had thoughtfully begun their own holiday tradition of attending Mass at Little Flower Catholic Church, followed by hot cider garnished with cinnamon sticks, and the opening of their gifts to each other. She was determined to make this holiday season as memorable as the last two. Nuttah was too little to appreciate the meaning or traditions of Christmas, but Carrie was certain her eyes would light up at the sight of her first Christmas tree.

Nate went out one afternoon and cut down an eight-foot blue-green Engelmann Spruce, dragging it back to their house and setting it up with great enthusiasm. After about thirty minutes and at least a dozen exclamations of pain caused by the sharp needles, he finished adorning the branches with twinkling white lights. While Nuttah napped, Carrie hung Native American-themed ornaments she had purchased her first Christmas on the reservation.

She had begun a tradition of selecting a special ornament each year to hang on their tree. Last year, it had been their engagement photo displayed in a small oval frame, hung on the tree with a red ribbon. With this, their first Christmas together as a married couple, she had a little more trouble deciding between two ornaments she loved: a log cabin that bore a remarkable resemblance to their house and a small snow globe with a little girl and a dog playing in the snow. It reminded Carrie that if Nuttah stayed with them, she would learn to play in the snow with Annie.

In the end, a decision was impossible, and she purchased both and hung them prominently on the tree. When Nuttah awoke from her nap, Carrie brought her into the living room to see the tree. The baby smiled, waving her tiny hands and feet at the sight of the beautiful twinkling tree.

Nuttah was blossoming, hitting her three-month developmental milestones. One week before Christmas, just after bath time, she rewarded Carrie with a beaming smile and a chortle of glee when Carrie blew bubbles into her tummy.

"Did you just laugh at me? Did you just laugh at Mommy?" Carrie exclaimed, calling for Nate to join in the fun. "She just laughed!"

Nate stood by grinning as Carrie blew bubbles into Nuttah's soft tummy, evoking yet another shriek of delight. Carrie fastened the tapes on the disposable diaper and dressed the baby in her onesie undershirt, jersey pajamas, and booties.

"Okay, now it's Daddy's turn," Nate said, scooping up the baby and holding her aloft. "Don't spit up on Daddy's face again," he said.

Carrie laughed heartily, remembering what had happened a day earlier and Nate's shocked response. "Learned your lesson, eh? She did that to me yesterday just before I went to work. I was at the clinic for three hours before Peg pointed out that I was wearing spit-up down the front of my sweater." She kissed the baby's nose. "I wear that badge of motherhood proudly. Yes, I do," she cooed to Nuttah, who smiled, showing a deep dimple.

"I can pick her up at Violet's this afternoon," Nate said.

"Perfect. Our patient schedule is full today, and I need to induce one of my overdue mothers-to-be, so who knows how long that will take? That little guy has overstayed his welcome in there," she said and met Nate's lips in a quick kiss. "As miserable as that poor woman has felt, I want baby out of there so that they can both be home for Christmas."

"Anything else we need to get for the party?" Nate asked. They had decided on the spur of the moment to have a holiday open house for all their friends, neighbors, and co-workers who had opened their hearts, providing everything Nuttah needed, and offering encouragement on the adoption. So many people had sent gifts and well-wishes for Nuttah, Carrie knew that expressing their appreciation in a tangible way was long overdue.

The only close colleague of Nate's who had not sent a card or gift was Beth Bradley who had recently returned from Kansas City after several days of defending herself over a malpractice suit. Nate had no details about how things had gone for her. Nor did he particularly want to discuss the situation. Without more information, it felt like gossip, and Nate never gossiped.

"At some point, I'm sure she'll tell me what's going on," he said. "It's hard for me to believe that anything she's being accused of could possibly be true. She's too good at what she does."

"I guess if I was under that kind of stress, maybe I'd be standoffish and curt, too," Carrie said. "Well, I hope it's over for her soon."

She was more than a little relieved that they had been able to include Beth in a blanket invitation to the open house without having to invite her to dinner on her own. With Nuttah's appearance in their lives, it had been easy for Carrie to procrastinate on that dinner invitation. Besides, relations between Beth and Carrie had only grown more strained in recent weeks. It was likely that any invitation extended by Carrie would be declined by Beth.

Following surgery on his feet to remove only those toes that were too badly infected to save, Carrie's diabetic patient was learning how to walk with the help of a physical therapist and a walker. Not surprisingly, Beth had taken criticism of her surgical plan to remove both feet as an affront, seemingly oblivious to the fact that Nate had agreed. She had gone so far as to suggest that Margaret Blue Sky hated her because she was a female surgeon and jealous of her skills, a point that Carrie knew to be completely unfounded. This did not endear Beth to others on staff, who already found her arrogant and prickly.

Whenever Nate was around, Beth became an entirely different person: smiling, charming, and quick with a joke. Yet, Carrie reasoned, everyone on staff was on their best behavior around Nate. He brought out the best in others by modeling respect and compassion. It seemed silly and immature to believe that she had anything to fear from Beth's relationship with Nate. Still, there was something about the way Beth fixated on Nate that irritated Carrie. With any luck, Beth would decide not to attend the open house.

"We've got plenty of cheeses, crackers, and spreads," Carrie said. "I'll pick up a tray of veggies and fruit. We've got soft drinks, water, tea, coffee, wine, and beer. What were you thinking of making for appetizers? Bruschetta, I hope? And your hummus?"

"Yes, to both of those, plus meatballs in sauce, stuffed mushrooms, phyllo squares—easy stuff," he said.

Carrie raised her eyebrows. "Easy for you," she said. "You're the most talented husband ever. Too bad you married such a dolt in the kitchen. Your mother was horrified when she realized I don't cook."

"You have other redeeming qualities." Nate smiled sweetly at Carrie and deposited Nuttah in her swing. "Speaking of my mother, she called yesterday."

"Everything okay with her and your dad?"

"Yes, although of course, she's disappointed that we couldn't come for Christmas after not making it for Thanksgiving, either. I explained that nonstop or direct flights from here to Kansas City are out of sight. We also needed to give a month's notice to the caseworker, and we've missed that deadline, already."

"I know. It really wasn't an ideal time to travel, anyway. We could get stuck somewhere and be late getting back. What else did your mother have to say?"

"She asked if we were sure about this, I mean about adopting Nuttah. I told her yes." Nate pulled on his jacket and grabbed the sack lunch he had packed.

"She doesn't approve?" Carrie bit her upper lip.

"She didn't exactly say that." Nate leaned in to kiss her. "But you know my mother. Sooner or later, we'll know exactly how she feels."

"True. At least, we won't have to wonder." Carrie had looked forward to introducing Nuttah to both their families. She already knew how her parents and Gran—especially Gran—felt about the baby.

"I hardly have words to express how proud I am of you," Gran had said when she heard that Carrie and Nate wanted to adopt Nuttah. "To care for this special little girl . . . well, I knew Providence brought you to the reservation. Now I see even more evidence that you are meant to be there."

"Medicine Owl said Nuttah belonged with me," Carrie told her. "She won't say more, but I think there is something going on with the family that she knows about."

"That is extraordinary for her to have such faith in you," Gran said after a few moments. Carrie could hear the catch of strong emotion in her grandmother's voice as she spoke. "With all that her people have endured, she has the most forgiving, generous spirit. I never thought I'd live to see the day when a Native American medicine woman would go to such lengths to teach and support a white female doctor."

"Gran?"

"What, honey?"

"I'm happy that Medicine Owl is sharing all that she knows with me. But, remember, you were the first medicine woman who taught me."

"Now isn't that just about the nicest thing you could ever say to me? I miss you, Carrie. Come and visit us soon," Gran said. "And bring your daughter of the heart."

LATER THAT MORNING, AS CARRIE ROUNDED a corner in the hospital corridor, she nearly smacked into Beth Bradley, who was reading a message on her cell phone while walking. "Oof!" Carrie exclaimed, holding out one hand to keep from bumping into her. "That was close!"

Beth looked up from her phone. She looked distracted and upset. "Sorry."

"Are you okay?" Carrie asked. "I didn't mean to startle you."

"I'm fine." The edge was back in Beth's tone. "I've got a lot going on. Now if you'll excuse me . . ."

"Tis the season," Carrie said and started to walk on, and then turned. It was, after all, a time of goodwill toward others. Now was the time to extend kindness to Beth, to make the effort to let bygones be bygones. "Hey, Beth, we hope you'll be able to stop by our place tomorrow for the holiday open house. There will be lots of people who would like to know you better. Plus, Nate is cooking up some wonderful appetizers."

Beth swiveled on one foot to face Carrie. The exasperated expression on her face wavered a bit as she considered the invitation. "That's right. I almost forgot he liked to cook," she said, pursing her lips. After a moment, she offered a noncommittal smile and said, "That's how he burned off stress when he was a surgical resident. I remember that anything he brought me to taste was fantastic." She made direct eye contact with Carrie and let out a deep breath. "Sure, why not? I'll enjoy trying whatever Nate is offering."

"Great," Carrie said, certain that Beth's comment was laced with innuendo. "Any time after four. Just bring yourself." *Do whatever you like but leave Nate alone.*

"Thanks." With that, Beth was off like a shot, still reading her phone as she walked.

"You're welcome," Carrie mouthed silently. With a shrug, she headed back to the clinic.

ON SATURDAY, NATE GOT UP EARLY to begin prepping appetizers for the party, and Carrie did a speed-clean around the house, dusting, vacuuming, and scrubbing both bathrooms. As delicious aromas filled the house, she made her way into the living room with her Swiffer, humming along to iHeart radio songs on her iPod. From her swing, Nuttah fixated on a mobile of black-and-white farm animals circling her head to a twinkling nursery tune. Occasionally, she drifted off to sleep while her best friend Annie lay nearby, on guard for the slightest cry or movement. The old dog had taken the baby's appearance in their household in stride and seemed to consider it her job to babysit.

"Annie, is your baby still sleeping?" Carrie asked. "Thanks for taking such good care of her." She bent to stroke the animal's soft fur and planted a kiss on Annie's long nose.

"Are you making rounds today?" Nate entered the living room, wiping his hands on a dishtowel. "If so, I wondered if you'd mind checking on my gall bladder patient. See whether you think I need to order a different pain med for her."

"Be glad to. The census is way down, and I've discharged most of my patients," Carrie said. "Is there anything you need me to pick up on the way home?"

"Nope. What time does Nuttah get another bottle?"

"She'll be making noises in another forty-five minutes, I think. Don't worry, Annie will let you know the minute she hears the slightest peep out of her. Back soon," she said. "I love you." She kissed him lightly on the lips.

After making rounds, she decided to stop by the house where Medicine Owl lived during the winter with her grandson, a man in his sixties. He answered the door and smiled at Carrie, who handed him a fruit basket. "Is Medicine Owl able to see me now?" Carrie asked him. "I didn't have time to let her know ahead of time that I was stopping by."

"Come in," Medicine Owl said as she heard Carrie's voice. She moved quickly from her chair to greet Carrie at the door and admired the fresh apples, oranges, and bananas. "I was hoping you would stop by. But you didn't bring the baby." She looked disappointed.

"I had to see patients at the hospital. Then I had errands to run. I'll bring Miss Nuttah over some evening next week, if it's okay." Carrie's eyes took in Medicine Owl's appearance. The elderly woman, wrapped in a shawl, appeared more fragile than she had ever seen her. For the first time, Medicine Owl looked her age, which according to Carrie's quick calculation must be about ninety-seven. "How are you feeling today?" she asked Medicine Owl. "I stopped by to see if you would like to come over to our house and be part of the holiday gathering. I could drive you. Both of you," she indicated Medicine Owl's grandson.

"That is very nice of you to think of us. But we will stay here today."

"You look a bit tired today. Are you well?"

"I am well enough," Medicine Owl said. "When you have seen as many moons as I have, you learn to be grateful for however you feel. At least, I *can* feel." She smiled, displaying the twinkle in her eyes that let Carrie know she had made a small joke.

"Call me, please, if I can do anything for you? I'll bring Nuttah over soon," Carrie promised, leaning in to embrace the tiny woman. She added, "We haven't heard a word about what is happening with the adoption."

Medicine Owl waved away her concern. "There is no reason to worry. I have spoken with the tribal elders," she said, wrapping her shawl more tightly around her.

"It's so hard not to worry," Carrie said. "I'm only human."

"To be human is to forget what your spirit already understands—the power that is possible when we believe. Worry is not good because it weakens that power we hold in here," Medicine Owl said, touching her chest. "When we think fearful thoughts, we forget that there is a greater power that knows what is best. We get in the way of the Great Spirit, who can make anything possible. Look at how much has happened to you. Everything you desired has all come about."

"It's true," Carrie said, taking in a deep breath. "Thank you for reminding me."

"Concentrate your thoughts on what is good, not what you fear, daughter." Medicine Owl walked Carrie to the door. "I will look forward to seeing the baby."

Chapter Ten

꠸

As guests began arriving late that afternoon for the holiday open house, Carrie forgot her usual concern about Nuttah's future. Instead, she concentrated on enjoying the party. She and Nate stayed busy filling and re-filling plates and drinks for their friends and coworkers. By six o'clock, nearly forty people had come and gone. A few closer friends, including the Leathers family, congregated in a semi-circle around the fireplace.

Carrie looked over to find Nuttah on Nadie's shoulder as she patted the baby's bottom. Earl and Nadie sat side-by-side on the sofa surrounded by their growing family. Nadie looked majestic in a wine-colored pantsuit, her hair in a thick braid, pinned into a crown around her head. She turned Nuttah to the front and introduced her to her grandson Charlie sitting on Gali's lap. Carrie smiled. No doubt, Nadie was already playing matchmaker, planning for Nuttah and Charlie to be married someday. That was how many Blackfeet couples ended up together.

Nearby, Mike Leathers stood with his bride Naomi, a pretty, plump woman with a shy demeanor. Mike leaned in to whisper something in her ear. She touched his arm and smiled, the expression of a woman in love. Carrie was relieved that Mike appeared content with a bottled water while others enjoyed wine and beer. This was a sure sign that he could remain successful in his recovery from alcoholism. There also could be little doubt that true love with a supportive woman would aid him in maintaining his sobriety. Mike's success as an artist ensured the couple's future was bright. Carrie wondered if his notoriety as an activist for wolf preservation might overshadow his art career, at some point.

"You two look happy," Carrie said, giving Mike and Naomi quick hugs. "I'm glad you could come today."

"My wife is expecting a baby," Mike said with the slightest of smiles, his eyes giving away the joy he felt at sharing the news.

"Oh? I hadn't heard that," Carrie said, offering a hug to Naomi. "How far along are you?"

"About two months. You were not working, so I saw the nurse-practitioner," Naomi said. "But I would like for you to bring our baby into the world."

"I would be honored," Carrie said. "When are you due?"

"July, probably during North American Indian Days," Naomi said. "All of our families will be here, so they can welcome the baby."

"Well, what baby in their right mind would miss Indian Days?" Carrie asked, laughing. Next July would be Nuttah's first Indian Days, as well. The annual North American Indian Days celebration took place over four days in July in Browning and drew visitors from all over the world. There were sporting events, crafts, and traditional carnival food. The Blackfeet Volunteer Medical Corps led by Dr. Jim always scheduled its week on the reservation during Indian Days.

Hearing a knock on the front door, Nate hurried to answer it. Carrie turned just in time to see Beth lift her face for the chaste welcoming kiss Nate planted on her cheek. As he took her stylish fur-trimmed coat, Beth raised her eyes to Nate's for several seconds and said something that caused him to look back at Carrie quickly—too quickly. Carrie waved at Beth—certain that whatever Beth had said had been about her. This was unsettling, if only because of the uncomfortable expression on Nate's face. She went to retrieve Nuttah from Nadie's arms, then headed over to greet their newest guest.

"Hi, Beth," she said. "I'd like you to meet Nuttah."

Beth held out her finger to the baby, who grasped it and squeezed. "She has a good grip." Beth looked directly at Carrie. "Are you thinking that you'll be allowed to keep her much longer? It will be hard to give her up."

Carrie felt her throat tighten. "Nate and I have started adoption proceedings, so yes, we're planning to have her a *lot* longer." Realizing the comment sounded curt, she softened her tone. "Of course, we have no way of knowing how long it will take, but we're optimistic."

"That's nice." Beth retrieved her finger and combed back a lock of long luxurious dark-brown hair with her fingers. "I can't wait to taste some of Nate's amazing food," Beth said. "It's all I've thought about all day."

Beth looked stunning in high-heeled black boots and a red sweater dress with a round neckline that accentuated the curve of her full breasts. Far from revealing too much, the dress spoke of expensive tastes and an unlimited clothing budget. Square-cut diamonds glinted at her ears, matching the infinity band of fiery diamonds she wore on her right ring finger. *Right hand not left.* Although Beth wore her nails cut short in a practical style befitting a surgeon, her manicured fingers shone with a simple nude gloss. She had a manner of dress that appeared carelessly elegant, as if she made no effort at all to be this beautiful. It was a style that Carrie had always felt she could never quite pull off. She knew, however, that Nate preferred a more natural look. He had told her so. Still, how could any man not admire a woman this beautiful?

"Help yourself. There's plenty of everything," Carrie said. She held Nuttah facing to the front with one hand beneath her bottom, gently bouncing her. It was the witching hour—that time each afternoon when Nuttah turned cranky. "We have wine and beer, soft drinks, and water. Enjoy."

Beth made her way to the kitchen in a subtle cloud of expensive scent. Nate put the finishing touches on a pot of chili with a platter of vegetable garnishes, sour cream, and grated cheeses. Carrie smiled. He appeared as intent on getting the details of his food presentation right as he did when performing an intricate surgery. Beth walked over to stand beside him, watching while he put the finishing touches on the garnishes. She accepted the glass of red wine he poured for her. From there, they moved into the dining room, where he prepared a small plate of appetizers for her to sample.

The sight of Nate fixing a plate for Beth irritated Carrie. What? The woman couldn't serve herself at a buffet like everyone else? Beth followed him as close as an overeager puppy, occasionally touching his arm or indicating something else he should add to the plate. Carrie rolled her eyes. She headed over to join Peg and her husband Ken by the fireplace.

Peg took one look at Carrie's perturbed expression and let out a low throaty chuckle. "I see the Snow Queen has arrived. And, of course, she's stuck like glue to Dr. Nate."

Carrie took a deep breath and decided to take the high road. "I think she's probably more comfortable talking with him. She's known him a lot longer." She bit her upper lip as Beth broke into peals of laughter at something Nate said, and he joined in, albeit more subdued. "I hope she'll step out of her comfort zone and get to know other people this evening," Carrie said between clenched teeth.

Yet as she watched the animated expression on Beth's face as she tossed back her mane of dark hair and bit daintily into a piece of perfectly seasoned bruschetta, her eyes closed in ecstasy for Nate's benefit, Carrie knew that the only person Beth Bradley cared to know better was Nate.

As the hour wore on, Beth monopolized Nate who made occasional apologetic eye contact with Carrie, indicating that he knew he needed to excuse himself and socialize with their other guests. She finally decided it was time to rescue him.

"Nate, do you want to help put Nuttah to bed?" she asked, entering the kitchen and grabbing a bottle of formula from the refrigerator. She ran hot tap water in a small container and set the bottle in the water to warm the formula. She never microwaved formula for fear of causing hot spots that could burn Nuttah's mouth.

Nate seemed grateful for the interruption. "Excuse me, Beth," he said. "We're going to put this little one down for the night. I'll be back in a while, and I'll introduce you around."

"That's okay, I've got to leave," Beth said. "I'll make my good-byes now." She leaned up and kissed Nate's cheek. "To be continued," she said. "Good night, Carrie. Thanks for inviting me."

"Good night, Beth," Carrie said evenly. She waited while Nate walked Beth to the door, helped her on with her coat, and ushered her out—but not before Beth embraced him and marked him with her signature matte rose lipstick just beside his mouth.

"Here, allow me," Carrie said and scrubbed at the lipstick with a paper napkin. When they reached Nuttah's room, she asked, "What did she mean by that 'to be continued' remark?" She changed Nuttah's diaper and put her into her pajamas and sleep sack.

"We were just talking about old times," Nate said. "Did I remember this person or that surgery we did back in Kansas City? Do I talk with people we used to work with? You know, it was just talk. None of it matters."

"Sounds like she's homesick," Carrie said. "Well, do you?"

"Do I what?" Nate settled into the rocker with the baby and began feeding her.

"Do you talk with people the two of you used to work with?"

"Occasionally. Why?" Nate glanced up at her, his brow furrowed. Then he focused on the baby, who gobbled down the bottle and watched him with her large brown eyes. She grabbed his index finger and held tight. A smile softened Nate's expression as he stroked the soft tiny fingers.

"No particular reason," Carrie said as a troubling thought took root. "It's just . . . I wonder what other people at the medical center in Kansas City think of her decision to come here—why she came here—the timing, I mean."

"I share your concerns, believe it or not. But any surgeon knows how easy it is to be accused of mishandling a procedure just because the outcome isn't what the patient or a family member expected. It's only fair to give her the benefit of the doubt. If I hear anything that I think needs to be reported to Margaret Blue Sky, I'll handle it. Okay?"

"Okay."

He glanced up at her, his blue eyes sincere, without guile. "All Beth wanted to know was what I remembered about someone from my time there. It was someone else on the medical staff. I don't know why it matters to her. I sort of remember the guy."

At this point, Beth's behavior was off-limits to Carrie's speculation lest it appear to be criticism. Nate had made himself clear on that point. Yet Carrie was more certain than ever that there was more to the story of why Beth left Kansas City than Nate was willing to consider. It wasn't uncommon for surgeons to have legal action brought against them when a patient had post-surgical complications or died during or after a procedure. That was the reason for internal review boards. Families grieving loved ones sometimes took out their anguish through the legal system. But depending on the seriousness of the accusation, Beth might be on permanent waivers from the medical center. In that case, it might be beneficial to know the full story.

"Nate, I have to be honest. We've always been truthful with each other." Carrie took a deep breath and sat down on the ottoman near the rocker where Nate was feeding Nuttah. "It bothered me tonight seeing the way you act with Beth. She said something to you, and you laughed and looked at me. It was like you had a private joke, and I was the joke."

"I'm sorry. I remember that." Nate looked directly at her. "Beth said she hoped you wouldn't hand her the baby. Babies throw up on her, and that was a new dress."

"Why would I force her to hold a baby?"

"It was a joke—not a good one. But she was trying." Nate shrugged. "She isn't good at making small talk."

"You think?" Carrie frowned. "She hung all over you, and you even fixed her a plate! Let her fix her own plate."

"You have no reason to feel threatened by Beth." Now it was Nate's turn to frown. "I have never—nor would I ever—do anything disloyal to you. I was uncomfortable by what she said, and I'm sorry. What more can I say?"

"Okay, I'm satisfied with that. It isn't that I don't believe you. I just get a little tired of you standing up for Beth, especially when she treats me like I crawled out from the plumbing or something. I look like the bad cop, and you're always the good cop."

"I stand up for you all the time. I took your side when you two were sparring over the patient with the infected feet. I stand up for you all the time, Carrie. You just don't hear it."

Carrie reached out and touched his arm. "I'm sorry. I hope you take it as the ultimate compliment that I get jealous. It's just that I'm crazy about you."

"And I'm crazy about you, too, even when you're acting a little crazy." He crossed his eyes and waved his finger in a circle in the air.

"I used the word 'crazy.' I guess I deserve that." She smiled, then kissed him on the mouth in that way that let him know she intended to do more later, and left Nate to finish feeding Nuttah.

She returned to the party, only to find that Gali and John had taken Charlie home. "I should have said goodnight before I went upstairs," Carrie said to Earl and Nadie. "The time got away from me." She grinned. "I understand congratulations are in order. Another baby is being added to your family," she said, indicating Mike and Naomi sitting close together on the sofa.

"Yes, our son is doing well, thanks to you, Dr. Carrie," Nadie said. "I thought there might be no way to save him from his troubles. But now, he has everything I hoped for him." Her eyes focused on Mike, then filled with concern. Her mouth became a thin line. "He needs to settle down with his family and give up trying to save the wolves."

Carrie gave her a questioning look. "He loves wolves."

"He has started leading people to the ranches of those who are killing wolves. He could get himself hurt or killed. I tell him, 'Stop. Let other people fight this battle.'"

"I wasn't aware that he was taking such an aggressive stance," Carrie said. "I thought he just spoke at public meetings."

She had been very impressed after reading about Mike's group in a newspaper editorial that was critical of Native Americans protesting the numbers of ranchers and farmers killing wolves. Wolves sometimes strayed onto private property. Mike viewed it as the way of nature. But there had been altercations between property owners and those who protested. There had even been a few arrests.

"It's good that he has something to keep him focused and busy," she said. "But, yes, he needs to be careful." She decided to change the subject. "I'm glad he's doing so well at his art, too, following in your husband's footsteps. She paused for a moment. "Nadie, I wonder how everything is going for you." She meant in general but hoped Nadie would say something about her husband's progress with daily diabetes blood testing, diet, and exercise.

"I have talked with Medicine Owl," Nadie said. "She says to me that our diet is not what it once was, in the days when men hunted, and women cooked whatever the man brought home. There was meat that our men hunted, fish they caught themselves, and whatever vegetables and fruits could be picked or grown. The women grew corn and ground it for bread. We ate berries. Later, we raised chickens and had eggs—good eggs that tasted better. It is not that way anymore. Now we have two grocery stores." She shook her head in wonder. "I go to the store, and the only work I have to do is carry bags of food into our house. We have milk and eggs, meat, vegetables, bags of fruit, even cornbread from a mix. I don't have to do any work except put it in my mouth. When I was a young girl, my mother did not have it so easy."

"It's true. The old way of eating was much healthier," Carrie said. "But I'll admit, if it weren't for convenience foods, I'd have starved by now. I am not a cook like you are." She laughed, and after a moment, Nadie joined in politely. She would never have made fun of Carrie.

"You know what I think?" Nadie leaned in and patted Carrie on the knee. "I think we were better off not having it so easy."

Carrie looked over at Earl. "He might not have diabetes if we didn't have all these pre-packaged foods—I mean, if he had to hunt for his evening meal."

"Yes, but Dr. Carrie, if he spent all his time hunting for our food, he wouldn't have time to make such beautiful paintings." Nadie smiled at the large oil painting hanging over the fireplace. "That one is my favorite," she said. "The mother and the little girl. Do you have any idea who they are?"

"I've wondered," Carrie said. "The woman in the painting looks familiar."

Nadie's face crinkled into a grin. "It is me, when our daughter Cheryl was very small. She was little Charlie's age. She works with me now making moccasins, you know. Seeing me with our daughter touched Earl's heart." She put her hand over her chest. "He is a man who feels things deep inside here. Our Mike is like him, I think. Earl said he had to make something to keep the beautiful picture of me with Cheryl alive in his heart forever. That was his first painting."

"I'm honored to have it in my home," Carrie said, studying the painting through new eyes. "I wanted it because it was such a beautiful image of a mother and daughter. When Nuttah came to live here, the painting took on an even deeper meaning. But now that I know it is you and Cheryl, I love it even more."

Chapter Eleven

﹀

JANUARY

A WEEK AFTER THE START OF THE new year, Carrie picked up Nuttah from Violet's house, intent on taking her to see Medicine Owl. It was important to keep up regular visits with the baby to the medicine woman. But just as important, Carrie relished time with her friend. Since Medicine Owl avoided going outside during the coldest months, she too looked forward to their visits. Nuttah was as much a beloved child to Medicine Owl as she was to Carrie and Nate.

Medicine Owl always brewed a pot of herbal tea and served a special kind of cornmeal cookie sweetened with molasses that Carrie loved. "These are traditional, from the time of my mother and grandmother," Medicine Owl said. "This was before the buffalo began disappearing, when my people roamed these lands."

"I would love to know how to make these," Carrie said as she bit into a warm cookie.

"I will share the recipe with you, along with many other things," Medicine Owl assured her. "My time on earth is nearing its end, daughter." She touched Carrie's hand. "I cannot stay forever. What I know, I will give to you. I am preparing now, a little at a time."

"When I come here, I learn something new each time," Carrie said. "Everything you have ever told me is in here," she said, touching her heart.

Although Nuttah was growing like a weed and hitting all her developmental milestones, Carrie wanted Medicine Owl's assurance that she was doing everything possible for the Blackfoot baby. As if the usual infant concerns involving teething and fussiness weren't enough, Nuttah had recently caught her first cold. Carrie may have been a doctor, but like any new mom, she fretted.

She had more empathy now for new mothers who suffered right along with their unhappy babies. Nasal aspirators were no fun for either babies or their parents, especially in the middle of the night. Over-the-counter remedies for congestion, sore throats, and coughs weren't safe for infants. Carrie preferred a more natural approach to healthcare in children this young. Still, it was frustrating, when so little could be done to relieve a baby's congestion and misery. Medicine Owl had taken care of many Blackfeet babies and might know something Carrie didn't.

But the medicine woman simply shrugged. "Sniffles happen to every little one," she said, turning the baby over on her tummy and patting her bottom. "Nuttah will be fine. This may be harder on you. Now, let us talk of other matters. How is your husband?"

"He's fine. He's been talking with a counselor about the nightmares and what happened to him in Kansas City."

Medicine Owl sat in silence for a moment as if viewing a scene in her mind. "It is good that he talks out his concerns. He is troubled," she said finally. "There is another woman who works with him who makes this trouble."

"Yes. She is a surgeon he used to work with. She taught him. She also operated on him when he was shot."

Medicine Owl nodded. "He doesn't understand why she says or does certain things, although he is glad that she is here. His thoughts are confused. I think you are not fond of this other doctor, the one who comes from Kansas."

If this statement had been uttered by anyone other than Medicine Owl, Carrie might have made a joke about a wicked witch from Kansas. But the medicine woman was never unkind in how she spoke of others, so Carrie bit her lip. "I wouldn't say we get along very well," she admitted, twisting her mouth. "Actually, I'd welcome your advice. You always know how to handle difficult people."

Tensions between Carrie and Beth had escalated. A new hospital budget under discussion that week had resulted in a confrontation between them. Beth took issue with the new childcare center that Carrie had proposed—a proposal the hospital's CEO and board of directors supported—saying the resources could be used for other more important needs.

"Let's face it," Beth said to Carrie across the conference table. "You have to figure out somewhere to put your baby. Not everyone here wants that kind of benefit. There are other more important needs at this hospital." She looked at Nate who reddened. He started to speak, but Carrie was too fast for him.

"Somewhere to put our baby?" Carrie was incensed, but she remained polite, keeping her tone neutral. "Yes, Nate and I do think quality childcare is important, but that's not the only reason I'm advocating for a center. It's for any employee who needs care for their child while they work."

"We need another surgical nurse," Beth said. "Yesterday, we were short-handed. Nate, you know we were." She looked pointedly at him. But before Nate could answer, Margaret Blue Sky stepped in.

"You two were short-handed because a surgical nurse called in sick," Margaret said. "In fact, I have reason to believe she had to be home with her sick child. Employees often call in sick themselves when they don't have someone to care for their kids." She smiled at Carrie. "I thank Dr. Nelson for taking a leadership role in helping us maintain a strong, stable staff."

Nate gave Carrie a look of solidarity. "It's true that the childcare center does help Carrie and me. But we've been trying for a year to recruit another emergency medicine specialist and a new pharmacist. Having services like childcare available strengthen our chances of being able to recruit good people who happen to have kids."

"I can see I'm outnumbered," Beth said, her ice-blue eyes leveled at Carrie.

Carrie relayed this story to Medicine Owl. "We need Beth Bradley, but she often creates tension, even between Nate and me," Carrie had said. "He wants to be supportive of her, and he has asked me to try harder to get along with her. I really do try. Today, at least, I won."

"There will be no winners in this matter. You must keep trying to find common ground," Medicine Owl said. "Choose peace, always. Remember the lessons you have learned in the past about forgiveness. It takes just one person to forgive before change is possible."

"But what woman doesn't get upset at having to put up with her own husband who defends another woman's bad behavior, especially when his wife and this other woman don't get along? Shouldn't the husband care more about what his wife thinks and how she feels?"

Medicine Owl was quiet for a moment, but now, Carrie saw the characteristic twinkle in her eye. "Of course, he must care about his wife's feelings. In this situation, there are two women in his life. You are his wife. Your life together is important to him. Yet, he also cares about this other woman, for a different reason. He depends on her, too—to save lives."

"That's true." Carrie felt a little ashamed. "You're saying I haven't been fair."

"You have been as fair as any woman who loves a man can be," Medicine Owl smiled. "I believe you can trust him. He has many responsibilities, and he takes them all seriously. The nightmares show that he is human. He has fears, too. He just doesn't want to show them to you."

"He's wonderful at everything he does." Carrie felt tears sting her eyes. "I'm the one who needs to grow up."

The medicine woman held Nuttah up, and Carrie took her. "Daughter, you will have to be a bigger person than you have ever been in this matter."

Although she knew Medicine Owl was right about the importance of forgiveness and being fair to Beth, it was hard to do. Every day, it seemed, Beth said or did something that created tension in their work relationship. Was Carrie supposed to ignore insensitive comments or approve of Beth's behavior?

In this case, maybe it was about making the effort to see another point of view and to avoid judgments. Beth had good points, too, even if Carrie had trouble seeing them. Although their mannerisms were different, what they had in common was a commitment to patients.

THE TWENTIETH OF JANUARY DAWNED AS one of the coldest days on record. With life-threatening below-zero temperatures, the furnace labored to keep the house warm. Nate built a fire in the big stone fireplace to help ward off some of the chill. Today was a rare day off for him, and he wanted to keep Nuttah at home while Carrie worked.

"It's too cold to take her out, even across town," he said. "Besides, I want time with her."

Carrie bundled up in a down coat, hat, scarf and Arctic mittens, and called to Annie. "Let's go outside!"

The old dog trotted to the front door and waited while Carrie fastened the retractable leash to Annie's collar and led her outside. Predictably, Annie sniffed the snow before doing her business, her attention focused on wild smells her sharp nose picked up, even with a strong north wind. It was far too cold for Annie to be outside too long, and after five minutes, Carrie sent her back in the house. It was then she saw the wolf emerge from a grove of trees on the edge of their property.

"Hello," Carrie called out in a conversational tone. "I miss seeing you when you don't come by."

She noticed that the animal walked more slowly than usual. Was she lame? Had she been injured? Or was she simply weak from hunger?

Winter in such a harsh, unforgiving climate was especially hard on older animals not able to hunt as easily as others. It was likely that being one of the oldest females, other wolves provided food for her. But was there enough to nourish her? She watched the wolf turn and go back through the grove of trees, where she disappeared as suddenly as she had appeared.

"I just saw the wolf," she told Nate. "She was moving slow."

"I'm sure a lot of older animals like her don't survive winters like we're having," Nate said. Seeing the look that crossed Carrie's face, he hastened to add, "I hope she'll be okay." He put his hands onto Carrie's shoulders and kissed her.

"I hope so, too. She's like a symbol of older women in my life. In a way, I think of her as being an animal version of Medicine Owl . . . or Gran. I hope seeing her today isn't a foreshadowing of something bad."

"My, aren't we positive this morning?" Nate handed her a travel mug of coffee. "Go. Be a force for good."

MIKE LEATHERS WAS HER FIRST PATIENT that morning. She hadn't seen him in at least two months, although she saw Naomi regularly for prenatal visits. As she did a physical exam and reviewed Mike's lab work, she realized that he was a much healthier, happier man than when she had first met him.

"Clearly, marriage plus your painting and wolf activities agree with you. You're fit as a fiddle," she said. "I'm proud of you for remaining sober, too. You're a success story in every way, Mike."

He glanced down at his shoes, clearly embarrassed by the compliment. Still, he looked pleased. "I'll be at the Capitol in Helena next Tuesday to talk with lawmakers," he answered. He appeared confident. "I've spoken with the Governor. I am anxious to share with other political leaders the news that the movement is growing and how many people from around Montana, Wyoming, Washington, and other states are joining us."

"It's become a big deal under your leadership," Carrie said. "I've never been part of any kind of protest movement, but if I did, it would be this one. Is there anything I can do to help? I'd be glad to write a check."

"We have an account set up at the bank. We are not a non-profit organization yet, but donations are appreciated. I am not drawing a salary. The money is being used for mailings, a phone line, and a website."

"Speaking of wolves, I saw my wolf this morning. She looked weak. She seemed unsteady on her feet as she walked," Carrie said. "I worry about her."

"She came to you on a day like today?" Mike stroked his chin. "Ordinarily, an old female would remain in the den on a day like today. She must have wanted to see you."

"I hope she made it back okay," Carrie said. "I had to go inside, but I watched her as she went back into the trees. I look forward to seeing her more often when the weather improves."

"One of these days, she will pass," Mike said. "She is your friend. It will be a sad time for you. I know how that feels."

THAT AFTERNOON, A LITTLE AFTER FIVE o'clock, Carrie's cellphone vibrated in the jacket of her white coat. She reached for it immediately and saw 'Nate' on caller I.D. "Hey, how's it going?" she asked. "Is Nuttah up from her nap?"

"She just woke up and had a bottle. What time do you think you'll be home?"

"I can be out of here in a few minutes, I think," she said. "Should I pick up anything at the store for dinner? Do we need diapers?"

"Yes, and yes," he said. "I'll cook if you shop."

"You've got yourself a deal."

When she arrived home at six-thirty, after making a quick pass through Glacier Foods, Nuttah was awake. Carrie picked her up and cuddled her while Nate unpacked the groceries and began preparing dinner.

"By the way, I had a call from the caseworker a little while ago," Nate said. "Nuttah's grandmother cancelled this week's visit."

"Why?"

"No idea, but while I had her on the phone, I double-checked to make sure it was still okay for us to take Nuttah to Philadelphia at the end of the month. We asked way in advance, but you never know. I've got that surgical conference, but you and Nuttah can just have fun with your folks and Gran."

"I'm glad her grandmother cancelled," Carrie said in a blunt tone, then added, "It might have been the weather, but still, it doesn't show a commitment to seeing her granddaughter."

"While I had her on the phone, I also requested permission to take Nuttah with us to Kansas City in March. That's assuming nothing happens in the meantime, of course."

"We're going to Kansas City in March? I didn't know you wanted to do that."

"I just decided this week. Is that okay with you? We can see my parents. My mother pointed out that she hasn't seen me since our wedding. I'd also like to visit the E.R.—return to the scene. My counselor thinks that would be a good test—to see the place and find out if it brings up any other feelings. I still don't think the nightmares are about the shooting."

"One of these days, you'll figure it out." She kissed him. "Hopefully, Nuttah and I can join you. But we won't know for sure until closer to that time. Anything can happen between now and then."

"It would be good to see some old friends, too," Nate said. "The chief of surgery asked me to stop by."

Carrie was quiet for a moment. She knew that the medical center hoped Nate would return someday. But if they were able to adopt Nuttah, they would need to remain on the reservation. "Are you starting to have second thoughts about the adoption?"

"Not at all." Nate began sautéing chicken in garlic and olive oil in a pan. "I just think it's important to maintain connections, for professional reasons."

Chapter Twelve

—٭—

"**I**S ANYTHING THE MATTER?" CARRIE ASKED, peering into the guest room, where Nate sat in semi-darkness in the rocking chair. He had removed his surgical scrubs and now sat in a pair of boxer shorts and a tee shirt. "Aren't you cold, babe?"

Nate shook his head. "I was about to take a shower. I just didn't make it that far."

"Did you just get home from the hospital?" She shivered and rubbed her arms. The furnace struggled to keep up with the chill in the house. She had dressed Nuttah in layers under her sleep sack. Outside, the wind howled.

"About an hour ago. I just didn't feel like making the effort to sleep yet."

Carrie sat down on the bed across from him. "As tired as you obviously are, you shouldn't have to *try* to sleep. Do you want to talk about it?"

"Not now." He leaned over and squeezed her hand. "All I want to do is take a hot shower and let go of this day. I'd like to forget it happened."

Carrie paused, watching him. "How did the surgery go?"

"I wasn't able to save him. He came in with advanced colon cancer. I opened him up and knew it was over. He died two hours later in the recovery room."

"I'm sorry." Carrie was quiet for a few moments. "It must be hard to want to help and know there was absolutely nothing you could do."

"Yeah. His wife said he'd been having stomach pain for a while. But of course, we don't have a specialist here to do routine colonoscopies. People wait and hope that Dr. Jim can bring one with him in the summer. Then they hope they can get on the schedule. It's like playing Russian Roulette. In this case, earlier detection could have made all the difference." Nate rose from the rocking chair. "It gets to me sometimes."

"It gets to me, too," Carrie said, standing and wrapping her arms around him, listening to the steady beat of his heart. "But you've reminded me before, when

I feel that way, that even with all the limitations we have here, what we do still matters. We do the best we can with what we're given."

"I could do more colonoscopies."

"You could," she said, stroking the small of his back. "But there would still be cases like this. You can't save everyone." She felt him relax under her touch. "Why don't you take a shower and unwind; then come to bed. I'll even let you sleep." She intended it as a mild joke and was rewarded with a weak smile.

Nate got up from the chair. "Okay. Get back into bed and warm it up for me."

After his shower, Nate came into their bedroom, a towel wrapped around his waist. His curls were still wet. As he approached the bed, Carrie lifted the sheets and comforter from his side of the bed and patted the mattress. "Care to join me?"

"Where are your clothes, lady? You're going to catch your death," Nate said, eyeing her with appreciation.

"I seem to have lost them someplace. You'll have to warm me up," Carrie said. In the semi-darkness, she noticed that Nate had lost weight he couldn't afford to lose.

He flicked off the towel and crawled into bed, drawing her to him. "Can we make this just for fun tonight? No baby-making pressure?"

Carrie took in a deep breath. The comment stung, even though she knew he didn't mean it to hurt her. Clearly, their efforts to conceive were putting more stress on him than she had realized. Their lovemaking had always been playful and spontaneous. Now it was practically prescribed. No wonder Nate felt under the gun. She let out the breath she had been holding. "What I want most right now is for you to be as close to me as possible." She kissed him. "It's just about us tonight."

THAT FRIDAY, AS CARRIE WALKED FROM the E.R. to the clinic, she stopped to get a bowl of chili in the cafeteria. She had spent the past two hours in the emergency department because one of her middle-aged female patients with high blood pressure suddenly began exhibiting signs of a heart attack. With women, cardiac episodes were often stealth attacks, difficult to diagnose. There might be vague pain or discomfort in one or both arms, the back, neck, jaw, or stomach. The patient might have cold sweats or nausea that could be attributed to other conditions. Many complained of shortness of breath with no other symptoms. Women often said they weren't sure what was going on but knew they didn't feel well.

In this case, the patient had a nagging pain in her mid-back accompanied by shortness of breath. Her daughter became concerned and forced her to go to the clinic. Carrie assessed the situation and knew within a few minutes the woman was likely experiencing a cardiac event. Fortunately, the patient was doing well now, but it had been a close call. If she had waited any longer to ask for help, she might not have survived.

Carrie only had ten minutes to eat before her next patient. As she sank into a chair in the dining area, feeling more tired than usual, she dug into her lunch. As she ate, she wondered whether Joseph Red Feather had made any headway in finding out what was happening with Nuttah's grandparents and their custody case. She had avoided calling him this week, mostly because she was afraid to hear potentially disappointing news. Besides, she mused, if there had been any news, good or bad, he would have called.

The last time she had talked with him, he had said that she and Nate would need to arrange for Nuttah to visit her birth family on their home turf, a piece of news that produced grave concern. It seemed to Carrie that once that happened, it might be a natural next step for Nuttah to be sent there permanently. She knew that it was only Medicine Owl standing firmly in their court that allowed Nuttah to remain in their home. There were Native American foster families in other parts of Montana who could take the baby.

Carrie's heart beat faster just thinking about what could happen next. The law was clear on this issue. If the child's birth family wanted her, it would take a near miracle for a white couple to adopt her. There would have to be extenuating circumstances for her and Nate to get the nod. It was a fluke that Nuttah had been allowed to remain with them this long.

Carrie took comfort in the knowledge that Nuttah's grandmother had not shown up for a meeting to discuss the upcoming home visitation. At the very least, this demonstrated irresponsibility and the potential for negligence. But a part of Carrie understood that many Native Americans didn't live by clocks and would show up for appointments late, even days later. It was called Indian Time for a reason.

"She may have arrived later in the day or the next, but she still didn't come to the meeting. That may bode well for you," Joseph Red Feather wrote in an email. "Try to relax. The moment I hear anything, I'll let you know."

After work, Carrie picked up Nuttah from Violet's house and drove home, intent on spending a relaxing evening with Nate. After they put the baby to bed, they could have a late dinner and watch a little television. Downtime was important. It had been a more stressful week than usual for both.

She planned to make her mother's recipe for spaghetti, one of Nate's favorites. She wanted him to have a home-cooked meal, even if what she cooked wasn't nearly as good as what he could make for them. It was the thought that counted. She stopped at the grocery store and hurried inside, protecting Nuttah from the wind. Placing her car seat/carrier in the grocery cart, she started down the produce aisle.

She picked up salad greens before turning the corner to head down the other aisles. She located spaghetti, crushed tomato sauce and tomato paste, and lean ground beef. As she concentrated on finding the next item on her list, she looked up just in time to see Gali who had Charlie perched on one hip.

"Oh, hi, Carrie," Gali said. Her parka looked as if she was carrying a beach ball underneath. "I was planning to call you tonight."

Carrie embraced her friend. "Sorry I haven't been in touch lately. A lot has been going on. Between work and all the stuff going on with Nuttah, I've been preoccupied. What's new with you?"

"Someone broke into our house the other night. You might want to start locking your doors."

"That's terrible! You weren't at home when it happened, I hope."

"We were over at John's parents. Whoever did it came right in the back door and took off with a little money, not much—just what John had on his dresser." Gali frowned. "It was an amateur. The police said it was probably a kid looking for money for beer or drugs."

"I've never worried about break-ins before, not way out where we live. I guess we've had a false sense of security."

"There's a lot of crime that doesn't get reported here. Whoever it was broke a window and unlocked the back door. There were blood smears on the door."

"Not a very smart burglar, but it might make it easier to catch whoever did it. Fingerprints." She smiled at her friend. "Are you feeling any better?"

"I've replaced nausea with heartburn," Gali said.

"My grandmother always says heartburn means a baby with lots of hair."

"Well, I hope this kid doesn't come out looking like a grizzly." Gali rolled her eyes. "Is everything okay with you? Any news, good or bad?"

"No news is good news, I think," Carrie said. "Nuttah's grandmother cancelled a visitation and came way late to another meeting about a home visit. Not very responsible, if you ask me."

"John says his dad told him there are concerns about the house where her family lives," Gali said. "I shouldn't say anything that Earl says, but I'm your friend. The family has been given a certain amount of time to bring their house up to minimum standards. It was pretty bad, Earl said." Gali let out a huge breath and shifted Charlie to her other hip. "I need to get this guy out to the car. He's so heavy, he's about to break my arm. I'll talk to you later."

Carrie finished her shopping, packed the groceries in her Subaru, and fastened Nuttah's car seat securely. A heavy snow had started again. She'd have to hurry if she wanted to get the spaghetti sauce done before Nate got home from work.

He arrived home ninety minutes later, planted a kiss on Carrie's cheek, and washed his hands at the kitchen sink. "Mm, smells good in here." He tickled

Nuttah under the chin. She smiled and blew a spit bubble, waving her hands and kicking her feet. "How was your day?" he asked Carrie.

"A heart attack caught just in time. Two new pregnant teenagers. The usual. Hey, I just ran into Gali at the store. She says someone broke into their house and took money. Whoever it was broke a window on their back door and left bloody fingerprints."

Nate poured himself a glass of wine and another for Carrie. "I'll check and see if anyone showed up in the E.R. requiring hand stitches. I've caught a couple of bad guys that way."

At the end of January, Nate flew to Baltimore for a surgical conference, and Carrie took Nuttah to Philadelphia to visit her family. Nate planned to join her and Nuttah at her parents' house the Sunday after the conference. Although the trip was long, requiring two flights and a two-hour layover in Denver, Nuttah was a perfect angel, eating and napping on schedule. Unaccustomed to air travel with an infant, Carrie felt like a pack mule, with a large diaper bag over one shoulder and her purse in the other. She released the combination stroller and car seat on the jetway and took her seat.

They arrived at Philadelphia International Airport late that evening. With a drowsy Nuttah nearly asleep in the stroller, Carrie hurried to baggage claim. Her parents were already there, waiting for them. Their eyes lit up at the sight of Nuttah.

"Mom! Dad!" Carrie said, falling into a group hug.

"So, this is our little Nuttah," her mother said, her eyes joyful as she stroked the baby's plump cheek. "Oh, she's even more gorgeous than in her pictures!"

Her father bent over to get a closer look at the child. "Hello, Miss Nuttah. I'm your Grandpap," he said, touching her hand.

Nuttah stared in wonder at her grandparents, her brown eyes taking in their smiling faces, her mouth a perfect rosebud. Carrie expected her to cry, but she seemed more curious than frightened. Perhaps she was too tired to fuss. Her parents collected Carrie's suitcase from the conveyer belt, and her mother took the diaper bag, slinging it over her shoulder, while her father commandeered the stroller and car seat, and went to retrieve their car.

"Dad, I'll help you install the car seat," Carrie said. "It's tricky."

"We already put one in the back seat of the car—for when she visits," her mother. "We also have a new crib and changing table in the guest room."

"Why am I surprised?" Carrie said, laughing. "You do realize we're here for just five days, right?"

"I know." Her mother raised her eyebrows at Carrie, a mother's way of discouraging further comment. "It was fun shopping at the baby store. I had to exercise serious restraint."

"Apparently, not that much restraint. Maybe you and I could go there together while we're here," Carrie suggested. "Nuttah needs some new outfits. She's growing out of her sleepers." She blew a strand of blonde hair out of her eyes.

"You must be exhausted," her mother said, studying her. "Traveling with a baby as far as you did is a lot of work. Here, let me take her." She wriggled her fingers in her eagerness to hold the baby. Carrie undid the restraints holding Nuttah in her car seat and picked her up. She went willingly to her new grandmother, although her eyes darted to her left, searching for Carrie.

"I'm right here, baby girl," Carrie reassured her, rescuing her mother's expensive handbag that she had dropped in her haste to hold the baby.

Within fifteen minutes, bundled into the car, they headed toward the suburbs. Carrie looked out the window at the scenery speeding past her. It had been a warmer winter than usual in the east, without much snow. This would be a welcome change from their Northwest Montana weather with its frequent bouts of double-digit sub-zero temperatures and deep snow.

"Gran can't wait to meet the baby," her mother said with a backward glance over the seat. "She shares every email you send her. Every photo of Nuttah goes on her refrigerator."

"I'll take Nuttah over there tomorrow, first thing," Carrie said. "How is she doing?"

"She still sees patients in her office every day, and she still makes house calls. Your dad and I try to convince her to cut back, but you know Gran."

"She sees more people than I do," her father said with a chuckle. "Oh, by the way, she was after me last week to make sure I had signed up for the volunteer medical corps. She'll be there again this year."

"I'm glad. We need both of you," Carrie said. "Medicine Owl asks about Gran all the time. Those two really bonded last summer."

"They're birds of a feather," her mother agreed.

"Medicine Owl has been under the weather lately—nothing she'll allow me to treat, of course. It seems like she's wearing down," Carrie said. "I'm worried."

"Well, at her age, it's tougher to bounce back," her father said. "Even the medicine woman is human."

They were silent, thinking of the elderly woman who had impressed all of them with her gentle manner and openness to share what she knew of her native medicine. Carrie was glad she had checked on Medicine Owl a day earlier. Despite an obvious wheeze in her breathing, the medicine woman had waved off Carrie's attempts to listen to her heart and lungs, saying she felt much better. She had been more interested in seeing Nuttah.

Carrie thought of that visit now. It was important to remember everything Medicine Owl had shared with her. There had been an intensity to every word the medicine woman spoke, and Carrie listened carefully, imprinting the message.

Now she wondered if she should have asked more questions.

"She is a good baby," Medicine Owl had said, stroking the fine dark hair that curled around Nuttah's face. She smiled. "I know you think about this child's future."

"Every day, every hour. I love her so much."

"My eyes see that. I have reasons for thinking she should stay with you."

"Medicine Owl, is it her family situation that concerns you?" Carrie had asked. "Do you think she would be safe if she left us and went to her grandparents' house? Would she be hungry, cold, mistreated?"

Medicine Owl was silent for a moment. "I keep notes," she said. She looked at Carrie, impressing what Carrie knew was a bond between healers, trusting her with this information. "Like you, I am bound to keep what people say to myself. I don't share what they tell me, unless it is necessary." Her eyes met Carrie's. "The notes are in our language."

"Oh." Even if Carrie saw the notes, she wouldn't understand what they meant. But it was good to know that the notes existed. She hoped that someday, Medicine Owl would share them with her.

As her father's car pulled into the garage at their stately Bucks County, Pennsylvania home, Carrie's mind returned to the present. After feeding Nuttah a bottle and putting her to bed, Carrie joined her parents in the living room. Her mother poured her a glass of wine and set it on the end table. Carrie picked up the glass and held it as she surveyed the room, noting a few changes among the comfortable furnishings and art. Although she had grown up in this house, she had been away for fourteen years. First, she had gone to Princeton, followed immediately by Philadelphia College of Osteopathic Medicine, before completing her residency at Mayo in Rochester, Minnesota. She had been on the reservation now for almost three years. Although this house was familiar, it was no longer her home. Now she and Nate had their own home on the reservation, a place where she had put down roots. She had a strange sense of disembodiment for a moment, as if part of her was still in Browning.

"Are you hungry?" her mother asked, watching her. "I made some chicken noodle soup, and there are fresh cookies and some fruit cobbler in the fridge."

Carrie shook her head. "No thanks, Mom. I'll make up for it tomorrow."

Her parents were quiet. Carrie knew they were holding back questions. It was only natural that they would be concerned about the adoption, about how she would handle the loss if Nuttah was returned to her birth family. She decided to put them at ease so that they could enjoy the weekend together.

"Sorry to be so vague about the adoption. We haven't heard anything new, but Joseph Red Feather is still hopeful things will go our way," Carrie said. "We're lucky to have Medicine Owl on our side. For as long as she insists that the baby remain with us, I think we stand a chance."

This was wishful thinking, but if the Tribal Council continued to follow Medicine Owl's request, everything could turn out well. The wild card now was that any new members of the Council might not view the situation in the same way. That could change everything.

"We'll continue to think optimistically," her mother said. Her face was filled with concern, and Carrie knew it was for her. "We can't even begin to imagine how hard this must be for you and Nate. We keep trusting that everything will work out for the best, whatever that means."

Carrie nodded. She started to take a sip of wine, caught herself, and put down the glass. Her period was four days late. She didn't want to drink any alcohol if there was even a chance that she might be pregnant. Her mother's eyebrows went up, missing nothing. Carrie was grateful, knowing that with her mother's experience with infertility, she would be sensitive enough not to ask a question that might end up in disappointment.

At ten o'clock the next morning, Carrie drove Nuttah over to Gran's house. It was a beautiful winter day in southeast Pennsylvania, with a clear blue sky shining on the rural landscape. A powdering of snow dusted furrowed fields. Here and there, she saw barns—many repurposed into workspaces, even an art gallery. As she drove down one of the country roads to Gran's house, she passed the barn belonging to one of Gran's neighbors and saw the old bison that still lived there. Her name was Beatrice. As a girl, Carrie had loved visiting Bea the Buffalo. No doubt, Beatrice was the reason Carrie had such fondness for bison. She smiled, thinking of all the miles between this bison and its kin in Montana.

Gran's house was nearly a hundred years old, a white farmhouse that had recently been painted. Off to the side sat a greenhouse where Gran grew herbs and flowers, many used in her healing remedies.

The painted boards of the front porch creaked as they always had when Carrie made her way to the door, evoking memories of all the times during her childhood when she had skipped up the stairs and into the house. She knew the door would be unlocked if Gran was seeing patients. Predictably, there were a few people waiting their turn in the casual family room that Gran used as a waiting area.

Carrie went through to the kitchen, calling out a cheery hello. She unzipped Nuttah from her jacket, removed her hat and mittens, and waited for Gran, who hurriedly washed her hands before hugs and kisses were exchanged. Gran accepted the baby from Carrie and walked her into the waiting area to show her off.

"This is my great-granddaughter," she said to her waiting patients. They looked up in surprise, smiling broadly, as she quickly explained. "Nuttah is a member of the Blackfeet Nation. My granddaughter Carrie and her husband are doctors on the reservation. This little one is the newest member of our family. Isn't she gorgeous?"

Smiles and compliments were exchanged. Yet Carrie could see the questions in a few of their expressions. This was to be expected.

"Is your husband an Indian?" one older woman finally asked.

"No. We're adopting Nuttah," Carrie explained. There were more curious stares at the baby and then at Carrie.

"Do you have other children, your own children?" the woman persisted.

"We plan to have more children," Carrie said, bristling. "Nuttah is so much our child that it's hard to think that we could be any happier than we are right now. Of course, we'd love to have at least one or two more. Nuttah would love a brother or sister, wouldn't you, baby?" She smiled at Nuttah, who rewarded everyone with a dimpled smile so much like Nate's that Carrie felt her heart swell.

After a few minutes, she knew Gran needed to get back to work. "We'll come back and pick you up for dinner," she said, kissing her on the cheek. "Mom and I are going shopping so that she can make sure Nuttah is the best-dressed baby on the reservation."

Gran nuzzled Nuttah's chubby cheeks. "Nothing wrong with that," she said.

It wasn't until Carrie picked up Gran later that afternoon, having left Nuttah with her parents, that she was able to speak freely. No matter what the subject, whatever challenge she faced, Gran was her rock. Gran would know what to say, how to guide her, how to support and encourage her. It was also Gran's way to ask a question in such a way that Carrie would find it impossible to dodge an honest answer.

"How are you holding up?"

"I'm doing okay." Carrie slowed the car to a stop at a traffic light.

"Are you still trying to get pregnant?"

"Yes, I never seem to stop trying. I'm four days late. It's happened before, though. I don't want to get my hopes up."

Gran reached over to squeeze the hand Carrie held out to her. "It will happen."

Carrie thought of those words the next morning when she got her period. Thank goodness, she hadn't mentioned to Nate that she was late. He would have been as disappointed as she was. Maybe it was time to take further action.

Chapter Thirteen

⁓ˎ↓ˏ⁓

FEBRUARY

O N SUNDAY, NATE ARRIVED IN PHILADELPHIA from his Baltimore surgical conference. He looked energized, and shared details of his continuing education sessions in a way that told Carrie he had benefited from this time away to focus on his career. Surgeons needed to stay abreast of all the newest techniques, especially when they were responsible for so many different procedures.

But she also knew that Nate had looked forward to this trip to Philadelphia for personal reasons. He genuinely enjoyed spending time with her parents, especially her dad. Father and son-in-law had become the best of friends based on mutual respect and shared interests. She wished their time in Philadelphia could last a little longer, but they needed to get back to the hospital. A backlog of patients awaited them.

She could remember the anticipation she had felt in the past about returning to the reservation after being in her hometown for even a few days. Living in the vast, quiet splendor of Glacier, she had felt out of her element when visiting Philadelphia. The hub bub of a big city unsettled her. But on this trip, she felt content—even safe—there with her husband and baby, surrounded by the people they loved and who loved them. There was acceptance and support, yes. But more than that, there was a deep understanding and empathy for the situation she and Nate faced. It was easier not to think about what might happen when they returned to Browning.

Carrie admitted her ambivalence to Gran as she drove her home after dinner that evening. She was surprised at her grandmother's response. "I can control things here," Carrie said. "I can pretend nothing will change."

"You can't run from this, Carrie," Gran said after a moment of silence. "You have no idea what might happen, good or bad. Nor can you decide for Nuttah what is best for her life. As tiny as she is, this is her life, and she must be allowed to live out that life, including the good and the not-so-good."

"That sounds like something Medicine Owl would say, except in this case, she thinks Nate and I are the ones who are the best parents for Nuttah." Carrie heard the defensiveness in her tone and caught herself before she said anything more. She hadn't answered Gran that way since high school.

"I didn't say you aren't the best people to be Nuttah's parents," Gran replied, not offended in the least. "What I said is that you cannot choose for her. You already know that this matter will be decided by others. Whatever happens, you'll have no choice but to accept it, even if you don't understand or agree. You want to control the outcome of this, and my love, surely you know by now that control is an illusion. You can pray and wish and hope and dream. You can envision something good, yes. I believe that optimistic thoughts about a good outcome can absolutely make the difference. Whatever happens, you have done a good thing for this child—the very best thing. You have loved her when she needed love. Fearing the worst won't help. Enjoy this time with Nuttah and allow the situation to resolve itself."

Carrie knew Gran was right. Every minute she spent with Nuttah was meant to be cherished. If she concentrated on her fears, she couldn't be fully present with her.

"Gran, you know what it's like to lose someone you love. I don't think you ever got over losing my grandfather. If I lose Nuttah, I will never get over it."

Gran had lost her young husband from cardiomyopathy after he succumbed to a severe respiratory virus. He was gone within a few hours. For years, Gran grieved the loss of the man she loved. She had never remarried but had concentrated instead on her son and her medical practice.

"It's true. You never completely get over the loss of someone you love," Gran said. "Some days are harder than others. But there is also a sweetness to the memories, and I smile when I think of our wedding day, how much in love we were, the joy we felt the day your father was born. He was such a good man, the best husband in the world. I think of how proud he was of my career. He called me 'Doc.'" She let out a quick laugh. "He used to say he married someone smarter so that he didn't have to work so hard. In those days, a man who was proud of a wife with a career was an unusual man indeed."

"I wish I had known him," Carrie said. "He must have been a wonderful man." She thought for a moment. "He sounds like Nate."

"Your grandfather would have loved Nate. After he died, I wondered whether I ought to do more to try to love again, to give my son a father. It was easier to let that part of my life go by the wayside. I always had a good excuse: I had patients!" She shook her head. "The truth was I never had the heart."

"Oh, Gran. That's sad."

"I could have chosen differently, and I did have a chance to love again, but I didn't take it. Don't waste precious moments thinking of the worst, Carrie. And if Nuttah does have to go back to her family, don't feel guilty about having a joyful life without her. You and Nate deserve to be happy."

"Gran, it's just that life seems really overwhelming right now. First, Nate and I were newlyweds. We had just bought our house from Dr. Jim and Lois. Our future was an open book, and we had all the chapters planned. Wedding, check." She made a check in the air with her finger. "House, check. We figured it would be a piece of cake to have kids right away, only it wasn't happening as easily as we thought it would. Then, we were leaving the hospital on our way home to have a romantic dinner, and bam! Along comes this abandoned baby to change our lives. We never thought anything like this could happen. It just . . . did. Now we're in limbo, and it's causing stress in our relationship."

"You talk as if all your happy plans are kaput, and all you face now are troubles. You're still newlyweds, and your future is still an open book," Gran said, reaching across the car seat and patting Carrie on the leg. "Every marriage has its rough spots. If it was all smooth sailing, you'd never get to know the true character of the other person—how they handle problems. I'd venture to say this is the hardest thing any couple faces—infertility and adoption issues. The way you handle it will be the measure of how the two of you define your life together."

Carrie managed a smile. "I know you're right. You're always right."

THAT NIGHT, AS THEY SPOONED IN Carrie's girlhood bed, Nate said, "I've slept better the past few nights than I have in months."

"I'm glad." Carrie nestled closer to him, bringing his hand to her mouth for a kiss. "I think you needed time to focus on yourself and your career."

The truth was that in the four days he attended the conference, she had missed him more than she thought possible. They hadn't been apart in over two years. His presence seemed as vital to her as the air she breathed. When she had news, he was the first one she told. When she was stressed or angry or sad, it was Nate who knew just how to comfort her. It was remarkable, really, how the right man— such a good man—could convince even a strong, independent woman that being together was better than being alone.

BACK AT THE HOSPITAL TWO DAYS later, Carrie was busier than ever. The month of February tended to be hectic as patients showed up with viruses, strep, and respiratory infections, in addition to the usual maladies. But the health conditions of two of her patients concerned her more than any others. Violet High Tower's routine bloodwork showed a slight decrease in kidney function, the result of the many cysts choking off healthy cells in her kidneys.

Carrie pondered what else she could do to help her. She advised her to drink more water, eat less salt and sugar, cut back on animal food products, and eat more vegetables. Violet was more active than she had been when they first met, especially now that she had Nuttah to look after. This would help her keep an optimistic attitude so important to good health. The mind/body connection was crucial to health. There was one approved treatment, but she wasn't convinced it was time to prescribe it yet. She wanted to get Gran's advice and have her examine Violet in July when she volunteered at the hospital.

It appeared that the hospital's childcare center could open as early as July. Margaret Blue Sky had approached Violet about working there. Carrie knew she and Nate would feel much better about leaving Nuttah at the childcare center if Violet was there. She and the baby already had a strong bond. With the erratic hours Carrie and Nate worked, they could spend more time with Nuttah during their shifts.

The other patient causing concern for Carrie was Earl Leathers. Earl still balked at having his blood tested with finger sticks throughout the day. Nadie was frustrated with her husband and called him a stubborn old mule.

"He is like a child, Dr. Carrie," she said. "I have to chase him down to test his blood, and he whines about it like a little kid. His blood sugar isn't what it should be because he doesn't want to test it after eating something that could make it go up. I say, 'Earl, we have fruit for dessert. I will not bake for you anymore if you can't control yourself. One cookie is okay, not three or four.'" She shook her head. "Why should the rest of my family have to be without my cookies because Earl won't even try to stick to his diet?"

Carrie patted Nadie on the hand. "That must be hard on him. You're such a wonderful baker. I think you're doing a wonderful job supporting him," she said. "And, yes, he does need to make healthy choices on his own. This is a disease that requires continual monitoring. I'll talk with him and explain what could happen if he doesn't regularly test his blood."

But when she described to Earl, with Nadie present, the effects of too-high or too-low blood sugar, he said nothing. Stony was the only way she could think to describe the expression on his face. She knew he heard and understood what she was saying. Yet he still resisted following doctor's orders. He might have to learn the hard way what could happen if he didn't keep his blood glucose level in check. Nadie's face showed concern as she listened. Watching her, Carrie knew that Nadie had already seen some of these symptoms in her husband.

She noted Earl's lack of progress in her electronic patient notes. It would be important for emergency room personnel to know about his condition and the difficulties he faced if he required emergency care for a dramatic spike or drop in blood sugar. This would be a life-threatening event.

And of course, there was Medicine Owl. Although she was seeing patients at her grandson's home in Browning, she was seeing fewer of them lately. She had chest congestion that concerned Carrie, and she began to suspect heart failure. Medicine Owl had been self-treating with a combination of herbal remedies that had merit and were known to work. But she was in her late nineties, after all. Carrie checked on her more frequently under the guise of consulting with her about patients, and even took over a large container of homemade chicken soup she made. When she served it to Nate for dinner that evening, his eyes widened in surprised delight.

"This is great, honey!" he said. "Was this your mom's recipe?"

"It's Gran's recipe. I always thought it was this mystery soup that could cure anything, and that she was the only one who had the power to make it. Who knew I could do it, too?"

"I never doubted you for a moment," Nate said, pulling her onto his lap. "I've known you long enough to know that when you put your mind to something, it's only a matter of time before it happens."

As SHE HEADED TO HER CAR that afternoon, Carrie saw Beth Bradley getting out of her SUV in the parking lot. Carrie's greeting got lost in the howling wind as Beth wrapped her scarf around her more tightly and hurried past Carrie into the hospital. Had Beth heard her call out, or had she chosen to ignore her? Probably the latter. Nate reminded Carrie again that she hadn't yet invited Beth to dinner. "What makes you think an invitation from me will even be accepted?" Carrie asked.

"What makes you think it won't?" he countered. "Just ask her, would you? Do it for me? I want you two to get along."

Thinking back to her conversation with Medicine Owl about the pressures Nate faced, she raised herself up on tiptoes and kissed the side of his mouth. "For you, anything."

Meanwhile, Beth's lack of popularity hit a new low. She had been reprimanded the day before by Margaret Blue Sky for a nasty comment she made to one of the operating room nurses. The nurse, who was new on staff, handed Beth an instrument too slowly. Beth had given her a scathing rebuke, saying in front of others in the operating room that the nurse had obviously been trained by idiots and that she needed to go back to nursing school. The nurse had remained quiet but reported Beth to Margaret Blue Sky. Margaret tolerated no such behavior to her nurses and called Beth to her office.

In this matter, Nate had broken with his practice of not commenting on things that happened at the hospital involving Beth. "No matter where you work, whether the hospital is big or small like ours, that kind of behavior is unprofessional. It's beneath her," he said. "I do remember she had a sharp tongue when we worked together. Apparently, she hasn't learned her lesson about being respectful to the nurses. Nurses are our right *and* left hands."

"It must have been like getting called to the principal's office," Carrie said. "I would've been mortified. I'd never mess with Margaret Blue Sky. She's a nurse, too, so of course, she'd be upset that one of her nurses experienced that kind of disrespect." She paused for a moment. "Do you think you'll hear an update about Beth's situation when you go back to Kansas City in March?"

"I don't plan to do an official inquiry, if that's what you mean. But when I talk with other surgeons, the subject of Beth is bound to come up."

"I'm looking forward to seeing your hometown," Carrie said. "Dr. Jim and Lois have invited me many times to visit them, but I never made it."

"I think you'll like Kansas City. We'll do some sight-seeing, have some barbeque. I want my parents to spend time with the baby. It might help with their concerns."

"Concerns about losing her or concerns about us being allowed to adopt her?" Carrie chewed on the side of her mouth. She knew Nate's mother wasn't in favor of the adoption.

"The latter: us adopting a Blackfoot child," Nate said. "My parents aren't quite on the same page as yours."

"Good to know. Well, maybe meeting Nuttah will make the situation real for them. Who can resist such a cute baby?" She tucked her hair behind her ears. "I'm glad I can get away for a few days, too."

"I hope nothing happens to keep us from taking Nuttah with us," Nate mused. "I know we have permission, but if a hearing gets scheduled, we probably would be considered a flight risk."

"We've traveled with her before and always returned." Carrie frowned. "And her grandmother didn't show up for the last meeting to discuss visitation. I also heard there are concerns about the home, and those must be fixed within a certain amount of time. To be honest, all it did was make me feel more nervous about Nuttah going there, even for a visit."

Nate sat at the kitchen table, his head resting in his hands. He was silent for a moment before looking up. "I feel the same way. I don't like it, not one bit."

"There are already enough concerns about her grandfather's drug abuse and her aunts and uncles being in trouble with the law." Carrie sat down across from him. "Let's face it. If we lose her, it's going to be hard knowing where she's going, and that we can't do a thing to help her."

FEBRUARY PASSED WITHOUT INCIDENT. NOTHING MORE was heard about Nuttah's status, although her grandmother applied for benefits to cover the cost of raising an extra child. This seemed premature since nothing had been decided legally. Carrie immediately assumed this meant that the grandmother had been told she would get custody of Nuttah, and she went into a tailspin. It was only after John assured her that nothing had been decided yet, and that there were still concerns about the family's home that Carrie was able to relax.

If Nuttah was returned to her birth family, it was only natural that her grandmother would need money to support her. But Carrie was deeply resentful. "This family hasn't got the money to raise this child, but the law says she's still better off with them," she fumed to Peg.

Peg bit her lip, her eyes clear and direct yet full of compassion. "Most families on the reservation live in poverty, Dr. Carrie. You know that. Grandma would need the money to feed another mouth."

"Forget I said that," Carrie replied, blowing a wisp of stray hair off her forehead. "I want Nuttah to know she is Blackfoot and be proud of it. I'm willing to do whatever it takes to help her with that, and I know that means . . . Well, it means nothing. I'm just frustrated that this hasn't been resolved. If we're going to lose her, it would be better if it happens before she gets much older. It will be so traumatic for her to have to leave us."

"I don't mean to sound unsympathetic, but babies are resilient. Whatever happens, it is in much larger hands than yours." Peg handed Carrie a clipboard with paperwork on their next patient. "You're going to need to prepare yourself for the worst and hope it doesn't come to that." Seeing the stormy look that crossed Carrie's face, Peg changed the subject. "So, what are you serving the ice queen for dinner tomorrow night?"

To Carrie's surprise, Beth had accepted her email invitation to dinner. She was even gracious in her response. Maybe it was easier to communicate with Beth in a way that allowed her to think before responding. Beth seemed to lack filters and often responded to the simplest comment in a clipped manner.

"Um . . ." Carrie looked perplexed. "I don't know, and I don't want Nate cooking. Beth expects that he'll be the one to cook for her. I'd like to surprise her." She offered a mischievous smile. "Hopefully, the surprise will be a good one."

Peg chuckled. "Mashed potatoes are always a hit. I've got turkey gravy in my freezer that you can heat up. Go get a turkey breast at the store and call me before you do anything with it. I'll walk you through how to roast a turkey breast my mother's way."

Carrie kissed her nurse on the cheek. "Peg, what would I do without you?"

"You might poison our two surgeons. Then where would we be?" Peg swatted Carrie on the back with the paperwork. "Now git. You have a patient to see."

When Beth came to dinner that Friday evening, Nate wasn't home from his shift at the hospital. Carrie greeted Beth, invited her in, and then took a leap across the living room to stop Nuttah from snacking on the dog food Annie liked to hide under chairs. "Nuttah, no, no. That's Annie's." Turning to Beth, she explained. "Annie, our dog, was abandoned. She hides food."

Beth cleared her throat. "Well, at least it's protein." She looked mildly amused. "It wouldn't hurt a baby, I guess. It's a shame, though—about the dog, I mean. No animal should ever be abandoned."

"Do you have any animals?" Carrie asked, thinking this might be a safe topic of conversation.

"No, but I really like dogs." She held out her hand to Annie who sniffed her hand and licked it. The corners of Beth's mouth turned up in a way Carrie had never seen before—a genuine smile. Annie settled at her feet. Beth said nothing more.

"May I get you a glass of wine? We've got red and white." Carrie asked, falling back on social niceties to hide her discomfort.

"Red wine would be nice. Thank you."

Carrie could tell that Beth was equally uncomfortable in her presence. The strain on her face was evident, and she had trouble making eye contact. It was hard to tell whether she was uneasy because she was with Carrie or because she was uncomfortable with people in general. Was Beth naturally shy?

Carrie brought a glass of cabernet sauvignon to her. "Here you are. I'll have dinner ready soon."

"I thought . . ." One of Beth's eyebrows shot up.

Carrie thought for a moment before responding. "I suspect my reputation as a terrible cook probably precedes me, and you have every right to wish Nate was cooking. But I've improved a lot. We're having a roasted turkey breast and homemade gravy—although my nurse made it, not me—mashed potatoes, green beans, and cherry pie and ice cream for dessert."

"Sounds good. Thank you." Beth sipped her wine.

Carrie sat on a chair across from Beth. "I know that you and I haven't always seen eye to eye on things. I guess it's normal for doctors to disagree sometimes. But I hope you know how glad I am that you're here at the hospital. And I really do hope you're happy."

Beth's expression stiffened, but she seemed to at least consider the generosity in Carrie's comment. She picked at the fabric on her slacks. Finally, she said, "I haven't had the easiest year. Selling my house, moving here, getting used to the way people live here. You've got to admit, it's different than anywhere else. I'm a little homesick, I guess."

"It takes a while to get used to being here," Carrie said. "I cried so often my first year, I had a chapped nose for four months. Winter can be hard. But hey, it's halfway over," she said with a smile. "Pretty soon, the restaurants will open again. You can hike and explore. It's a beautiful place."

"I don't know if I can ever get used to it," Beth said, reaching down to pet Annie. "I don't fit in. Surely, you see that."

"I'm sorry you feel that way." Carrie's eyes met Beth's. "Maybe I can help." She remembered Nate's comment a few months earlier that Beth thought Carrie had turned the nurses against her. It wasn't true, but maybe now was the time to do something to prove it.

"I'm not sure there is anything you can do." Even as she said the words, Beth looked curious.

"Well, for starters, I can let the nurses and other people at the hospital know that you and I have spent time together socially. That will help. They'll naturally assume I like you."

Beth bit her lip. "But you don't."

Carrie let out a deep breath. "I don't know you, Beth. We'll have to figure out how to learn to like each other."

When Nate arrived home from the hospital, Carrie and Beth were arranged at opposite ends of the sofa, glasses of wine in their hands, discussing their experiences as women in medical school and residency. On this subject, they found much in common.

"Something smells good," he offered.

Carrie's eyes widened as she leapt from the sofa. "Oh my gosh! I forgot about the turkey!"

Nate laughed. "You two keep talking. I've got this."

Chapter Fourteen

_~\l/~_

MARCH

"HAPPY BIRTHDAY TO YOU, HAPPY BIRTHDAY to you, happy half-birthday, dear Nuttah..." Carrie sang, waltzing her round the nursery. Nuttah closed her eyes as if she were flying, a wide smile showing a couple of new baby teeth.

Nuttah had just turned six months old. How the time had flown. She had begun sitting up now, propped up by sofa pillows, and had learned to propel herself across the floor by rocking and scooting. Her best friend Annie was always nearby, encouraging her with a nudge of her long nose to roll over. Nuttah and Annie were inseparable. Even when Nuttah put Annie's tail in her mouth one day, the old dog barely reacted except to yank her tail away in surprise.

"Nuttah, no," Carrie said in a firm voice even as she stifled a grin. "Sorry, Annie." She petted the dog's head. "I'm sure you've had your tail nipped before—just not by a baby."

In every way, Nuttah was a normal, happy baby. She ate well, slept eleven hours at a stretch during the night, and had an agreeable personality and an irresistible smile. Every day she spent with Carrie and Nate cemented the bond between parents and child.

The night before, Carrie had dropped by with Nuttah to see Medicine Owl for their regular weekly visit. "Nate and I are taking Nuttah to visit his parents in Kansas City," she said. "We'll be visiting Dr. Jim and Lois, too." She watched her friend's face. "We're going to be back early next week. Is there anything you need before I leave? How are you feeling?"

Medicine Owl still sounded wheezy. She had treated herself the way she would treat any of her Blackfeet patients: with herbal tea, poultices, and steam. "I am much better," she insisted.

Still, the shortness of breath worried Carrie. The symptoms were pointing to heart failure. She broached the subject carefully, receiving only a shrug in response.

"I have lived through many moons, daughter, and my body is wearing down," Medicine Owl answered. "I know that frightens you."

"I can't stand the thought of losing you, ever. I need you so much, especially now, to help me with Nuttah and everything that is going on." She stopped and thought for a moment. "Medicine Owl, don't you ever get frightened of death?"

"It is the Circle of Life." Medicine Owl patted Carrie's hand. "Death is never to be feared. I will always be with you. Just think of me, and I'll be there."

"Promise you'll take care of yourself while I'm in Kansas City," Carrie said. "If you don't feel well, please go to the hospital. Allow them to help you. You and I have worked together to help people. What we do there has value, too."

"Yes, I know that." Medicine Owl smiled. "I have never thought otherwise. I am giving you notes I have for remedies. They are in our language, but I have made pictures for you so you will know the plants. They are medicines for our people."

"Thank you, Medicine Owl," Carrie said in a breathless voice. "I will treasure them." She could hardly believe what she was hearing. This was an amazing gift.

"I have something else for you, too, daughter," Medicine Owl said. "I will give you patient notes so that you have information about how I have treated people over the years. They also are in our native language, but you will be able to find someone to help you read them. There are still tribal elders who read our language."

"Medicine Owl, you may need your notes," Carrie said, wanting to protest, yet understanding that her friend was giving her more than her patient notes. The medicine woman was entrusting her with tribal knowledge no one else had. She sensed that this was a turning point—that Medicine Owl was acknowledging and preparing to die. "When you give them to me, I will put them in a safe place." The thought was painful to Carrie. She felt nervous about leaving her to go to Kansas City.

"There is information about everyone I have treated on the reservation, back many years," Medicine Owl said. "Great-great-grandmas and grandpas. Remember this."

"As soon as I return from Kansas City, I want to talk with you about a few of those people," Carrie said. It was important that she ask about one family, in particular: Nuttah's family.

"I will be here." Medicine Owl said, struggling to regain her breath.

"As soon as I get back, I'll bring Nuttah over for a visit." Carrie knew as she watched her take deliberate breaths that Medicine Owl was failing fast.

"I will look forward to it."

THAT EVENING, CARRIE TOOK ANNIE FOR a walk on the land surrounding their house. The old dog loved to sniff all the good smells of the outdoors, submerging her snout deep into the snow and pulling it out so that she looked as if she had a white beard. This time of the evening was their special time together. In the summer, they would begin running together again, just maybe not as far. She knew that like Medicine Owl and her wolf, Annie was older, too—at least eighty-four in dog years.

While she loosened the retractable leash so that Annie could explore safely, Carrie watched the back yard for her wolf, searching through the trees beyond to the field. There was no sign of her. It hadn't escaped her notice that there had been no wolf cries at night for at least a week. Whenever a wolf howled, Carrie always imagined it was her wolf. Minus those comforting cries, she couldn't help but wonder about the wolf's whereabouts.

There had been many heavy snowstorms, and they weren't over yet—not by a long shot. Food was a challenge for animals to find, young or old, large or small. Deer had stripped trees and bushes bare. Even predators like wolves had to work harder at hunting. This was nature, predictable and often cruel. Carrie was tempted for just a moment to ignore Mike Leathers' advice and leave something for the wolf to eat. But she resisted the urge, knowing Mike was right.

The next morning, as she and Nate prepared to leave for Great Falls Airport on their trip to Kansas City, Carrie went outside again, searching every corner of their property for the wolf. There was no sign of her. With a heavy heart, she went inside and packed Nuttah's clothing and toys in a small suitcase. The sight of Nuttah in the play yard, watched over by Annie, brought a smile to Carrie's face and lifted her spirits.

"Miss Nuttah, you're only six months old, and this will be the third time you've traveled away from the reservation," she said. "Many of your people never leave the reservation their entire lives. You are such a lucky girl!"

Nuttah grinned, showing her new white teeth. Carrie changed her out of her fuzzy yellow bunny pajamas and into a pair of Baby Gap jeans and a long-sleeved shirt. Her parents had sent the outfit, along with the smallest pair of sneakers Carrie had ever seen. Nuttah looked adorable in them. She quickly snapped a photo with her phone and sent it to her mother with a message. *Nuttah says thanks for the great new outfit! XOXOXO*

"Are you ready to go?" Nate appeared in the doorway. His eyes lit up when he saw Nuttah. "Hey, punkin,' don't you look beautiful!"

Nuttah grinned and danced in place on her chubby legs as Carrie supported her under her arms allowing the baby to test her legs. Nuttah's glossy dark hair had grown and was long enough that Carrie could catch some of it in a ponytail atop her head. Nuttah shrieked with delight, her dimples popping, as she danced in place. Carrie and Nate watched in adoration, laughing with her, until Nate snapped back to attention. "We need to get going, girls."

"THEY'RE HERE! OH, IT'S SO GOOD to have you home!" Dana Holden said, grabbing her son and kissing him on both cheeks as Nate entered the foyer of his family's Kansas City, Missouri home.

Carrie followed, holding Nuttah, who appeared bewildered at the unfamiliar surroundings as Nate's mother and father took in the sight of her in her pink snowsuit and mittens. They wore uncertain smiles on their faces, as though they weren't sure whether to react to the child or hold themselves back. Carrie accepted a peck on the cheek from her mother-in-law and an awkward hug from Nate's dad. His eyes were wary at the unfamiliar child his daughter-in-law carried on her hip.

Carrie thought Nuttah had never looked more irresistible than she did at that moment, with her chubby cheeks and velvety-brown eyes with long dark lashes. She was such a beautiful child. How could anyone keep from loving her on sight?

It was surprising and disappointing when Nate's parents turned away from Carrie and Nuttah and hurried into the living room, clearly more intent on talking with their son than acknowledging that they were meeting a prospective grandchild. But wasn't this a normal reaction by parents who rarely got to see their adult son? Carrie decided to let it go.

As she unzipped Nuttah from her snowsuit and hung her own coat in the closet, she looked around, taking in the gracious features of the older home in an established neighborhood, where towering trees had existed for decades. The house was just as Nate had described it: charming with distinctive architectural features including wainscoting and a stained-glass window at the stairwell landing. White shiplap stretched between the foyer and the entryway to the large country kitchen. The Holdens had owned their home for over thirty-five years, raising Nate and his two brothers there.

The dwelling was a bungalow style: spacious and airy with tall windows, French doors separating all the downstairs rooms, dark hardwood floors, and classic woodwork that still smelled of the fragrant Murphy's oil soap his mother used on it each week. Eclectically decorated with antique collectibles and overstuffed, comfortable furniture, the entire house was spotlessly clean—a testament to her meticulous care.

As Carrie looked around the house, admiring its gracious style, she wondered how Nate's upbringing had contributed to the man he had become. While his parents were more conservative, Nate took a more moderate approach to most issues. His strict upbringing had included numerous youth service projects, which had given him a broader worldview, especially about the health concerns of developing nations. Although the Blackfeet reservation was part of the United States, it had some of the same health issues that Nate had seen during his church mission projects in developing nations. In many ways, these volunteer stints had prepared him well for life and his work as a doctor on a Native American reservation.

Nuttah started to fuss as her naptime came and went. She hadn't slept much on the flights to Denver or Kansas City. Carrie mixed a fresh bottle of formula with bottled water and shook it. "Dana, would you like to help me change her?" she asked her mother-in-law. "Then I can feed her and put her down for her nap."

Nate's mother's mouth opened, then shut. She looked decidedly uncomfortable. "I'm not sure how much help I'd be, dear," she said. "It's been ages since I changed a diaper. Let me know when you're ready to put her down for her nap, and I'll show you where to go."

With that, she left the kitchen to join her husband and son in the living room. Carrie watched her back as she retreated. She changed Nuttah on a fluffy mat in the downstairs powder room and carried her to the living room, where she sank into a corner of the roomy sofa to feed her.

Nate's eyes brightened when he saw Nuttah. "Are you tired, baby girl?" he asked, kissing her forehead. Nuttah forgot about the nipple in her mouth and grinned at him for a split second before returning to her bottle.

"Flirt," Carrie said to Nuttah and grinned at Nate. "She has you wrapped around her little finger." Nate's parents exchanged glances.

"I put that porta crib I borrowed from my sister in the same room where you and Nate will be sleeping," Dana said. "Whenever you're ready . . ."

"Why don't I just take her up there now? That way, I can feed her and put her to bed."

Together, they went up the stairs to Nate's childhood bedroom, which still looked much as it probably had when he lived there. Carrie saw sports memorabilia, including a Royals baseball ball and bat, and a Kansas City Chiefs ball cap. A model airplane, painstakingly assembled and painted, appeared ready to take off from atop his dresser. Carrie noticed a prom photo of Nate at seventeen, his hair curly and wild as dandelion fluff, as he stood next to a willowy blonde girl with pony-like arms and legs, who looked a lot like Taylor Swift. On the wall, she saw his diplomas from high school and college. In another photo—taken the summer after his graduation from the University of Kansas—he appeared remarkably as he did today, although his golden curls had been shorn in preparation for osteopathic medical school. Years later, Nate was as strikingly handsome as ever, she thought, except now there were laugh lines around his twinkling blue eyes.

"I haven't done much with the boys' rooms," his mother said. "I like to pretend the boys still live at home."

Carrie sat down on an old rocking chair beside the bed to finish giving Nuttah her bottle. "This room even smells like Nate," she said with a soft laugh. Turning her eyes to the drowsy baby, she added, "She's beyond tired. I couldn't get her to nap much on either flight. There was too much to see. Come to think of it, I might just take a nap with her. Do you mind?"

"Not at all. We can catch up later," Nate's mother said. She studied the baby, whose eyes were closed. "She's very sweet. I hope she can have a happy childhood."

The comment pierced Carrie, who glanced up at her mother-in-law with a questioning expression. Dana had a habit of being direct, sometimes with results she didn't necessarily intend. "Of course, she will. We're determined that will happen."

"Don't you think that caring for this little one might somehow be *delaying* you in having your own children?" Nate's mother asked, perching on the edge of the bed. "I mean, having a baby is exhausting. It might be why you haven't yet . . . well, you know."

"My mother was delayed a bit when she wanted to have a baby," Carrie said in a careful tone, not stressing the word 'delayed' as Dana had. "But, eventually, I came along. I'm sure we'll be announcing happy news any day now. Then we'll have two littles to love."

"Of course, you will." Nate's mother got up, offered a semi-smile, and left the room, closing the door softly behind her.

Carrie breathed in and out, slowly. The comment about delayed fertility hurt. Nate's mother didn't understand. That much was clear. But it wouldn't help to allow herself to be upset by her comments. She was Nate's mother, and Carrie wanted a good relationship with her.

She continued breathing in and out until the feelings of annoyance passed. Even if she did get pregnant in the coming weeks or months, how could she even question that she already had a baby, a baby who needed her, a baby—this baby—she loved? She buried her face in Nuttah's fragrant black hair. As she gently stroked the baby's petal-soft cheek with her pinkie finger, she said the words she knew to be most true. "You are *my* daughter of the heart."

ON MONDAY MORNING, NATE DONNED A suit in preparation for his visit to the medical center. Then he yanked off the tie. "Too much," he said. "It's not a job interview."

"Are you sure about that?" Carrie asked. He had spoken recently by phone with the head of surgery, and she couldn't help but wonder if this meant he would be recruited to return to the medical center.

He ran his hand through his damp curls and flicked off a tiny piece of toilet paper he had pasted on a razor nick. "This morning, I'm meeting an old friend from the E.R., and then I'll catch up with a few of the surgeons I used to hang with." He splashed aftershave on his face and let out an expletive when it hit the razor nick, which evoked a quick laugh from Carrie. "I might have lunch with some other colleagues, too."

"Well, if you're putting on the expensive aftershave, I have to ask if these colleagues are guys or girls."

"Girls, of course." He playfully flicked a towel in her direction and gave her a come-hither look that made her snort as she tried not to laugh out loud. Nuttah was still sleeping.

"Just wondering," she said in a throaty voice. "You're looking pretty darned handsome there. Are you sure you don't want to come back to bed for a quickie? We might have, oh, five minutes." The baby rolled over, lifted her head, and then laid it down again.

"Let's not press our luck." He grinned. "I'm pretty sure my mother knew what we did last night. It's probably why she put the porta crib in here. Infant chaperone."

Carrie held her hand over her mouth to quiet her laughter. She lay propped up in the big bed, feeling more like a college coed surreptitiously spending the night in her boyfriend's room than his wife of eight months.

After three days, Nate's parents continued to treat her as if she was a visitor who might or might not ever return. Her mother-in-law insisted on introducing her as Carrie Holden, even though she knew Carrie had maintained her own name for professional reasons. 'Nelson' was on her medical school diploma and her license. Carrie hadn't minded, not really. She *was* Mrs. Holden, and she rather liked that distinction. What bothered her more was that Nate's parents continued to treat Nuttah with detachment.

"Maybe they're afraid of loving her and then losing her," Carrie had suggested to Nate.

"My parents have their own views on the world and those who inhabit it," he answered. "I don't share most of those views, and sometimes it can be hard to be around them. I love them, but I'm not really like them."

"I've noticed that," she said. "But they sure did a good job raising you." Already recognizing the stark contrast between Nate and the rest of his family only made Carrie love him more. She wondered how a young man from such a conservative household, where differences among people were not necessarily tolerated, had become a man who valued service to others over self-interests. Nate had given up a lucrative career at a major medical center to serve a remote Native American population at a tiny federal hospital in Montana. He loved the life he had chosen.

She marveled at this. Although her father also tended to be on the judgmental side, she had always had Gran to open her mind and heart to a worldview that embraced differences between people. Her father had made great progress in the past several years, thanks to his volunteerism on the reservation.

Carrie tried not to show her discomfort with Nate's parents, but she felt awkward around them. Conversations became stilted as she weighed her responses, choosing her words with care. By the end of the second day, she was more than ready to go home.

Nate had quietly made love to her last night—with the covers over their heads—so as not to wake Nuttah. Afterward, he had rolled over, drawing Carrie to his side and kissing her hair. "Are you okay?" he asked. "You've been awfully quiet—unusually so, if you don't mind me saying."

"Don't think anything of it. It's just weird being in the house where you grew up, sleeping in this bed. You probably read comic books in this bed." She tickled him underneath one arm. "So, how many other girls did you sneak in here?"

"Just one. Marisa." Marisa had been his college sweetheart and fiancée.

"I'm guessing your mother likes Marisa better than me," she said, snuggling against him.

"I married you, not Marisa. That ought to tell you something. That means I like you better."

She ran her fingers through his chest hair. "I hope so. But seriously, don't you think it's time for your mother and dad to at least want to hold Nuttah? They act like she's on display or something. 'Look at the Indian papoose and Nate's squaw.'"

Nate chortled. He was quiet for a few moments before speaking. "This is a really unusual circumstance in their circle of friends."

"You mean adopting a child from a difference race."

"My parents are great people, but you have to admit what we've done is unusual. They thought they'd have a grandchild who resembled one of us, at least."

"Well, with any luck, one of these days, we'll present them with a child who looks more like you." She was quiet for a moment. "Your mom asked whether it might be possible that having Nuttah is keeping me from getting pregnant—like maybe she's too much for me to handle on top of a job and stuff."

"Carrie, sometimes things do or don't happen for a reason. Maybe the timing just isn't right." Nate let out a deep breath and stroked her arm. "There might be a reason why you aren't meant to be pregnant yet. It's just not time."

She took in a deep breath and let it out. "I get that. Sometimes we wish for something and realize later that it was better that we didn't get what we asked for, at least at that moment." She pulled the sheets up to cover them. "Just because I want something right now doesn't mean I'm going to get it right now."

"Carrie, we *are* parents now. We'll continue to be parents, one way or another," Nate said, drawing up her face and kissing her lightly on the cheek. "No matter what, this little girl is in our lives for a reason. We're the ideal people to love her, and one way or another, we'll continue to do that. It's our destiny."

Carrie met the eyes of the man she loved. "You are the most wonderful person. How can you stand me? I'm so . . . well, you know how I am. I worry too much. I stress over every detail. I want to control the outcome of everything. I have so many fears. How do you do it? How are you always so calm?"

Nate lay back on the pillow and stared at a spot on the ceiling. "Don't be so hard on yourself. You're the most organized, conscientious person I know. You give a hundred percent of yourself to everyone. As for those fears, at least you admit having them. I'm the one with nightmares, remember?"

Carrie had remained awake long after Nate went to sleep, listening to the quiet in and out of his breaths. He had slept soundly—a good sign. In the dark, with the light of a streetlamp shining between a crack in one of the blinds, she thought about their life on the reservation. She hoped they could continue to stay there. Whatever came next, they would weather it together. A marriage went through changes, just like seasons. Springs followed winters. No matter what happened, they would be there for each other.

As Nuttah woke up and began sucking on her fingers, Nate picked her up before she could fuss. "Hey, baby," he said.

He handed Nuttah to Carrie, who lay back against the pillows. Nate put on his suit jacket and stood over them, a tender smile on his face. "You two have a good day," he said.

"Don't let them pressure you into coming back." She was only half-joking. With Beth Bradley no longer on staff there, it was highly likely the medical center needed Nate to return. They might make him an offer he couldn't refuse.

"I'd only agree to that if you wanted to work there, too," he said. "We can talk more when I get home." He shut the door behind him.

Carrie hadn't expected him to respond that way. She knew that working on the reservation was everything Nate had ever wanted in his career. He loved it.

And then she suddenly felt it: the inner knowing. Nate didn't believe they would be allowed to keep Nuttah. He was hedging his bets, preparing to leave the reservation—for her sake and perhaps for his, too.

WHILE NATE WAS AT THE MED center, Carrie took Nuttah to visit Dr. Jim and Lois, who lived in Leawood, an affluent suburb across the Kansas state line. She rang the doorbell and heard excited voices and footsteps. Then the door flew open, and Carrie and Nuttah found themselves scooped into Lois's waiting arms as she exclaimed, "Come in, come in, both of you! Jim! Jim, they're here! Carrie's here with the baby! Hurry up, Jim!"

Chuckling, Dr. Jim strolled to the front hallway, wiping his glasses on the front of his blue argyle sweater. He leaned in to embrace Carrie, who turned Nuttah outward, holding her under her bottom. "Here she is, the little girl who changed our lives," she said.

Lois chucked Nuttah under the chin. "Hello, sweetheart," she said. "Aren't you the prettiest baby on the entire reservation! In all of Montana!"

Dr. Jim grinned. "Nuttah, it's nice to meet you."

Nuttah looked directly at Dr. Jim and smiled, kicking her legs and waving her arms in delight. Dr. Jim's eyes crinkled in delight. He chuckled and said to Carrie,

"When I think of how she came to be in your lives, really how you came to be in *her* life, it fairly boggles the mind."

"I know. If I hadn't first gotten to know you . . . if I hadn't been given that research award to study Native American medicine . . . If I hadn't fallen in love with Nate . . . If we hadn't been at the hospital the night Nuttah's father left her there . . ." Carrie shook her head. "You're right. It's been a perfectly serendipitous life I've led."

"Take off your coat and stay a while. Where's Nate?" Lois asked, peeking out the doorway.

"He's over at the hospital. There were a couple of people he wanted to see. He's been there most of the day." She removed Nuttah's snowsuit and sat her down on the carpet near the sofa, surrounded by decorative pillows. Dr. Jim, Lois, and Carrie sat on the sectional sofa in a semi-circle, watching the baby as she investigated her surroundings with her doe-like eyes.

"Look how she can sit all by herself!" Lois said. "You can tell how smart she is by the way she's taking everything in. I wonder what she's thinking."

Nuttah shook her head as if to say, "Really, lady? I've been doing this sitting-up thing for more than a month," and let out a hearty belly laugh. All three adults reacted in kind. Then Nuttah reached out and touched Dr. Jim's pant leg. She looked up at him and smiled again.

"I could swear she knows you," Lois said. "Look how she watches your face, Jim."

Indeed, Nuttah was watching Dr. Jim with wonder. Dr. Jim bent over and caressed the baby's face. "Do you know me? Do I know you, little one? Perhaps we've met before somewhere."

Carrie swallowed the lump that came to her throat. She had come to believe over the past several years that she had once lived as a Blackfoot and had returned to help her people. Nate had felt the exact same way—had said he could sometimes remember scenes that were so vivid, he had to believe they came from memory. Now they had to consider that Nuttah, too, might have known Dr. Jim in a previous lifetime. Now here they were, all together again.

Chapter Fifteen

—◟⁄◞—

NATE ARRIVED AT HIS PARENTS' HOUSE around four-thirty, just as Carrie and Nuttah returned from visiting Dr. Jim and Lois. He looked cheerful, even whistling as he dropped his car keys on the hallway table and removed his overcoat. He kissed Carrie, then Nuttah, and took the baby in his arms, holding her up in the air and jostling her playfully.

"Did you have fun today, baby girl?" he asked, kissing both chubby cheeks. Nuttah tried to put both fists into her mouth.

"She had a terrific time, didn't you, Nuttah? She and Dr. Jim got along like they were old best friends," Carrie said. "Nate, you would have sworn they already knew each other. She beamed at him and stayed glued to his side the entire time."

"He's got that way about him." Nate smiled.

"How are things over at the hospital?" his father asked. "Did they ask you to come back?"

Nate let out a little laugh. "It's a major medical center, Dad. They can have their pick of anyone they want."

"Yes, but if you ever decided to come back here, could you get your old job back?" his mother asked, a gleam of hope in her eyes.

Nate and Carrie exchanged a look. "Mom, we have a home and careers on the reservation," he said. His mother's expression went from hopeful to disappointed in a split second.

Carrie knew that this discussion about Nate returning home was repeated at least once a year, usually around a major holiday. Now that she understood on a gut level that Nate was considering the idea, Carrie felt uneasy. Regardless of what might happen with Nuttah, they had purchased a house and had put down roots on the reservation. It wouldn't be that easy to leave—for either of them.

"The truth is that Blackfeet Community Hospital could never hope to replace him," Carrie said. "The work he does there is heroic—a calling, really."

Nate looked uncomfortable. "I need to change out of this suit," he said. He surveyed his parents, sitting side-by-side on the sofa. "I was wondering if you two would babysit this evening, so I can take my wife out for dinner. I want to take her out on the town—let her try some of the best barbeque Kansas City has to offer."

"Er, well, I guess we could do that," his father said, making eye contact with his wife. "Maybe you could plan on a later dinner and help us put the baby to bed. That way, she won't feel strange with just the two of us."

"Sure," Nate said, nodding. "That would be ideal. It's time I took Carrie out. We haven't had a night out alone since Nuttah came home with us."

That night as they drove to the restaurant that Nate promised would be a memorable barbeque experience for Carrie, he provided more details about his day. "It was different than I thought it would be. I stopped in the E.R. and saw quite a few people I knew. Everything looks the same. It's still as crazy as ever."

"Did being there make you feel anxious?"

"Not really. I walked through the area where I used to work, the room where I got shot, and . . . nothing," he said. "I can clearly remember everything that happened, hear the screams, the shots, but not with the same intensity as I used to. It was like visiting a battlefield where a lot of lives were lost, and you feel a deep emotion, but you're still able to remain detached and view it from a historical perspective, if that makes sense."

"Time does heal wounds, physical and emotional," Carrie said. "Maybe the nightmares really did help you process negative emotions. It's only normal that you'd want to forget what happened, or that you'd compartmentalize what happened . . . put it in a safe place where you could consider it later, maybe when enough time had passed."

"What did Medicine Owl say about the reason we dream? That what we don't want to think about during our waking hours must visit us in our sleep?"

"She says dreams are more important than we realize. They tell us many things we need to know about ourselves on a soul level," Carrie said, her brow furrowing. "Clearly, you must have processed what you needed to know because you aren't having the nightmares anymore. You've closed that chapter of your life." She paused and said carefully, "Returning here wouldn't really move you forward with your career, would it?"

"I haven't decided anything, Carrie. I'd never do that without talking with you first. It's always a possibility, though, because, well, we never know what's going to happen in life. What if the hospital on the reservation gets closed? What if we wanted to be closer to either of our families?"

"But if we have Nuttah, we can't really leave, Nate. We are promising to raise her there." Carrie took in a deep breath. "That's a commitment we have to make for life, at least until she's grown."

"I know. It's still important for us to have these discussions. We need to be on the same page," Nate said.

Carrie waited a moment before continuing. "Nate, you and I always agree. The only serious disagreement we've ever had has been about Beth."

"I know." He turned from the main street onto a side street, looking for a parking space. "I'm sorry for that. I think back to things I've said, and I wish I had explained better how I felt."

"It's okay. You and Beth have a long history, and I have no right to judge the way you communicate with her. I told her one time that I'm grateful she saved your life. I meant that."

"She is difficult. I don't deny that."

"Has it gotten worse since she's been on the reservation?" Carrie asked. "Okay, I'm just going to ask this: While you were talking with people today, did anybody mention anything about her being on the reservation? Aren't they curious about how she's making out there?"

"They are curious, and they also doubt she'll stay. Coming to the reservation was an escape hatch for her. She left the hospital under a shadow of suspicion, and she left in a hurry. She's still under investigation."

Carrie's eyes widened. "What happened?"

"Allegedly, she did emergency surgery on a woman who came into the E.R. with a cardiac dissection. It didn't go well, and the woman died."

"Well, a dissection is pretty dicey," Carrie said. "By the time the diagnosis is confirmed, the patient can be past saving. So, there must be evidence of some kind, and Beth must be accused of bungling the surgery. I think that would be tough to prove, in that case."

Carrie's father was a cardiologist. She had heard several stories of patients experiencing aortic dissection, a life-threatening condition where the aorta, the main artery in the body that originates in the heart and extends into the abdomen, spontaneously tears. As blood courses through the tear, the inner and middle layers of the aorta separate. If the patient received immediate diagnosis and surgery, it was possible to recover fully. But it was just as likely that the patient could die. From her own experience in medical school and residency, she had seen three cases. Only one patient survived.

"Beth doesn't bungle surgeries. Like I said, she's good at what she does. The patient was brought in near death. Beth diagnosed cardiac dissection and got her into the O.R. The patient died on the table."

"Did her family think she could have been saved?" Carrie was intrigued. She also felt sympathy for Beth. Cardiac dissection was one of the more serious conditions a patient could present with in an emergency department. Every second meant the difference between life and death. No matter how good Beth was, she could still lose a patient who was that critically ill.

"Apparently, there is a rather nasty accusation against Beth as a result of the patient's death."

"What kind of accusation?"

"I don't know the specifics, and I'd rather not listen to gossip."

"Aren't you curious?" Carrie was.

"I did ask, but my friends say they don't know the particulars, either—just that Beth obviously is in a lot of trouble."

"So, she left town and came to the reservation to wait until this situation is resolved or at least simmers down. Wow, no wonder she's so uptight and edgy all the time."

"The thing is, there's something that's been bothering me ever since she came to the hospital. If memory serves, she had a relationship with another doctor. I think he was a hematologist/oncologist. If that romance went south—for whatever reason—that could account for her saying she needed to get away for a while. A break-up with a guy plus the loss of a patient plus a lawsuit could contribute to that."

"You're right. It would be a triple-whammy for her." Carrie took in a deep breath. "I've been feeling much better toward her since she came for dinner," she said as Nate held open the front door of the restaurant for her. "I don't get as irritated with her, even when she talks *at* me instead of *to* me."

"We're a small staff, and we really need her, so it's in everybody's best interests for us all to get along," Nate said. "I just hope it doesn't turn out that she really did something wrong."

"Do you trust her to be completely truthful with you?" Carrie asked as the host seated them at their table.

Nate bit his upper lip. "I trust her fully—at least until I have information that she can't be trusted. How's that?"

"Fair enough," Carrie said, turning her attention to the menu in front of her. "So, what should I order? Not being from Kansas, I feel as if I'm in Oz. This is overwhelming."

The menu offered a wide array of options, with entrees, appetizers, sandwiches, and desserts that looked so tempting, Carrie already knew what Nate's game plan would be. He would order as many items as possible, so they could try them all.

Predictably, he looked up and grinned. "Let's have a little of everything," he said. "What do you want to drink?"

"Am I allowed to have wine in a barbeque restaurant?" Carrie asked.

"I'd suggest one of the local craft beers," Nate said.

"Why don't you pick one for me—nothing fruity. If I want fruit, I'll order wine."

"You're such a purist," Nate said, rolling his eyes. "I'm getting you a dark beer with chocolate undertones."

"That works," Carrie said. She sat back while Nate ordered a large plate of brisket, pulled pork, burnt ends (considered a Kansas City barbeque must-have), spicy chicken, and the restaurant's famous wings. He also ordered onion straws.

"I want a salad, too."

"No, Carrie. You are not eating a salad at a barbeque place. I forbid it." Nate waggled his finger at her. "You just have to trust me on this. Do you trust me?"

"I trust you fully until I have information that you can't be trusted," she replied, giving him her most beguiling smile.

"Touché." Nate touched his water glass to hers.

When their beers arrived, she took a sip, appreciating the smooth creaminess of the brew as she surveyed the atmosphere of the restaurant. Warm and cheery, the spacious dining room had a modern-rustic vibe with exposed brick. The place was packed—typical, Nate said, any night of the week. The conversations of diners around them provided a layer of insulation as they talked.

Carrie realized she was enjoying herself and didn't feel a moment's guilt about leaving Nuttah. She had a sense of peace that all would be well—helped along by the beer. The adoption might not fall into place immediately, but hadn't life always turned out fine, even when it felt chaotic? Medicine Owl was right. It was important to trust that the Great Spirit knew best.

She held up her glass in a toast. "To us, to our baby, and to all the people, places, and events that contribute to our wonderful life together."

Nate touched his glass to hers. "To the woman who makes me happy to be alive."

ON THEIR FIRST DAY BACK ON the reservation, Carrie and Nate had a terrible shock. Although she wanted to trust in Medicine Owl's assurances that all would be well, they learned via the hospital grapevine that Nuttah's grandmother had told others that she had been given custody of Nuttah. This was not, in fact, the truth. Joseph Red Feather assured Carrie of this.

"Nuttah's grandmother has lost her daughter Kimi and now wants Kimi's baby," he said. "That is the basis for wanting the baby, and it is a sympathetic plight, to be sure." He paused for a moment. "However, she also says she needs money to feed another mouth, and she says this must happen before she takes this baby—that she needs it now. I'm not judging, and it's only natural she would need that kind of assistance. But it also could be about more income for the family. I'm hoping it will appear that way to a judge."

Carrie was heartsick but had no choice other than to allow the process to resolve itself, hoping for the best—whatever was best for Nuttah. *Do I really know what that means? I am not a Blackfoot.*

She could understand that the grandmother had been surprised by Nuttah's birth and hadn't had adequate time to adjust to the idea that she might be helping to raise her daughter's child. After meeting Nuttah and holding her, the grandmother naturally would want her granddaughter to live with her. What grandmother could resist her own grandchild? Carrie let out a long sigh. The truth was that Nuttah had another family—a family other than Carrie and Nate. Yet it made her sick to her stomach to think that Nuttah might be the best way for the grandmother to earn more public assistance.

"If Nuttah is given back to the family, it will be because of the law," Peg had said, laying her hand over Carrie's. "The law was passed for a reason, Dr. Carrie."

"Yes," Carrie said, her voice sounding more like a whisper. "I understand. We knew this might happen."

Peg took in a deep breath and pursed her lips. Then she said, "Not so very long ago, Indian children were taken away from their families, and parents lost their right to raise their own sons and daughters. The children never knew their families or what it meant to be a member of their Indian Nation. The children were told their parents were dead."

"I know. That was terrible," Carrie said. "But this situation is different. Isn't it?"

"I believe it is. Sometimes what is best for the child must be decided based on other things." Peg shifted her weight to her other foot, waiting for Carrie's response. From the look on Peg's face, Carrie knew Peg didn't have confidence, either. Despite Peg's feelings that the birth family's home environment wasn't stable or suitable, the situation didn't look good.

"That's why it's more important than ever that I have Medicine Owl in my court," Carrie said. "And you, Peg. And Violet, too. And John and Gali, Nadie and Earl, Pete and Naomi. All our Blackfeet friends."

"And we will be there for you. There are people who don't agree with me, Dr. Carrie," Peg said. "There are people who think the baby should be with her grandmother. They say the Tribal Council is bowing to Medicine Owl's wishes that Nuttah stay with you. At one time, I might have thought Nuttah should not be with a white couple, but not this time. I am not in favor of the baby going back to that house—not with that grandfather and some of those troublemaker aunts and uncles."

"Thank you, Peg," Carrie said. She embraced her nurse, who returned the hug. "You're always there for me."

"You are part of us now," Peg said. "We take care of our own."

Despite a heavy flow of patients, Carrie needed to see Medicine Owl. She didn't have much time, but she had to talk with her. She was also worried. Medicine Owl had stopped seeing patients that week, which was highly unusual during the cold and flu season. When Medicine Owl saw patients, there were fewer people who came to the clinic seeking help. Now, with even more patients than usual streaming into the clinics because they couldn't see the medicine woman, Carrie's workload had increased. In addition, she had been called to the hospital to deliver babies two out of four evenings that week.

Carrie drove over to Medicine Owl's house right after work. The elderly woman didn't answer the door, but her grandson did, and ushered Carrie into his grandmother's bedroom. Medicine Owl was sitting in a rocking chair, wrapped in her shawl.

"Medicine Owl, Nuttah's grandmother says she will get the baby." Carrie spoke in a rush, unable to catch her breath for a moment. "She may have heard something."

Medicine Owl shook her head. She let out a raspy cough before answering. "This is not the truth," she said.

"You don't look well, Medicine Owl," Carrie said, moving toward her. "Will you let me listen to your lungs?" She pulled her stethoscope out of her white coat.

"My heart is very old. I'm resting and drinking fluids. I'll be fine," Medicine Owl answered. "I thought it best that I do not see patients this week."

"I agree you should rest," Carrie said. "It will put my mind at ease if you let me take a quick listen."

"Very well," Medicine Owl said, and allowed Carrie to listen to her heart and lungs. Carrie heard congestion. Carrie placed her hand on the medicine woman's forehead. No sign of fever. The normally energetic woman seemed to be conserving what strength she had left. She refused medication.

"I will come back in a day or so," Carrie said, biting her lip. "Can I bring you anything? Do you have enough food in the house?"

"I don't need much," Medicine Owl said with a kind smile. She wrapped the shawl more tightly around herself. "I am more concerned about you," she said. "I can see that you are tired, and I am sure this waiting is difficult for you and your husband."

"We feel helpless."

"There are things that he does not tell you. It is his way to be strong and quiet. It does not mean he does not feel things as deeply are you do."

"We are trying to be patient, but when we hear nothing, we—I mean, I— think the worst. He doesn't say much. But sometimes, I think he believes we will lose Nuttah."

"He understands what he can see with his eyes and fix with his hands. He cannot see a good outcome, and this troubles him. In this matter, you must be his vision. I believe you will hear news soon." She coughed again. "There will be a time for sadness, and you will question things that I have said to you."

"What do you mean?" Carrie asked. "Why will I be sad?"

"Sometimes there are difficulties that we must go through. It is necessary. There is a reason for everything that happens, whether we understand or not. A lost item may be found later by someone who needs to see it. Information may come in unexpected ways."

"That has happened before," Carrie said. "I believe that."

"You are making progress." Medicine Owl rocked in her chair.

"Sometimes I think I am letting you down—that I disappoint you when I say things like what I just said. You tell me over and over to be patient and optimistic, and yet my mind still goes to that place of fear."

"This is something you must train your mind to do. You are still young. You will learn and grow, and it will be easier when you have more experience. It is important for you to remember that we are all connected. What affects one, affects all. What you want does not matter more than what another wants."

"I do sympathize with Nuttah's grandmother. It would be terrible to lose your daughter."

"It is a sad situation. It is right that you should hold loving thoughts about her. She has suffered for many years. I know this."

Carrie wondered if there was domestic abuse in addition to all the other concerns in that household. She had never seen Nuttah's grandmother as a patient. This must mean that she went to Medicine Owl for her care. At some point, it might be up to Carrie to be this woman's doctor.

"The best outcome cannot benefit just one person. Everyone matters. What each person needs must be considered. That is the work of the Great Spirit. In your heart, you know this, daughter."

"I worry that Nate will want to leave the reservation if we lose Nuttah," Carrie admitted.

"I am aware of this." Medicine Owl closed her eyes for a moment as if viewing a scene. She opened them again before speaking. "You and your husband will be strengthened in your marriage if you work through these hard times together. I cannot say more at this time."

Chapter Sixteen

_⁓\|⁓_

APRIL

As HARSH WINTER WEATHER CONTINUED INTO the month of April with blowing snow and ice, it seemed impossible that spring would ever come. One night, Carrie awakened to a cry on the baby monitor from Nuttah who fussed for about a minute before going back to sleep. Carrie rolled over to face Nate and found his side of the bed untouched. Concerned, she went looking for him and found him asleep, fully clothed on the sofa, wrapped in one of Lois's afghans. A surgical journal lay open on the floor, where he had dropped it when he fell asleep while reading.

She lightly touched his forehead and kissed it. How she loved this beautiful man. He stirred slightly, but not even her touch and the kiss could wake him from his exhausted sleep.

She took in the bluish circles under his eyes, the growth of beard from a long shift at the hospital. In addition to surgeries, he had regular shifts in the E.R. When he came home, he also helped with housework and cooked. He was always more than willing to care for Nuttah.

For a few moments, studying his tired face, she wondered if Nate was happy. She knew he rarely voiced any concerns he might have. What she wanted, he wanted for her. He did what he could to fix problems. But this challenge of Nuttah's adoption couldn't be as easily fixed. Medicine Owl was right. He did feel things deeply.

She wrapped the blanket more tightly about his shoulders and went back to bed. Lack of sleep—from anxiety—was taking a toll on her, too. She wondered if in addition to stress, a lack of sound sleep might be preventing her from getting pregnant. Restorative sleep was so important. Without enough sleep, her hormones could be out of balance.

The next evening after work, Carrie went again to Medicine Owl's house. She decided to take Nuttah with her. It would do the medicine woman good to see the baby. Snow had drifted up the front door of the ramshackle house, making entry difficult. While she waited for Medicine Owl's grandson to answer the door, she covered Nuttah's face against the fierce wind.

When the door opened, she nearly fell inside, so strong was the wind at her back. She deposited Nuttah on the worn sofa and removed the blanket covering her. Only her tiny face was visible, but she smiled and blew a spit bubble.

"Peek a boo," Carrie said. "Peek-a-boo, bubbly boo." She covered Nuttah's face again and removed the blanket. The baby laughed.

Medicine Owl stood to the side, wrapped in her shawl. As she watched Carrie play with Nuttah, a smile appeared on her wrinkled face. Then she moved with difficulty to join Carrie on the sofa. Carrie put Nuttah into Medicine Owl's outstretched arms.

Medicine Owl touched her fingers to the baby's forehead and encircled her face in a gentle, continuous motion. "Even as a baby, she has the mark of a wise one. She is a fighter. She will go far in life, and you and your husband will make sure she has an education. I see that she will be a leader for our people."

Carrie's smile was small and sad. "I would do anything for her. And I believe you are right that she's a fighter. She survived a hard delivery and being abandoned on that cold night."

"That was a night that changed many lives," Medicine Owl said. "This child was sent to you because she would have died. I believe her mother was ill for weeks before giving birth."

"Her blood pressure was too high while she was carrying the child," Carrie said. "We call it preeclampsia. She didn't come to the clinic for prenatal care. We might have been able to save her."

"She also did not come to me for care," Medicine Owl said. "This can run in families."

Medicine Owl handed the baby back to Carrie and stood up. She walked, taking tiny shuffling steps, to a wall with a jagged plaster crack reaching from ceiling to floor. Hanging on the wall was a crude medicine wheel constructed out of thin tree branches bent and fashioned into a large circle. Around the circle were totems in varying colors that symbolized north, south, east, and west; the four seasons; natural elements such as fire, water, and wind; and animals such as bears, wolves, eagles, and butterflies. Each had significance for the person or family for whom the wheel was fashioned.

"I made this wheel for you and your family," Medicine Owl said. "Do you remember what I taught you about the sacred hoop?"

"I think so," Carrie said, moving in for a closer look.

"Your life is part of nature. It comes and goes in a circle like the seasons," Medicine Owl said. "You must be more like nature and join in the joyous flow of life. Do not worry. Do not hurry. Does the moon worry that the sun will not rise? Do flowers worry that they will not bloom next spring?"

Carrie smiled. "Only humans worry, it seems—especially me. I wish I could stop looking for trouble."

"You think that if you worry about this and about that, you can stop that thing from happening. But it is not true. By worrying about something, you bring it closer to you, like a circle."

"I understand that. You're telling me that what I think about returns to me as my actual experience. I need to choose my thoughts more carefully, so I can have the best experience."

"This, too, is part of the circle of life, daughter. Love this child Nuttah with all your heart. Feel the joy she brings to you, and never fear. If a child is separated from her real mother, she will find her again."

"But doesn't that mean . . .?" Carrie stopped. "I am not her real mother."

"When a woman gives birth to a child, it does not make her a mother. Loving and caring for a child is what makes a mother. You did not carry this child. But she lives in your heart. She will always be a part of you."

Carrie felt a lump in her throat. She blinked away a tear. "This is a beautiful wheel, Medicine Owl. Thank you." She looked closer. "I see the wolf, my spirit animal."

"The wolf is black, which is the color of power," Medicine Owl said. "That is your power, and you must not give it away to anyone, for any reason."

"How would that happen, Medicine Owl?"

"We give away our power when we allow our behavior to be dictated by fear. When we are afraid, we behave and react in ways that are harmful to ourselves and others."

Carrie was silent for a moment, considering how her fear of losing Nuttah had caused her to be less than compassionate toward Nuttah's birth family. The truth was that she didn't want Nuttah to visit them, even though it would be in the child's best interest to know her relatives on the reservation. After all, she could hardly keep Nuttah away from them forever. Browning was a small town.

Carrie also realized that insecurity and underlying fears about Nate's working relationship with Beth had caused her to lash out, fighting for what she imagined was being threatened: her relationship with her husband. She had chosen to fight Beth rather than trying to understand what might be happening with her—or even what was happening in her own dear husband's life. Now she was afraid of losing Medicine Owl, even though the medicine woman was clearly ready to die.

It was important to be fully present with a loved one during such important life experiences.

Carrie continued studying the wheel as Medicine Owl explained the significance of each totem she had placed there. She recalled reading a book Gran had given her about the medicine wheel. Native Americans believed nature expressed itself in circles and cycles, never in straight lines. Birds' nests were round. Eggs were ovals. The earth, sun, and moon were spheres. Spring, summer, autumn, and winter evolved in a perpetual cycle in the overarching cycle from birth to death.

Medicine Owl had explained that a medicine wheel was arranged with its directions of north, south, east, and west. "Every living thing—people, animals, plants—even rocks and gemstones—are connected in this wheel," she had said.

By creating a medicine wheel, a person could learn how to live with the Great Spirit. Physical conditions could be healed. Life experiences could be changed for the better. Since Carrie had lived on the reservation, she had seen medicine wheels erected for problems facing the entire tribe, including alcoholism and drug abuse.

Carrie's eyes made their way around the wheel. "I see dried corn. Does that mean harvest time, autumn?"

"Very good. What significance does autumn have for you?" Medicine Owl asked.

"Nuttah was born in September."

"Yes, and now we are in another cycle, the spring season. Soon, the snow will end and there will be new growth. This is when new beginnings are possible, daughter."

Carrie looked closer. "What does the sun mean on this wheel?"

"The sun is yellow and gives much light. This is happiness. On your wheel, I have placed it in summertime, when everything in nature blooms." Medicine Owl's eyes twinkled.

THREE DAYS LATER, ON FRIDAY MORNING, Carrie looked up from a stack of paperwork she was reviewing to find Peg standing in the doorway to her office. Her expression grim, Peg said, "I've got things covered this morning with the nurse-practitioner. You need to head over to see Medicine Owl. She hasn't left her bed since Tuesday evening."

"That was when I last saw her," Carrie said, her face turning pale. "She showed me the medicine wheel she made for Nate and me." She set her mug of coffee on the desk so hard, coffee sloshed onto her paperwork. Her stomach felt as if she had just been punched. "I'm leaving right now," she said, shoving her arms into her coat sleeves. Her heart thumped wildly. "She has been so weak lately. I knew I should have insisted on doing something more for her. I blame myself."

"She is very old, Dr. Carrie. It may be her time. Just go to her and be with her," Peg said. "Here is your bag. I packed a few things in it you may need."

"Thanks, Peg," Carrie said, grabbing her medical bag. She ran to her car and drove faster than normal down the snowy roads, praying she wouldn't be too late to help Medicine Owl. Surely, her friend would allow her to help.

When she arrived at Medicine Owl's home, she noticed that the shades were drawn in all the windows. She hurried to the front door and knocked as loud as she could to be heard over the wind. The medicine woman's grandson appeared at the door and, with a nod of his head, invited her in. He appeared somber.

Medicine Owl lay on her bed, wrapped in multiple blankets, her head raised on several pillows. Even from the doorway, Carrie could see and hear that she was in respiratory distress. But her blue eyes were clear as they met Carrie's. "Thank you for coming, daughter," she said between shallow breaths.

Carrie pulled out her stethoscope and listened to Medicine Owl's heart and lungs. "I am calling an ambulance," she said. "You need oxygen, and I can take care of you better at the hospital. Please, Medicine Owl. Let me help you be more comfortable."

Medicine Owl shook her head. "Stay with me," she said, patting the bed. "This is where I want to be. I will leave from here."

Carrie took her hand and held on for dear life, watching the elderly woman's face as she struggled to breathe. Yet there was no fear in her expression, just acceptance. The word that came to mind was *peaceful*.

Carrie knew it was important to say what was in her heart. "Medicine Owl, you have been more than a friend to me. From the day I met you, when I first arrived on the reservation, you have been dear to me. I have often felt that I knew you long ago."

The medicine woman's eyes closed for a moment, and she nodded.

"I asked you to teach me, and you did. You have taught me everything I need to know to help your people."

"They are . . . your . . . people, too," Medicine Owl said, lightly squeezing Carrie's fingers. Her eyes flickered.

"You gave me my child," Carrie said, tears oozing from the sides of her eyes. "You knew how much I wanted a baby, and you gave her to me."

"The Great Spirit . . . gave her . . . to you. She is . . . yours now," Medicine Owl said.

Carrie thought it best not to say anything more. The medicine woman had done what she could to help with this adoption case. Now it was up to a Montana judge to decide.

"She will always be mine, thanks to you," Carrie said. She kissed the old woman's forehead, felt the coolness of her skin. "Let us get you some water," she said.

She motioned to Medicine Owl's grandson. He took a step toward the kitchen, and then stopped when he heard his grandmother say, "No. Water is not . . . what I need."

Carrie watched in agony as the span between Medicine Owl's breaths lengthened. This was the hardest death she had ever had to endure. "I love you, Medicine Owl," she said, tears streaming down her cheeks. "When you arrive wherever you are going, will you let me know?"

There was no answer. Carrie laid her head lightly on Medicine Owl's chest, listening to her heartbeats. They slowed and stopped. Carrie looked up at Medicine Owl's grandson and shook her head. His face crumpled.

"Come and be with her," Carrie said. "I will leave the two of you alone."

"She would want us both to stay," he said and took his grandmother's other hand so that the three of them were joined as one.

Chapter Seventeen

⁓⁖⁓

Two hours after Medicine Owl took her last breath, Carrie looked up from where she lay curled up on the bed beside her friend, and found Peg standing over her. She struggled to sit up, not sure how long Peg had been there. Carrie felt as if she had taken a journey somewhere, and she needed a moment to acclimate herself.

"Peg, how long have you been here?"

"A little while. I thought I'd still find you with her," Peg said. She handed Carrie a handful of tissues as fresh tears flowed.

"How did you know?" She blew her nose.

"The drums." Peg eased onto the bed beside Carrie and watched Medicine Owl's peaceful expression. "I am glad you could be with her at the end."

"I didn't even hear the drums," Carrie said. She directed her red, swollen eyes to Peg. "Medicine Owl wouldn't let me to take her to the hospital. We talked for a little while, and then..."

"She wouldn't have gone to the hospital. It wasn't her way." Peg looked directly at Carrie in that compassionate, wise way that experienced nurses do when comforting someone who has lost a loved one.

"I could have helped her with oxygen and IVs. I could have fixed this."

"Yes, and she knew that. The fact that she chose not to go to the hospital wasn't about her not trusting you. She knew it was her time," Peg said. "There was nothing you could have done, Dr. Carrie. It was her choice to go."

"I guess it's like a Do-Not-Resuscitate order." Carrie thought for a moment. "You're right. She would've hated all the tubes and machines keeping her alive."

"Yes. She was ready, and you allowed her to go. You helped her on her way," Peg said. "That was what she needed most from you."

Carrie nodded and took a deep breath. "What comes next?" she asked. "There will be a funeral, right?"

"We'll hear from Tribal Council when we will honor her with a ceremony," Peg said. "Her wishes were to be buried in the foothills near that cabin she loved."

"Peg, you knew she was dying. I'm glad you didn't say that to me this morning. I wouldn't have been able to hear it. I had to see for myself."

"I know. Yesterday, I got a call from her grandson. He said Grandma wasn't feeling well. She told him on Tuesday evening that it was time for her to take a long rest, and then she went to bed. She ate a little soup on Wednesday. He said she was touching the middle of her chest. He thought she was praying, and said she seemed to be in a different place far away."

"It sounds as if she knew death was coming. She may have decided to go to bed so that she wouldn't collapse in front of her grandson. That would be just like her. I'm *sure* she knew," Carrie said. "She knew everything." She grew silent for a moment. "Oh, Peg, what will we do without Medicine Owl? What will I do without her? She taught me everything."

"Dr. Carrie, Medicine Owl loved you," Peg said. "She taught you many things that have not been shared with outsiders. She would want you to carry on her work."

AT A LITTLE AFTER TEN P.M. the next night, Carrie received a text message from Gali. *My water just broke. The pains are coming fast! John's mom is on her way to stay with Charlie.*

Carrie stretched and stood up from the sofa, where she and Nate had been watching the news. "Gotta go. Gali's in labor."

Nate put down the surgical journal he was reading while listening to the news. "You're going over to the hospital now?"

"Yes, I'm going right now." She grinned and rolled her eyes. "I'm her doctor, but she's also my best girlfriend. Sounds like things might be moving fast. I'll go over now and plan to stay with her until it's over," Carrie said. "John was a basket case when she was in labor with Charlie. He almost passed out when he saw Charlie's head."

"Okay. Let me know if you need anything from me. Give her my love."

"I will. And hopefully, I won't need additional services from you." She smiled and dashed upstairs to change into a pair of clean scrubs. Pulling her hair back, she quickly arranged it in a French braid. She clambered downstairs and donned her parka and boots and grabbed her purse. "I'll be back as soon as I can."

As she leaned in to kiss him, he gently took hold of her braid as if rooting her in place. "Let me know as soon as the baby comes."

"I will."

She drove to the hospital where Gali had been admitted to labor and delivery. A nurse was about to insert an intravenous line into the back of her hand. As Carrie entered the room, a hard contraction hit. John sat by his wife's side, timing it.

"Nice one," he said, when it was over. "Take a rest."

"Hey, you," Carrie said, leaning over to embrace her friend. "I'll do it," she said to the nurse, taking over insertion of the needle into the vein. "Take a breath. Now just a little stick . . . all done."

Gali watched while Carrie taped the needle in place. "You still want to go all natural? Are you sure I can't talk you into a little pain relief?"

"I did the epidural the first time. I wanted to see if I could do it on my own this time," Gali said.

"Up to you," Carrie said. "You don't have to be a hero, you know."

"Can I change my mind?" Gali suddenly looked fearful as another hard contraction hit. Carrie sat beside her on the other side of the bed, holding her hand until it was over. She looked at the strip from the fetal monitor and saw that the baby's heartbeat was strong and steady.

"There's no shame in having an epidural," Carrie said. "I've already told you that. But let me see how far along you are first." She pulled on exam gloves, certain of what she'd find. Yes, this labor was progressing fast. She looked up at Gali. "When you have a baby, you don't mess around. You're already at six centimeters. Now is a good time to decide on that epidural."

"Okay, I want it," Gali said, flashing a weak grin. She looked over at John, her labor coach, as if seeking agreement. He nodded his head up and down in relief.

Carrie smiled. "You got it, my friend."

Two hours later, Lucy Leathers made her way into the world—not without a bit of drama when the umbilical cord got in the way. Fortunately, the baby was born two minutes later with no ill effects. Carrie breathed a sigh of relief as she lifted the newborn up to show her to Gali and John. Gali reached out her arms, and Carrie laid the baby on her chest. There was no such thing as a routine delivery, as far as Carrie was concerned. Each mother and baby presented a unique set of challenges and concerns. She examined the newborn, glad to see that she was completely normal and a healthy seven pounds, six ounces.

"Welcome to the reservation, Miss Lucy," Carrie said as the nurse treated the baby's eyes with drops and checked her reflexes. The nurse swaddled the newborn in a receiving blanket and tugged a pink knit cap over her head. Carrie picked up the baby, thinking how much she resembled Nuttah as a newborn. Turning to Gali and John, she formed a smile. "Congratulations, Mom and Dad. She's perfect."

IN THE WEEKS FOLLOWING MEDICINE OWL's death, Carrie often felt adrift on a sea of emotions that ebbed and flowed, ranging from intense grief over the loss of her friend to a lack of confidence unlike anything she had felt before. Could she continue the medicine woman's work? She moved woodenly from task to task, endeavoring to stay focused and present with everyone who needed her.

Medicine Owl's death left a huge void in her life that couldn't be filled by anyone else—not even Gran's ever-comforting voice across the miles. The only way to manage her emotions was to fill each waking moment, working at a feverish pace and going into overdrive on the home front. She cleaned the house compulsively and taught herself how to make three new recipes. Now more than ever, she needed to be the perfect doctor, the perfect wife, the perfect mother.

But the feelings of emptiness lingered. It was nearly unbearable. Each patient reminded her that Medicine Owl was gone. It was as if Medicine Owl was speaking in her ear, whispering suggestions about how to treat each person's malady or what emotional issue might be contributing to an illness. These insights kept Medicine Owl alive in her heart and mind—painfully so. Only time with Nuttah and Nate relieved her sadness.

During the month, Carrie took advantage of the quiet to reflect on her memories of Medicine Owl and everything the wise woman had taught her. She gave thanks in the silence for this great blessing in her life.

She wanted to do something to honor the memory of Medicine Owl— something visible. But she needed to be careful, since anything she did could be misconstrued as an attempt to buy favor with the tribal elders. Nate agreed.

"I want to do something meaningful to celebrate her life—something the people can see and enjoy," Carrie said. "To remember what she meant to them. That way, I can see it, too."

As the days ticked by with no resolution of their adoption case, Carrie tried hard to remain optimistic, remembering Medicine Owl's advice to be positive and trust that all would be well. But this was becoming increasingly difficult, since she knew through the grapevine that Nuttah's grandmother expected to receive custody. There had been no word from Joseph Red Feather or anyone else from social services about how the matter was progressing, adding to her worries. Their caseworker was frustratingly slow to return calls, too.

"If the home is viewed as satisfactory, if there is food and a place for her to sleep, you would assume she'd get immediate custody," Carrie fumed to Peg at lunch one day. She stabbed her spoon into a container of strawberry yogurt.

"Count your lucky stars above that things are still in limbo," Peg said, clucking her tongue. "The longer it takes, the more likely it is that someone in child welfare suspects a problem or has already identified one. From what I know of that family, there will be more than one issue." She lowered her glasses and looked over them at Carrie. "It might also be possible that Grandma cannot meet the list of things she is required to do. She might not be able to get them done. No news is good news. That's what I think."

This insight from a member of the Blackfeet tribe, a nurse who had professional and personal knowledge of the family situation, gave Carrie fleeting hope. Still, she knew that the odds were stacked in favor of the family getting custody of Nuttah. She and Nate were temporary caregivers in the eyes of the law.

"I want to see the house where they live, Peg," Carrie said. "I want to know where my baby girl might end up. If it's bad, it will make me fight even harder to keep her."

Peg pursed her lips, considering this. "If I drive you over there to see the house, you will need to keep quiet about it. I need to remain neutral on this because you might need me, at some point. If anyone wants to know what I think, I'll tell them, but not now."

"Would you? Would you testify on our behalf, Peg? You're a tribal member. Your words would hold a lot of weight."

"Someone else's words would mean more to those in power. John Leathers is the one who can help you the most." Peg gave Carrie another significant look. "He is your friend, and his grandfather is an elder. Now his father is on Tribal Council. The three of them can take this matter on, since Medicine Owl isn't around to do it."

"John has already said he will help us. He said we must wait and 'not stir up the dirt.'" Carrie said, making air quotes. "I wasn't sure about his grandfather. He knows first-hand why that legislation was enacted."

Adding to the uncertainty was the news that another Native American healer had taken on the role of medicine man for the surrounding region. The elders called him Medicine Bear. He was not from Browning, but lived about thirty miles away, just beyond Heart Butte. Heart Butte was where Gali Leathers had taught high school math before marrying John and moving to Browning.

"He isn't like Medicine Owl." Gali looked intently at Carrie as if considering how much to tell her. "He won't be as friendly toward you as she was." Gali cleared her throat, taking a moment to consider her next words. "I think you shouldn't get your hopes up that the two of you will have any kind of working relationship."

That week, Gali and John and their babies came over for Sunday dinner. While Nate prepared a roast chicken, John stayed in the kitchen with him. Their discussion about sports erupted every now with a louder comment and then, predictably, laughter. It was clear that Nate had missed John and Gali as much as she had while their friends adjusted to the challenges of a new baby along with an active toddler.

Gali sat at one end of the sofa, nursing baby Lucy. Carrie sat across from her in the wingback chair Dr. Jim favored. It was her favorite chair, too. Charlie was toddling now, launching himself from chair to sofa to coffee table, creating havoc wherever he went. Carrie was glad she had baby-proofed the house, even though Nuttah was still mostly rooted to one area. Not for long. Carrie kept a close eye on her, watching as she moved like a combat soldier under barbed wire. Once

Nuttah realized she could go faster on her knees, she would be unstoppable. For the moment, she seemed intent on watching Charlie to see how he did things.

"That's not what I wanted to hear right now," Carrie said, looking away from the children for a moment. "I thought if the medicine man knew about my relationship with Medicine Owl, he would feel more favorable toward me."

There had been occasions over the past several years when patients living in Heart Butte came to the hospital, much sicker than if they had sought medical help right away. Peg had told her that Medicine Bear's way of treating illness was to speak words that were supposed to bring about spontaneous healing.

"I'd be curious to know how well or how often that works," Carrie said, raising one eyebrow. "Last week's strangulated hernia certainly didn't listen to whatever Medicine Bear told it to do."

No matter what she thought of his methods, she would have to forge some sort of working relationship with him. They shared patients. It had been so easy to work in tandem with Medicine Owl, who understood that Carrie's intentions were never to overshadow Native American medicine, but rather to work in complementary fashion. Medicine Owl practiced herbal medicine and had considerable skill and experience using plant-based remedies like those Gran used in her practice. Carrie had grown up understanding the value of these traditional remedies.

But Carrie couldn't just pick up the phone and call Medicine Bear. She had to wait for an invitation to visit him. This had been made clear to her from the start. In her early days on the reservation, she hadn't met Medicine Owl for a few months, and then only at her invitation. John Leathers had accompanied her on that first visit. There was a protocol to be followed.

Carrie set the table with cloth napkins and the set of china and silver her parents had given them for their wedding. With John's help, Nate brought the roast chicken and side dishes of roasted potatoes, glazed carrots, and a green salad from the kitchen to the dining room. As they ate, the couples talked about recent events in Browning.

"What is going on with Mike and his work with the wolves?" Carrie asked John. It was a sensitive subject with the Leathers family. Because of their concern for Mike's safety, Nadie and Earl Leathers were not in favor of their son's work on behalf of the wolves. Carrie was certain that John was aligned with his brother.

"It's heating up," John noted, wiping his mouth with his napkin. "Ranchers and farmers want to protect their animals. That's understandable. Those who want to protect the wolves don't like the way that some of the property owners go about eliminating their problem."

Carrie speared a perfectly roasted quartered potato seasoned with garlic and rosemary. "Mike told me it's not just that they shoot wolves. He says they also poison them."

"Mike gets upset that animal carcasses—deer and elk—are laced with poison and left for the wolves," John said.

Carrie sat back in her chair and observed, "That would kill several wolves at a time."

"It could kill an entire pack. Other members of the pack—and pups—eat the meat the wolves take back with them." John shook his head. "As you know, there aren't a lot of fenced-in properties in these parts. Wolves come down from the hills and have easy access to animals that are grazing. They don't know those animals belong to someone. They are just living as they have always lived. They are predators. That is their role in nature."

"I worry about my wolf," Carrie said. "I haven't seen her in a long time. I know she's old, and it's even possible she could have died already. Because of her, I care about the wolves, too." She indicated the painting Mike had done of the she-wolf, which now held a place of honor on one wall of the dining room.

"That is an important connection you have with Mike." John was quiet for a moment. "My brother has come a long way in his life. This work he does for the wolves is important to him. He's on the front lines. We can stand behind him."

"I want to stand *with* him," Carrie said. "What more can I do?"

"You can write letters to elected officials, to start with. Mike won't want you in harm's way. That I can tell you. But there are steps we all can take to support Mike's work."

"It's one thing to want to do something about a lone wolf that is preying regularly on a rancher's herd. I could understand killing the animal if it threatened or attacked people," Carrie said. "But killing an entire wolf pack including pups by poisoning them is unconscionable."

"It definitely has more serious implications for Glacier," John agreed. "There is a balance to nature. Predators thin out herds of deer and elk that would reproduce and then struggle to find enough food. When there are too many deer or elk, they starve when there isn't enough grass. They end up stripping the trees of their bark in the winter, which then threatens the trees. Wolves were killed off in years past, and we saw that imbalance. As their numbers grew, the balance was restored. So many positive things happened in nature when the wolves came back."

Nuttah began to fuss. Carrie took her out of her swing and held her cheek to cheek. "Nuttah, you care about the wolves, too. Don't you? We have to do something to save them."

"Next thing I know, Carrie will be holding up a sign and demonstrating," Nate said, smiling indulgently. "She thinks of the she-wolf like a member of the family."

"I do, and I just might," Carrie said, winking at John. "Although, I don't know how I'd fit a demonstration into my schedule. It seems that every minute I'm not working or taking care of the baby, I'm researching information about Native American adoptions and re-reading everything Joseph Red Feather has sent me that sounds the slightest bit hopeful."

"I hate watching you go through this," Gali said. "I want what's best for Nuttah, and I think that's to have you as her parents."

Carrie held Nuttah on her lap and handed her Sophie the giraffe, her favorite toy. "We've heard nothing in weeks. It's the waiting that's hard, although I'd rather this never be resolved if it means we can keep her," she said. "What else can we do?"

John cut into his chicken, took a bite, and considered the question. Gali, who was chopping up tiny bites of chicken for Charlie, looked anxious as they waited for his response. Gali's discomfort was not lost on Carrie, who wondered whether Gali knew something she hadn't yet conveyed to her.

"I will arrange a meeting with my grandfather and my father," John said. He put down his knife and fork and leaned his elbows on the table, resting his chin on his hands, looking pensive. "I think if you talk with them about your intentions to raise Nuttah as a Blackfoot, with help from the tribe, it could help. But I can't say for certain."

Carrie poured a little more wine in his glass. "With Medicine Owl gone, we're worried that we won't have an elder standing with us."

Gali bit her upper lip. "John, I think they need to know."

John cleared his throat. His expression was pained. "My grandfather Pete White Cloud bowed to Medicine Owl's wishes. They were friends. He does not know you well. He would rather the baby live with her birth family. My mother has tried to talk with him, but he will not listen."

"It seemed wrong not to tell you what we know." Gali fastened Charlie's bib.

There was silence around the table. Carrie had a momentary urge to pick up Nuttah and run away with her. Why had she thought there might be a chance of keeping her? The deck was clearly stacked against them.

"Grandpap is one of the few elders who still speaks our language," John said. "He wanted me to become an educator so that I could help our children understand what it means to be Blackfeet." He paused. "He was one of the elders who fought to have the legislation passed that restricts adoptions by those who aren't Native American. As for my father, he knows and respects both of you, but he will not go against his father-in-law."

Carrie held Nuttah even tighter. "I see."

Nate began taking dishes to the kitchen. Carrie remained at the table, her thoughts swirling as she considered what to do next. "John, I do want to talk with your grandfather," she said.

"Nate should go, too," John said.

After John and Gali left, Carrie and Nate put their baby to bed. Neither spoke as Nate changed Nuttah into her sleep sack and Carrie warmed her nighttime bottle. Nate handed Nuttah to her.

"It's your night to put her to bed," he said, turning away quickly, but not before she saw the look of despair on his face.

Chapter Eighteen

_.\l/_

MAY

THE FIFTH OF MAY DAWNED CLEAR and balmy for an early spring day in Northwest Montana. The wind had died down considerably, and most of the snow had melted. The mountains were still snow-covered and would remain snow-topped until early summer. Although trees stood barren, and the landscape was a monochrome of gray and ochre, the mountains were luminous in shades of blue, rose, and lavender. Carrie looked out the kitchen window, searching the fields for her wolf, as she made a pot of coffee.

She saw a Mourning Dove perched on top of the wood porch railing. She opened the kitchen window a few inches to listen to its melodic warbles. It landed on the windowsill as if arriving for a visit. At that moment, Carrie wondered if the dove was a messenger. She already knew from Medicine Owl that birds were believed to be messengers of the Great Spirit. Doves were a special bird in many cultures, signifying everlasting love and peace.

"Doves are a sign of good health and a happy home. They are a message of hope, renewal, and peace," Medicine Owl had once told her. "When such a bird visits you, ask yourself what it was you were thinking about. It is a sign to bring you peace."

In fact, when Carrie saw the dove, she had been thinking about their adoption case, wondering how much longer it would take to come to a decision. She felt anything but peaceful about their chances now. Had Medicine Owl sent the bird as a hopeful, positive sign? She missed Medicine Owl so much. She felt afraid and needed her friend more than ever. As she grieved the medicine woman, she had cried herself to sleep many nights, her silent tears soaking the pillowcase. She needed desperately to talk about her feelings, but this was not done on the reservation. The very people to whom she would have turned were silent, dealing with their grief in their way.

Carrie decided that the best way to help herself was to focus on helping others, doing the very work that Medicine Owl had entrusted to her. In this way, she was honoring her memory. There was more she wanted—no, needed—to do. But healing took time, and she would make more of an effort to go within to hear the messages that Medicine Owl had called whispers of the Great Spirit.

Medicine Owl sometimes appeared in Carrie's dreams. When she awakened, she could barely remember the details, which frustrated her. What if Medicine Owl was communicating important information to her in dreams that she couldn't retain in her waking hours?

She wished she had a photograph of Medicine Owl to look at each day, but like so many Native Americans, Medicine Owl avoided having her photograph taken. Then, two nights ago, Carrie had dreamed that she was hanging a painting on a wall in the hospital. The painting was covered by a canvas. Last night had been a continuation of the dream, and this time, she had seen the face in the painting. It was Medicine Owl. An idea took root. Of course! This was the perfect way to celebrate the medicine woman's memory and to have her close by. She decided to ask Mike Leathers to paint Medicine Owl's portrait. She could make a gift of the painting to the Blackfeet people and have Medicine Owl's photo in the hospital lobby, in a place of healing where she could see it every day.

The funeral for Medicine Owl took place at Little Flower Catholic Church on a mild early spring day. Carrie was surprised to learn that Medicine Owl had been raised Catholic. Although this was a Blackfeet memorial service to honor the tribe's medicine woman, Carrie and Nate were invited. Carrie hoped the experience would bring her comfort and the closure she needed.

She carried Nuttah into the church, Nate's arm around her shoulders, to the solemn beat of drums. The people wore their best Native American attire, some adorned with traditional feathers and beads. The church was full to capacity. And still they came, standing outside with the doors open to hear the priest speak of Medicine Owl's work on behalf of her people, of her goodness, patience, and her healing skills.

"There will be a celebration of her life in a year," John Leathers said after the service. "It will be part of North American Indian Days so that more people can honor Medicine Owl and her good works."

Even as Carrie nodded, she wondered what would happen over the course of the next year. Would she and Nate still be on the reservation? She didn't feel certain of anything anymore.

THE NEXT AFTERNOON AFTER WORK, CARRIE picked up Nuttah at Violet's house and drove home, intent on a quiet evening. It had been a hectic day, not made any easier by a difficult delivery of a baby to a fourteen-year-old girl. Mother and baby would be fine, but it had been a traumatic experience for the frightened teenager. To make matters worse, Carrie believed the baby was the result of a rape by an older relative. She had called social services after the girl's mother refused to allow her daughter to answer any questions. Domestic and sexual violence were realities on the reservation. Again, she wondered about Nuttah's birth family and what kind of home life they had. Would Nuttah be vulnerable to physical or sexual abuse?

She decided to make tomato soup and grilled cheese sandwiches for dinner—comfort food. After putting Nuttah to bed, she and Nate could sit in front of the fireplace and watch a movie. But when she pulled into the driveway and reached for the garage door remote button, she saw Nate standing outside on the porch. He motioned to her to stay where she was. She stopped and rolled down her window.

"There's been a break-in," he said. "Stay in the car with the baby until the police arrive."

"This happened to John and Gali, too," she said. "I wonder what was taken. We don't really keep a lot of cash in the house." Her eyes flew open. "My wedding rings!" She always left them in her jewelry box before going to the hospital.

"They're insured. If they've been taken, we can replace them," Nate said.

"We can never replace them," Carrie said. "They won't be the rings we exchanged."

"I know that. But it's good we weren't home at the time," Nate said. He stood with his hands on his hips, looking around. "Whoever did it is probably long gone." He got into the passenger side of Carrie's car. "I walked into the living room, and thought something was strange, so I went into the kitchen. I noticed the window on the back door was broken. That's how the burglar got in: broke the window, reached in, and unlocked the door."

"Same as what happened at John and Gali's house," Carrie said. "This is scary." She glanced back at Nuttah in her car seat. "We now have to think of a baby's safety, too."

Within half an hour, the police arrived and began their investigation. They dusted for fingerprints and took photos of the damage to the back door, made a list of what had been stolen, and left two hours later. Less than forty dollars had been taken from Nate's sock drawer, along with an antique watch his grandfather had given him. The thief or thieves had overlooked Nate's wedding ring on a tray on the bathroom counter, but Carrie's wedding and engagement rings were gone, along with the pearl necklace her father had given her. The police said the items might turn up if they were pawned in any nearby shops.

"I'm getting us an alarm system," Nate promised. "I never thought we'd have to worry about this—not here. But with a baby in the house, we can't take chances."

"I guess we've been living with a false sense of security," Carrie agreed. "Let's do it."

While Nate got Nuttah ready for bed, she called Gali to let her know that they, too, had been burglarized. "It happened sometime today while we were at work."

"There hasn't been much in the newspaper about it, but the police have a few suspects. They think the burglaries are drug-related."

"Well, whoever did it has my wedding set," Carrie said. "I never wear my rings at work. Too easy to drop them down the sink when I'm washing my hands."

"Oh, no," Gali said. "Your rings are so beautiful. But maybe they'll turn up. I'm sure they'll be pawned or sold for quick cash. What would the thief want with your wedding rings, right? Money. We just have to hope for the best."

"Frankly, I'm losing hope—on a lot of fronts," Carrie admitted. "Sorry, I didn't mean to be Debbie Downer. I haven't had the easiest week."

Gali was quiet for a moment. Then she spoke the words that Carrie needed to hear most. "I'm here for you. You are my best friend, and I love you. John and I are always here for you."

TEN DAYS LATER, NO PROGRESS HAD been made on the investigation into the person or persons responsible for breaking into homes on the reservation. Three more break-ins occurred at homes in East Glacier. The third time, the homeowner surprised the thief, described as a teenage male Blackfoot, as he rummaged through a chest of drawers. A scuffle ensued, resulting in a deep knife wound to the young man's shoulder. Nate was on red alert in the emergency room, waiting for someone with a knife wound to seek treatment. But no one showed up at Blackfeet Community Hospital with a knife injury to the shoulder.

"It makes more sense for the burglar to get as far away from the reservation as possible before seeking treatment," Carrie said.

"Or the guy didn't think he was seriously hurt and decided not to seek medical care." Nate chewed on his upper lip.

Carrie hoped she would get her wedding rings back but wasn't optimistic about it. In the meantime, Nate filed an insurance claim and told her to pick out a new set of rings. Reluctantly, she agreed.

"It's just a darn shame that you've had such a difficult year, you and Dr. Nate," Peg said. "Between the adoption and Medicine Owl's death, and the burglary at your house, I think your luck is due to change."

"I heard from Joseph Red Feather, our attorney, yesterday. He said a ruling could come as early as next month on whether Nuttah will stay with us." Carrie leaned against the sink in one of the exam rooms. Peg pulled out a length of white paper to cover the table in preparation for their next patient. "John Leathers tells me that he'll arrange time with his grandfather and maybe the Tribal Council in hopes of swaying them to our side. But we might run out of time."

"I think you and I need to drive over to the house where Nuttah's grandparents live," Peg said. "You need to see the place, so you can begin to prepare yourself mentally and emotionally for what may come. We'll do it in secret, you and me."

That afternoon, Carrie climbed up into the passenger seat of Peg's truck and put on her seatbelt. Peg liked to drive fast, and Carrie didn't relish riding over bumpy roads at Peg's usual breakneck speed. But today, Peg took her time. It was as if she, too, was reluctant to face Nuttah's future.

The house where Nuttah's birth mother Kimi had grown up was half trailer, half shack. It was situated among about fifty other homes in an area known for its desperate poverty. There were not the same kind of building codes or standard requirements in Browning as in other places. Construction could be downright shoddy. The kindest thing Carrie could say about Nuttah's grandparents' house was that it was still standing. Two broken-down rusty cars and a truck on concrete blocks were adjacent to the house. There was trash everywhere. Carrie wondered if the house even had indoor plumbing.

She took in a breath and let it out, feeling sick to her stomach. "Oh, Peg. She can't live here. Nuttah can't live here."

Peg idled the car at the side of the road. "This is where her people live, Dr. Carrie. This is where Kimi, her mother, grew up."

Carrie put her face in her hands. "I can't bear this. Please, let's go."

As they drove back to the hospital, Peg remained uncharacteristically quiet. Carrie stared out the window at the passing countryside, weighing their options. There were no words to describe the despondency she felt at the thought of losing Nuttah—worse, of having her baby live in that depressing, desolate area of Browning. Thoughts paraded through her head: of running away with Nuttah, abandoning their house, going somewhere else. Surely, if they went far enough, they could find sanctuary.

"I know you well enough to know what's goin' through your head, Dr. Carrie," Peg said after a little while. "You're thinking that you can run from this. Sure, you can run. But wherever you go, you'll never know peace. I am going to speak for you at Tribal Council next week. Let me talk with the elders before you and Dr. Nate speak. I will tell them what I know about Grandma and that family."

Carrie looked over at her nurse and dear friend, grateful beyond measure. "Thank you, Peg."

"DID YOU SEE THE PAPER TODAY?" Nate asked Carrie during dinner that evening.

"No time today. After Peg and I went over to see Nuttah's family's house, I went directly to pick up Nuttah at Violet's. Was there something I should read?"

"Mike and three of his supporters were arrested a few days ago while protesting in front of a ranch." He handed Carrie the newspaper as she sat down at the table. He speared a piece of meatloaf and took a bite, closing his eyes in bliss before speaking again. "This meatloaf is great. It might even be better than my mom's." He grinned.

"It's your mother's recipe. Don't you dare tell her what you just said." Carrie read over the story, her brow furrowing. Someone could have been hurt or killed. "I'm worried something will happen to him, Nate. This incident got out of hand fast. I'd rather Mike get arrested and go to jail than get injured or killed."

"Yeah, no kidding. He didn't spend much time in jail. I called John to ask what happened. He said the rancher is someone who poisons deer carcasses and leaves them for the wolves to feed on. Animal protection activists are all over this issue. But it sounds like Mike's group has attracted a bigger following from Montana and Wyoming—people who care about the wolves and are willing to stand with the Native Americans."

"Naomi is in her third trimester now," Carrie said. "I don't want stress affecting her blood pressure or causing her to deliver prematurely. She needs Mike to think of her welfare, too."

"John told Mike to be careful. The more heated these standoffs get, the more people join the protests, it seems. There were television stations there when Mike got arrested." Nate helped himself to another slice of meatloaf. "The national media is starting to take notice of what's going on. That can be a good thing. But emotions are already high. Turn a camera on someone who doesn't want to be filmed, and it could get nasty."

"I know. I keep thinking of what happened to all the Native Americans who protested the oil pipeline project." Carrie grimaced and folded up the paper. "When it comes to protecting the environment or endangered species versus business interests, Mother Nature gets the shaft every time." She spooned pureed green beans into Nuttah's mouth. "It's a complicated situation. I understand that. I just don't want Mike to become a martyr for the cause."

"EARL, IT'S GOOD TO SEE YOU," Carrie said, entering the patient room where Earl Leathers sat on the exam table. She glanced at his chart, noting with concern that his blood sugar was still too high. She checked his vital signs before sitting down on the chair across from him. "So, tell me how you're doing with your diet and glucose testing," she said.

"I cannot get my blood sugar down, and I hardly eat anything," Earl said, not making eye contact. This was not true, and Carrie knew it. His blood glucose numbers were all the evidence she needed.

"Well, you have to eat. It's important to eat regularly. You need to keep your blood sugar regulated. There is no reason to starve yourself. Just make the healthiest choices you can. Are you sticking to the plan the dietician gave you?"

"Yes."

She raised one eyebrow at him. "Are you testing your blood at the same time every day?"

"Yes."

"You're going to need to test more often," Carrie said.

Earl's eyebrows shot up. "I can't do that," he said.

"Why not?" Carrie already knew the reason. But she needed to hear it from Earl.

"I just don't . . . I can't . . ." he faltered.

"I understand," Carrie said. "You don't like needles, and testing your blood is hard for you. But you must keep a closer watch on your blood sugar level. I don't want you passing out. You could fall and get hurt or have a car accident."

"I am careful, always."

"I'm sure you are. But it could happen suddenly. You could lose consciousness. Please, Earl. Test your blood right after breakfast and again after dinner. We have got to get your blood sugar under control. This is important."

She had hoped the office visit would go better than this. If he was upset with her, as he might be now, his feelings might spill over into the area of Nuttah's adoption. She needed Earl's support as a member of Tribal Council. But she was his doctor, and that was what mattered most, in this situation. She couldn't mince words. Still, she felt compassion for what he was going through.

"Earl, I wish this wasn't happening to you," she said, looking down. "I know you are still adjusting to having diabetes. I am taking care of your health, but I also care about you. Very much."

Earl lowered himself from the table and stood before her. She reached out and placed her hand on his arm in a gesture of support. "What can I do to make this easier for you?" she asked. "More practice with the glucose monitor? I'll help you myself."

He shook his head. "You are a good doctor. This is my problem."

"Earl, you are important to this community, to your family. You have children and grandbabies that you love, and they need you in their lives. I need you," she said, and stopped. Now was not the time to ask anything of him. "We need you to be as healthy as possible," she finished.

He nodded and made his way to the door. Opening it, he walked through and then stopped and looked back at Carrie. She smiled reassuringly. "I'm here if you need me."

PEG KEPT HER PROMISE TO TALK with the Tribal Council at their May meeting. The next morning, she pulled Carrie into one of the examination rooms and shut the door. She said she believed her words had been heard. "I told them you and Dr. Nate are part of our community. You have made your home here and you care for our people. You took that baby when she had no home, and you treat her as your own. I said you ask for advice from me, from others about how to raise her in our ways."

Carrie listened intently, holding herself back, wanting to ask a hundred questions as Peg described the scene. "Nuttah knows no other mother than you," Peg said. "I told them I am in favor of you keeping Nuttah. I reminded them that Medicine Owl thought Nuttah should stay with you. Many people in the room were surprised by that."

"What will happen next?" Carrie asked.

"The men will talk. They will decide. Their words will carry some weight with the adoption authorities. But," she said with a sigh, "it may not be enough. The law is clear." Peg patted Carrie's hand. "I did what I could."

"I know you did, and I couldn't ask for more. Thank you," Carrie said. "Peg, actually, you could do one more thing."

"What is it?"

"Could you go to Little Flower and light a candle for Nuttah?"

Chapter Nineteen

—◦✦◦—

JUNE

WITH LESS THAN A MONTH UNTIL the volunteer physicians arrived on the reservation, Carrie called Dr. Jim to say that all the doctors were credentialed to work in the federal hospital. It had taken several months to get all the paperwork back from a few of the doctors. It was an arduous process that sometimes frustrated those wanting to help.

"I thought I'd lose my mind, at one point," she said. "But Margaret Blue Sky stepped in and helped me. She doesn't want to lose potential volunteers because they get upset with the credentialing process."

They were about to hang up when Dr. Jim said, "Wait, Carrie. I want to tell you something, if you have a minute."

"Of course. What's up?"

"I've weighed telling you this against keeping quiet," he said. He was silent for a moment. "But you probably need to get back to the baby. This can wait until I see you."

Carrie leaned against the kitchen sink, one eye on Nuttah who was bouncing in her jump seat and making screeching noises, her newest talent. "What is it, Dr. Jim?" Carrie wrinkled her forehead. "You know you can tell me anything."

There was a part of her that continued to be worried about Dr. Jim's health. He had undergone surgery, chemotherapy, and radiation for prostate cancer. He was cautiously optimistic about his prognosis. Yet she knew he might require additional treatments. She hoped whatever he wanted to say wasn't bad news about his condition. "Are you doing okay, Dr. Jim? No more chemo or radiation?"

"I'm fine. This isn't about me. I was talking with one of my classmates who works at the med center. He was thinking of joining us for the volunteer medical corps this year, and he mentioned that he knew Beth Bradley was working on the reservation. I said, 'What a coincidence.' He said he wasn't anxious to see her."

"Why?" Carrie asked. "Other than the fact that she can be sort of disagreeable and difficult. For the record, I've seen improvement."

"I heard that about her." Dr. Jim paused. "I'm not one to spread rumors. You know that. But she has serious trouble." He told Carrie the details of what he had heard. "She could lose her license to practice, if she doesn't end up in jail," he said.

Carrie was stunned at what she heard. She'd have to tell Nate right away. He'd know what to do.

A half hour later, Nate arrived home from work. He headed straight to the kitchen, kissed Carrie, and picked up Nuttah. Carrie leaned against the kitchen counter. "Nate, I have to tell you something."

"You look pale. Are you okay?"

"You won't want to hear this. I know how you feel about gossip and rumors, and I understand that you don't like to hear criticism about Beth."

Nate frowned. "Carrie, I'm not blind to her faults. I just don't want to dwell on behavior or personality traits that have nothing to do with her surgical skills."

"I know, and I respect you for that. But Dr. Jim just told me something, and you know he would never say anything unless he thought he had to. He says he trusts the person who told him." She chose her words with care. "Dr. Jim said Beth was having an affair with another doctor who happened to be the husband of the patient who died on Beth's operating table, the one with the cardiac dissection."

"Oh, geez." Nate looked as if he might be sick. "Beth had no business performing surgery on that patient," he said.

"Right. The patient's best friend came forward with the accusation that Beth might have allowed her friend to die so that Beth and the woman's husband could be together."

"I don't know how they'd prove that, unless another member of the O.R. team observed her doing something wrong that caused the woman to die." He bit his lip. "Even if there is a ruling that she wasn't negligent, even if the family doesn't end up winning a lawsuit, there will be a cloud of suspicion over her for years to come. That's a career killer for a surgeon."

"Dr. Jim said he heard she won't be returning to the med center, no matter what the outcome. I don't know where else she'll go if she decides to leave here. That kind of situation follows you the rest of your life."

"If she doesn't lose her license, that means she could be here for the long haul." Nate was silent, considering this. "I don't know how I feel about that now."

"I know. Me either. I'm glad we have another surgeon. I'm glad you and I have more time together. But knowing that it might even be a possibility that she could do something so unethical, so . . ."

"Potentially criminal?" Nate's mouth was a grim line. "Now that you've told me this, what happened yesterday with Beth makes more sense."

"I'm almost afraid to ask." Carrie removed a bottle of formula from the refrigerator and set it in a pan of hot tap water in the sink.

"We were sitting in my office, talking about an oncology case that will require surgery. She said it reminded her of a procedure we did in Kansas City. I said I remembered that one. She got a funny look on her face. Then she said she guesses I remember a lot of things, not all of them good. I asked what she meant."

"What *did* she mean?"

"She asked again who I talked with in Kansas City and what they said. I mean, about her. I said I didn't go to Kansas City to talk about her. I was there to work through my own stuff."

"If she continues to ask about it, she must be worried."

"It went beyond questions. From the time she arrived here, she has always wanted to know what I remember about this person or that person. Yesterday, she started to grill me. I got really annoyed. Who did I talk with while I was there? What did I hear? I understand she's anxious to know anything that pertains to her case, but there seemed to be more to the line of questions. She said she had to know."

"What did you say?"

"I came right out and asked about the status of her position at the med center. She's already told me she is under investigation for the death of a patient. She said the patient who died was a woman and that the trouble lies with the fact that she wasn't exactly a stranger. I said, 'What do you mean?' She said the woman's husband is a physician, too. Then she laughed—kind of nervously—and said she told him about the volunteer medical corps—that he should sign up and come here and try it out. I didn't think anything about it at the time. But now, what Dr. Jim said makes sense."

"Nate, if she's still involved with him, she was trying to get him to come here to Browning so she could see him." Carrie wet her lips. "What if she really did cause his wife's death?"

"I don't want to think about that. It's too ugly."

"You're right. It is ugly. It's also potentially a big problem for us—I mean the hospital. Is this something you think Margaret Blue Sky ought to know about right now? I think so."

Nate was silent for a moment before he spoke. "Let me talk to Beth again. I need to get clear on some things. Maybe she'll be honest with me."

"She cares more about your opinion than anyone else's, Nate. If she can't be honest with you, she won't be honest with anyone."

"I knew she and this other doctor were close. I didn't know if it went beyond friendship. It wasn't any of my business. She and I worked together. We weren't friends. Then I got shot. I ended up leaving after that. It's been a long time since I worked there. I don't know why, but I suddenly remembered this guy Beth was "friends" with." He made air quotes with his fingers. He was quiet again. "Maybe the nightmares really were something I needed to know. I may have been observing a surgery where Beth was the surgeon, and the patient was about to die at her hands."

"Medicine Owl said the truth comes through in dreams."

"Well, those nightmares mostly stopped when I realized they had nothing to do with the shooting. But I still have a dream occasionally. Every time it happens, I remember something else. It's as if my subconscious is still feeding me information."

"You've always had a kind of sixth sense," Carrie said.

"Oh, I don't know about that." He let out a quick laugh.

"Don't discount your intuition. Everyone has it. What matters is whether we pay attention to it. I've learned the hard way to pay attention to mine. If I don't listen, I regret it," Carrie said.

"Women have better intuition than guys. That's why they call it 'women's intuition.'" Nate raised his eyebrows.

"Not true. How many times during a surgery has something suddenly occurred to you that led you to do something different, something you realized later was the best way to handle that procedure? You went into that surgery not knowing what might happen. What was it that guided you to do a procedure a certain way?"

"Experience, for one thing. Doing a procedure over and over leads to being skilled at it."

"That's true. Okay, but what about when you do something instinctively, something you haven't been taught? I've seen you in surgery try something because you had a sense that it would work. Nate, that's intuition. That's taking something you might not know consciously and acting on it. What comes to you in dreams or in a flash of insight is super important in processing experience and leading you to new insights. You sensed something about Beth, but it was in your subconscious. Those nightmares brought the clues to the surface. I think Medicine Owl was right."

"Well, let's face it: I don't know anything about this, Carrie, not really. An insight isn't fact. Just because I might think or remember something doesn't make it true. I can't prove it."

"Yes, but you also can't just let this go. This is happening for a reason."

Nate leaned against the kitchen counter. "I have no interest in throwing a colleague under the bus if she's innocent."

"Margaret Blue Sky knows Dr. Jim. She would consider what he said to be credible information," Carrie pointed out. "She's in charge of all these patients, all these staff members. If something is going on with Beth, she needs to know. Nate, if Beth loses her license, she won't be able to practice any longer. Margaret needs to know it's a possibility."

"Carrie, it's important that I talk with Beth and get the truth from her first."

"The truth or her version of the truth?"

He gave her a look of such reproach, she bit her lip. "I'll handle this," he said.

Carrie felt her stomach tighten. She reached over to squeeze his hand. "I get it. Beth deserves to be considered innocent until proven guilty."

Nate rummaged through the refrigerator and pulled out a bottled water. "Yes, but what is going on with her is troubling on a number of levels. I can't ignore it. I'll talk with her tomorrow."

JUST BEFORE TWO O'CLOCK THE NEXT day, one of the nurses knocked on the door of Carrie's office as she was placing a call to Joseph Red Feather. He had called earlier, but she was with a patient and couldn't talk. Carrie was anxious to talk with him. But when the nurse knocked on the door, Carrie put her phone back in the pocket of her white coat.

"Doctor, there is someone to see you," the nurse said.

It was Medicine Owl's grandson. Carrie greeted him with a hug. She hadn't seen him since the day Medicine Owl died.

"Is there anything I can do for you? Are you well?" Carrie asked.

"Well enough, yes," he said. He handed her a large manila envelope. "My grandmother said that if anything happened to her, I should go to the hut and get this for you. But when she died, the weather was too bad, and I couldn't make it up into the hills. No one has been able to get to the hut. Yesterday, I went there to get some of her belongings, and I found the envelope."

"Thank you for going to all the trouble to do that for me."

Curious, Carrie opened the envelope. Inside were notes from Medicine Owl, written in her slanted script on rough paper yellowed with age. The words were unintelligible.

"They are written in your language," she said, looking up at the man. "Do you know any of these words?"

"Only a few—not enough to be helpful. But White Elk can read them for you."

"White Elk?" Carrie asked and then remembered this was the Blackfeet name of John's grandfather and Nadie's father, Pete White Elk.

"I'm glad to have these notes, even if I don't yet understand what they say." She smiled at the beloved grandson who had shared his home for decades with Medicine Owl. Then she tucked the envelope in a large side pocket of her handbag. "I can't thank you enough for your help."

"My grandmother told me they were very important. I hope they help with whatever you need them for," he said.

"I hope so, too." Her stomach flip-flopped, telling her the notes were of vital importance.

She would need John Leathers to take these notes to his grandfather right away. There was no time to lose. *What did the notes say?*

Chapter Twenty

—◦∖⊹∕◦—

"CARRIE," NATE SAID WITHOUT PREAMBLE WHEN she answered her cell phone. "Mike Leathers is on his way to the E.R. by ambulance. He's got head and internal injuries."

She gripped the phone and took a deep breath to steady herself. "What happened?"

"I don't have many details. I only know what one of the EMTs told me. He said Mike was leading a group of protestors on a highway near one of the big ranches. Some sort of scuffle broke out and Mike was on the wrong end of a rifle butt. Shots were fired, but he doesn't have gunshot wounds. A couple of other people were shot, but they went to other hospitals."

"I'm coming right over," Carrie said. "You might need me." At the very least, she could help triage and treat any other patients who came to the E.R. while Nate was busy assessing Mike's condition.

She had feared this sort of danger to Mike as the result of his increasingly confrontational efforts to protect his beloved wolves. He had a mission, and even his artwork took a back seat to saving the wolves. Fights had broken out before at other demonstrations, but fortunately no one had been seriously injured . . . until now.

Peg entered the exam room, her expression telling Carrie she already knew what had happened. "I heard the drums," Peg said. "How bad is it?"

"Nate isn't sure yet. I'm heading over to the E.R. now. Can you hold down the fort here until I get back?"

"Of course," Peg said. "I hope Mike will be okay. He's a good boy, and Naomi is just weeks away from having their baby."

The ambulance arrived as Carrie entered the emergency department. Mike's head was wrapped in a blood-soaked cloth, his face a ghostly shade of pearl-gray. Nate assessed his condition as Carrie stood by, prepared to assist. She watched with concern as nurses took Mike's vital signs and hooked him up to an EKG monitor and an I.V.

"Let's get some x-rays so we know what we're dealing with," Nate said to one of the nurses. "Call Dr. Bradley. We need four hands on this surgical case."

He turned to Carrie. "I already know he has internal injuries, but I'm more concerned about trauma to his brain. Beth and I can at least fix the internal injuries."

"Whatever you can do to help, he'll be better for it." Carrie said in a firm voice, her eyes meeting her husband's intense gaze. She took Mike's hand and leaned over to talk quietly in his ear. She knew that even if patients seemed unreachable, they were still aware, on some level. "Mike, it's Carrie. You're going to be fine. Nate is taking extra-good care of you."

There was no response, not even a flicker of movement under the eyelids. As emergency room personnel prepared Mike for x-rays, Nate removed the bloody gloves he was wearing and disposed of them in a nearby can. Then he reached his hand out to Carrie, who grasped it between both of hers.

"Are you okay?" he asked, running the fingers of his other hand along the back of her neck, squeezing lightly. She nodded, biting her lower lip. He glanced at the clock on the wall. "I'm guessing his family has arrived by now. Could you . . .?"

"Absolutely," she said. She hurried over to the waiting area where a very pregnant Naomi sat stoically alongside Earl and Nadie Leathers on one of the sofas. John sat across from his parents on a chair. His head was bent, his arms clasped across his knees.

When she walked in, four sets of dark, frightened eyes fixated on Carrie. "Mike has just gone for x-rays," she told the assembled family members. "Nate and Dr. Bradley need to operate."

"Is he awake?" John asked at the same moment that loud, angry voices erupted from the hospital lobby.

"He's unconscious. He has a head injury—not sure how bad," she answered, cocking her head to listen as the sounds coming from the lobby grew louder. What the . . .?" she asked and hurried down the hall, where she saw people trying to force their way past the lobby toward the emergency department. A television crew filmed the entire scene, and a female reporter holding a microphone did a live spot. The hospital's two security guards were hard-pressed to keep the crowd under control. Where had all these people come from?

She ducked out of sight and hurried back to the Leathers family. "There is a mob in the hospital lobby and a television crew! John, what happened?"

"I wasn't there. My sister Cheryl's husband saw it, though. He goes with Mike to all the protests." John glanced over at Nadie. "My mother begged them not to go today. She said it is getting more dangerous, and Mike is playing with fire."

"Where is your brother-in-law now?" Carrie asked, looking around.

"He stayed behind to answer questions. He told me that Mike and the biggest group of protesters they've ever had—more than two hundred—demonstrated on the road across from one of the ranches. The guy who owns the place is known to poison wolves."

"Someone who would poison animals, knowing that poisoned meat would go back to wolf pups, could be capable of much worse," Carrie said fiercely. "Nadie is right to be worried."

"Mike wanted the rancher to see for himself how many people are against killing wolves, but the rancher stayed hidden. Then, from what my brother-in-law said, the trouble started—no warning. The rancher walked straight up to Mike as if he wanted to talk. He got in Mike's face and told him to leave the area and take the others with him. He said not to come back, or he'd kill him." John stopped, biting his lower lip. "Mike said something to him and then started to walk away. The rancher hit him in the back of the head with his rifle."

Carrie flinched. "Sounds like the rancher has no self-control."

John nodded. "That rancher is known to be a hothead. While Mike was on the ground, the guy kicked him until Mike stopped moving. The protesters went nuts and took off after the rancher. The rancher started running and then turned and fired shots at them." John paused and glanced again at his mother who sat rigid beside her husband. He lowered his voice. "Two other protestors were wounded. Mike was brought here. The others were taken straight to Great Falls."

"I don't understand," Carrie said. "Why weren't the others who were wounded also brought here? Our hospital is closer."

"Mike was the only Native American who was injured. The others were white, Carrie," John said.

"Oh, of course." Carrie was silent, taking this in. As a federally funded hospital serving Native Americans, Blackfeet Community Hospital saw mostly Native Americans. Other emergency cases were usually transported to other public or private hospitals.

"I didn't realize how large this protest movement had gotten," Carrie said. "I knew Mike's group was getting bigger and they were getting more news coverage, but I had no idea how widespread this had become—that so many others who aren't Blackfeet are involved."

"At first, it was all Blackfeet and a few other tribes from the region—that is until about a month ago. That was when a story appeared in a Missoula paper. Then Mike had a lot more people showing up to demonstrate with him. After that, Mike started a Facebook page and posted on Instagram. He said he needed more people to come and help fight for the wolves."

"In some ways, there is safety in numbers. But I think it's remarkable that so many people who aren't Blackfeet want to stand with Mike on this issue. People really care about the wolves. John, your brother is a hero."

"Don't I know it? He saved my life once. He has more courage than anyone could have guessed, especially those who remember him from the days when he was drinking," John said. There was pride in his voice. "This is going to put him and his organization on the map."

If he survives. Carrie prayed Mike wouldn't end up being a martyr, dying for his cause. Would she have had the courage, as Mike did, to stand up to a rancher with a gun? Somehow, she doubted it. What had happened today demonstrated the passion Mike felt for the wolves—caring more for them than he did about his own safety. Now he was paying a high price for his dedication to the defense of these helpless creatures.

"John, what about the rancher? Did he get arrested?"

"I didn't hear what happened after that," John said, a grim expression on his face. "There were a lot of witnesses, so the guy won't get away with it, especially since he shot his own kind. It wasn't just my brother." He shook his head and a look of bitterness crossed his face. "If it had just been Mike, I wonder if he would even face charges. I doubt it."

"Surely not." But as she said it, Carrie understood that what John said might be the truth. Thousands of Native Americans had been injured or killed at the hands of other Americans, and the perpetrators of these crimes often acted with impunity.

"Nate and Beth are taking Mike into surgery. After that, it's likely he'll need to be flown over to Great Falls for more care. Head injuries require special attention." Carrie studied her friend's face and noted how the muscles tightened in his jaw. John was angry, but he was also scared. The brothers were close.

She glanced over at Naomi who sat in silence, her eyes fixated on the doors of the emergency department. Her husband was in critical condition with injuries he might not survive. Their baby was due in a few weeks.

There were other victims here, too, not just Mike. Carrie moved to a chair across from Naomi and placed her fingers around the pregnant woman's wrist, taking her pulse. Naomi didn't seem to notice as Carrie took her hand and gently kneaded her cold fingers.

"Naomi," Carrie said, and waited until Naomi made eye contact. "Mike is in good hands. My husband is an excellent surgeon, and we have another surgeon who taught my husband. She will be working with him."

Naomi nodded but said nothing. Carrie went to get a cup of water for her. As she crossed the room, she saw Nadie Leathers' frightened eyes. Naomi was

Mike's wife and the mother of his child, but Nadie was Mike's mother. Nadie had feared something like this could happen to her oldest son. She had been his most stalwart supporter over the years as Mike fought the effects of his alcoholism. She never gave up on him. Nadie was like a mother bear, watching over her cubs. Now that she was a mother, Carrie understood that fierce determination to protect her young.

Mike's head trauma could produce lasting negative effects, if he survived. Yet he had already shown in his recovery from alcoholism that he possessed the kind of strength and determination that would serve him well in this recovery process, too. He had to heal and get back to his life. Naomi needed him to be there when their baby was born.

"Come with me, Naomi," Carrie said, holding out her hand. "You can see your husband before he goes to surgery."

Naomi rose and took Carrie's hand. Wrapping her arm around Naomi to support her, Carrie led her into the room where Mike was being prepped for surgery. Carrie guided Naomi close to Mike and released her hand. "It's okay. You can touch him and talk with him. He can hear you. I'm sure of it."

She listened as Naomi spoke gentle words. "I will take care of you as you take care of me. For now, you must rest. Dear husband, I love you so much. Please care for your child and your wife as much as you do for your wolves. They are important, yes. You know that I love the wolves, too. But our baby needs a mother and father."

Carrie bit her lip and stepped out of the area, allowing the couple their privacy. If Mike survived, he would need months to recover from his injuries. Even so, it was unlikely he would give up his activities to protect the wolves. More likely, his protests would be curtailed, at least until after their baby was born. But it was more likely that media attention would fuel the movement.

Chapter Twenty-One

—⚬—

As the afternoon wore on, Carrie scurried back and forth between the emergency waiting area and the clinic, where she continued to see patients, returning every so often to check on the Leathers family. She sat with each of them, in turn, offering comfort and answers, when she had them. Most of her attention, however, was on Naomi whose baby was due the first week of July. This much stress wasn't good for a mother-to-be. It could lead to an early delivery with complications.

A strong point in Mike's favor was that his head injury wasn't as severe as Nate had feared. Trauma to the delicate brain could cause internal pressure and lead to long-term or even irreversible brain damage. That was what had concerned Nate most. It was a relief that, although Mike had sustained a serious concussion, he likely would recover with bedrest and therapy. His internal injuries were more life-threatening. Ribs broken in the savage attack punctured a lung.

Despite fears for his brother's life, John needed to be strong for the rest of the family. "It's a relief that the head injury isn't worse. I have always told my brother that he has a hard head." The joke was an attempt to coax a smile out of Naomi. It didn't work. The knuckles on both hands shown white through her dark skin.

Carrie joined John on a sofa in the waiting area, gratefully easing into the cushions to relieve her tired legs and feet. "We need to keep an eye on Naomi. I don't want stress to bring on premature labor," she said, lowering her voice. "Can someone make sure she eats, has enough water to drink, and a chance to lie down?"

"Naomi's mother and my mother are best friends. They will take care of Naomi. When Mike comes home, and when the baby comes, both mothers will be there to help," John assured her. "It is what we do."

This was not a surprise to Carrie. Throughout her time on the Blackfeet reservation, she had witnessed first-hand the abiding love demonstrated by Blackfeet family members toward each other. The Blackfeet were an intensely loyal, loving people, protecting and defending each other as they had for centuries.

As Carrie sat with John, she sipped the stale lukewarm coffee a nurse handed her, and anxiously watched the clock. She wanted to remain with the family but would need to leave soon to pick up Nuttah at Violet's house. She rose from her seat. "John, I'm going to pick up the baby in another hour or so. Will you be okay? I could ask Violet to keep her longer, if you need me."

"I am fine. Nuttah needs you, too." He glanced up at her and smiled, started to say something, and stopped. Then he laid his hand over her smaller hand in a gesture that spoke volumes. "I'll talk with you later."

Carrie stood. "Tell Gali I'll call her tonight after all the kids are in bed."

Concern flickered across John's face. "Carrie, wait. Before you talk with Gali, I need to tell you something," he said, rising to his feet. "I think I should be the one to say this."

"What is it?" Carrie's heart did a flip, sensing unfortunate news.

"The person responsible for breaking into all the homes in this area has been arrested."

Carrie's face brightened. "That's great!" Noting John's grim expression, she was confused. "The burglaries will stop now. Maybe we can get our belongings back." She glanced down at her hands. "I lost my engagement and wedding rings in the break-in."

"It is Nuttah's uncle, Carrie. He is the younger brother of Kimi, Nuttah's mother."

Carrie's face whitened several shades, and she sat down hard on the chair. "I don't know what to say. Why would he break into our home? Was he trying to take Nuttah away from us?"

"I don't think so. It wasn't the baby he was after." John let out a long whoosh of air. "He is the one who has broken into all the homes. He's looking for whatever he can find to sell. He uses and sells drugs. And that's not all. He lives with Nuttah's grandparents."

"Oh, John." Carrie stared off into space for a moment, processing this information.

It was terrible that Nuttah's family had an active criminal element living in their midst. Here was evidence of yet another family member with a drug problem. But wouldn't this bode well for Carrie and Nate in their pursuit of an adoption? Perhaps the uncle's crimes would be enough to prove that the birth family's home was not a suitable environment for Nuttah! An abandoned baby living in a household with drug abusers and thieves? Surely this did not help the grandparents' case to have Nuttah returned to them. Yes, she decided. This surely was a good thing.

"Carrie, I know what you're thinking," John said, taking her arm. "Come with me." They walked down the long corridor, continuing their discussion. "Remember, he is innocent until proven guilty. There will be a trial on the reservation, yes. He will face other penalties for burglaries not involving tribal members. But it won't necessarily keep the authorities from returning Nuttah to her grandparents. You must face that. Tribal law is still on their side."

"I don't understand, John." At that moment, Carrie had an urge to run as fast as possible to pick up Nuttah and take her far away. But what place was far enough to escape this law? Her hands dropped to her sides as she stood, feeling numb. Peg was right. Nowhere was far enough.

John pulled her to him. "I'm so sorry. You don't understand, and likely, you never will. You love Nuttah. But this is an uphill battle you are fighting, and the law is clear." He held her at arms' length, impressing his words on her. "I don't want to give you false hope. I am willing to do whatever it takes to help you. But I don't think . . ."

Read the notes. Carrie suddenly remembered the notes Medicine Owl's grandson had dropped off for her. "John, I just remembered something! Medicine Owl left patient notes about Nuttah's family. She wanted me to have them. Would you translate them for me? I have a feeling they could shed light on something we need to know."

John's eyes met hers. "Do you have the papers with you?"

"They're in my office, in my purse." Her eyes filled with hope.

"Let's get those notes. I don't know our language, and neither does my dad. But my grandfather Pete White Elk can speak and write it. Those notes could make a difference. Medicine Owl was always very intentional about what she said and did."

They hurried over to the clinic to Carrie's office. She reached into her desk drawer and pulled out her handbag. Removing the envelope, she held it against her chest. "You're right, John. These notes must be important, or she wouldn't have put them aside for me. She told her grandson to make sure he gave them to me . . . if she couldn't. John, she knew she was dying and might never make it back to her hut to retrieve them for me."

She looked at the envelope, hesitating for a moment. These precious notes were all she had of Medicine Owl—notes in the medicine woman's handwriting, her native language. What if they couldn't be returned? She cherished everything Medicine Owl had ever given her.

"May I?" John asked. Carrie nodded and reluctantly handed the envelope to him. He opened the flap, withdrew the stack of papers, and glanced over the slanted script. "I only recognize a few words here and there. May I show this to my dad now?"

"Of course. But now is not the time, John," she said. "He can't think of anything else except Mike right now. It's not right. We'll have to pick another time."

"You are running out of time," John said in such a point-blank tone, Carrie understood the gravity of his message: Nuttah might be removed from their home sooner than she might think. "Anyway, this will give him something else to think about while we wait for word about Mike."

John showed the notes to Earl whose face registered something Carrie didn't completely understand, although she could tell he was impressed by what he saw. From the way Earl's eyes met John's, then Nadie's, Carrie was certain that whatever was in those notes was important. Was it something bad about the birth family? Was it about Nuttah's mother?

Carrie had a sense that even in death, Medicine Owl had come to her assistance. Her spirit lived on. Of this, Carrie was certain. Overcome with the solemn nature of this deep knowing, she dabbed at her eyes with the corner of her scrub top, missing Medicine Owl more than ever. Hadn't Medicine Owl promised to always be with her? When she needed to feel the medicine woman's presence, her friend was there. She was always there.

"What do the notes say?" Carrie asked, trying not to be impatient, and failing. Earl looked at his son and nodded. They seemed to understand each other without benefit of words.

John looked at Carrie and said, "My father will take these notes to my grandfather. He needs to see them."

"Will they help us? Can you give them back to me afterward?" Carrie asked. "Medicine Owl wanted me to have them."

"You may go with us to see Nadie's father, Pete," Earl said. "I don't understand all of what she says, but these notes tell quite a story."

Chapter Twenty-Two

—٠٧/٠—

NATE SPEAKS

IT WASN'T THAT NATE DIDN'T HAVE confidence in the surgical work he and Beth had just completed, bringing Mike through a four-hour operation. He was in recovery now, and Nate knew he would live. Due to the severity of his injuries, the surgery should have taken place at a bigger hospital with an intensive care unit. But he and Beth had agreed Mike might not survive a ride by helicopter.

At first, their goal had been to stabilize him and have him sent by helicopter to a hospital with more extensive trauma capabilities. But when they saw the punctured lung, they knew they had to take immediate action. Fortunately, Mike could have their full attention. Other victims of the attack had been taken to such hospitals in neighboring communities—facilities that tribal members called "white hospitals."

Mike and another Blackfoot man had been the only victims of the attack taken to Blackfeet Community Hospital. The other Blackfoot, who suffered a broken leg, had been treated and released. Mike, on the other hand, was in for a longer recovery.

It was fortunate that the head injury hadn't been as life-threatening as Nate and Beth had feared. There had been a severe concussion, but not as much intercranial bleeding as they expected. Although thirty stitches had been needed to close the laceration on the back of his head, Mike had been lucky on that score. Yet, his internal injuries had been so serious, he would need post-surgical monitoring until he was out of the woods. Nate blew out a long breath. It was up to him and Beth to oversee Mike's post-surgical care and, if necessary, arrange for physical therapy. It was fortunate that Mike's livelihood was in the arts, painting and showing his work. He would be able to continue painting at home while he recovered.

Meanwhile, Carrie was right to be concerned that the stress of Mike's injuries could bring on premature labor in Naomi. Naomi would stay with her mother until the baby arrived. If anything happened, her mother and Nadie Leathers would know what to do. He hoped he wouldn't have to deliver a baby by emergency C-section because Naomi had complications.

His thoughts turned to Carrie, waiting for him at their house with nine-month-old Nuttah. Hard to believe it had been that many months since they brought her home from the hospital. He had intended to be home by now, but there had been a backlog in the E.R. after the surgery, so he stayed.

Although it would be too late to help put Nuttah to bed, he could shower, change into something comfortable, and have some time alone with Carrie. "Caddy Shack" was on television tonight. They could both use the comic relief. Carrie had a great laugh—lusty and contagious. Too bad he hadn't heard that laugh as often the past year.

It wouldn't be much longer until they heard a decision about Nuttah's adoption. In a way, being in limbo felt safer. On this, they agreed. Yet the stress was taking a toll on each of them—and on their marriage, at times. They were less patient with each other lately. For the first time, he had snapped at Carrie when she forgot to set the security alarm on her way out of the house. The shocked look on her face hurt him more than her reaction, which had been to mumble an apology and retreat into silence for a day.

When he asked whether Joseph Red Feather had said anything hopeful on her last call with him, she averted her eyes and mumbled, "No news is good news."

He tried to apologize again, but Carrie waved him off and left with the baby. They couldn't go on like this much longer. The situation was unfair to everyone involved. If they won their case, the baby's grandmother would lose the only link to her daughter. If they lost, they would lose the baby they loved. There would be no clear winner.

Nate had learned from John that there were safety and hygiene concerns about the birth family's home environment, but that after several bungled attempts, they had been addressed to the caseworker's satisfaction. This situation would need to be monitored, however. Would that happen?

Then came the arrest of Nuttah's young uncle for the rash of home burglaries. At first, Nate shared Carrie's optimism that this could make the case stronger for them to keep the baby. But John had shaken his head and explained that it would be up to the Tribal Council to make a final determination. There were older members who would be unlikely to allow an adoption by a white couple, no matter what negative circumstances were happening with another family member. It was a sad reality that on the reservation, substance abuse and this type of crime were not unique. Blood was blood. That seemed to be all that mattered.

Now, with the death of Medicine Owl, their biggest ally was gone. He had spoken briefly with John, hoping for additional information about what might happen with the Tribal Council. Was there anything he or his father could do? John had made it clear that the law was the law. Whether he and other family members agreed or not, in this case, Native American children were placed with Native American families, whenever possible. As helpless and frustrated as this made him feel, Nate understood John's position.

He wasn't sure how much more heartache Carrie could take. Medicine Owl's death had affected her like a beloved family member. And why not? In many ways, the medicine woman had become as much a role model and confidante to Carrie as her beloved Gran. Carrie had looked to Medicine Owl for more than just her opinions on the healthcare of Native Americans. She had depended on Medicine Owl for the sort of advice that an older woman could provide to a younger woman, offering life experiences freely while understanding that each woman had to find her own way. In every way, Medicine Owl had been a surrogate grandmother.

Carrie had returned home after Medicine Owl's death a different woman: stronger even in the fragility of her grief, determined to carry on the medicine woman's work. Nate had seen the determination in her sad blue eyes. The medicine woman's death left Carrie responsible for the health of the Blackfeet people. Medicine Owl had made it clear that Carrie was her apprentice. She was the teacher, Carrie the student.

Yet, the medicine woman's time and attention had meant so much more to Carrie. She had given Carrie confidence and helped her to see that her lifelong goal to help underserved Native Americans was achievable. If the medicine woman believed Carrie could do this, who was Carrie to doubt her? Despite intense grief over Medicine Owl's death and stress over Nuttah's adoption, Carrie still showed the same strength of character that had attracted Nate to her in the beginning. Medicine Owl's confidence in Carrie had not been misplaced.

Although there was a medicine man in a nearby town, members of the Blackfeet Nation who lived in and around Browning had come to trust Carrie. She had earned credibility with them, with the assistance of Medicine Owl. Nate had benefited, too, from Medicine Owl's benevolence. He had performed countless surgeries on Blackfeet men, women, and children with the full blessing of the medicine woman. For this reason, he and Carrie felt they belonged here. But this could change. Would a decision to remove Nuttah from their home end up being the catalyst that could force them to leave the reservation? His heart sank at the thought. He deeply loved the baby and considered her his daughter.

How difficult would it be for Carrie to provide healthcare for Nuttah and the baby's birth family if she was returned to that dreadful home? Although Carrie would do the right thing by the child and her relatives, what price would she pay for her devotion? Everyone had their breaking point, even Carrie.

But there was more. Each month, when Carrie realized once more that she wasn't pregnant, it eroded a little more of that indominable spirit. Oh, she put up a good front. Work was a major part of her identity. But it had to be hell to deliver babies to other women, to care for them in the most joyous time of their lives, when she wanted to experience pregnancy so much. After delivering Gali and John's newest baby, Lucy, he had heard Carrie crying in the bathroom after she returned home from the hospital. It broke his heart.

He felt helpless to comfort her. And what if he was the reason she hadn't conceived yet? They hadn't gone through a fertility work-up yet. Dr. Jim had been able to recruit a fertility specialist to the reservation this year as part of the volunteer medical corps. But there were other Blackfeet women needing the same assistance. Carrie had insisted she would wait until all the other patients were seen, putting her own desires after their needs.

"You and I can afford to see a specialist somewhere off the reservation. They can't," she had said firmly. How hard must that have been for her to say?

Feeling weary after so many hours at the hospital, Nate sat down at a table in the lunchroom and nibbled a day-old huckleberry muffin. Running his fingers through two days' beard growth, he sipped stale black coffee, grimacing at the bitter overheated taste. When had he last eaten anything other than hospital food?

He had just checked on Mike, who was awake, and had given him a little more pain medication. Since Mike was in lifelong recovery for alcoholism, Nate needed to be careful not to overmedicate him. Mike was a trooper and had nodded in understanding when Nate explained his concern about narcotics. But he wouldn't allow the man to suffer. Members of the Leathers family were as dear to Nate as they were to Carrie.

He thought about the years he had spent on the reservation, nearly four at last count, and how much he had come to enjoy working under such challenging conditions. There was never a dull moment at Blackfeet Community Hospital. One day, he might be removing a cancerous growth. Another day might find him delivering a baby by caesarean section. The E.R. saw every kind of emergency, and it was up to Nate to deal with each. Before he arrived, the hospital had been without a general surgeon and a chief of emergency medicine. He had been glad to fill both roles and relished the variety of responsibilities. Of course, it was too much, which was why he had been so glad to see Beth. Would she stay? More to the point, would she be allowed to stay?

He frowned, remembering a conversation with a fellow surgeon in Kansas City. It was clear that Beth faced further legal action, possibly the loss of her medical license. No one questioned that she had made an error in judgment, operating on a patient when it would have been better to turn the surgery over to a colleague. Had she, consciously or unconsciously, killed a woman? This would be tough to prove, given the desperate condition of the patient when she arrived at the hospital.

For whatever reason, she had insisted on performing surgery on a woman suffering a cardiac dissection. Although there had been another surgeon assisting, along with a surgical resident, the woman's condition was so high-risk, so grave, the chances of success would have been, at best, forty to fifty percent. Did he believe Beth was guilty? The case was largely circumstantial, and so far, Beth had answered questions honestly and to the satisfaction of the hospital's review board and investigators.

She had been a valuable addition to Blackfeet Community Hospital's surgical staff, doing many surgeries that had helped people recover from serious, life-threatening conditions. If she lost her license to perform surgery, she would have to leave, and the hospital would have no back-up surgeon. This was painful for Nate to consider, for Beth was gifted at what she did. It was true that she could be difficult and short-tempered. He didn't blame Carrie for her earlier opinions about Beth—not really. Beth had been beyond rude to her. Nevertheless, it was important to be fair to all concerned, and it was up to him to stand up for Beth, to provide another opinion.

He thought about the improved relationship between Beth and Carrie—who had done everything he had asked of her—had, in fact, gone out of her way to be supportive. Beth now had a more positive view of Carrie, albeit begrudgingly. Nate chuckled to himself. It was just like Carrie to fight for the underdog. Once she realized Beth was vulnerable and homesick, she rose to the challenge and worked hard to get along with her. It had helped a lot. The nurses became more forgiving toward Beth.

As for the situation in Kansas City, the dead woman's best friend believed, whether it was true or not, that Beth had been having an affair with the patient's husband, a fellow physician. What did the widower think? If he and Beth were involved romantically, and he loved her, it would stand to reason that he would defend her. Isn't that what any man would do for a woman he loved? But if he thought she was guilty, he would, as a physician, have a moral obligation to let the hospital's review board and the authorities determine her fate.

Beth had never revealed to Nate whether she'd had an affair, but he didn't find this hard to believe. Beth was a beautiful woman whose career left precious little time for a romantic relationship. It was a reality of hospital life that physicians often turned to each other for companionship and emotional support, and this often led to romantic entanglements. Nate had certainly had his share of opportunities with female doctors at the med center. But until he met Carrie, he hadn't thought it wise to date at work. Even more important, he hadn't been certain of what he wanted in a woman. He had wondered whether it was even desirable to date or marry another physician.

His engagement to Marisa, his sweetheart since college days, ended when he took the job in Montana. Marisa was a wonderful woman, but life on a remote Indian reservation wasn't her style. In contrast, the moment he met Carrie, saw the delight in those blue eyes as she surveyed the expanse of mountains, witnessed the passion she had for her work with the Blackfeet people, he had known she was the woman of his dreams. Smart as a whip, an expert at her chosen career, loving, loyal, and full of fun, she had captured his heart in an instant.

He could have been intimidated by her. She was a winner of the coveted Roosevelt prize, a national award that came with a $50,000 stipend. It was this income that had allowed her to study Native American medicine on the reservation before the hospital was able to pay her a salary. She was the brightest woman he had ever met, and she continued to fascinate him. The fact that she was so lovely, with long blonde hair, cornflower-blue eyes, and a slender runner's figure, only added to her appeal. She was a wonderful wife and mother. He was still as much in love with her as he been at the start.

Naturally, the course of their relationship hadn't been without its challenges. She had been engaged to another doctor, although it was evident to Nate from the moment that he met the guy that he wasn't right for her. Along with Carrie's father, her fiancé had tried to control her. But there was no controlling a woman with Carrie's strength of mind and heart.

She was strong, yes, but also human. The infertility they were experiencing and the threat of losing Nuttah were taking a toll. She loved Nuttah and wouldn't let her go without a fight. Nate wasn't certain that either of them would fully recover if they lost Nuttah. If the worst happened, he would need to think seriously about getting them off the reservation, at least for a while—maybe several years. They could always come back later or volunteer during the summers.

It would be difficult to live so close to Nuttah and worry about her wellbeing in her grandparents' rundown home—little more than a shack, really, slapped onto a small trailer and constructed of plywood walls and a tin roof. He had figured out where they lived and had driven by the house a few days after Nuttah's grandmother came forward asking to see her. There had been old cars in the yard, trash, and rusted metal. In many ways, the reservation was like a developing nation, with dilapidated housing and water that wasn't safe to drink. Poverty was a way of life in this remote part of the country. Nuttah wouldn't have everything he and Carrie could give her if she moved back to that life.

He hadn't admitted yet to Carrie that, after meeting briefly with the therapist to talk about the nightmares, the chief of surgery had offered him his old job back. The money he offered was incredible. Carrie's father also had spoken with him about a job in Philadelphia, and even an appointment to the faculty at the medical school where he taught. Carrie would always be welcome to join her father's group practice. Together, they would recover from their grief with the help of Gran and Carrie's parents. They had options.

The thought of moving away filled him with dread. It wasn't something he wanted to do, not for a moment. From the day he first set foot on the reservation as part of Dr. Jim's volunteer medical corps, he had known this work was what he was born to do. He loved working on the reservation, and so did Carrie. Now that they owned a home here, it would be more difficult to leave. But perhaps, they could rent the house back to the hospital.

His job at Blackfeet Community Hospital had helped him to heal, emotionally and physically, from his past. He had been too busy working to give much thought to the traumatic experience that had been the catalyst for resigning from the medical center in Kansas City. Time in the outdoors had given him back the full use of his injured leg. He had met and married Carrie. Life was better than he could ever have imagined.

During the past few months, as he underwent remote therapy with the psychologist, he had begun to understand that the nightmares were of his own creation. They didn't just happen through random association. Subconscious images and repressed memories fueled the dreams. He was now certain that the scene he relived over and over in those dreams had been a series of clues, precognitive in nature.

He no longer feared the dreams; he welcomed them, for they revealed more details each time. He now knew that the surgeon in the dream was Beth. The intense emotions of fear he experienced in the dream were hers. She was terrified of what was happening to her patient. Deep down, he believed her to be innocent of the charges.

Yet the dreams also helped him realize that the flow of life had moved him forward, propelled by each experience, each choice he made. He could cease judgment and examine any situation, his or that of another, with compassion and empathy. He could view that terrible night in the emergency room when he was shot as an episode that helped him grow as a man and a surgeon. Instead of bitterness toward the shooter, he chose to feel lucky to be alive, to be able to live each day and appreciate each moment. An unexpected benefit had been that he had more empathy toward his trauma patients, for he had been one of them. He understood their fears, their worries for their futures.

There was no villain in the dreams. That he knew. Sometimes terrible things happened. But from those experiences came new understanding of what was most important in life. It was about finding joy and holding onto those happy moments for dear life. And it was this knowledge that also enabled him to judge less, love more.

He stood up from the table and stretched. Glancing at the clock on the wall, he realized that if he hurried, he could still get home in time for a late dinner with Carrie. He texted to ask if she wanted him to pick up something at the grocery store for dinner.

She responded immediately. *Made spaghetti. Hurry home! Can't wait to see u.*

What's for dessert? he texted back and grinned at her response.

"Me."

Chapter Twenty-Three

—⟩⟨—

AT HOME WITH NUTTAH THAT EVENING, with her mother's signature spaghetti sauce simmering on the stove, Carrie waited for Nate. He had texted earlier to say he was on his way. They had shared a light-hearted text message that promised special time together. But she also was impatient to hear about Mike's condition, and she wanted to hear Nate's thoughts about Medicine Owl's notes.

She gave Nuttah her bedtime bottle and rocked her to sleep, savoring quiet time with her baby girl. She kissed her soft forehead and held her close, breathing in the clean scent of baby wash and lotion. Her breath was sweet, too. These moments were precious. As she had done so often the past year, she stored this moment away for safekeeping, into the memory album in her heart.

With Nuttah tucked in for the night and the baby monitor turned on, she decided to call Gran. It was nearly ten o'clock on the east coast, but Gran would still be awake. She rarely went to bed before the nightly news was over.

As soon as she heard her grandmother's voice, she said, "Gran, I just had to talk with you tonight. You wouldn't believe what happened today."

"Carrie! I was just thinking about you and wondering how things are going. Just let me turn down the volume on this news program so I can hear you better."

Carrie waited a moment until Gran returned to the phone. "There, that's better. I may not hear as well as I used to, but I'm all ears now. Tell me everything, and don't leave out a single detail."

"A terrible thing happened to Mike Leathers at one of his rallies." She related details of Mike's accident and injuries. "Nate and Beth operated. I'm expecting Nate home any time now. I'll know more then. Mike is lucky to be alive."

"I suspect he knew the dangers and was willing to face them, anyhow. That's the definition of true courage," Gran said. "Isn't their baby due soon?"

"Naomi is due the first week of July. But that's not all that happened today." Carrie told her about Medicine Owl's notes. "Gran, there has to be a reason why I received those notes today from her grandson. It was as if Medicine Owl was reaching out to offer more help."

"She had big plans for you," Gran said. "She probably hoped you wouldn't need to see those notes—that the situation would resolve. But at some point, she knew she had to go that extra step. She may have seen a foreshadowing of what was coming."

Carrie took a deep breath to steady herself and heard Nate's footsteps on the front steps. "Nate just got home," she said and hurried to open the front door. "How's Mike?"

He gave her a quick thumbs-up. That irresistible dimpled Nate-smile melted her insides. She let out a quick whoop of joy and clapped a hand over her mouth. Nuttah was sleeping. "Is he awake yet?"

"He's awake, although he's still got a breathing tube," Nate said, dropping his car keys onto the table in the foyer. "He was conscious about two hours after surgery. He'll have a doozy of a headache for a while, but he'll be fine."

Carrie relayed this news to Gran. She wanted to hear more details of the surgery and trusted her grandmother to understand. "Gran, I need to go. I'll fill you in on more details by email tomorrow. Can't wait to see you! It won't be long now. Love you so much!"

"Not nearly as much as I love you," Gran said. "Keep me posted on how Mike is doing. As for the rest of what is happening, I believe in benevolent outcomes, as you know."

Now more than ever, Carrie needed to believe that. "Thanks, Gran. Keep believing. We can use all the help we can get."

Although it was late June, the night air was cold. Carrie lit a fire in the hearth while Nate showered. She closed the front door and turned the deadbolt, locking them off from the rest of the world. She programmed the security system, feeling relief as she heard the now-familiar female electronic voice, "System on. Stay or exit now."

Nate came downstairs wearing just his pajama bottoms, his lanky body even leaner than usual, the result of long hours and stress. He dried his curly hair with a towel and then looped it around his neck. Carrie went to him and pressed her face to his chest, listening to the reassuring beat of his heart, savoring the feeling of his arms around her, holding her close. For several minutes, they did not speak as Nate lightly ran his fingers up and down her back. She wrapped her arms around his waist, unwilling to let go.

So much had happened today. In a senseless act of violence, they had nearly lost a friend. How could anyone know what the road ahead might hold? At any moment, tragedy could strike.

And yet, in the blink of an eye, you could receive an unimaginable blessing—Nuttah. That blessing could just as easily be taken away. Fate could change their lives again, bringing heartache. But for now, they had each other and Nuttah.

They stood together, heart to heart, for several minutes. Then Nate kissed the top of her head. "Let's eat. I'm starving." He threw another log on the fire, bringing a rush of orange sparks, before leading her by the hand into the kitchen.

"I hope you like what I made." Carrie ladled spaghetti sauce onto zucchini noodles and set the plate in front of him. "I used that spiralizer thingie my mother gave us for Christmas."

Nate smiled. "You're becoming a regular gourmet."

They enjoyed a quiet leisurely dinner together discussing their day. Nate offered more details of the surgery, but she also thought he seemed distracted and troubled. Carrie listened, sensing that he needed to debrief by sharing the process he and Beth had followed. Hopefully, it would allow him to let go of this day and sleep.

He drew a hand wearily across his forehead. "Everything is fine, but it might not have turned out that way."

"What do you mean? What happened?" Carrie waited.

"Nothing, thanks to a second pair of eyes." He became quiet for a moment. "I screwed up. It's easy to think if you have enough training, enough experience, you can fix anything. I was reminded today that mistakes happen."

"Well, of course. Surgeons are human."

"It was a tricky situation with that lung. I was focused on that and not on the liver. If it hadn't been for Beth . . . Well, I'm convinced we took care of everything. There was a bleeder I missed, but she saw it. That's why we need two surgeons—for situations like this."

Carrie nodded. "I understand. But mistakes happen, babe. You can't expect perfection from yourself. As good as you are, things happen."

"Exactly. Things happen, and we either do something the right way or we mess up. What I did could have killed him. I could have been responsible for Mike's death."

"Mike is fine. Even if it was a close call, there was a good outcome. That's all that matters now."

"We'll keep him in the hospital for a while. He'll need some rehab. We'll figure that out as we go along."

Nate took their plates to the sink. "Any ice cream?" he asked in a hopeful voice.

Carrie peeked into the freezer and pulled out Moose Tracks, a decadent mixture of vanilla, peanut butter, and fudge. It was their favorite. As she scooped enough for two small bowls, she suddenly remembered the other big news of the day. "Oh! There's one other thing I have to tell you. With everything else that has happened today, I didn't have a chance earlier. Medicine Owl's grandson came to see me today. He went to her hut in the hills and brought me an envelope of patient notes she wanted me to have. They're about Nuttah's family."

"Really?" Nate's eyes widened. "What do they say?"

"They're in the native language. John thought they were important, and he shared them with Earl."

"Can Earl read them?"

"Not very well. But he thinks the notes tell an important story. That's all he said. He also thinks there could be an invitation to meet with Pete White Elk, his father-in-law, who reads and speaks the language."

Nate sat down and pressed his elbows against the kitchen table, resting his head in his hands. When he looked up again, she could see the determination in his eyes. "I want to go, too."

"It's important they hear from both of us," Carrie agreed.

"If they invite us to talk with them, that will be a good sign," Nate said. "John said if they avoid speaking with us, that will be our answer."

"When did he say that?" Carrie asked. "You never told me that part."

"It was before we went to Kansas City. John said it would be a positive sign if the tribal elders want to meet with us, to ask questions about how we intend to raise Nuttah."

"That's true. They haven't heard anything from us. We've had people speaking on our behalf."

"I had to ask him. We'd gone for so many months without hearing much of anything," Nate said. "To tell you the truth, I took it as a bad sign that no one wanted to hear from us."

"I've sensed you weren't feeling as hopeful," Carrie said, shaking her head. "I think what John said is right. If they don't care what we plan to do to raise her, they obviously have no intention of giving her to us." She was silent for a moment, considering this point.

"I wonder sometimes . . ." She paused, considering how best to phrase her next thought. There was more at stake here than what was happening with their marriage and family. They had careers to consider. "I have to know something, and I need for you just to tell me straight out. Are you thinking we should leave the reservation if Nuttah is given back to her birth family?"

"Don't you think that would be healthier for us? I mean, it doesn't have to be forever—just a few years, maybe. We could go to Kansas City or to Philadelphia, wherever you want. We could still volunteer here in the summers."

"You sound as if you think we've already lost her." Carrie looked down at her plate. It was more important than ever that they were on the same page. "Nate, we have not lost this case. We need to believe in what is possible, and we need to believe in it together. I can't do this myself."

"I don't want to leave here," Nate admitted. "I've never loved a job more. But I don't know if we can stand . . . if I can deal with . . . being here if we lose Nuttah. I thought I could handle it. I know what the law says and what our chances were of being successful in this. What I didn't expect was how fast I would come to think of her as my own daughter. She didn't just wrap me around her little finger. She grabbed hold of my heart."

Carrie knew at that instant that she had to be strong, for Nate's sake, too. Sometimes in a marriage, one person had to try harder, give more, even if it seemed impossible. He needed her encouragement, too. This situation was as hard on him as it was on her.

"You're a wonderful father. She's a lucky little girl that you love her as much as you do. She'll always benefit from that. I understand how you feel. I think of her as my real daughter, too."

"Maybe if we hadn't wanted to be parents so much, if we hadn't been trying so hard, we might have been less vulnerable," Nate said. "We might have been able to be more objective. As it was, we were a heartbreak waiting to happen." Tears glistened in his blue eyes.

Carrie took a deep breath, considering her next words. "When we were approved as foster parents, we knew what we were doing. We knew we could lose her at any time. We signed up to be this child's parents for however long that lasted, and we took the risk because we cared about her."

"If I had to make the decision all over again, I'd still choose to do what we did," he said. "I will always love her, no matter what."

Carrie reached over and took Nate's hand. "We came here to do important work. Heartache and tragedies are a part of life. They're a part of our career, too—caring for people from birth to death. You know how hard I grieve when I lose patients. I know you do, too. We do our best to remain objective, but that's not entirely possible. In the end, the people we help become a part of us. I still think it's worth the emotional investment."

"I agree. But can you honestly tell me you've never thought about leaving?"

"Yes, a few times," Carrie admitted. "On days when I'm full of fears, I've thought about running away—of taking Nuttah as far away as possible. But Peg reminded me that's no way to live. Running away isn't the answer. If we lose Nuttah, we'll take it a day at a time, together. This place is too important to us."

"I love you, Carrie, and that means taking care of you. I'll do whatever it takes to make sure you're happy. That's why I thought it might be better to leave."

"Nate, we take care of each other. This is the biggest challenge we've ever faced together, and whatever happens, we'll be okay."

"We will." He brought her hand to his lips and kissed it.

"Let's not think any more about leaving. Let's concentrate on taking each day that we have here, each day that Nuttah is with us, and make the most of that time."

The irresistible sounds of the popping, crackling fire drew them into the living room. Carrie uncorked a bottle of red wine that had been given to them as a wedding present. Their one-year wedding anniversary was coming up soon. This seemed like the ideal time to think about what had drawn them together as a couple and what kept them closely connected.

"Give me a minute to look in on Nuttah? I didn't get to kiss her goodnight." Nate went upstairs for a few minutes.

Carrie poked at the logs in the fireplace, setting them ablaze. She glanced at the clock on the mantle. Almost eleven o'clock. With everything that had happened that day, she and Nate should be thinking about sleep. Yet, sleep was the furthest thing from her mind.

When Nate returned, she handed him a glass of wine. "To good outcomes," she said and clinked her glass to his.

"To good outcomes," Nate said. Then he drew her into a deep kiss.

THE NEXT MORNING, CARRIE DROVE NUTTAH to Violet's house, her thoughts hop-scotching to the hectic day ahead. A full schedule of patients awaited her, and now a patient was in active labor. She felt exhausted already, and the day hadn't even officially begun. When they arrived at the High Towers' tiny frame house in the center of town, the aroma of French toast wafted through the front screen door. Carrie followed the irresistible smell of vanilla and cinnamon to the kitchen, where Violet was cooking breakfast for her two sons.

"Smells good in here," Carrie said, depositing Nuttah into the highchair at the table.

"I will fix you a plate," Violet said. "Sit and eat. You are getting too thin."

Carrie laughed. "Don't mind if I do. Thank you." She sat at the table and visited with Violet's two sons, now eleven and nine, until they finished their breakfast and went outside to ride their bikes. While Carrie's French toast browned in the skillet, Violet cut up tiny pieces of banana and laid them on the highchair tray. Nuttah chased one of the slippery pieces around the tray, working to pick it up between her thumb and forefinger. She put it in her mouth and grinned.

"Her manual dexterity is getting better and better," Carrie noted, beaming. "See how she uses her fingers like a pincer. You are the smartest baby!"

Violet gave Carrie an odd look. "I don't know what that means, but Nuttah loves bananas," she said, kissing the baby on her round cheek. In response, Nuttah picked up another piece of banana and held it out to Carrie. Before Carrie could taste it, Nuttah put it in her mouth and gave Carrie a look of pure mischief, wrinkling her nose and grinning.

"You monkey!" Carrie laughed.

Setting Carrie's plate in front of her, Violet said, "I hear they have caught the man responsible for the burglaries."

"It's her uncle," Carrie said, with a nod of her head toward Nuttah. She drizzled maple syrup over the two pieces of French toast. It seemed rude to speak of Nuttah's relative in front of her, even if she was an infant.

"I am not surprised," Violet said as she wiped up the sticky mess her sons had left on the kitchen table.

"What else have you heard?" Violet had many friends on the reservation. She and Peg were often Carrie's conduits for information.

"I hear that the boy's mother is upset and blames her husband for this trouble," Violet said. "The boy is like his father. I'm sure he is stealing to buy the drugs."

"Ugh. I hate to hear that." Carrie picked up her fork to take a bite, but her appetite was gone. She felt queasy. Still, Violet had gone to the trouble of cooking for her. She took two bites, resolving to call Joseph Red Feather later and stress the gravity of this information about drugs in that household.

Violet sat down at the table across from her. "It is hard for some people to understand why you want this baby when she has a family already. I say, 'It is not hard for me to understand because I know Dr. Carrie and Dr. Nate.' I say Nuttah belongs with you. But not everyone agrees. I don't know what it will take to change their minds."

"We always knew that trying to adopt her might not work out," Carrie said. "Medicine Owl wanted us to keep Nuttah. I found it easier to believe that if she thought it was the right thing to do, everything would be okay. Everyone else would agree automatically. That wasn't the case. Now that Medicine Owl is gone, I'm not sure what will happen."

She didn't share with Violet the fact that she now had information from Medicine Owl about the family. It was privileged patient information. In any case, she had no idea what the notes contained. They might change the course of events or they might mean nothing. Did the medical history say there were drugs in the home? With so many households on the reservation affected by alcohol and drugs, would it even make a difference?

Though she felt unsettled, it was important to eat the food that had been prepared for her. She speared another bite of French toast and dipped it in maple syrup. Putting it in her mouth, she chewed and then took another bite. As she ate, Violet watched her, caring that the breakfast she made nourished and comforted Carrie. Maybe food *was* love.

When Carrie finished the last bite, she sat back and smiled. "Violet, thank you. That was exactly what I needed."

Carrie kissed Nuttah good-bye and hugged Violet longer than usual, so grateful was she for her steadfast support. Then she drove to the hospital. She parked about two hundred feet from two horses tied to a post in the parking lot. She recognized the larger of the horses, Tall Boy, belonging to one of her patients, Vernon Eagle Spotter.

A wave of nausea hit her. Before going to the clinic, she headed straight for the restroom, where she emptied her stomach. Standing in the restroom, pale, feeling light-headed, she realized for the first time the strain she was under. There was no doubt that stress was affecting her health now.

She rinsed her mouth out with water, patted her face with cool, damp paper towels, and took several deep breaths, feeling better. Then she headed for the inpatient unit, needing to see for herself that Mike was doing well. She peeked inside and saw Naomi asleep in a padded chair by her husband's side. Nadie was there, too, dark circles under her eyes. The older woman tucked a blanket around her pregnant daughter-in-law and turned, touching a finger to her lips. Carrie nodded, and the two women tip-toed into the hall to talk.

"I'm glad you are here. My son is still sleeping. He shows no sign of life today."

"He is very much alive." Carrie wrapped her arms around Nadie and kissed her on the cheek. "Your boy is strong, Momma. Sleep is what he needs. It will help his injuries to heal."

"Yes, I believe that. Thank you." Nadie took Carrie's hand in hers and held it for a moment.

It occurred to Carrie at that moment that at no time during the family's vigil had a single tear been shed by Nadie. It was not her way. "Nadie," she said, "This experience has been so hard for you. I watch as you care for the others in your family, and you're so strong, as if nothing can break your spirit."

"That is because I feel the larger arms around me," Nadie said. "Those arms are there for you, too, Dr. Carrie. Feel them around you. They will hold you up and carry you through anything."

Chapter Twenty-Four

⁓⁓

As if Mike Leathers' injuries weren't enough to jangle everyone's nerves, more troubles were on the way for the Leathers family. A little after nine o'clock that evening, Carrie's cell phone rang. She saw John's caller I.D. pop up. "Hello, John," she said. "How are you?"

"Carrie, we need you. Dad is unconscious. I've called for an ambulance."

"Let me know when it arrives. I'll stay on the phone with you." Carrie swung into action, pulling her jacket from the hall closet and slipping her arms into it. "I'm still here, John." Nate stood by, a question mark on his face.

"It's Earl. He's unresponsive," Carrie said to him. She turned her attention back to John as she headed out the door. "What happened and how long ago?"

"About twenty minutes ago. My mother says he got very white and started to shake. She tried to get him to drink some orange juice, but he got more agitated and fought her. That was when she called me. Now he won't wake up. My mother called the ambulance. I got here a few minutes later." Carrie could hear the ambulance siren through the phone. "Oh good, the ambulance is here," he said.

"Did he take his medication today?"

"Mom says she didn't see him take it, and he didn't test his blood, either. He, uh, rarely does that, even though she says she'll do it for him."

"I'll meet the ambulance at the E.R.," Carrie said. "The EMTs will stabilize your father and get him on the right track. I'll check him out when he gets there. I'm on my way now."

"Thanks, Carrie. Do you think there will be any complications?"

Carrie decided not to outline the cardiovascular implications of untreated diabetes, including the potential for kidney failure. "We'll work to minimize any issues."

She ended the call and ran to her car. Starting the engine, she carefully navigated the ruts in their winter-ravaged gravel driveway and eased onto the highway, taking the curves a little faster than usual on the rough, rutted road. As she drove, she watched the sides of the road ahead for deer. With so much open space for wildlife to roam, it didn't pay to let your guard down.

To say that Earl was a non-compliant diabetes patient would not begin to describe the concerns she had. He remained fearful of needles and stubborn about changing his diet. There was only so much Nadie could do to manage what he ate. Now that she was spending so much time at the hospital to be near their son, it was up to Earl to be proactive about his health. He seemed not to understand the severity of his illness and the potential risks.

She parked near the E.R. entrance and hurried inside. Attendants unloaded Earl from a gurney onto a hospital table. He seemed alert, having received an intravenous solution that returned his blood sugar to normal levels, and he answered questions in a coherent manner. When he saw Carrie, he looked sheepish.

"Dr. Carrie, I am so sorry that you had to leave your home tonight because of me." He waved his hand at the equipment now surrounding him, including an EKG machine, intravenous bags of fluid on a pole, and oxygen tubes in his nostrils. "I was a little careless today."

Carrie accepted a stethoscope from one of the nurses and began to assess his condition. "Earl, this is a lesson about the importance of good diabetes self-care. I hear that you might not have checked your blood sugar today or taken your medication."

"I saw Medicine Bear yesterday," Earl said.

Carrie frowned for a moment before recognizing the name of the new medicine man. She had not yet been introduced to him. "Oh?" she asked, watching the expression that crossed Earl's face, as if he had been caught cheating on Carrie with another doctor.

She took his pulse. "Did he give you any medicine to take?" She hoped not. While Medicine Owl had been wise in her use of native plants and roots, Carrie wasn't sure about the skill and knowledge level of the new medicine man.

"He spoke words of healing." Earl let out a deep breath as if now considering their questionable results.

"He spoke words of healing," Carrie repeated, stressing the word 'healing' as she took in the deeper meaning. "I think I hear you saying that he spoke words that were supposed to make you healthy. Is that correct?"

"Yes. He said these medicines that I am taking for my diabetes are the white man's medicine and will hurt me."

"Earl, the words of good health are important, yes. But you must follow the plan I gave you. Those medicines are keeping you from what just happened—a blood sugar attack that brought you here to the hospital," Carrie said with as much patience as she could muster. She leaned closer. "I would never give you anything that would hurt you. Do you believe that?"

Earl's eyes met hers. She had her fingers on his wrist, and he moved to take her hand. "Yes, I do believe that you are a good doctor. I will try harder to listen to you and to do what you say. I am sorry."

"There is no reason to apologize," she said laying her cool hand on his forehead. "It takes time to learn how to manage diabetes. Earl, the blood testing is important. Without it, you cannot handle this disease. As your doctor, as your friend, I want you to feel good and live a long life with Nadie and all those wonderful grandchildren."

He let out a low chuckle. "Yes, there are more of them than Nadie can handle without my help."

Carrie shook her head. She wanted to scold him, but there was more she wanted and needed to say. "I'm counting on you to be there to help us with Nuttah." She impressed these words on him with her eyes. "Please take care of yourself . . . for all of us who care for you. We need you around."

"Yes. I will do that," he said.

THE NEXT DAY, CARRIE'S PATIENT SCHEDULE did not allow for many breaks. It was nearly noon before she called Joseph Red Feather. She had already emailed him news that Nuttah's teenage uncle was responsible for the burglaries. Today when she called, she said, "Joseph, in addition to burglarizing over thirty homes in the area, including ours, this young uncle has a history of drug abuse, and so does his father. A baby shouldn't have to grow up in that environment."

"I am expecting a decision by next Monday afternoon," Joseph said. Today was Wednesday .

"I'll have other information to share with you, hopefully by the weekend," Carrie said. "The medicine woman left notes for me about Nuttah's birth family. What she wrote may shed light on why she thought it was important for Nate and me to adopt Nuttah. I can't read the language. There is only one person we know who can do that."

"Can you get those notes translated by tomorrow or Saturday?" Joseph asked.

Carrie let out a sigh. "There has been an accident in the family." She explained what had happened to Mike Leathers. "His grandfather is the one I need to talk with. You know how difficult it can be to communicate with people who don't have telephones. There is no way to reach him. I have to rely on family members to help me."

"Do what you can. It would be best to find out by this weekend what is in those notes. We need all the help we can get."

THE NEXT AFTERNOON, CARRIE AND NATE sat side by side on chairs, their hands linked, as Pete White Elk, Nadie's ninety-year-old father, read the notes Medicine Owl had written. The ink had faded on many pages. But there were newer pages, too. The old man's lips moved as he read, his fingers following Medicine Owl's tiny script across the pages. He took his time reading while Carrie tried not to fidget.

John had moved mountains to get Carrie and Nate an audience with his grandfather. It turned out Pete White Elk was one of only three Blackfeet elders who spoke the native language. He was the only one living in Browning. His home was just two doors down from where Medicine Owl had lived.

"She was my friend and neighbor for many years," Pete said. "She was a good medicine woman."

"Yes, she was," Carrie said with a sad smile. "She was a great healer, and she taught me about her medicine. She helped me write a book about Native American medicine. Did you know that? I was honored to call her my friend."

Pete frowned. "I am not in favor of our children being adopted by someone who is not one of us," he said. "Surely, you understand why. Our children were taken from us—taken off the reservation."

"We understand, and we are deeply sorry that happened," Nate said. "It was wrong. My wife and I respect the Blackfeet culture. We came here to live and work among your people. We weren't planning to adopt a baby, but she was abandoned and needed a place to live."

"No one else stepped forward to take her, Grandpap," John pointed out. "The baby would have gone to foster care somewhere else—somewhere far away. Nuttah lives here now, on the reservation. She is near her family, at least, and Dr. Carrie and Dr. Nate will support her in learning about them and spending time with them. They have been good parents to her."

"We own a home on the reservation, and we want to stay," Nate said.

"Medicine Owl told us the girl baby should live with you," Pete White Elk said. "Not everyone agreed, but we listened to what she said. She insisted that the baby needed to live with you. I respected her and knew she had reasons for saying this, although I did not know what those reasons were. Out of respect for our friendship, I went along with this plan and convinced the other tribal elders to give permission for the baby to live with you for a time. But it was only until a Blackfeet family could be found. Now we know she has a Blackfeet family."

"The child is safer living with Dr. Carrie and Dr. Nate," John insisted. "You have heard about the boy, her uncle who has stolen from so many people, including my wife and me."

Pete held up his hand, silencing his grandson. "I am not finished. There has been much sadness in this family," he said. "I am aware of the troubles. The baby's mother, the girl called Kimi, died in childbirth. The mother of Kimi also died."

Carrie and Nate looked at each other in confusion, and then at John. He, too, seemed not to understand. Carrie opened her mouth in surprise and started to say something. John sent her a look that silenced her. "Grandpap, Kimi's mother is still alive," John said. "It is Kimi's mother who wants to adopt the baby."

"No," Pete said. "The grandmother is dead. She died giving birth to Kimi."

There was utter silence. After a few moments, Carrie could remain quiet no longer. "Mr. White Elk, I don't understand."

"The grandmother who lives in that house is not Kimi's mother," Pete said. Carrie and Nate looked at each other again. "Kimi's mother died in childbirth. She left four other children in addition to Kimi. Another woman took care of the children. She is not married to Kimi's father, but they have lived together all these years."

"Is that what you read in Medicine Owl's notes? What else do the notes say?" John asked. "Does Medicine Owl know what killed Kimi's mother?"

"Medicine Owl delivered Kimi but was not able to save her mother. She said there are many problems for the women in this family. Some die in childbirth or shortly afterward."

Carrie guessed that Nuttah's real grandmother had also died of eclampsia in childbirth. She remembered when she and Nate had delivered a baby by caesarean section from a woman who came to the E.R. with preeclampsia. Medicine Owl had told this patient's sister that she approved of Nate's and Carrie's work, and said the two doctors had saved the mother and baby.

This had happened early in Carrie's time on the reservation, but she hadn't realized that Medicine Owl had lost one of her patients to the same condition. It had been Kimi's mother. No wonder Medicine Owl understood that surgical intervention had been necessary to save the life of a young mother with this dangerous condition.

"So, Kimi died from the same thing that killed her mother," Nate mused. "A pregnant woman with high blood pressure must be monitored carefully. There is a genetic component to high blood pressure."

"We'll need to watch Nuttah carefully as she grows up," Carrie said to Nate, forgetting for a moment where they were. "So far, she has been fine. It's important that we found out about the family's health history."

Pete's eyes remained fixed on the papers he held in his lap. "Medicine Owl says there have been other deaths in childbirth on the mother's side of the family. Medicine Owl writes that the new girl child could face the same troubles. It says here," he pointed to the last notes Medicine Owl had written, translating them into English. "The baby is living with the two doctors. She must stay with them."

"Does this change how you feel about us adopting Nuttah?" Carrie asked. "Medicine Owl was concerned that Nuttah wouldn't receive the kind of healthcare she needed, living with her birth family. Now I understand why she said the baby belonged with me."

"Grandpap, what do you think? Will you allow this?" John asked. "They are good parents to Nuttah."

"I will need for them to tell me how they will raise the girl," Pete said.

"Mr. White Elk, my husband and I love Nuttah, and we want only the best for her," Carrie said. "We promise that Nuttah will remain on the reservation and go to school with other Blackfeet children. We will raise her with lots of help from our Blackfeet friends. We will ask for help in teaching her about your culture. Will you help us, too?"

John leaned forward in his chair. "Grandpap, I promise that I will make sure Nuttah understands what it means to be a member of the Blackfeet Nation. My entire family and I will stand with Dr. Carrie and Dr. Nate to raise the child."

The old man was quiet for several minutes. To Carrie, it felt like an eternity. Finally, he spoke. Looking directly at Nate, he said, "I know of your work. You have saved the lives of both my grandsons when they were hurt, first John when he was in the car accident two years ago," he pointed at John who nodded. "Then Mike."

"I was glad to do what I could," Nate said.

Pete turned his attention to Carrie. "You have helped my daughter's husband Earl. He was very sick with the sugar disease. He saw the medicine man, but his words did not help Earl. You saved him with your medicine." Carrie's face turned rosy. "I know that Medicine Owl thought you belonged here with us." Pete gave her the slightest smile. "You have delivered two of my great-grandchildren, and there will be another child born soon."

"Yes, sir," she said. "I look forward to delivering another healthy baby for your family."

Pete nodded. "We are grateful to both of you for your good works. I will give you my blessing."

This was just one vote on the Tribal Council, but Carrie and Nate whooped with delight and hugged each other, then John, then Pete White Elk. With this initial hurdle overcome, they stood a better chance of winning their adoption case. Pete White Elk was well-respected. Others on the council might vote with him.

Before they left Pete White Elk's home, he stopped them. "Dr. Carrie, Medicine Owl said she taught you everything she knew about healing. She said you already understood these truths. I think you are a medicine woman, too."

Carrie bowed her head to hide the tears forming at the corners of her eyes. This was unexpected high praise coming from Pete White Elk. "Thank you," she said in a choked voice.

Nate took the old man's hand. "We thank you. We will continue to do our best."

As soon as they were back in the car, Carrie called Joseph Red Feather to give him the good news. "Really, I don't know where to start," she said, doing her best to recount the entire discussion.

"This is huge," he said. "I'll call the judge right now and let him know about the notes and what this tribal elder said to you. We are building a case that I believe is historic in its unique detail. Every bit of information counts now."

THE NEXT DAY DAWNED, AS PERFECT a summer Friday in Glacier Park as Carrie had ever seen. The mountains were clearly visible, white snow dusting their peaks. Fields of emerald green and gold provided a backdrop for wildflowers that dotted the landscape in an array of vivid colors. Carrie took an early morning run with Annie, who despite her age, was able to keep up the pace. The old dog still loved to run.

With Violet looking after Nuttah, Carrie took a leisurely shower before heading to the hospital to check on Mike. He looked better and seemed stronger but was still confined to a wheelchair when he wasn't in bed. Nate had started him on physical therapy to keep up his muscle tone. Since two of Mike's ribs had been broken, puncturing his left lung, he still suffered pain and labored to breathe. It was normal for a patient with broken ribs to take shallow breaths to avoid pain, but it was important that he took in enough oxygen. For this reason, he was still receiving oxygen through a tube in his nose, along with respiratory therapy to prevent pneumonia.

Naomi sat in a chair by her husband's bed, weaving what looked to be an oversized placemat using dried corn husks and corn silk. Her strong fingers moved deftly, crossing the strands of husk and silk under and over to create a fabric the texture of satin ribbons. Watching Naomi with her craft reminded Carrie of all the times she had watched Gran crochet, each of her stitches intricate and controlled, yet seemingly effortless, in and out like breath. Gran often said that crocheting gave her a sense of calm and peace like meditation. Carrie had never had the patience for sewing or handiwork. But as she watched Naomi weave, a look of serenity on her face, Carrie longed to learn how to do these traditional crafts. Maybe it would help her mind to quiet itself.

"What are you making?" Carrie asked.

"It is a mat for changing a baby's diapers. When one mat gets dirty, you can throw it away," Naomi said, glancing up at Carrie. "These cornhusks and silk don't get used after we eat the corn. But I say they have another use."

"It's pretty. But doesn't it feel rough?" Carrie touched the surface of the mat and was surprised at the smoothness of its surface. "Wow, it's soft."

Naomi looked pleased. "Yes, a baby's skin is sensitive."

"I've never seen anything like this before," Carrie said, thinking Gran would be fascinated and would want to learn how to make one.

"It is Naomi's idea," Mike said with pride. "She makes beautiful art. We are a good match." He looked at his wife, who returned the smile he gave her. The love in this room was palpable. What a lucky baby these two would have, born to such loving parents.

"You're so talented, Naomi." Carrie stroked the mat again, thinking of the many ways that Native Americans used by-products from nature in their daily lives. Rarely was anything wasted. If it came from the Great Spirit, it was used with appreciation for its innate value.

"This one is for you, for little Nuttah," Naomi announced, her voice happy. "It is my way to thank you for what you do for my husband and me."

"You don't need to thank me. I love taking care of both of you. But I sure do appreciate this mat," Carrie said with a smile. "And so will Nuttah, if I can get her to keep still. She wants to flip over now when we change her." She glanced at the large baby bump nearly covering Naomi's lap. "How are you feeling? I think you have an appointment with me later next week."

"Yes, I will see you on Friday. I am a little scared of what will happen."

"I don't want you to worry. You'll do fine when you have this baby. I'll be right there with you."

"Thank you." Naomi flashed her shy smile. Her eyes crinkled. "I don't want to be a baby myself. I don't want to yell and cry and scare my husband."

Carrie grinned. "You're allowed to do whatever you want. When I have a baby, I'm going to be the loudest mouth anyone has ever heard."

Naomi laughed politely. "I will be a good patient and not cause you any trouble. I promise."

"And my promise is that I'll make sure you are as comfortable as possible."

Mike and Naomi's baby was due during North American Indian Days, an ideal time to be born into the Blackfeet Nation. Every Leathers family member would attend the festival, some arriving from Canada to take part in the fun. The tribe would welcome all new babies.

Carrie looked forward to meeting this newest member of the Leathers family. She couldn't wait to see the look on Mike's face when he laid eyes on his first child. She knew he wanted a boy. But, knowing Mike, he would adore a little girl.

After assurance that Mike was on the path to a full recovery, Carrie excused herself and went in search of Nate. She rounded a turn in the corridor on her way to his office. Hearing low voices, one of them female, she slowed down as she approached Nate's office door. What she saw made her pause in mid-step.

She put a hand on the door frame to steady herself. Her heart beat wildly against her chest, and for a split second, she felt sick to her stomach. Beth's head rested against Nate's chest. His arms were around her. But when he saw Carrie, he pulled away, putting distance between himself and Beth.

Carrie froze, taking in the scene, assessing it. But Nate's expression was innocent. He beckoned to Carrie, inviting her in, before saying to Beth, "You know what you have to do."

"Yes." Beth dabbed a tear from the corner of her eye. "You might as well know, too," she said to Carrie, taking in a ragged breath. "It doesn't look good for me."

Realizing once and for all that what she had just witnessed had nothing to do with anything romantic between Nate and Beth, Carrie took a deep breath. "If I can help, I will," she said, feeling relieved even as she took in the wretchedness of Beth's condition. Maybe she *could* help.

The irritation that so often appeared on Beth's face whenever Carrie spoke, was gone. In its place, Carrie saw raw emotion: sadness and regret. Her heart contracted in sympathy.

"I'm innocent of what they say I did, killing a patient. But who would believe me?" Beth sat down on one of the chairs in Nate's office, looking defeated. "All I'm guilty of is loving a man I couldn't have—who happened to be married. It's his wife who died."

Carrie and Nate exchanged glances as Beth continued. "He loved me. He also loved his wife, and I accepted that. I knew we couldn't be together the way I wanted. But I never would have harmed her. I'm a surgeon. I save lives. I don't end them."

"But you should have let someone else do the surgery," Nate said. "Beth, you know that."

"I do," Beth said in a quiet voice. "When she came into the E.R. by ambulance, he was with her. I could tell she didn't have much time." She paused, looking off into space. "I had never seen him cry before. I knew what he wanted. He wanted her to live." The tears began again in earnest. "I loved him so much, I wanted . . . what he wanted. I wanted to save her—for him—so he would know that my love for him was real and pure."

"Beth, even so . . ." Nate said, exchanging a look with Carrie.

Beth knotted her hands together. "I was being stubborn." She looked at Carrie. "I'm sure you have no problem believing that." She let out a humorless laugh. "I thought I was the only one at the hospital, at least at that moment, who could do the procedure correctly." She wiped her nose and looked at Nate. "I knew what to do! I had done successful procedures on cardiac dissections at least four times and assisted with others. I thought I could save her." She was quiet for a moment. "But maybe it was more about wanting to be a hero, in his eyes." She turned back to look at Nate. "Do you think anyone will ever believe me? Do *you* believe me?"

"I want to." Nate rubbed his hands together. "Does it really matter what I think?"

"Yes, it matters! You've known me for years, way before this happened. You know I'm a good surgeon. You've worked with me to save lives. I saved your life!"

Nate wearily ran a hand through his curls. "You did, and I'll always be grateful. But I think you've got to tell Margaret Blue Sky about this. Whatever happens, she needs to have a heads up. It wouldn't be good for her to hear it from anyone else, and that is bound to happen. If you want, I'll go with you," Nate said. "I owe you that."

He turned to Carrie who nodded. "I will, too, Beth—if you want me to," she said. She reached out and took Beth's hand. "I know all about loving someone so much he becomes a part of you." Carrie's eyes met Nate's. "All you care about is his wellbeing, his happiness."

"I'm not an easy person to love," Beth said, wiping her nose again. "This man understands me like no one else ever has, and I still love him. But how . . . how can we ever be together now? He may honestly think that I killed his wife."

"Are you sure he thinks that?" Carrie asked. "Have you spoken with him?"

"No, not in almost a year. We spoke after the surgery, and I told him she was gone. He has grown children, and there was a funeral to plan. Then came the accusations and the lawsuit, and we needed to keep our distance. He hasn't responded to any of my phone messages or emails or text messages in a long time. I think, deep down, I might be a bad person, since no one really cares about me. Maybe I deserve that."

"You are not a bad person," Nate said. "We are your colleagues here, but we also care about you. If this incident doesn't result in losing your license to practice, I don't know that we have a right to pass any kind of judgment about the decision you made that day. Good doctors sometimes make mistakes. It happened to me," he said with a meaningful look at Carrie. "Beth, if you hadn't been with me in the O.R., working on Mike Leathers, there would have been a life-threatening complication, even death."

For the first time, Beth met Carrie's eyes. "I have no right to ask for your forgiveness, but I am asking for it now. I haven't been fair to you. It's not easy for me to relate to other women. I would like to know you better."

Carrie squeezed the hand she held. "You don't have to ask for my forgiveness. You've already got it."

"Thank you." Beth offered Carrie a small smile that spoke volumes.

Nate squeezed Beth's shoulder. "Tell Margaret Blue Sky what happened. Don't leave anything out. Margaret is a good person. She'll be fair."

AT HOME THAT EVENING, AFTER TUCKING Nuttah into bed, Carrie watched the silent battle going on in Nate's head. She knew him too well to believe he could stop thinking about what had happened that afternoon with Beth. He was troubled, fighting an instinct only a fellow surgeon could understand. Beth had crossed a line by operating on a patient under such questionable circumstances.

On the other hand, Carrie knew that Nate was indebted to Beth on two fronts. She had trained him as a trauma surgeon. She had saved his life after the shooting. It was only natural that he would have conflicting emotions about someone he admired. She also knew that Nate would stand by Beth until there was incontrovertible evidence of wrongdoing. Carrie admired him for his loyalty and sense of justice.

In a case like this one, the patient could have died at any point before, during, or after surgery. No matter which surgeon had operated on her, the woman's life had been in jeopardy. It was difficult for Carrie, as a physician, to believe that a skilled surgeon like Beth could willfully end a life entrusted to her care. Yes, Beth had loved the patient's husband, and it was this fact that negated any good motive she might have had for performing the surgery. It would be up to others investigating the case to rule for or against her actions.

The patient's family had brought a lawsuit against Beth. Even if she was found not guilty, it would still be on her professional record for the rest of her career. The case might be settled, but that would never fully clear her name. She still might lose her license to do surgery. One decision made in the heat of emotion could end up ruining a brilliant career. Worst case, she could end up in prison.

Nate patted the sofa cushion next to him. "It's been quite a week. Thanks for what you said to Beth today. I was proud of you."

"Of me?" Carrie leaned into him and laid a hand on his leg. "At first, I thought . . ." She shook her head. "But then I saw the look on your face, and I understood she isn't a threat to me, to us. I used to worry about that, the way she flirted with you, the way she would touch you as if she had that right. I tried to believe what you said at the holiday party. But I saw what I thought I saw."

"I won't deny that she hasn't tried to get closer to me, Carrie." He took her hand. "It happened early on, months ago. I told her there was no chance of anything happening between us. Anyway, I don't think it was real romantic feelings she had for me. She just wanted me to stand with her, so she wouldn't be alone. I couldn't be with her. I wouldn't ever do that to us. You're the one I love."

"I know that." Carrie lifted her face up to his for a kiss.

She knew his love for her could withstand any hardship, any difficulties they faced. They had found each other while doing the work they were meant to do. They were ideally suited, compatible in nearly every way that mattered. They were on this reservation for a reason, and that bigger purpose was more important than anything else. For the past two years, it had been their work on the reservation that became the glue holding them fast to this place. Now it was their marriage, their love for Nuttah, their home here that kept them rooted. No matter what happened, they were members of this tribal community.

He cupped her face between his hands, looked adoringly into her eyes. As he kissed her, more urgently now, she knew she could count on him to be there for her and for their future together. It was in his kiss, in the gentle way he touched her. It had always been that way with Nate. He had promised to love her for the rest of their lives. But she sensed that even before this lifetime, she had been his true love.

Chapter Twenty-Five

ON FRIDAY AFTERNOON, NATE BROUGHT THE car to a full stop two seconds before Carrie flung open the door and propelled herself out like a shot, sprinting to the front door of Earl and Nadie's home. He followed her up the front porch steps, Nuttah in his arms, just as Nadie appeared in the doorway. When Nadie saw the look on Carrie's face, she called out, "Earl! Come to the door! Dr. Carrie and Dr. Nate are here with the baby!"

"Hi, Nadie," Carrie said, giving her a quick hug. "We're sorry to just show up like this, but we're on pins and needles. We heard there was a meeting of Tribal Council last night, and it went on for a long time."

Earl appeared in the living room. "Hello, Dr. Carrie," he said. "Please sit down. You, too, Dr. Nate." Earl glanced at Nadie. "Mother, do you have some coffee and maybe some cookies for our guests?" He gave a wry glance at Carrie. "None for me. I don't need cookies."

Carrie offered a little smile. "I am proud of you for taking care of yourself."

"Yes, yes. Everyone is proud of me," Earl said with a grimace. "But my wife can still bake for others." He accepted the cup of coffee Nadie handed him.

"Thank you, Nadie. These cookies look great," Carrie said, taking an appreciative bite of a warm cookie as she waited for Earl to speak again. But the bite of cookie didn't want to go down. She put the cookie back on the napkin and took Nuttah from Nate.

Earl sat down on a chair opposite Carrie and Nate. His expression serious, he said, "I wish I had better news for you. My father-in-law spoke to other members of the council last night. There were others there, too, speaking on your behalf. The medicine man was there. He had words to say. The others listened. He was not helpful in this matter."

"Medicine Bear? Why was he there?" Carrie asked. "He isn't on Tribal Council, is he?"

"He is not on the council. He was there because he heard what Medicine Owl wrote in her notes. He does not agree with what Medicine Owl said. I am sorry."

"How much power does he have in this situation?" Nate asked as Carrie visibly shrank into the sofa cushions. It was as if all the air had gone out of her lungs. Pressing her hand to her chest, she struggled to take a full breath. This couldn't be happening. Not now. She had been so sure all was well after Pete White Elk gave them his blessing.

"Medicine Bear has a say in this matter. There will be another meeting of the council Sunday night, and they will vote. I will do what I can to say my piece."

"How many others might vote against us because of the medicine man?" Carrie asked in a voice that sounded strangled. Nate put his arm around his wife and the baby.

"I cannot say. As soon as the vote is done, I will tell John. He will let you know."

"Thank you, Earl," Carrie said. She held Nuttah closer to her. "I guess the best we can do is wait and hope."

Nadie's eyes filled with sadness. "We will pray for your family at Mass tomorrow morning at the Little Flower," she said. "You should come. Be with the people. Let them see you with the baby before the vote."

"That's exactly what we have to do," Carrie said, but her face was full of discouragement. "Nate, can you go with us? You're scheduled to work." She put her hand on his arm, and their eyes met.

"I'll ask Beth to fill in for me," he said. "She said she wanted to help us."

They left the Leathers' home in a despondent state. Nate opened Carrie's car door for her and waited as she settled into the passenger seat. Then he put Nuttah in her car seat and strapped her in. Carrie fumbled for the seat belt, her hands shaking as a feeling of nausea overtook her. She turned on the air conditioning in the car. Nate closed the rear passenger seat door but remained standing outside the car. She looked over at him and saw that his head had dropped to his chest.

Unfastening her seatbelt, she got out of the car and ran around to his side, throwing her arms around him. "What is it?"

"We can't lose her," he said in a choking voice. "We love her too much to let her go." He bent over and vomited, retching over and over, as Carrie held onto him. When he could speak again, he said, "I try so hard to hold things together. But the truth is, I can't stand this." He leaned against the car, breathing hard.

She wrapped her arms around his waist. They clung together, embracing each other for dear life. "We can get through this," she said, letting out a deep breath. "Whatever happens, we have each other."

"I know. I'm sorry," he said. "I didn't mean to . . ."

"You have no reason to be sorry—for anything. We are feeling this together."
They held hands for a moment before they got back into the car.

"Are *you* okay?" Nate asked when they were seated again. "You're so pale."

"I felt sick to my stomach, too. I guess now you could say I'm a real pale face." She let out a long breath. "I think Medicine Owl would be mad that this is happening, Nate." She glanced into the rear-view mirror at the baby mirror fastened to the car seat. It allowed them to watch Nuttah, even though her seat was rear facing. The baby was sound asleep, one tiny fist resting against her rosebud mouth. "Darn it," Carrie said after a moment, and pounded the dashboard with one fist. "Medicine Bear could screw this up for us." She couldn't contain the bitterness she felt.

"It's not over yet." Nate started the engine and reached over for Carrie's hand, interlacing his fingers with hers.

He pulled out onto the main street, heading for home. This might be their last weekend as a family with Nuttah. They would make every minute count.

SATURDAY PASSED QUIETLY. WITH SUMMER IN full bloom, Carrie and Nate took Nuttah on a hike, enjoying time in the outdoors. Montana was a paradise, but the warm season never lasted long enough. This time of year, Glacier National Park put on its best and most public performance. Wild residents, large and small, emerged from winter dens with their young.

It often seemed as if the animals were proud to show off their newest family members to the appreciative humans who came from near and far in hopes of catching a glimpse of them. But today, Carrie, Nate, and Nuttah saw only a brown hare that hopped across their path, delighting Nuttah.

In the distance, they saw a young elk grazing in a field. Soon, it was joined by its twin. The greens and golds of the plains in summer were stunning, flowers of every hue waving in the warm breezes. Insects darted from plant to plant, the low hum of bees at work the only sound that could be heard, assuring a new generation of flowers. Every being, large or small, had its role here.

The mountains shown today nearly iridescent under a periwinkle blue sky with just a hint of puffy white clouds. Carrie breathed deeply of the fresh clean air, so different from the antiseptic smells of the hospital. These mountains always brought her peace. Somehow, when she looked out on these ancient mountains, she had a sense of an underlying order, a belief that all was well. This was exactly where she needed to be today.

Nuttah rode along on Nate's back in an infant sack, her tiny brown feet hugging Nate's ribcage, taking in the mountains and their surroundings as if she knew precisely where they were going. And why wouldn't she? This majestic land belonged to her people—had been their keepsake for a century and more. The Blackfeet were Plains Indians who had settled along the rugged terrain and often harsh climate of the Northern Plains states and Canada. This land belonged to Nuttah, too. It was her birthright, and Carrie and Nate wanted to explore her homeland along with her, intending that she would have a full understanding of that legacy.

"This land is your land. This land is my land . . . This land was made for you and me," Carrie sang softly. Nuttah flashed a toothy grin and crooned a song of her own creation. It was melodic yet not familiar. Did Nuttah recall a song of her people?

Carrie's eyes took in the expanse of land in all directions, still searching, ever hopeful that she might see her wolf. Would the animal dare to appear when Carrie was with Nate and Nuttah? It wasn't that Carrie feared the animal. She knew her too well. They were safe in her presence. The wolf would honor the space between them, even as their spirits communicated a language of their own.

But the wolf was nowhere in sight. A deep inner knowing told Carrie the she-wolf was dead. She had been old the first time Carrie saw her three years ago. The wolf had appeared ill when she last saw her in March. She wondered if the wolf had died around the same time as Medicine Owl. Why the two deaths might be related, she couldn't say. But she believed this to be true.

Hadn't the medicine woman been the one to tell Carrie the wolf was her spirit animal? In her mind, Medicine Owl and the wolf were inextricably connected. Carrie had longed to take Nuttah outside in the summer in hopes of showing her to the wolf, to say, "*This is my daughter of the heart.*"

A stiff breeze lifted Nuttah's fine dark hair. Her lips opened in an "ah," and she closed her eyes, allowing the wind to caress her face as if welcoming an old friend. Carrie saw the look of profound peace and joy that crossed her baby's face and was utterly in awe of this child. On a soul level, Nuttah already understood the profound truth that Native Americans revered nature, believing themselves to be one with all the elements. For a fleeting moment, Carrie wondered what gave her the right to think she could mother and teach this child of an ancient race, a child whose heritage was synonymous with nature. More likely, Nuttah would become her teacher.

She dismissed the doubts that crept in and remembered something Medicine Owl had told her. "Yours is a journey that must be taken. That is why you are here. Everyone and everything you experience here is part of your journey."

Nuttah had shown up unexpectedly in their lives. To everyone's surprise, the medicine woman had approved of Carrie and Nate as Nuttah's parents. Medicine Owl had advised Carrie to let go of her fears and trust. "The Great Spirit knows what to do," she had said. "Get out of the way."

Yes. Walking along this woodland path, faced with the infinite expanse of mountains and sky, it was possible to believe in almost anything. Carrie linked her arm in Nate's as they continued walking. Here, they found it easier to believe in a benevolent spirit that could work miracles.

When they returned home, they turned a corner of their property, and saw a minivan parked in front of the house. "Dr. Jim! Lois!" Carrie yelled, and made a beeline for the front door.

She had hoped they'd arrive earlier that week, but Dr. Jim had a medical practice he was in the process of closing. "I can't leave until I see all my patients at least once more before I refer them to another doc," he had said. "This retirement process is more complicated than I thought."

Carrie wouldn't have expected anything less from Dr. Jim. He had said he would volunteer the entire summer at the hospital before he and Lois returned home to Kansas City. "You'll be tired of us by the end of August," he joked.

As if that could ever happen. She cherished the time they spent together. He had been her mentor and friend since medical school.

"Dr. Jim? Lois?" Carrie called out, peering into the living room before heading to the kitchen. They were sitting at the kitchen table, drinking iced tea.

"Carrie! There you are." Lois sprang to her feet, catching Carrie in a hug. "I hope you don't mind that we let ourselves in without so much as a 'Hello, we're almost there,'" Lois said. "Jim got itchy to get on the road day before yesterday. We threw some clothes and supplies in the van and took off. Cell service can be so sketchy in these parts."

"Of course, I don't mind! I'm thrilled you're here," Carrie said. "To tell you the truth, you're coming at the best time possible. Nate and I sure could use your support."

Dr. Jim gave her a quick hug. "What's happening now?"

"We're supposed to hear day after tomorrow whether we can keep Nuttah." She filled Dr. Jim and Lois in on the back story. She included the most recent revelation about the new medicine man's objections. "Dr. Jim, do you know him?"

Dr. Jim had been given the tribal name Medicine Wolf by the people in thanks for his good works. He knew many leaders in the tribal community, and it was likely he might have met the new medicine man when he volunteered in the Heart Butte area. It was worth asking.

"Is that Medicine Bear?" he asked.

"Yes, do you know him? Apparently, he has a say in what happens." She blew out a frustrated puff of air. "Sometimes I think he's dangerous."

"Why? What happened?" Dr. Jim asked. "I know Medicine Bear. He isn't Medicine Owl; that's for sure. But he is a good man."

"I'm glad to hear that. I'm not feeling very kindly toward him right now." Carrie told him about Earl's recent catastrophic drop in blood sugar brought on by Medicine Bear's assertion that Earl didn't need to follow his diabetes diet and medication. "Earl wasn't the most compliant patient, to begin with," Carrie said. "He never wanted to test his blood. He was probably thrilled to hear that he shouldn't listen to me."

To her surprise, Dr. Jim laughed out loud. "Earl is a smart guy, just not in this case. He didn't want to hear what you were telling him, so he went looking for advice that wouldn't involve needles and a change in diet. I'm betting that will change now."

Nate deposited Nuttah in her highchair, and Carrie gave her a snack of graham cracker tidbits. Nate settled into the chair beside the highchair and pretended to steal Nuttah's crackers. Normally, this would result in squeals of delight as Nuttah held out a piece for Nate to take, then snatched it back and put it in her own mouth. To their surprise, Nate opened his mouth, and Nuttah fed him the cracker, allowing him to chew and take another bite.

"Thank you for sharing, baby," Nate said. He caressed her cheek with his hand. "I love you."

"Dada," Nuttah said.

FOLLOWING LOIS'S DINNER OF SUCCULENT ROAST chicken, whipped potatoes with rivulets of butter, steamed fresh vegetables, and oven-warm huckleberry pie, it took every ounce of willpower Carrie had to stay awake. "Must be all that fresh air today," she said, yawning for the fourth time.

Watching Carrie's eyelids flicker during coffee, Lois insisted that she and Dr. Jim would do the dishes. "You and Nate concentrate on Nuttah tonight," she said. "We're here now to take care of things. Reminds us of the old days, right, Jim?" A look of pure mischief crossed her face. "Oh, wait, I forgot. You never helped with dishes." She kissed him on the lips. "You can make up for it now."

Carrie and Nate gave Nuttah a warm bath, allowing her to splash with her toys for an extra fifteen minutes. Then they each read her a favorite book. "You go ahead," Carrie said, handling Nate the bottle. "I need something for this acid reflux. I ate more than I usually do."

"You ate way less than you normally do," he pointed out. "You're starting to worry me. Acid reflux has more serious ramifications. Don't let this go on too much longer. We might need to find you a specialist."

As he fed Nuttah, Carrie sat across from them on the bed, loving the sight of them together. As Nuttah drank the last of her bottle, Nate laid her down in her crib. They stood there for several minutes in silence, watching her sleep, her head to one side, one chubby fist next to her cheek.

With Dr. Jim and Lois insisting they were exhausted from their long drive and that they planned on going to bed early, Carrie and Nate said good-night and crawled into their four-poster bed, intent on getting a good night's rest.

But at three o'clock in the morning, Carrie's cell phone rang. "This is Dr. Nelson," she answered in a voice heavy with sleep.

It was one of the nurses from labor and delivery. "Dr. Carrie, Naomi Leathers is in labor. It started while she was with her husband in his room. She's already at six centimeters. Don't take too long getting here."

"Well, that was a short night," Carrie said, swinging her legs out of bed. She had a moment of slight vertigo and sat for a moment at the edge of the bed until she felt better. Fortunately, she was used to middle-of-the-night calls to deliver babies. Even so, she had hoped to have an uninterrupted weekend. The bracing mountain air had clearly done its job of tiring her enough to sleep soundly.

Nate," she whispered. "Naomi is in labor."

He groaned and rolled over on his side, facing her. "A little early, isn't she?"

"Not much. I'm not concerned. Sounds like she'll deliver fast." She kissed him on the forehead. "I'll be home as soon as I can."

She donned a clean pair of scrubs, grabbed her stethoscope off the chest of drawers, and headed for the car. Driving to the hospital, she kept the window open, knowing that drowsiness could overtake her without warning. She parked close to the front door of the hospital and walked down the long hallway to the obstetrical department. There she found the Leathers and Prairie Hen families already camped out in the waiting room. At least this time, it was for a joyous reason.

"Why am I not surprised that all of you would beat me here?" she laughed. "Sounds like we're going to have a new addition to your families very soon."

"Naomi wanted Mike to be there with her," Nadie said. "He will be sad to miss the birth of their baby."

"There's no reason he has to miss the big event," Carrie said. "He's been doing physical therapy, and we're sending him home soon. He can be with her. In fact, I'll go check on Naomi and then have someone bring Mike over."

Twenty minutes later, Mike was by his wife's side as she labored. He was still too weak to stand for long, and hospital policy required that he be in a wheelchair, but he was there. He had wanted to be a supportive husband during the birth. Within the hour, Naomi delivered a healthy boy who entered the world with the most peaceful expression Carrie had ever seen on an infant's face. She held the baby out to Mike so that he could cut the umbilical cord uniting mother and baby.

"Congratulations on your handsome son," she said, watching as the first tears rolled down Mike's cheeks. He cut the cord with the scissors a nurse handed him.

Carrie handed the baby over to the nurse, who weighed and measured him, treated his eyes, and swaddled him in a blanket. Mike held his son while Carrie tended to Naomi.

"You did well, Momma," Carrie said with a grin. "Congratulations on a perfect baby. Now comes the fun part: raising him."

Carrie retrieved the baby from the nurse and handed him to Naomi. "Do you have a name for this boy?" Carrie asked.

"Michael, Jr.," Naomi answered, smiling at Mike. "I want my son to share the name of the most wonderful man I have ever known."

Carrie swallowed the lump that formed in her throat as Mike took Naomi's free hand, an expression of love and gratitude in his eyes. Carrie had once heard Medicine Owl use the term "twin flames" to describe a love between two spirits that burned so brightly, anyone could see and recognize it as true spirit love. Here it was. It was exactly how she felt about Nate.

After Naomi went to her room, both sets of grandparents stopped by to visit and meet the new baby. John and Gali were home with their children and planned to visit tomorrow. After about a half hour, Carrie shooed everyone away, assuring them they could come back later in the day. "Naomi needs to sleep now," she said in as firm a voice as she could manage. She was exhausted, too.

After making sure Naomi was comfortable and the baby tucked into the nursery, Carrie wrapped a blanket around Mike's legs. "You must be tired. This was a big night for you. I'll take you back to your room."

"Could I stay here with my wife just a while longer?"

"For just another fifteen minutes, okay? You need your rest, too." She sat down on a chair near Naomi's bed, too tired to stand a moment longer.

"Thank you, Dr. Carrie, for giving Naomi and me our son."

"Hey, I was just there to catch him. You and Naomi did all the important stuff," Carrie said with a chuckle. Naomi was already sleep.

"I am glad you are here," Mike said.

"Thank you for saying that. I'm glad I can be here, too. And it means a lot to deliver such a beautiful baby for friends like you and Naomi."

"It is more than that." He took a deep breath before continuing. "I did not know how I would stop drinking," he said. "You helped me to become the man I am now."

"You've come a long way from the day I first met you in the clinic," Carrie said, touching him lightly on the arm. "Not everyone can do what you did. But *you* were the one who did it."

"It was painting that helped my spirit." Mike looked out the window next to Naomi's bed. From here, they could see the shining mountains. The sun had just risen in tones of rose-gold, lemon yellow, and coral, promising another beautiful day. His eyes searched for a point in the distance, one of the highest peaks still covered in snow. Carrie knew this summit was his favorite. "I painted a wolf," Mike continued, "and I remembered. There was more I needed to do. That mountain is where I learned about my journey."

"The wolves? Is that what you mean?"

Mike nodded. "When I was a boy, all I cared about was wolves. I wanted one as a pet." His smile was serene, though his eyes crinkled with good humor. "My Grandpap Pete took me into those hills." He pointed into the distance. "He said if I found a wolf, I could ask it to be my friend."

"And did you?" Carrie was fascinated. She was thinking of her wolf.

"I saw three pups playing near a river. Their mother was nearby. Grandpap taught me to be careful, to keep my distance. One of the pups had a white star on his forehead. I remembered him and thought he might be the one who could be mine." He took a deep breath. "For years, he came to me in my dreams. He is the reason I do this work, to protect wolves like him."

Carrie waited. Mike was a man of few words. He spoke when he had something important to say, and everyone listened. Clearly, there was more he needed to tell her. In a few moments, his attention turned to his sleeping wife. "Naomi knows this story. It is why she supports me in what I do." He smiled gratefully in her direction. "When I was a young man, I saw a wolf lying at the side of the road. He had been shot. Whoever did it cut off his paws." An expression of grief crossed Mike's face. "He had a white star on his forehead."

"Oh." Carrie's stomach turned over. "I'm sorry you had to see that." Having loved a wolf as a friend, Carrie could empathize with the feelings Mike must have felt seeing the dead wolf.

"I *had* to see it, Dr. Carrie. I needed to understand that what happened to the wolf must be stopped. But by then, I was drinking. I couldn't stop. I lost my way." He looked sad. "I wasted years I could have been doing something to save others like him. Now that I am well again, I must continue to help other wolves."

"I understand. I really do," Carrie said. "But I hope you can be safe while you're helping them."

"I would do it again," he said. "I would face that rancher."

"I know you would. You'll probably have to face him in court, you know. He needs to be punished for hurting you, for hurting the wolves. But, Mike, you have Naomi and this little baby. Please be careful."

"Yes." He bit his upper lip. "I don't wish this rancher any harm. All I want is for him and others like him to stop shooting and poisoning wolves. That is enough for me."

Carrie pulled out her smart phone from her pocket. "Not everyone would still feel as you do after what happened." She typed in the URL of a website. "Here, I'd like to show you something."

It was a news story about the arrest of the rancher who had beaten Mike. He was out on bail until his court date. "He will be punished for what he did to you, Mike," Carrie said. "But there is more. Listen." She read a paragraph to him. "What started as a mission by one man to save wolves has turned into a national movement. After being critically injured, Leathers' work is being carried on by his supporters, who have turned out by the thousands across the country with a goal of protecting wolves."

There was a look of wonder on Mike's face. "I never thought . . ."

"Mike, you're a hero," Carrie said. "Your dreams about the wolf led you to take action. I understand now that our dreams guide and teach us. There are important things we need to know, that could change our lives or the lives of others, and the dreams show us. What you've started through these protests will save many more wolves." She paused, watching Naomi as she stirred slightly. She lowered her voice to a near whisper. "Did I ever tell you that a wolf came to me in my dreams? The she-wolf wanted me to come here and help the people. I think it was the same wolf who visits me sometimes. But I haven't seen her in a long time. I don't know whether she is still alive."

"You do understand," Mike said. "Dr. Carrie, I probably shouldn't tell you this, but I found an old female wolf in the woods about a mile from your house. She was dead. It was in March. I can't be sure, but . . ."

"You think she might have been my wolf," Carrie's finished for him. "Could you tell how she died? Do you think it was natural causes?"

"She was poisoned. I'm sorry to be the one to tell you."

Carrie was silent, processing this information. Her wolf had appeared ill the last time she had seen her. She never saw her again. It was likely the old she-wolf Mike had found was her wolf. "So, I lost two dear friends in March, Medicine Owl and my wolf."

She took in a deep breath. Somehow, it would have been easier thinking that the wolf had died of old age. It was unimaginable that her wolf had been poisoned. She felt angry. "Mike, I want to do more to help you."

In that moment, she understood in a way she never had before how Mike could face danger to save wolves. The anger she felt at that moment might have caused her to face down that rancher, too. She and Mike had both shared soulful relationships with wolves. Her wolf had been more than her spirit animal. She had been a real friend who came to her in good times and bad.

Now Carrie was determined to take a more active role in Mike's movement to protect wolves. She would add to the money in the bank to support his work. She would ask her parents and Gran to do the same. She would speak out, participate in the protests, write to government leaders. This was even more personal now.

She remembered something she had wanted to ask of Mike. "You will be recovering for several months. You will be busy being a new father. But I wondered if you would do a special painting of Medicine Owl. I don't have any photographs of her. I would like it to be a gift to your people and be displayed in the hospital lobby. I will pay you," she finished quickly.

"I will do this for you," he said. "There will be no talk of money."

"Thank you, Mike," Carrie said. "That is what I need to finish healing from her death."

Mike glanced again at Naomi, who was waking up. A nurse brought their baby back to the room and laid him in Naomi's waiting arms for her to nurse. The look on Naomi's face was beatific, the morning sun creating beams of light around her face. The Madonna image of Naomi holding a baby was unmistakable.

Mike looked at his wife holding their newborn son. Carrie knew he also would paint this vision of her and their baby. He looked back at Carrie and smiled. "I hope my son will honor the wolves."

"He will have his own journey, too. But one thing I know, Mike: he will grow to be a great man, just like you."

Chapter Twenty-Six

—∿—

JULY

O n Sunday morning after breakfast, Dr. Jim asked to borrow Carrie's trusty Subaru. He had the unmistakable look of Dr. Jim on a mission. "I need something rugged with all-wheel drive," he said. "Where I'm going, I'll need it."

"I thought you were going to church with us," Carrie said as she finished loading the dishwasher.

"I'd like to, but there is something just as important I need to do," Dr. Jim said. "While the rest of you are at church, I'll go visit Medicine Bear."

"I'd send my love, but I'm not feeling it," Carrie said.

Carrie dressed Nuttah in a yellow smock dress sent by her mother, and the tiniest pair of moccasins she had ever seen—a gift from John and Mike's sister, Cheryl, a moccasin-maker. She was finally big enough to wear them.

Carrie, Nate, Lois, and Nuttah arrived at morning Mass, and found the Leathers family in their usual pew. Nate waited until Carrie slid into the seat next to Gali who was there with three-month-old Lucy. Charlie sat on his father's lap, content for now, but probably not for long. Nate took his place at the end of the row, fully prepared to take Nuttah for a walk outside if she got fussy.

As the Mass continued through readings and time-honored songs, Carrie and Nate were happy to be with their friends and neighbors, appreciating the traditional Mass infused with Native American elements. Even though they were not Catholic, Carrie sensed that Nate, too, felt as much at home in this beautiful church adorned with hand-painted murals as if they had attended here all their lives.

Her eyes met those of Nadie who had encouraged them to come today. Nadie smiled and patted the hand of Lois who sat next to her. During one of the responsive readings, followed by a prayer, Carrie saw that the two women—one white, one Blackfoot—held hands, united by concern for her and Nate. It was a powerful moment for Carrie.

As she offered and accepted handshakes of peace, she understood that, at least here in this church, they were not outsiders. They were just another young couple attending Mass with their little girl. In this sacred space, they were one with everyone else. In the eyes of the Great Spirit, there were no differences between people.

Carrie was a blonde, fair-skinned woman who had come here to take care of the Blackfeet people. They called her Dr. Golden Hair. She had asked for nothing except their patience as she learned how best to serve them. All she wanted now was their trust that she could mother one of their smallest members. *Please, please.* She closed her eyes and sent up a silent prayer. Here, surrounded by so many well-wishers, she could believe anything was possible.

AFTER A SIMPLE LUNCH OF TOMATO soup and grilled cheese sandwiches, Carrie put Nuttah down for a nap, and waited with Nate and Lois for Dr. Jim to return. Medicine Bear lived about thirty miles from Browning. Over back roads, however, the drive each way could take an hour. Dr. Jim had been gone nearly three hours. Carrie hoped this was a sign that he and the medicine man were having a productive discussion. She tried to think good thoughts about Medicine Bear.

Although it was considered highly unusual for a white man to have influence with tribal elders, especially the medicine man, Dr. Jim had served the Blackfeet people for almost twenty years. His medicine was respected on the reservation because he was equally respectful of their healing traditions. This was the most important lesson Dr. Jim had taught Carrie.

At two-thirty, they heard a car in the driveway. Peeking out the front window and seeing her dusty green Outback slow to a stop, Carrie went over to sit beside Nate on the sofa. He wrapped an arm around her. Lois set a tea tray with a pot of brewed tea and freshly-baked snickerdoodles—Carrie's favorite— on the coffee table. Although the cookies smelled wonderful while they baked, Carrie had no appetite.

Dr. Jim strode into the house and put his keys on the table in the foyer. Carrie and Nate stood in unison, their expressions equal parts anticipation and agony. Dr. Jim's face was impossible to read, but he didn't appear positive. He would never relay hope where there was none.

"How did it go?" Lois asked. "Were you able to talk with him?"

"Yes. He offered the pipe. I took it. That was a good sign, I thought. I told Medicine Bear about Carrie's dream about the wolf, telling her to come here. I said that a she-wolf visited Carrie. He seemed impressed by that. I said I believed Carrie and Nate belong here and that they are committed to his people." Dr. Jim paused and bit his upper lip. "He is not in favor of this adoption. At the end of our time together, he said he will pray and do what he believes is right for the child. He didn't say what that was." He couldn't hide his disappointment. "I'm sorry not to be more hopeful."

"That's okay. You tried. Thanks," Nate said. His pager buzzed. "Excuse me. I need to take this." He went into the kitchen to call the hospital. When he returned, he looked disgusted. "Unbelievable! Jimsonweed poisoning. It doesn't even grow here!"

Dr. Jim shook his head. "Nate, you stay here with your family. I'll handle this." He let out a sigh and retrieved the car keys. "No matter how long I live, I will never understand the incessant need some people have to escape reality."

Carrie shook her head. Jimsonweed, which went by numerous other names, was highly toxic. "Might be a suicide attempt," she said.

"It's called loco weed for a reason," Nate said. "I'm betting Dr. Jim is right. Someone was looking for a cheap way to get high. Unfortunately, those hallucinations come with a high price."

"Maybe the E.R. staff got the diagnosis wrong. I hope so. It's just weird."

She went to the Physician's Desk Reference and looked up symptoms of jimsonweed poisoning, which included incoherent speech, rapid heartbeat, blurred vision, impaired coordination, and dry, and flushed skin often hot to the touch. In extreme cases, patients experienced seizures, visual and auditory hallucinations, and potentially cardiac arrest. Gardeners sometimes ingested it accidentally. Regardless of whether it was taken accidentally or on purpose, swallowing even a tiny amount of jimsonweed could result in death.

"I hope it's no one I know," she fretted.

Dr. Jim returned a few hours later. "The patient survived," he said. "It was definitely jimsonweed, although this kid wasn't saying how he got his hands on it."

"If you're intent on getting high, I guess you'll figure out a way," Nate said. "Did you report it to poison control?"

"I did. The police brought him in, so they got all their information, too," Dr. Jim said, lowering himself with a groan into a nearby chair. "I swear, it fairly boggles my mind, the level of stupidity," he said. "Sometimes these young people think they're indestructible."

"Thanks for handling that," Nate said. "I owe you one."

"Eh, it's good for me to have a little excitement in my day now and then," Dr. Jim said. "The few patients I have left in Kansas City these days tend to have fairly routine concerns. The worst thing I've dealt with lately is a lady taking two blood pressure pills, instead of one. Pretty tame stuff."

"How old was this kid?" Carrie asked. "I hate hearing this kind of thing."

"He's sixteen. While I was cleaning out his G.I. tract with charcoal, a woman came in claiming to be his mother. She had no idea what had happened."

Just then, Carrie's cell phone rang. She picked it up and saw that the caller was John. "Hi," she said in a hopeful voice. "Have you heard anything?"

"I did, actually. There may be a development. Did you hear? Nuttah's uncle was in the emergency room this afternoon."

"The one who committed the burglaries? What happened to him?"

"Not the one who broke into our houses. It was another brother. Jimsonweed poisoning."

THAT MONDAY MORNING, CARRIE STAYED HOME from work, intent on being available when word came from Joseph Red Feather. He had emailed her over the weekend twice, assuring her that he would call the moment he heard anything. She had reported to him the additional news that yet another uncle of Nuttah's had gotten into trouble, and that it had almost killed him.

"Imagine what could happen to a baby if she got into jimson weed," she typed.

"I'll make sure I share that information," he had replied. "Carrie, keep the faith. A lot has happened recently."

Almost sixteen hours had passed since Tribal Council met the evening before. Earl had voted, as had Pete White Elk. Surely John knew something by now. She had attempted to call John the night before, but her message went into his voice mail. What did his silence mean?

She had forgotten to ask whether proceedings of the council were public information. Although she had heard drums the night before, she couldn't discern their meaning. She tried to call Peg, who didn't answer. Surely, if either Peg or John had heard the result of the vote, they would immediately tell her and Nate what they knew. Or would they? Would they feel comfortable being the ones to share potentially heartbreaking news? The Blackfeet people tended to be noncommittal, not answering yes or no, even when asked a specific question.

While she waited to hear from Joseph Red Feather, a steady stream of friends and neighbors appeared, bringing offerings of food. Although Carrie understood their intent was to be supportive, she couldn't help thinking of funeral food. Food was often solace for the survivors of loss.

"Thank you," she said over and over, immediately handing the covered dishes and pans to Lois, who raved over each item, exhibiting the enthusiasm Carrie couldn't quite muster.

Carrie insisted on carrying Nuttah around everywhere on her hip. "Go get a warm shower," Lois finally said. "You need a little break. I'll watch her."

Carrie stood under water as hot as she could stand as tears she had held in check for too long flowed freely. Her chest heaved with sobs. Gran often said a good cry was better than any medicine. She held onto the tiled wall for support, lowering herself into a sitting position. With her back against the wall, knees pulled against her chest, she continued to cry while the water ran hot to cold. A nap would feel so good right now.

It was too bad that Gran and her parents wouldn't arrive for another four days. She needed her family here now. They had offered to come earlier, but she couldn't ask that of them. Gran and her father had medical practices to run. Her mother would arrive at a moment's notice, but Carrie sensed she might need her later.

As sobs wracked her slender frame, she suddenly felt quite ill. She pulled herself up, crawled out of the shower, and leaned over the toilet. Then she threw up everything she had eaten that day—admittedly not much. How long could she possibly endure this much stress? Despite seemingly insurmountable evidence that she and Nate would be far better parents to Nuttah than a troubled birth family, they were fighting a system stacked against them. In this case, legislation enacted to protect children was likely to accomplish the exact opposite.

She stood in front of the closet door, studying her too-thin body. She tried to eat a normal meal—at least soup or a salad—but had little appetite. Whatever she attempted to eat seemed not to want to go down, anyway. *Classic gastric reflux caused by stress.* It didn't take a doctor to see that these past months had taken a toll. She hadn't felt like herself in weeks. Between the ever-present exhaustion (not helped by middle-of-the-night deliveries) and fears of what might happen if Nuttah went back to her birth family, Carrie's usual high energy was at a low ebb.

As soon as they heard the outcome of their adoption case, positive or negative, she would insist that she and Nate get away for a short vacation. They could return to the Isaak Walton Lodge, where they had honeymooned. If the baby was able to remain with them, they'd take her, too.

Yesterday had been their one-year wedding anniversary. They celebrated with a quiet dinner at home with Dr. Jim and Lois. They defrosted leftover wedding cake, although neither felt like smooshing fingerfuls in each other's faces. Instead, they gently fed pieces to each other. Nate had been so sweet, insisting they renew their vows this year. They had done that at dinner in the presence of Dr. Jim and Lois. Nate's anniversary gift to her surprised and touched her. He presented her with her original engagement and wedding rings, along with the pearls her father had given her that also had been stolen. The items had turned up at a pawn shop on the other side of Glacier Park. Nate had driven over there without her knowledge and picked up her rings and the pearls. He had also picked out a diamond anniversary band at a jewelry store to go with them. His thoughtfulness brought her to tears. She had given him a gift certificate for a round of golf, something he enjoyed but rarely did. Somehow, she felt that she had slighted him.

No matter what, she needed to make more of an effort to show Nate how much she loved and appreciated him. He was suffering, too. It had been a long year, and they needed more time together as a couple. Their lovemaking had been particularly sweet lately, comforting in its gentleness.

She dried her hair and dressed quickly, then went downstairs to feed Nuttah lunch. As she arranged macaroni and bits of cooked carrots and peas on her tray, her cell phone rang. It was Joseph Red Feather.

"Hello?" Her voice quavered. She nearly bobbled the phone in her haste to answer it.

"Hi, Carrie. Are you and Nate together right now?"

"He's at the hospital. Should I call and tell him to come home? Do we need to do something, be somewhere?"

"I'd suggest going out to dinner to celebrate. Congratulations, Carrie," he said. "Nuttah is officially yours."

Lois and Dr. Jim stood nearby, looking as nervous as expectant grandparents. As Carrie's expression changed from fearful to stunned to gleeful, Lois finally dared to ask, "Yes?"

Carrie nodded and burst into happy tears. "Council voted unanimously last night that we can adopt Nuttah! The judge agreed."

Dr. Jim laughed and shook his head. "Something tells me Medicine Bear relented and gave his blessing, after all."

They hugged and went in search of tissues, alternating between exclamations of joy and more tears. Dr. Jim danced Nuttah around the living room, producing baby giggles of delight, before returning her to Carrie. Then he spun Lois around the room.

"I have to tell Nate right now," Carrie said. "I'm taking Nuttah with me. But wait, I should call my parents and Gran, too!"

"I'll be glad to call your folks and Gran while you tell your husband this exciting news," Lois said. "You can talk with them yourself when you get back. And while I'm at it, I'm going to call the Leathers and Bright Fishes and all our other friends and tell them to get over here. We have a mountain of food to eat up. This calls for a celebration!"

"Sounds great to me," Carrie said, laughing. "I'll be back as soon as I can to help."

Carrie put Nuttah in her car seat for the short drive to the hospital. With the car hot from sitting in direct sunlight, Carrie opened all the windows. The air smelled fragrant. For the first time in close to a year, she could relax and look forward to their future.

As they drove, Nuttah sang another song of her own creation. It was at that moment that Carrie first heard the drums. Multi-tonal, fast, then slow. She slowed the car to a stop, listening intently. Nuttah stopped singing as they listened to the sound of drums coming from the campground. North American Indian Days would begin in three days. It was the perfect time to hear the news that Nuttah was theirs. From now on, Indian Days would be their time to celebrate as a family, together and with the broader Blackfeet community.

Carrie glanced back at her daughter, and the baby met her gaze. "Mama," Nuttah said.

Chapter Twenty-Seven

—⟋⎸⟍—

"Carrie, hello." Beth walked forward to greet her. She had a smile on her face, a change indeed from past interactions.

"Oh, hi, Beth," Carrie said, looking around the E.R. "I was looking for Nate. Have you seen him?"

"He's with a patient right now. Is everything okay?" Beth paused. "You look pale."

"Oh, that." Carrie waved her hand. "All the stress the past few weeks. It's just a little tummy trouble."

"Don't let it go on too long. If you don't mind me saying this, you're too thin." Beth appeared genuinely concerned.

"Thanks. I'm sure everything will be fine. But I really need to find Nate."

It was doubtful that Beth would ever become Carrie's best friend, but over the past few weeks, they had forged a more comfortable communication style. Beth was less edgy, more approachable. She smiled more these days and made the effort to be friendlier with colleagues.

There had been good news that Beth had been cleared of any criminal charges in the death of her patient in Kansas City. Even so, there had been questions about her judgment. She would not be returning to the medical center. Although Margaret Blue Sky and the hospital's board of trustees had expressed concern about what had happened, Beth's surgical skills were sorely needed, and she had been asked to remain at Blackfeet Community Hospital.

"I know where Nate is," Beth said. As they made their way down the hall from the lobby to the E.R., Beth tickled Nuttah under her chin. "I can't believe how much this baby has grown. What? Is she a year now?"

"She'll be a year in September." Carrie wanted desperately to share the happy news that Nuttah was theirs now, but she didn't feel right telling Beth before Nate. While they walked, she changed the subject. "So, I hear congratulations are in order. We're glad you're staying, Beth. We need you."

"Well, for now, I'm staying," Beth said. "There are some things I have to take care of—personal stuff. I'll make a decision soon, though."

They finally found Nate. "Hey, there!" he said, when he saw them approaching. Nuttah rewarded him with a one hundred-watt smile.

Carrie rushed into his waiting arms, unable to contain the words one moment longer. "Nate, she's ours! We won!"

He looked stunned for a moment as if not quite believing what he heard. Then a grin broke out on his face. "That's wonderful!" he said, grabbing Nuttah and lifting her high in the air before lowering her and holding her against him. Nuttah rested her head on his shoulder. "When did you hear?"

"Joseph Red Feather just called. I didn't want to tell you news this important on the phone."

Nate encircled Carrie and Nuttah in his arms, holding them close. Carrie raised her face to receive his kiss. Beth stood by, appearing uncertain whether she should stay or go.

Carrie reached out one arm to include her. "You, too, Beth," she said. "This calls for a group hug."

The celebration began almost immediately at Carrie and Nate's home. Within an hour, Peg arrived with her husband Ken. The entire Leathers family arrived moments later in two cars, spilling out into the driveway and rushing to the front door. Carrie and Nate welcomed their friends and opened the doors to the back porch, while Dr. Jim and Lois served up food and an assortment of soft drinks.

As John approached, Carrie said, "I was worried when I didn't hear back from you."

"I'm sorry. I was there when the council met. They asked me to offer my thoughts before they voted. But then, I was told I must leave before the vote. It was very late when the vote was taken, and my father and grandfather didn't return calls. By the time I heard about the vote late this morning, the judge had already made his decision. At that point, I thought it was better you hear it from an official source."

Nate and John embraced in a loose man-hug. John held on to Nate a moment longer. "This is a big day for you and Carrie," he said, his eyes meeting those of his friend. "But it's a big day for the Blackfeet. We want to thank both of you for staying, for taking care of our people. We thank you for taking in this child. On behalf of the tribe, we promise to help you raise her."

Dr. Jim held up a glass of sparkling water. "Friends, I'd like to make a toast to Carrie and Nate, and to Nuttah, their daughter. May they continue to be blessed with good health and happiness!"

Everyone cheered and clapped. Nuttah smiled at Dr. Jim and reached out her arms to him. He put down his glass and scooped her up. "Welcome to the family," he said.

As evening approached and their guests drifted out into the fragrant night air, Carrie went to the kitchen to help Lois with the dishes. Nadie was there, helping Lois. "Here, let me dry," Carrie said, pulling a dishcloth out of a drawer.

It was then that she saw her. With a sharp intake of breath, Carrie noticed a gray wolf lying in the grass about two hundred yards from the back porch. But it was not her wolf. This animal was a younger version of the she-wolf Carrie had come to know and love. Was she a daughter?

Carrie's breath caught, and she headed out to the back porch. "I'll be right back," she said. She walked down the porch steps and into the yard, keeping a safe distance from this unfamiliar animal. "Thank you, Medicine Owl," she murmured. "I know this wolf is a sign that you're here, too. You helped make this miracle happen. Nuttah is my daughter now, just as I was your daughter of the heart."

CARRIE'S PARENTS AND GRAN ARRIVED THE next day. "Dad! Mom!" she said, rushing out to meet them.

The back of their rented SUV was stacked high with suitcases. Her family never traveled light. She met each of them with tight embraces and kisses. It was then she saw her grandmother getting out of the car. "Gran!"

They embraced and held on to each other for a few moments. Gran stepped back, studying Carrie with practiced eyes. She smiled broadly. "I can see that all is well with you."

"Well, I think she looks thin and tired," her father said. "Are you eating enough? Taking a good multi-vitamin?"

"I've had a little reflux lately from all the stress. But now that everything is settled, I'm sure my appetite will pick up," Carrie said.

Gran linked her arm in Carrie's as they walked up the steps and into the house. "This will be a wonderful week," she said. "I've looked forward to getting back into the clinic with you. And we need to make time this week for you to have a check-up. How long has it been since you had a physical?"

"Me? Oh, I guess it's been a year or more. Doctors always seem to be the last ones to follow their own advice about preventive healthcare."

After dinner, Nate and Carrie put Nuttah to bed and stood over her crib, watching her sleep. It was their favorite thing to do. In the stillness of the darkened room, they listened to her soft breaths. They still thought of her as a miracle child.

"We need to start a college fund," Nate whispered.

Carrie chuckled softly. "And a wedding fund."

Holding hands, they left the nursery and went outside to the back porch. Settling into the glider, Nate pushed off with one foot, and they began a back-and-forth movement. It was still light outside, though the mountains were ringed in pink clouds as the sun made its slow descent.

"I saw a wolf today—a younger one," Carrie said. "She was lying in the grass not too far from the house—just the way my wolf used to do."

"How do you know it was a female?"

"I just do. I believe Medicine Owl sent her."

In the distance, they heard drumbeats. Nate took Carrie's hand, and they listened as more drummers joined in. It was a song of celebration. With North American Indian Days starting in just three days, hundreds of thousands of visitors were already arriving to watch sporting events, eat carnival foods, and enjoy traditional arts and crafts.

"I look forward to Indian Days every year," Nate said.

"Me, too. But this year, it seems different, doesn't it? We aren't visiting doctors or guests anymore. We really belong here."

THE FOLLOWING MONDAY, GRAN AND CARRIE'S father saw a steady stream of patients in the clinic. As a cardiologist, Mark's skills were sorely needed, and Carrie made sure that some of her most fragile cardiac patients had time with him. Gran was board-certified in family medicine and nephrology, and Carrie wanted her to see Violet High Tower. Violet's polycystic kidney disease had progressed over the past year. Her blood pressure was under control, but Carrie wanted her to have another ultrasound, when Gran could assess the continuing problem of growing numbers and sizes of cysts on her kidneys.

Carrie woke up later than usual the next morning, fed Nuttah, and left her with her mother for the day. Nuttah and her grandmother were going to read stories and sing songs. Carrie's status as an only child meant that her mother was particularly anxious to have special time with her only granddaughter.

"I know you two will have a super-fun time today," Carrie said, watching as Nuttah ate a breakfast of teddy bear pancakes fashioned by her grandmother— one of Carrie's favorite childhood breakfast treats—decorated with diced bananas. "Make sure she gets her afternoon nap, or we'll all regret it tonight," she advised.

She went to the clinic to see patients and to help oversee the volunteer work of the visiting doctors and other specialists. As usual, during North American Indian Days, the patient caseload involved visiting Blackfeet from other regions who had no access to doctors in their own rural communities. The waiting area was packed when Carrie arrived. She poured herself a cup of coffee, added a little milk to it, and nibbled on a bagel Peg handed her.

"Here, you need to eat something," Peg said. "I'll get you some peanut butter or cream cheese. You need some protein," she said. "Listen to me. I'm your nurse."

Carrie laughed. "Yes, nurse." She spread a little cream cheese over half a bagel and nibbled at it. Peg was right. She needed to make more of an effort to eat, but this annoying heartburn made even the most innocuous of foods difficult to swallow. She finished the bagel, hoping it wouldn't come back up later.

Violet High Tower was Gran's first patient. After bloodwork and an ultrasound, Gran analyzed the results. Although she could see that Violet's kidneys were covered with more cysts, her kidneys were still functioning within a normal range. At some point, her kidney function would decline. Without a transplant, she would need dialysis. For now, Violet was doing fine. Gran went to find Carrie to tell her.

"She's still doing okay," Gran said. "I'm concerned that the cysts are growing larger and there are more of them. I adjusted her blood pressure medicine and advised her to watch salt intake and to drink more water."

"What's the status on potential drugs?" Carrie asked.

Gran washed her hands and massaged lotion into them. "There is one treatment, but I'm not sure she could get it here. You might want to check into that. Let me know if you want me to prescribe it, since I'm a nephrologist. I'll send you information. I'm hopeful we'll have several more drugs in the foreseeable future. They take a while to be approved." Her forehead wrinkled. "Clinical trials take years to complete. Violet may not have that long before she needs dialysis."

"I know. It worries me. Her son has the disease, too," Carrie said. "Maybe one of the new treatments will be available for him, at least."

"I believe that," Gran said. "For now, all you can do is continue to monitor their blood pressure and overall health—and encourage Violet to avoid stress."

"She just started working at our new childcare center. She seems excited. I think it keeps her active and happy, and gives her a sense of purpose," Carrie said.

"You have a childcare center now?" Gran grinned. "How perfect for you and Nate."

AT FOUR O'CLOCK, GRAN ENTERED THE patient room where Carrie had just finished up notes on her last patient. In her white coat, her white hair pulled into an elegant French twist, Gran looked years younger than her eighty-seven years. Her cobalt-blue eyes were clear and direct as she approached her granddaughter.

"Gran, aren't you tired?" Carrie asked. "You've gone all day without a break. I'm exhausted."

"I can see that. To tell you the truth, today reminded me of the old days, when I was first in primary practice," Gran said. "It's good to know I've still got it." She smiled and bit into an apple. "I'm more concerned about you right now."

"Me? I'm fine. I just want to finish up these notes and get home to Nuttah."

"I didn't come all this way to spend time with you and not notice a few things," Gran said. "First, you're not eating like you should. Second, your coloring isn't good. Let's figure out what's going on with you."

She handed Carrie a urine sample cup. "After you go, I'll give you a physical. No arguments."

"Okay," Carrie said. "But please don't tell me I need to slow down. You know I can't do that. I promise, though, that Nate and I are planning a getaway as soon as we can."

When Gran finished her examination, she turned around, a twinkle in her eye. "Well, I'll say this for you. You're looking amazingly fit for someone who is, as far as I can tell, at least twelve weeks pregnant."

"What?" Carrie struggled to a sitting position. All the color drained from her face. "Gran, I can't be pregnant. I had a period about . . ." She stopped and calculated. "I'm not sure exactly when, but it wasn't that long ago."

"This heartburn, the nausea? Honey, you deliver babies. How can you have missed the signs that you're pregnant?" Gran was amused. "As for that last period, you may have had some spotting—a little implantation bleeding. Your urine sample clearly shows you're pregnant, and I know a three-month pregnancy when I see one," Gran said. "Congratulations. You and Nate are going to have a baby."

A look of wonder crossed Carrie's face. She touched her abdomen with her fingertips. It was too early to feel the flutters of fetal movement. But, yes, there was a slight rounding there. How could she have missed clear signs of pregnancy when she had wanted a baby for so long?

"I thought it was stress," she said, blushing. A smile crept across her face. "There's been so much going on, I just didn't dare hope . . . Maybe I was afraid to hope and be disappointed again."

"Why don't you find your husband?" Gran leaned against the sink in the exam room. "There are only a few more patients left out there. I can handle them."

Nate stood at the nurses' station in the E.R. when Carrie entered. He looked up as she skipped across the tile floor. A smile lit up his features. "Hi, there," he said. "Are you ready to head home? I can be done in a few minutes."

"Nate." She took a deep breath, unable to contain the happiness that had been building over the past fifteen minutes. She threw herself into his arms—behavior not normally seen in the E.R.

He lifted her off her feet and put her gently back on the ground, a look of delight on his face. "What's going on?" he asked, mystified.

"I'm pregnant," she said. "We're going to have a baby."

Nate's blue eyes widened as he reached for her. And then they were dancing through the E.R., Nate twirling Carrie in place, while their coworkers and even a few of the patients cheered.

Afterward

⟶⟍⟋⟵

THE FIRST DAY OF CLEAR SPRING weather that next year warmed Carrie's face as she stepped onto the Blackfeet campground. The entire tribal community was here today, sitting in the stands and watching as members walked one by one to the center of the circle. Each laid a gift on a table.

The sky was the palest of blues, the mountain peaks and hills still mostly snow-covered. It had been a long winter—the coldest Carrie could remember since arriving on the reservation. Influenza had arrived right on schedule, claiming a few older people. Carrie treated them with a careful mix of newer therapies and the time-honored methods Medicine Owl had taught her. They had proven their worth countless times.

Nate walked beside Carrie, holding Nuttah's hand. The toddler liked to run, and she was fast. Today, she wore a new pair of beaded moccasins, her pride and joy. Her long dark hair was woven in a braid that reached halfway down her back.

They followed the Blackfeet Chief to the center of the campground where a ceremony was underway, celebrating the life of the medicine woman. It had been over a year since her death. At first, Carrie had been confused by the delay. She needed closure. It was as if Medicine Owl had simply disappeared. She knew better, of course. Medicine Owl had been beloved by her people—had cared for them for over seventy years.

Grieving her friend, Carrie had listened as John Leathers explained that to Native Americans, silence and patience, the passage of time to allow healing, were ways to commune with the Great Spirit, honoring such an important member of the tribal family. Throughout the seemingly endless cold fall and winter months, as Carrie trudged back and forth between home and hospital, she thought often of Medicine Owl, and hoped she could carry on her healing tradition. It had been particularly difficult being pregnant and not having Medicine Owl there to advise her. From the time she had gotten married, Carrie had envisioned giving birth, assisted by the medicine woman. It helped that the painting Mike Leathers had done of Medicine Owl had a place of honor in the hospital lobby where Carrie could visit her every day.

Today, as Carrie walked behind the Chief, she carried a copy of the book she and Medicine Owl had co-authored. It was titled *A Natural Approach to Healthcare: The Confluence of Native American and Modern Medicine*. The book had done well in initial sales, and Carrie received numerous opportunities to speak and write about her experiences on the reservation, blending her academic medicine with the traditional Native American remedies Medicine Owl had taught her.

When she reached the inner circle, the Chief watched, nodding, as she laid her offering on the table, honoring her friend and teacher. She bent forward slightly, and as she did, the newborn she carried in a sling against her chest stirred, mewing like a kitten. She smiled and kissed the top of his downy blonde head. Holding her hand against his head and neck as she arranged the book with the other gifts, she felt tears at the corners of her eyes. But now, they were tears of gratitude for the elderly woman who had been so kind to her.

"Want me to take him?" Nate asked, watching as Carrie's face worked with emotion.

She lifted her face to meet her husband's. Nate's blue eyes were like pools of glacial water today. "Thanks. I'm fine. He needs to be fed soon."

They shared a tender smile. Their first son, born January twenty-first, had been given the name Nathan Mark in honor of the two most important men in Carrie's life. The baby had arrived on the coldest night in January, when the temperature dipped to thirty below zero. Nate diligently tended a fire to keep their log house warm. She could see he was nervous as her due date approached.

Carrie had gone to the clinic and seen as many patients as she could until the contractions became urgent enough that she was unable to concentrate on anything other than the major event taking place in her body. She needed to focus on the new life she was bringing into the world.

Violet came to the house to care for Nuttah while Carrie labored at home. Peg arrived soon after her shift and held Carrie's hand, rubbing her back, offering her ice chips and a cool cloth, as the pains intensified. Meanwhile, Nadie, Gali, and Naomi appeared throughout the evening and into the night, sitting with Carrie, encouraging her. This was the way women supported each other, here and elsewhere.

It had never occurred to Carrie not to give birth at home. She knew that if Medicine Owl was still on earth, she would be here, too, helping to deliver this baby. Even so, Carrie felt her presence. For the first time in her life, Carrie felt utter confidence in her own ability to give birth as women had done for centuries.

As Nate brought their baby into the world, Carrie heard his first cries. "It's a boy!" Nate exclaimed, laying him on Carrie's stomach. He waited until the umbilical cord stopped pulsing before separating mother and son.

As he examined their baby and pronounced him healthy, Carrie heard the first cry of a lone wolf. Was it the young female who had arrived so suddenly last year, as if foretelling that Carrie was finally pregnant? The wolf's cries were the sound of life, the assurance that all things natural and good would continue. Here, on the reservation, they were part of this Circle of Life.

Nate handed her their baby son, wrapped in a blanket, and kissed her. "Thank you," he said.

In that moment, Carrie understood—in the same way she had learned so many important lessons from her time on the reservation—that like Nuttah, this boy child had arrived with a purpose. Her daughter would share her talents helping her people. In his own way, their new son would fulfill his journey. Holding his warm body against hers, she touched her lips to his forehead, and his eyes fluttered open, meeting her gaze.

"I am so glad to see you," she said.

And then she heard the first drums with their message. "Welcome," they said.

About the Author

ROBIN STRACHAN IS AN AWARD-WINNING POET and the author of four novels. She splits her time between homes in Chicago and Pennsylvania.